About the Author

VOLKER KUTSCHER was born in 1962. He studied German, philosophy, and history, and worked as a newspaper editor prior to writing his first detective novel. *Babylon Berlin*, the start of an award-winning series of novels to feature Gereon Rath and his exploits in late Weimar Republic Berlin, was an instant hit in Germany. The series was awarded the Berlin Krimi-Fuchs Crime Writers Prize in 2011 and has sold more than one million copies worldwide. Kutscher lives in Cologne.

D1051749

About the Translator

NIALL SELLAR was born in Edinburgh in 1984. He studied German and translation studies in Dublin, Konstanz, and Edinburgh, and has worked variously as a translator, teacher, and reader. In addition to translation work, he currently teaches modern foreign languages in Harrow. He lives in London.

ALSO BY VOLKER KUTSCHER

Babylon Berlin

THE
SILENT
DEATH

THE
SILENT
DEATH

BOOK 2
of the Gereon Rath Mystery Series

VOLKER KUTSCHER

Translated from the German by Niall Sellar

PICADOR

NEW YORK

THE SILENT DEATH. Copyright © 2009, 2010 by Volker Kutscher. English translation copyright © 2017 by Niall Sellar. All rights reserved. Printed in the United States of America. For information, address Picador, 175 Fifth Avenue, New York, N.Y. 10010.

picadorusa.com • instagram.com/picador
twitter.com/picadorusa • facebook.com/picadorusa

Picador® is a U.S. registered trademark and is used by Macmillan Publishing Group, LLC, under license from Pan Books Limited.

For book club information, please visit facebook.com/picadorbookclub or email marketing@picadorusa.com.

The translation of this work was supported by a grant from the Goethe-Institut, which is funded by the German Ministry of Foreign Affairs.

Designed by Steven Seighman

The Library of Congress Cataloging-in-Publication Data is available upon request.

ISBN 978-1-250-18701-7 (trade paperback)
ISBN 978-1-250-18702-4 (ebook)

Our books may be purchased in bulk for promotional, educational, or business use. Please contact your local bookseller or the Macmillan Corporate and Premium Sales Department at 1-800-221-7945, extension 5442, or by email at MacmillanSpecialMarkets@macmillan.com.

Originally published in Germany by Verlag Kiepenheuer & Witsch GmbH & Co. as *Der stumme Tod*

First English translation published in Great Britain by Sandstone Press Ltd

First U.S. English translation published as an ebook original by Picador

First Picador Paperback Edition: September 2018

10 9 8 7 6 5 4 3 2 1

THE
SILENT
DEATH

1

Friday 28th February 1930

The beam of light dances through the darkness, more reckless and wild than usual, it seems. Until the flickering subsides and takes form in the gentle outline of a face, sketched on the screen by light alone.

Her face.

Her eyes that open.

And gaze at him.

Sculpted in light for eternity, preserved from death for ever and all time. Whenever and as often as he desires, he can project her into this dark room, into this dark life. A life whose wretched darkness only one thing can illuminate: a dancing beam of light on the screen.

He sees her pupils dilate. Sees because he knows precisely what she is feeling. Something that is foreign to her and so familiar to him. He feels so close to her. Almost like in that moment captured there forever on celluloid.

She looks at him and understands, or believes she understands.

Her hands grip her throat, as if fearing she will choke.

She doesn't feel any great pain, merely notes that something is different. That something is missing.

Her voice.

That unbearable false voice which doesn't belong to her. He has freed her from the voice which suddenly took possession of her like a strange, wicked power.

She tries to say something.

Her eyes display more surprise than horror, she doesn't understand that he loves her, that he has only acted out of love for her, for her true angelic nature.

But it's not about her understanding.

She opens her mouth and it's just like before. At last he hears it again, her own voice has returned! Her true voice, which is eternal and cannot be taken away by anyone, which stands outside of time and has nothing of the present day's dirt and vulgarity.

The voice that enchanted him when he heard it for the first time. The way it spoke to him, to him alone, despite the many others sitting alongside.

He can scarcely bear how she is looking at him. She has gazed out over the edge, has seen everything, not long now and she will lose her balance.

The moment she goes to ground.

Her gaze, which is suddenly so different.

The premonition of death in her eyes.

The knowledge that she will die.

That she will die now.

No going back.

Death.

Has come.

To her eyes.

2

The man in the tuxedo smiled calmly at the woman in green silk, one hand in his pocket, the other holding a glass of cognac. His eyelids didn't so much as flutter as she came to a halt just centimetres in front of him.

'Did I hear you right?' she hissed, shaking and breathing heavily.

He took a sip of cognac and smirked. 'Looking at those delightful ears, I can hardly imagine them hearing *wrong*!'

'You really think you can treat me like that?'

He seemed to enjoy her anger; the angrier she became, the more insolent his smirk. He paused as if giving the question serious thought. 'Yes, actually. If I'm not mistaken, that's exactly how you let Herr von Kessler treat you. Well, isn't it?'

'I don't think that's any of your concern, my dear *Count* Thorwald!'

He watched with amusement as she placed her hands on her hips. There was a flash of lightning from outside the window.

'That's not an answer,' he said, gazing into his cognac.

'Well then, how's *this*?'

She'd raised her hand before even finishing the sentence. He closed his eyes in anticipation of a resounding slap that never arrived. A loud shout, which seemed to come from another world, was enough to freeze all their movements with instant effect.

'Cu-u-ut!'

For a fraction of a second, they were both so rooted to the spot that it might have been a photograph. Then she lowered her hand, he opened his eyes, and together they turned their heads and gazed into the darkness, to where the parquet on which they were standing gave way to a dirty concrete floor. Squinting into the wall of light, she could just discern the outline of a folding chair and the man who had shut everything down with a single syllable. He now hung his headphones over the chair and stepped into the light, a wiry-looking fellow, tie loosely knotted and shirtsleeves rolled up. His speaking voice was velvety soft.

'You were facing the wrong way, Betty, my angel,' he said. 'The microphones didn't catch you.'

'The microphones, the microphones! I can't listen to it any longer, Jo! This has nothing to do with film.' A quick sidelong glance at the sound engineer was enough to make the man pushing the buttons go red with embarrassment. 'Film,' she continued, 'film is light and shadow, surely I don't have to explain that to the great Josef Dressler! My face on celluloid, Jo! My appeal isn't based on . . . *microphones*!'

She stressed the last word so that it sounded like a newly discovered and particularly revolting species of insect.

Dressler took a deep breath before answering. 'I know you haven't required your voice before, Betty,' he said, 'but that was the past. Your future begins with this film, and the future talks!'

'Nonsense! There are lots of people who haven't taken leave of their senses still shooting real films without microphones. Do you think the great Chaplin is wrong? Who's to say sound films aren't just a fashion everyone's trying to keep up with, only to be forgotten when something else comes along?'

Dressler looked at her in astonishment, as if someone else had been speaking. '*Me*,' he said. 'All of us. *You* as well. Talkies are made for you, just as you are made for talkies. Sound films are going to make you huge. All you have to do is remember to speak in the right direction.'

'Remember? It's not about memory! When I play a role, I need to *live* it!'

'Then live your role, but make sure you speak in Victor's direction—and don't raise your hand until you've finished your line.'

Betty nodded.

'One more thing. You only need to tap him. You're not supposed to hear the slap, just the thunder.'

Everyone on set laughed, Betty included. The trouble had blown over, and the atmosphere was relaxed again. Only Jo Dressler could do that, and Betty loved him for it.

'Starting positions, let's take it from the top!'

The director returned to his place and put his headphones back on. Betty resumed her position by the door, while Victor remained by the fireplace and reset his expression. As activity continued noisily behind the scenes, Betty concentrated on her part. She was a hotel employee, grappling with the consequences of pretending to be a millionaire's daughter for the sake of her boss, and outraged at the insinuations this conman was making. This conman whom she would still kiss at the end of the scene—and who, far from being an arrogant trickster, would turn out to be modesty incarnate.

Sound and camera came back on, and the studio fell quiet as a church. The clapperboard cut the silence.

'*Liebesgewitter*, scene fifty-three, take two!'

'And, action,' she heard Dressler say.

Victor said his piece, and she worked herself into her film rage. She knew exactly where the camera was, as she always did, but acted as if there were no glass eye capturing her every movement.

She assumed her position by the fireplace and laid into Victor. A heavy microphone was hanging over his head, which she ignored, just as she ignored the cameras. She just had to speak to Victor. It was quite simple, Jo was right, and she knew she was good. As long as Victor didn't fluff his lines, which was always a possibility, they'd soon have the scene in the can. She registered the lightning, which had come at the right time, and let herself be carried by her own rhythm. She counted slowly backwards and uttered the scene's final words.

'Well then, how's *this*?'

Now . . . but she had hit him too hard! Well, Victor would live. It would make their quarrel seem all the more realistic.

Only now did she realise something wasn't right.

There was no thunder.

Just a high-pitched, metallic noise, a soft *pling*. A small metal part must have fallen to the floor behind her.

She closed her eyes. No, please no! Not some stupid technical hitch! Not when she had been so good!

'Shit,' said Dressler. 'Cu-ut!'

Although her eyes were closed she noticed the lighting change. Then it seemed a giant hammer struck her on the shoulder, the upper arm, the neck, with irresistible force, and when she opened her eyes again she found herself on the floor. What had happened? She heard a crack and sensed it had come from her body. She must have broken something. The pain gripped her so suddenly, so brutally, that for a moment everything went black. Above her she saw the cloths and steel trusses on the roof of the studio, and Victor's horrified face staring at her before disappearing from her field of vision.

She tried to get up but couldn't; something was burning her face, burning her hair, the whole of her left side. It was unbearable, but she couldn't even turn her head. Something was pressing her to the floor, scalding her. She tried to escape the pain, but her legs wouldn't obey, they wouldn't move any more, no part of her body would. Like an army of mutineers, it refused every command. She smelt singed hair and scorched skin, heard someone screaming. It must be her own voice, and yet it seemed as if it was someone else, as if it couldn't be her. Whoever was screaming and writhing and refusing to move was no longer a part of her, but a separate entity that could do nothing now but scream, scream, scream.

Victor's face returned, not smirking anymore, but grimacing, eyes wide open and staring at her. His mouth was strangely distorted, not the face of his screen heroes, but resolute nonetheless. Only when she saw the water heading towards her, a shapeless jellyfish that seemed to hang forever in the air before reaching her, only then, in that endless moment, did she realise what he was doing and that this would be the last thing she ever saw.

Then there was only a glistening light that enveloped her completely. No, more than that: she herself was light, for a fraction of a second she was part of a luminosity never before experienced. Never before had she seen so clearly, and yet in the same moment she knew it was precisely this luminosity that would plunge her into darkness, irretrievably and for ever.

3

Sch. defended herself stoutly. Nevertheless, 'Baumgart' forced her onto her back and tried to pull down her breeches. In response to her threat that she would scream if he didn't let her alone, 'Baumgart' sneered that she could scream all she liked, no one would hear. In the ensuing struggle, Sch. said she would rather die than bend to his will, to which 'Baumgart' replied: 'Then you shall die . . .'

'Would the gentleman like anything else?'

'Then you shall die,' he mumbled.

'Pardon me?'

Rath looked up from his journal at a waiter standing at his table, a tray of dirty crockery in one hand. 'Forget it,' Rath said. 'It's not important.'

'Can I bring you anything else, Sir?'

'Not at the moment, thank you. I'm waiting for someone.'

'Very good.' The waiter cleared Rath's empty coffee cup from the table and moved off, a penguin in a huff, balancing his tray through the rows of chairs.

The café was slowly filling up. Soon he would have to defend the free chair on his table. She was unusually late. Hadn't she understood what this was about? Or *had* she understood and decided to stay away as a result?

She shouldn't have telephoned him at the office. She didn't get it. She had been trying to do him a favour, just as she was always trying to do him favours he'd never asked for. That was the only reason she'd wanted to go to the Resi with him. Surely he must approve, she had said, flourishing the tickets for the costume ball. He was a Rhinelander after all.

Fasching! The word alone was enough, but that was what they called Carnival in Berlin, Fasching. Rath could guess what awaited him there: the obligatory costume, the obligatory wine, the obligatory good mood, the obligatory I-love-you, the obligatory we-belong-together-for-evermore.

The abortive telephone call had been a cruel reminder of what his relationship with Kathi really was: a New Year's Eve acquaintance that had survived too long into the New Year.

He had met her just before midnight and they had toasted the coming year, both of them already somewhat worse for wear, before spontaneously locking lips. Next they had made a move for the punchbowl, where some clever clogs was holding forth, destroying everyone's hopes for the new decade by claiming it wouldn't really begin until 1931 since, mathematically speaking, 1930 was, in fact, the final year of the Twenties.

Rath had shaken his head and refilled their punch glasses while Kathi listened, spellbound by the mathematician's missionary zeal. He actually had to drag her away, back onto the roof garden and into a dark corner where he had kissed her again while, all around them, people laughed and cried out as the fireworks whistled and banged in the night sky above Charlottenburg. He kissed her passionately until she let out a short, sharp cry of pain. Her lip was bleeding, and she gazed at him with such surprise that he began to apologise. Then she laughed and pulled him towards her once more.

She took it for passion, but really it was rage, an unspeakable aggression that was blazing its own trail, venting itself on an innocent party, later too, when she took him back to her little attic room and he spent himself, as if he hadn't known a woman for a hundred years.

She called it *lovemaking*, and his rage she called *passion*.

She had been wrong about everything that came after too. Their *love*, as she called it, whatever existed between them, something he could find no name for, which had begun with fireworks and hopes for the future, had never had a future, not even at the start. He had sensed it even during those first kisses, as alcohol and hormones swept aside all reservations. He had known it at the latest by the next morning, when she had brought him fresh coffee in bed, and gazed at him adoringly.

At first he had been delighted at the smell of coffee, but then he had seen her lovestruck face.

He had drunk the coffee and smiled at her wearily.

That first lie was the first of many to come, sometimes without his meaning to lie, sometimes, indeed, without his even knowing that he was lying in the first place. With each day the lie grew bigger, and with each day more unbearable. He should have said something a long time ago.

Her voice on the line just now, her forced merry chatter about the Fasching ball, about arrangements, fun and fancy dress, and other trivial matters, had opened his eyes. It was time to put an end to it, but not over the telephone, and certainly not his work telephone. Rath had peered over at Gräf, as the detective leafed intently through some file or other, and without further ado asked Kathi to join him in Uhlandeck. So that they could talk.

'What business do you have on the Ku'damm? We need to get to Schöneberg,' Gräf had said, without looking up.

'*You're* going to Schöneberg.'

Rath had handed his car keys to the detective and hitched a ride to Uhlandeck. Kathi's workplace was nearby. Even so, there was no sign of her.

Rath reopened the *Kriminalistische Monatshefte,* the journal he had been reading before the waiter came. Superintendent Gennat, his boss at Alexanderplatz, was reporting on the spectacular investigation in Düsseldorf, a series of gruesome unsolved murders, in which he and a few hand-picked Berlin colleagues were assisting the local CID. Rath had declined the opportunity to go with them, despite knowing that his refusal disappointed Buddha and would most likely stall his own career.

Being chosen by Gennat was an honour, something you couldn't turn down so easily. Rath's father, however, had advised against a return to the Rhine Province, even if it was Düsseldorf and not Cologne. Too dangerous, Police Director Engelbert Rath had said, LeClerk and his newspapers could get wind of the fact that Gereon Rath was still working as a police officer, and everything they had put in place a year before would be for nothing.

But how frustrating! The Düsseldorf case was the most spectacular in Prussia for years: nine murders allied to a number of attempted murders within the space of a few months. The Düsseldorf police had assumed it was a lone perpetrator and in so doing triggered uncontrollable hysteria throughout the city. Gennat didn't believe in drawing such hasty conclusions and had set out the specific features of each individual Düsseldorf murder.

It was the perfect case for the *Monatshefte.* In each edition Gennat reported on the state of the investigation, which, despite the high-profile assistance of his Berlin team, was still going nowhere. Lacking concrete results, he had painstakingly listed the victims: the nine deceased, but also four with serious and five with minor injuries, all recorded in the Düsseldorf area during the past few months. The 26-year-old domestic servant, *Sch.*, whose fate he had so vividly described, had only survived with serious injuries because the perpetrator had been interrupted.

Rath had read each instalment while holding the fort at Alex, making do with the scraps that Detective Chief Inspector Böhm fed him under the table. Of all people, it was the bulldog Böhm whom Gennat had entrusted with leading the Homicide Division at Alex during his absence. For Gereon Rath that meant running tedious errands or, at best, accepting cases no one else wanted. Like that of Isolde Heer, who had turned on her gas stove in Schöneberg two days before without lighting it. There were any number of cases like that at the moment. Suicides were enjoying a boom this winter. They were hard work, and investigating officers had little opportunity to cover themselves in glory. Most cases were handled by local CID in their individual precincts, but every now and then a few found their way to headquarters. Once there, they landed unerringly on the desk of Gereon Rath.

He leafed through the journal to where his reading had been interrupted.

Thereupon, Sch. felt the sudden thrust of a knife to her throat, and cried loudly for help. She thought her cries were immediately reciprocated. 'Baumgart' again stabbed at her, wounding her seriously in the back. As mentioned elsewhere, at this point the tip of the dagger broke and became lodged in her spine . . .

'Telephone for Inspector Rath!' A boy moved through the rows of tables, carrying a cardboard sign containing the word *Fernsprecher* in big block letters. 'Telephone, please, Inspector Rath!'

It took Rath a few seconds to realise who the boy meant, then he raised his hand as if he were in school. A few customers turned to face him as the boy approached his table.

'If you would be so kind as to follow me . . .'

Rath left the journal face down on the table to save his place. As he followed the cardboard sign to the booth, he speculated on whether it was Kathi cancelling by telephone. Well, if that was how she wanted to play it . . .

'Cabin Two,' said the boy.

He was immediately confronted by two public telephones behind glazed doors made of dark wood. A lamp was shining over the one on the right. The boy pointed towards the gleaming brass 'Two' located next to the lamp.

'You just need to lift the receiver,' he said. 'Your call has already been put through.'

Rath closed the door behind him. The murmur of voices from the café could now scarcely be heard. He lifted the receiver, took a deep breath and identified himself.

'Rath? Is that you? At last!'

'Chief Inspector?' He knew only one person who barked like that into the telephone. DCI Wilhelm Böhm.

The bulldog had an uncanny knack of catching him on the hop. 'What are you up to, man? You should brief your colleagues a little more thoroughly! Fräulein Voss couldn't even say what you were doing out west!'

'Isolde Heer,' Rath muttered, 'her suicide has been confirmed. The report is as good as done. It'll be on your desk tomorrow.'

'Have you joined the literati? Or perhaps you can explain why you're writing your reports in a café?'

'A witness works close by and suggested that we mee . . .'

'Doesn't matter anyway. Forget all that and grab that assistant detective of yours . . .'

'You mean detective . . .'

'And head out to Marienfelde. Terra Studios. Fatal accident just came in. Our colleagues in 202 have asked for assistance. Seems more complicated than they first thought.'

Or they're worried about knocking off on time, Rath mused. 'An accident,' he said. 'Sounds exciting. What was the name of the studio again?'

'Terra. The film lot. Someone's fallen from the scaffolding or something. I've sent you a car, your colleagues know the way.'

'How can I ever repay you?'

Böhm pretended not to notice Rath's sarcasm. 'Oh, Inspector,' he said. 'One more thing.'

Shit! Never get on the wrong side of your superiors.

'Yes?'

'That Wessel is being buried tomorrow at five. I'd like you to keep an eye on things. Discreetly of course.'

Well, of course, the bulldog had found another way to ruin his weekend! The ideal combination: a thankless task, perfectly timed for his Saturday afternoon off, and of guaranteed insignificance to further investigations.

'And what exactly am I supposed to be keeping an eye on, Sir?' Rath didn't see the slightest use in hanging around the cemetery in such a politically charged case, whose sequence of events had long been established. It might be something for the political police, but not for a homicide detective in A Division.

'I don't have to explain how CID operates,' Böhm snapped. 'It's routine! Just keep your eyes peeled!'

'Yes, Sir.'

The bulldog hung up.

Visiting the funerals of murder victims was indeed part of A Division's routine—only it was clear that tomorrow wouldn't resemble a funeral so much as a political rally. Nor would it shed any new light on a case that was already crystal-clear. A few weeks ago, a pimp had fired a bullet into the mouth of a young SA Führer who had liberated one of his 'girls'. On Sunday the Stormtrooper had died, and Goebbels's newspaper *Der Angriff* had made a saint of the youth who had fallen in love with a whore and paid for it with his life, a martyr for the movement, or *Blutzeuge* as the Nazis called it.

The pimp had been in custody for six weeks and already confessed, citing self-defence, although he and his Communist pals had forced their way into the victim's flat. The public mood had been stirred and the police, expecting violence between Nazis and Communists, had stood a few hundred uniformed officers at the ready. This was where Böhm was sending him! Into this seething cauldron. Perhaps the DCI was hoping that some Nazi or Commie would fell him by mistake.

Rath stayed on the line and put a call through to Schöneberg, reaching Gräf in Isolde Heer's flat. Five minutes later, he was standing on the pavement by Uhlandeck waiting. Kathi still hadn't materialised but, by now, it was too late for a heart-to-heart.

Böhm hadn't let him use the murder wagon. A green Opel from the motor pool was double-parked on the Ku'damm. Detective Czerwinski peeled his overweight body from the passenger seat and opened the door to the back. Assistant Detective Henning was at the wheel.

Rath sighed. Plisch and Plum, as the inseparable duo were known at the Castle, were hardly the most ambitious investigators at Alex, which was probably why Böhm kept foisting them on him. Henning briefly tipped his hat as Rath squeezed into the back seat. Long, sturdy wooden poles and a cumbersome-looking crate meant he barely had any room.

'What the hell is that?'

'The camera,' Henning said. 'Shitty Opel can't fit it in the boot!'

'It would have fit in the murder wagon!'

Henning shrugged his shoulders apologetically. 'Böhm needs it.'

'To drive to Aschinger, or what?'

Henning gave a deliberate laugh, as was expected of an assistant detective when an inspector cracked a joke. No sooner had Czerwinski reclaimed his place in the passenger seat than his partner stepped on the gas. The Opel performed a screeching U-turn and switched to the oncoming lane, banging Rath's head on the roof hinge. As the car turned into Joachimsthaler Strasse, he thought he could just make out Kathi's red winter coat in the rear-view mirror.

4

The studio was situated near the racetrack. Henning parked next to a sand-coloured Buick in the courtyard. Gräf had hurried over, spurred on by the prospect of working on something other than Isolde Heer's suicide. A death in a film studio. Perhaps they would run into Henny Porten.

The studio rose a short distance from the road and looked like an oversized greenhouse, a glass mountain that seemed out of place in the midst of the bland industrial Prussian architecture surrounding it. A long brick wall lined the site, with a police officer from the 202nd precinct standing guard so discreetly it was barely possible to make out his blue uniform from the road.

'This way, gentlemen,' he said when Rath showed his badge, gesturing towards the large steel door. 'Your colleague is already inside.'

'What happened?' Rath asked. 'We only know there was an accident.'

'An actress copped it in the middle of filming. That's all I know.'

Behind Rath a panting Henning struggled under the weight of the camera. The officer opened the steel door and the slight assistant detective manoeuvred the camera and its bulky tripod through. Rath and Czerwinski followed.

Inside, they couldn't make out the enormous windows that moments ago had made the building seem like a palm house. Heavy cloths hung from the ceiling, and the walls were covered in lengths of material so that Henning had to take care not to come a cropper. There were cables snaking every which way over the floor.

Rath moved carefully through the cable jungle and looked around. The place was crammed with technical devices: spotlights on tripods, in between them a glazed cabinet reminiscent of a plain confessional. Behind the thick yet spotlessly clean pane of glass Rath discerned the silhouette of a film camera. A second camera stood on a trolley with a tripod, this time enclosed in a heavy metal casing with only its object lens peeking out. Next to it was a futuristic-looking console with switches, pipes and small, flashing lights, on which there lay a pair of headphones. A thick cable led from the console to the back, where a set of thinner cables connected it to a kind of gallows from which hung two silvery-black microphones. Expensive parquet, dark cherrywood furniture, even a fireplace—it looked as if an elegant hotel room had got lost and wandered into the wrong neighbourhood. There were no cables on the floor of the set.

The cluster of people seemed just as out of place amidst the elegance: scruffily dressed shirtsleeves alongside grey and white workers' overalls. The only person wearing respectable clothing was dressed in a tuxedo and sitting apart on one of the folding chairs between the tripod spotlights and cable harnesses, a blond man sobbing loudly into his hands. A young woman in a mouse-grey suit leaned over him, pressing his head against her midriff. The crowd on the parquet floor talked quietly amongst themselves, as if the stubborn claims of the flashing warning sign above the door still held. *Silence*, it said, *filming in progress.*

Rath squeezed behind Henning, past a bulky tripod spotlight and onto the set. The assistant detective dropped the heavy camera stand onto the floor with such a crash that everyone looked round. The crowd parted and when Rath spotted Gräf next to two officers he understood the quiet, why the most anyone dared to do was whisper. Dark green silk glistened by Gräf's feet, the folds almost elegantly arranged, as if for a portrait, but in reality shrouding the unnaturally hunched body of a woman. Half of her face had suffered scorched skin, raw flesh, seeping blisters. The other half was more or less obscured, but hinted at how beautiful the face must once have been. Rath couldn't help but think of Janus, of Dr Jekyll and Mr Hyde. The blonde hair, perfectly coiffed on the right-hand side, had been almost completely burned away on the left. Head and upper body glistened moistly, the silk clinging wet and dark to her breast and stomach. A heavy spotlight pressed her upper left arm to the floor.

Gräf made a detour of the corpse to get to him.

'Hello, Gereon,' he said and cleared his throat. 'Nasty business. That's Betty Winter lying there.'

'Who?'

Gräf gazed at him in disbelief. 'Betty Winter. Don't say you don't know who she is.'

Rath shrugged his shoulders. 'I'd need to see her face.'

'Best not,' Gräf swallowed. 'The spotlight caught her square on. It fell from up there.' The detective gestured towards the ceiling. 'Comfortably ten metres, and the thing's heavy. Apart from that, it was also in use. It would have been scorching.'

Rath craned his neck upwards. Under the ceiling hung a steel truss, a network of catwalk grating to which entire rows of different-sized spotlights had been attached. In between were dark lengths of cloth like monotonous, sombre flag decorations. In some places, the heavy fabric hung even lower than the lighting bridges it partially obscured. Directly above the corpse was a gap in the row of spotlights. Only the taut, black cable that must have still been connected to the mains somewhere above indicated that anything had ever hung there.

'Why do they need so many spotlights?' Rath asked. 'Why don't they just let the light in from outside? That's why film studios are made of glass.'

'Sound,' Gräf said, as if that explained everything. 'Glass has bad acoustics. That's why they cover everything. It's the quickest way to turn a silent film studio into a sound film studio.'

'You're well informed!'

'I've just spoken to the cameraman.'

The spotlight that had struck the actress was much bigger than those CID used to illuminate crime scenes at night. The steel cylinder's circumference was at least the size of a bass drum. The power cable had barely checked its fall, let alone prevented it. Only the lagging had slowed it, with the result that in some places naked wire was exposed.

'And this hulking brute has the poor lady on its conscience?' Rath asked.

Gräf shook his head. 'Yes and no.'

'Pardon me?'

'She didn't die immediately. The spotlight practically roasted her, especially as the connection hadn't been cut and the light was still on. And her partner was standing right beside her . . .'

'The heap of misery in the smoking jacket?'

'Yes, Victor Meisner.'

'I think I've heard of him.'

Gräf raised his eyebrows. 'So you do go to the cinema?'

'I saw him in a crime film once. He spent the whole time brandishing a gun, rescuing various women.'

'He was probably in rescue mode just now too. Only instead of a gun he used a pail of water. They're everywhere here, because of the fire risk. Anyway, it seems he gave old Winter a massive electric shock. At any rate she stopped screaming right away, and all the fuses tripped out.'

'She might have survived the accident?'

Gräf shrugged his shoulders. 'Let's see what the doctor says. At any rate her career as an actress was over the instant the spotlight struck her. Even if she had survived, she'd hardly have been making romantic comedies.'

'Looks as if that poor wretch realises what he's done.' Rath pointed towards the sobbing Meisner.

'Seems that way.'

'Spoken to him already?'

'Our colleagues have tried. Pointless . . .'

'Unresponsive?'

'Nothing we can use anyway . . .'

A loud crash stopped Gräf in his tracks. He glanced at Czerwinski and Henning, who had begun to unfold the camera stand somewhat awkwardly. 'Perhaps *I* should take the photos,' he said. 'Before those two dismantle the camera completely.'

Rath nodded. 'Do it. Let them question the rank and file. Most likely they all saw something.'

Gräf shrugged. 'The cameraman saw *everything*. The director too. That's part of their job.' The detective gestured towards a wiry-looking chap who was talking quietly but no less forcefully to a balding, well-dressed man in his mid-fifties.

Rath nodded. 'I'll have a word with him in a moment. Where's the man responsible for the spotlights?'

'No idea. I can't take care of everything.'

'Tell Henning to find him and send him to me.'

Gräf turned away and Rath moved towards the blubbing Meisner. When Rath was standing directly in front of him, he stopped sobbing and looked up. The woman in grey stroked his shoulders reassuringly as Rath produced his badge. The man gazed at him beseechingly until, suddenly, despair erupted from him.

'I killed her,' he cried, 'I killed Betty! My God, what have I done?' His hands dug into Rath's trouser legs. The woman in grey came to his aid.

'It's all right, Victor,' she said softly.

She took the actor's slender hands and dragged him away from Rath onto the director's chair, where he buried his face in her grey skirt.

'Surely you can see he can't talk now,' she said, 'he's in shock! I hope the doctor gets here soon.'

Rath knew that Dr Schwartz was on his way, but he doubted whether the acerbic pathologist was the right man to comfort a tender soul like Victor Meisner. He gave the woman his card.

'There's no need for Herr Meisner to make a statement just now. He can come to the station when he's feeling better. Monday at the latest.'

Rath had the feeling she was gazing right through him. He wrote the date on the card, as well as a time. Eleven o'clock. He couldn't afford to give the poor devil any more grace than that.

'You look after him for now,' he said. 'The best thing would be to take him to hospital.'

'Do what the man says, Cora,' a deep voice said, 'it's better if Victor doesn't stay here any longer than necessary.'

Rath turned to the balding man who had been speaking to the director. Cora led Victor Meisner to the exit.

'Bellmann,' the man said, introducing himself. 'La Belle Film Production. I'm the producer of *Liebesgewitter*.'

'La Belle?' Rath shook his hand. 'I thought this was Terra Film.'

'The rooms, but not the production. Very few film companies can afford their own studio. We're not Ufa, you know,' Bellmann said, and it sounded almost apologetic. He pointed towards the director. 'Jo Dressler, my director.'

'Jo?'

'Josef sounds too old-fashioned,' the director said and stretched out a hand. 'Good day, Inspector.'

'We still can't believe it.' Bellmann said. 'In the middle of the shoot!' He looked genuinely shaken. '*Liebesgewitter* was supposed to be screening in cinemas in two weeks.'

'So soon?'

'Time is money,' Bellmann said.

'We still had two days of filming scheduled,' Dressler explained. 'Today and tomorrow.'

'The film's nearly finished?'

Dressler nodded.

'A tragedy,' Bellmann said. Then he gave a nervous laugh and corrected himself. 'The accident, I mean. The accident is a tragedy. The film, of course, is a comedy. A divine romantic comedy, something completely new. Divine in the true sense of the word.'

Rath nodded, though he didn't understand a thing. 'Did you see how it happened?'

Bellmann shook his head. 'By the time I arrived she was already lying motionless on the floor. But Jo, you can tell the inspector . . .'

The director cleared his throat. 'Well, as I said to your colleagues . . . it was just before the end of the scene. We were already shooting it for the second time, and it was going well. We just needed the slap and the thunder, then it'd have been a wrap . . .'

'Thunder?'

'*Liebesgewitter* is the story of Thor, the Norwegian God of Thunder, who falls in love with a girl from Berlin and courts her as Count Thorwald. Whenever the two of them come together, it thunders.'

Rath thought it sounded completely insane. *This* was the film that was supposed to launch Betty Winter's sound career?

'Well,' Dressler continued, 'suddenly the flood crashed down from the ceiling.'

'The flood?'

'The spotlight that struck Betty. It knocked her to the floor and buried her underneath it. My God, the way she was lying there screaming, and no one could help her—it was just dreadful . . .'

'Why *didn't* anyone help her?'

'Do you know how hot a spotlight gets? It isn't just something you can manhandle.'

'But there was one person who tried . . .'

'You mean Victor?' Dressler shrugged his shoulders. 'I don't know what came over him. It was their scene and he was standing right next to her. Well, who knows what goes through a person's mind? There's someone right next to you, and you smell their burnt skin, hear them scream—you want to help, don't you? And the way she was screaming!' He shook his head. 'We all stood as if paralysed. Before we understood what he was doing he'd tipped the fire bucket over her.' He cleared his throat before continuing. 'She stopped screaming immediately, and started . . . her whole body started twitching . . . in protest, almost . . . and then there was a bang. All the fuses had tripped and the lights went out.'

'Then?'

'It took a few seconds before we could see anything again. I was first there, after Victor, I mean. Betty was dead.'

'How could you tell?'

'I . . . I felt her carotid artery. There was no pulse.'

'Incomprehensible, isn't it?' Bellmann said. 'A devastating loss for the German film industry.'

Rath looked at the producer. 'Do things like this often happen?'

'Like what?'

'Like spotlights falling from the roof? The structure up there looks a bit wobbly to me.'

Bellmann flew off the handle. 'Listen to me, Inspector, it might look a little temporary, but believe me, it's all checked and approved. Ask your colleagues from the Department of Building Regulations!' He grew louder. 'This is a glasshouse, perfect for shooting films, but not for recording sound. That's the reason for the renovations—we're still in the middle of them. Soundproofing, you see. With talkies it's more important than daylight, which is something we must unfortunately make do without. As far as lighting is concerned, we've always had the best equipment. Our spotlights are among the most state-of-the-art in the industry today, Nitraphot lamps . . .'

It was an inappropriate remark given that an actress had died under just such a modern spotlight. Bellmann fell silent and Rath did nothing to ease his embarrassment.

Some people allowed their reserve to be broken by this sort of thing, but Bellmann kept himself in check, probably a useful skill in his profession. The director seemed less assured, transferring his weight from one leg to the other as if he needed to go to the bathroom. Before he could say anything unguarded, however, Henning appeared with a slightly built man in tow whom he introduced as Hans Lüdenbach. In his grey work overalls he had the look of an underpaid caretaker.

'Are you the lighting technician?' Rath asked.

'Senior lighting technician.'

'Then you're responsible for the spotlight that grew a mind of its own up there?'

The little man opened his mouth to say something, but Bellmann got in first. 'It goes without saying that the responsibility is mine alone.' He sounded like a has-been politician attempting to forestall the opposition's demand for his resignation.

'Well, someone's messed up, and if it wasn't the manufacturer of the lighting system, then it must have been one of your people.'

'Impossible,' Lüdenbach said.

'Don't you make regular checks to ensure everything up there is screwed in tight? You are the *senior* lighting technician.'

'Of course we do! We can't do any filming until the light's right.'

'And everything with the flood was OK?'

'Optimum settings. The light was perfect. I don't know why the fixtures gave way. I'd need to have a closer look.'

'You mean you haven't done that yet?'

Lüdenbach shook his head. 'Your people prevented us. We shouldn't touch anything was the first thing they said.'

'Then show me where the flood was hanging.'

Lüdenbach made for a narrow steel ladder, which seemed to lead straight into the sky, and Rath wondered whether you needed to be as thin as Hans Lüdenbach for the trestles to hold. Heights of ten metres were enough to make him break out in a cold sweat, so he didn't look down as he climbed, focusing on the grey overalls moving above. Nor did he gaze downwards as he followed the technician across the rickety grating, the structure rattling and squeaking with every step.

He groped his way forward, hands gripping the rail, but couldn't help looking at the tips of his shoes whenever he took a step. The studio floor seemed impossibly distant through the iron grille beneath his feet.

A curious floor plan was beginning to emerge as viewed from above. Next to the fireplace room that housed the dead woman was a hotel reception and a simple servants' quarters, and next to it a pavement café. The door of the fireplace room, meanwhile, led straight into a police office with holding cell. Most likely all part of the *Liebesgewitter* set. From below came the glare of a flash. Gräf had started his work. Rath forced himself to look up. The senior lighting technician had disappeared.

'Hey!' Rath cried. 'Where have you got to?'

The maze of steel grates was more confusing than it looked from below, mainly because of the heavy lengths of fabric hanging everywhere from the ceiling and obscuring his view.

'Here it is.' The voice of the senior lighting technician sounded muffled, but seemed nevertheless to be close at hand. 'Where have *you* got to?'

Having worked his way forward by a few metres, Rath saw Lüdenbach again, crouched by the floor of the grating, three metres away at most. 'Be right with you,' he said. 'Don't touch anything!'

His hands were knotted in pain and there was sweat on his forehead, but he didn't let it show as he inched his way forwards. Lüdenbach indicated a mounting. 'Here,' he said as Rath crouched beside him, 'take a look at this. I don't believe it! There should be a threaded bolt here. It must have come loose. Impossible really, they're all secured with a cotter pin.'

Rath looked at the mounting close-up. 'Maybe the bolt's broken!'

Lüdenbach shrugged his shoulders helplessly. 'There's still the one on the other side.'

The picture was the same there, however: no threaded bolt.

Lüdenbach shook his head. 'I can't believe it,' he muttered. 'I just can't believe it!'

They stood up. Rath held onto the swaying platform and his sweaty hands immediately cramped up again. He felt decidedly queasy, while Hans Lüdenbach stood by the railing, as secure as a helmsman in stormy seas.

'This sort of thing shouldn't happen.' Lüdenbach said. 'That's why the spotlights are doubly secured.'

'Perhaps someone wanted to adjust the spotlight and forgot to screw the bolt back in place.'

'But not in the middle of a shoot!'

'Still, the spotlight must have come loose somehow. Double metal fatigue seems far less likely than the possibility that someone's been a little careless.'

'My people are not careless!' Lüdenbach was outraged. 'Glaser above all! He knows what he's doing!'

'Who?'

'Peter Glaser. My assistant. He's responsible for the flood.'

'Why, in that case,' Rath asked, with growing impatience, 'haven't I seen him already?'

'Because you wanted to come up here with *me*! Don't you think I'd have spoken to him long ago if I knew where he was?'

'Pardon me?'

'He was up here this morning setting everything up.'

'And now?'

Lüdenbach shrugged. 'Now he's not here.'

'Since when?'

'No idea. I haven't seen him for a while. Since lunchtime today, perhaps longer. Maybe he's sick.'

'He hasn't reported absent?'

'Not to my knowledge.'

Rath lost his patience. 'If you want to be of any use at all today, then I suggest you show me how to get down from here right now!'

Peter Glaser was not in the studio. Bellmann had provided his address, though not before emphasising what a reliable worker the man was, and Rath sent Henning and Czerwinski on their way. In the meantime, the men from ED, the police identification service, arrived with the pathologist, and began searching the floor for two threaded bolts. Dr Schwartz crouched next to the corpse and examined the burns to the head and shoulders. Kronberg's people searched as systematically as only ED officers could but it was Gräf who made the find, an unremarkable oily-black piece of metal that had rolled underneath a spotlight tripod.

Lüdenbach confirmed that it was from the mounting. It had no cracks and was unscathed. They consigned it to an ED crate for further examination.

The second bolt remained elusive, however, and they found no trace of the cotter pin.

'Have we just cleaned their floor for nothing?' asked an ED officer.

'At least we have one of the bolts,' Gräf said.

'Perhaps Glaser has the other,' Rath said. 'Tried to dispose of the evidence, only he couldn't find the second bolt before he had to scram.'

'Do you really believe he meant for the spotlight to fall?' Gräf asked. 'Maybe he was just too much of a coward to admit responsibility for the accident.'

Rath shrugged. 'What I believe won't get us anywhere. Someone here really messed up, that much is clear . . .'

'Inspector?'

A young man approached them, waving a film canister.

'The cameraman,' Gräf whispered. 'Harald Winkler.'

'Inspector,' Winkler said. Despite his youth, his hair was already starting to thin. 'I think this might be of interest to you.'

'What's this?'

'The accident. You can see how it happened for yourself.' Winkler raised the film canister. 'Everything's on here.'

'You filmed the accident?'

'I filmed the scene. The camera kept on running. I . . . well, it was instinct, I suppose. I just continued filming until the lights went out. Maybe it'll be of use. There's no better eyewitness than my camera at any rate.'

'When can we see what's on it?'

'Not before Monday. It needs to be processed. If you like, I can book us a projection room.' Winkler handed Rath a card. 'Give me a call . . .'

Suddenly the cameraman was no longer looking in Rath's eyes, but over his shoulder. Gräf, too, was looking to one side. Rath turned and gazed straight into half a dozen press lenses. A swarm of reporters had somehow managed to get past the policeman on the door. Before any of the officers could intervene there was a flurry of flashing lights.

At least the corpse was covered.

'Who let this rabble in?' Rath asked.

Gräf sprang into action. 'This is a crime scene not a press club, gentlemen.' He gave one of the officers a decisive nod of the head, but the boys in blue were already pushing reporters towards the door. There was a round of protests.

'Stop! You can't do this to us!'

Rath positioned himself. 'Please be so kind as to leave the room without disrupting our investigations, and no more photos please!'

The press bunch didn't stand a chance against the uniformed officers, but a few of them fired questions into the air as they retreated.

'Was it an accident or murder?'

'Who has Betty Winter on their conscience?'

'Gentlemen,' Rath said, 'thank you for your understanding. We will inform you of any developments in good time.'

'Do you mean during the press conference?' asked one as he was pushed through the door. There was a final flash of light, blinding Rath for a moment, before the steel door closed and the commotion passed.

'How did they get in?' Rath asked. 'I thought the door was being watched.'

'It is,' Gräf said. 'They must have come through a back entrance.'

'Well, why is there no one *there*?'

Bellmann poked his nose in. 'Pardon me, Inspector. Your colleagues were unaware of the back entrance. I forgot to point it out.'

'Then how did the journalists know? Come to think of it, how did they know anything at all?'

'You can't keep stories like this under wraps,' Bellmann said. 'That's why I called a press conference next door. I would be delighted if you and your colleagues would particip . . .'

Rath couldn't believe it. 'A woman has died here, and all you can think of is getting into the papers?'

'Do you mind, Inspector? Do you have any idea what has just happened? The great Betty Winter is dead! Her public has a right to know.'

Rath looked the producer in the eye. 'If you ever pull anything like this again, I will make a world of trouble for you, my friend!'

'How and whether I choose to inform the press on my premises is up to me.'

'Oh yes,' Rath smiled, 'and whether I choose to make trouble for you or not is up to *me*!'

5

He calls the waiter and orders another Eiswein. He needs more wine. Really, he should have started eating long ago. His body is crying out for sugar.

'Would the gentleman like to see the menu now?'

'Give me another minute,' he says, even if he suspects he'll be on his own today. She's more than an hour late.

He doesn't know why she's stood him up, but he's sure it must be something important. She wouldn't just leave him in the lurch. He knows by now she's swallowed the bait. No reason to change his plans, she'll be there for filming tomorrow.

Where has the waiter got to? He must have more wine!

Will he ever get used to the fact that sugar can save his life?

You'll get used to it.

Mother's smile.

You'll have to.

He gazes at the wine glass in disbelief. May I?

You must.

I must.

He takes a careful sip and tastes the sweetness, feels it running down his throat.

Eiswein. Sweet Eiswein.

A dream he has dreamed for years becomes reality. He and his mother are sitting in the restaurant in honour of the occasion. The first jab. The first time he has administered it himself after days at the clinic. After all those attempts with insulin.

Alive again. After all those years waiting for death.

His second birth.

The waiters arrive and place the crystal glasses on the white tablecloth. Mother's smile. Eat, my child.

He cannot eat, the tears are flowing. He sobs uncontrollably, sees her dismay through the veil of tears.

She strokes his hand but he pulls away. He cannot bear her touch. He is wary of her love. He doesn't understand it. Doesn't believe it is real.

It's over now. I'll make it up to you. Everything. You're still my boy.

He dries his tears, takes the fork and bites carefully. His tongue tastes fresh crab, dill, the sweetness of tomatoes. The sweetness overwhelms him, flows through his body.

Mother smiles, and picks at her food without eating. She just smiles and picks and stares at him, as he lifts the second forkful to his mouth and then the third. She shouldn't stare at him. He isn't a funfair sensation, an elephant man, a monster, a natural wonder.

You'll be able to live like everyone else. Live with other people.

Finally, she, too, takes a bite.

They eat in silence and a waiter refills their glasses. She dabs her mouth with the serviette and raises her glass. To life!

To life.

They drink Eiswein, sweet Eiswein.

What will you do now?

I'll study.

That's good.

Study medicine.

Again she tries to grasp his hand, but breaks off before contact, withdraws once more. Sadness in her eyes. My boy, my darling boy!

The waiters arrive with the next course, removing the silver covers from the plates at the same time.

He still can't believe it. His first proper meal. His first proper meal after years of starvation.

It's over. Everything will be all right.

He really believed that.

Back then.

He was wrong. So wrong.

———

He glances at the time. No, she won't be coming. He shouldn't hold it against her, can't hold it against her. It's the price he pays for their secret meetings. If something crops up, she has no way of letting him know. It doesn't really matter.

What matters is that no one learns of their plans.

What matters is that she is there for filming tomorrow.

What matters is that her destiny be fulfilled.

At last, the waiter brings the wine.

6

With little traffic on Berliner Strasse at this hour Rath put his foot down and flogged the Buick over the wet asphalt through Tempelhof and towards the north. Gräf was sitting in the passenger's seat, discreetly holding onto the door handle, probably regretting not having gone with Plisch and Plum.

Under different circumstances Rath might have shown more consideration, but not now. The speed soothed him and, besides, what the hell were sports cars for anyway?

'Gereon, I'm in no rush.'

'A car like this needs to be driven properly once in a while.'

'I'm just as mad about that arsehole as you are, but that's no reason to take your anger out on the gas pedal.'

Rath did in fact use the brake—the lights on Flughafenstrasse were showing red. 'He loses his lead actress and straightaway smells a business opportunity, and then all that affected grief! I'd like nothing better than to lock him up.'

They had taken part in Bellmann's press conference to keep things under control, answering questions about the actress's death as evasively as possible, and keeping an eye on the producer. The reporters had made no secret of the fact that they were still angry at police for turfing them out of the studio, which made them doubly attentive to Bellmann. The film producer, who had served them coffee and biscuits, gave an unbearably unctuous speech about the great Betty Winter's incomparable dramatic art, and how her desperately premature death had deprived German cinema of one of its biggest and brightest talents.

'We will do our utmost to ensure that *Liebesgewitter* reaches cinemas, even if only as a fragment,' he concluded, with a moist glint to his eyes. 'We owe it to the great Betty Winter, and please feel free to write that. This film is her legacy. It shows what kind of future German sound films might have had, if . . .'

When he broke off mid-sentence and turned away from journalists, a handkerchief to his eyes, Rath would have liked nothing better than to shout *Bullshit*. What a farce! Rath wouldn't allow these film types to take him for another ride, that much he had sworn to himself.

The lights changed to green and the Buick's wheels spun for a moment before the car shot forward.

'What an arsehole!'

'Bellmann is an arsehole, no doubt about it,' Gräf said, reaching for security again, 'but that isn't a crime. Nor is being business-savvy. We can't lock people up for attempting to make capital out of someone's death.'

'Unless they've helped cause it.'

'*Deliberately* helped cause it. The way I see it, there are two poor wretches who have that woman on their conscience: Glaser and Meisner. A regrettable chain of unhappy circumstances. One of them has broken down and the other has fled out of guilt. Even if it was the electric shock that killed her, the person really responsible for Betty Winter's death is the lighting technician, and he must realise that too. You can't help feeling sorry for the guy.'

'He fled the scene. That makes him a suspect.'

'He's suddenly confronted with the fact that he's got someone's death on his conscience,' Gräf said. 'Not everyone can take that. Could you?'

Rath stared at the road ahead. A taxi pulled out in front of him, and he took his foot off the gas. The further north they went, the heavier the traffic. Time to slow down.

'Fancy a beer in the Nasse Dreieck?' Gräf asked as they turned onto Skalitzer Strasse at Hallesches Tor.

'Not today. But I can drop you off if you like.'

'I'm not about to start drinking on my own just yet,' Gräf said. 'Take me home.'

The detective lived in a furnished room at Schlesisches Tor. No great detour for Rath, who gave Gräf a brief tip of the hat before heading back to Luisenufer. As he crossed the rear courtyard, he realised there was a light on in his first-floor flat.

He had barely thought about Kathi in the last few hours, but now saw her red coat in the rear-view mirror again and recalled the wait in the café.

He paused outside the door before opening it, and took a deep breath as if preparing for a lengthy dive.

There was a second coat on the stand next to Kathi's, a dark gentleman's coat. Music blared from the living room, muffled by the closed door. It was one of Kathi's awful pop records. Normally he could prevent her from putting that sort of thing on. Except when she was alone, of course.

Only she wasn't alone. Loud laughter came from the living room, Kathi's silly giggling accompanied by a deep bass. Who the hell had she dragged back to the flat?

Rath kept his hat and coat on, mentally raised his fists and opened the door. She had achieved at least one thing: he was in the right mood to turf her out—but the sight of her guest took his anger in a completely different direction.

Kathi had her back to him, still laughing. Opposite her sat an older gentleman with a neat white moustache, raising a glass of cognac, a man whom he hadn't seen for the best part of a year, and who now looked up in surprise and beamed at him expectantly.

'Gereon,' the white-haired man said, 'there you are at last!'

Rath didn't respond, but turned off the record player.

'Gereon,' Kathi said, nothing more. She would have a guilty conscience. Usually, he didn't let her near the record player.

He still said nothing, first putting on a new record, *Big Boy*, with Beiderbecke on the cornet, a present from his brother, Severin. After the first few beats, he turned it up.

Right away Kathi sensed there was trouble brewing. 'I'll take care of the washing-up,' she said, and disappeared into the kitchen like the perfect housewife.

Rath waited until the living room door had clicked shut before sitting in her still-warm chair. He gazed at the white-haired man.

'Evening, Papa,' he said. 'Make yourself at home, why don't you?'

Engelbert Rath cleared his throat before speaking. 'Can we turn the music down a little?' he said. 'It's impossible to hold a conversation with that racket!'

'It's how I relax after work.'

Engelbert Rath stood up. It took a moment for him to find the right button and turn the volume so low that the sound of running water could be heard from the kitchen. His gaze alighted on the record collection on the lower shelf and he shook his head. 'Still listening to that Negro music?' he asked.

'Have you come all this way to ask me that?'

'Records from America?'

'Do you really want to talk about America?'

Engelbert Rath didn't take the bait. 'You have a new case, Fräulein Preußner said?'

The waiter in Uhlandeck must have told her. 'A dead actress,' Rath said, 'in a film studio.'

'Shame you can't be there in Düsseldorf.' Engelbert Rath rummaged in his brown briefcase. 'Your mother sends her love. She gave me something for you. Here . . .' He produced an item decorated with colourful ribbons and bound in wrapping paper. 'Your birthday present.'

'Thank you,' Rath said, placing the package to one side. 'It's still a few days away.'

'Your mother thought I might as well bring it. It's safer than by post.'

'So you're not coming to visit me?'

Engelbert Rath shrugged. 'Your mother would have liked to come, but you know how she is. She won't take the train on her own.' He cleared his throat. 'And I . . . well, on Ash Wednesday of all days it's impossible to get away from Cologne. There's the reception in the town hall after early morning mass, and the fish meal in the casino that evening is something I really can't . . .'

'You don't have to give me your entire schedule.'

Engelbert Rath gestured towards the package and reclaimed his place on the sofa. 'At least you have our present.'

The men stared at each other in silence. From the kitchen came the gurgle of water and the clinking of china.

'She's nice, your fiancée,' Engelbert Rath said.

'She's not my fiancée.'

Engelbert Rath only looked surprised for a moment. 'I can never get used to these modern ways. She's a proper lady at any rate. You might have said something! I thought I'd come to the wrong flat. But Fräulein Preußner knew who I was right away!'

'Must be the photo I keep on my bedside table.'

Engelbert Rath pulled a sour face. 'Here I am visiting my son, and this is how he treats me!'

'What did you expect? I've been living in this city almost a year and neither of you has visited me even once . . . Now you turn up, completely unannounced, and expect me to roll out the red carpet?'

'People who live in glass houses shouldn't throw stones,' Engelbert Rath said. He didn't need to speak any louder to lend his words weight. 'Have you bothered to put in a single appearance at ours since you've been living in Berlin? You didn't even spend Christmas in Cologne, and you know how pleased that would have made your mother. Instead you put your name down for holiday duty—even though Karl would have given you the time off.'

'Have you been spying on me?'

'I don't need to spy on anyone. I'm a policeman.'

'How is it I always seem to forget?'

Engelbert Rath looked tired as he gazed at his son. 'We see each other so rarely, Gereon, we shouldn't spend the time squabbling. You're the only son I have left.'

Because you refuse to give Severin a chance, Gereon thought. 'Why are you here?'

'We have an appointment. A friend needs your help.'

'I don't recall any appointment.'

'I've already spoken to Fräulein Preußner.' Engelbert gestured with his head towards the kitchen. 'She's happy for me to borrow you for a while. It won't take long. You'll be back by nine, maybe half past. Keep your hat and coat on, we need to head to Kaiserhof.'

That was precisely what he hated about his father. Engelbert Rath had to be in control of everything, had to pull the strings wherever he went, take care of things you'd never asked him to, but Gereon hated himself even more for allowing his father to monopolise him like this. Something deep inside prevented him from putting up any kind of resistance.

'I knew you wouldn't let me down, Gereon.' Engelbert Rath rose to his feet. 'If we hurry we can still get there on time.'

His father's right hand pushed him towards the door and he obeyed, just like he always did.

As they stepped into the hallway, Kathi was standing in the kitchen door, tea towel in hand and smiling back at them, a monument to the German housewife. Gereon looked her briefly in the eye as he took his leave.

Her gaze told him everything he needed to know.

She knew something was up, and was refusing to accept it.

There was a build-up of traffic at Moritzplatz, with a battered truck blocking almost the entire lane and a policeman waving vehicles through one by one. It was a tight-lipped journey.

'An American car?' was all Engelbert Rath said as he slipped into the Buick's passenger seat. There was disapproval etched on his face, and Gereon had said nothing more out of sheer annoyance.

It wasn't until they were stuck at Moritzplatz that his father broke the silence. 'We'd have been better off taking a taxi,' he said.

'It'd be sitting here just like us,' Rath replied angrily.

The policeman waved the Buick through, past the accident and into Oranienstrasse. Before crossing Leipziger Strasse they had to pause briefly at a red light; otherwise they made good progress. Gereon was doing his best, but obviously his best wasn't good enough.

'Late,' Engelbert Rath said, as he climbed out of the car at Wilhelmplatz. 'We're almost ten minutes late.'

Go to hell, Gereon thought, taking his time to lock up. His father was already striding towards the hotel entrance.

The Hotel Kaiserhof and its cuisine were popular with politicians and high-ranking civil servants from nearby Wilhelmstrasse. Engelbert Rath led his son purposefully towards the restaurant on the ground floor. In its oak-panelled surrounds, the babble of voices seemed more refined than it would elsewhere, the clinking of glasses more subdued. People seemed to be talking, eating and drinking with the handbrake on.

Engelbert Rath was a man who knew what he was about. They made their way determinedly towards a table, where a group of formally dressed men sat, looking as if they had been driven straight from a session at the Reichstag. It was immediately clear who was in charge. The man with his back to the wall had a face like an Indian chief with high cheekbones and an implacable gaze that took in both Raths straightaway. His expression remained unchanged as he mumbled something to his table companions and stood up.

'Please excuse our being late, Konrad,' Engelbert Rath began, 'but the police service . . . even in Berlin . . . my son . . . !'

'It's fine, Engelbert, it's fine!' The Indian pronounced it 'Engelbäät'. He had a Cologne accent. 'My train isn't leaving for two hours anyway,' he said, those unknowable Indian eyes seeming almost friendly. 'So? How is the young Rath? Settled into the imperial capital?'

Gereon shook his hand. 'Thank you for asking, Mayor Adenauer.'

'Let's forget about the titles, shall we? Here I'm not the Mayor, or the President of the Prussian State Council. We're meeting on a purely private basis. Three Cologners in Berlin.'

Gereon gave a deliberate smile.

'Let's go to the bar,' Adenauer said. 'I've a table booked.'

A bottle of Zeltinger Kirchenpfad awaited them next to the reserved sign. Their host had left nothing to chance, which was perhaps why Police Director Engelbert Rath got on so well with him, their status as fellow party members notwithstanding. The truth was that Rath's father had always kept in with those whose acquaintance could benefit his career. Successfully too: he had been the youngest chief inspector in Cologne in his day, and was now police director.

'We can speak freely here,' Adenauer said, showing them to their places. The waiter filled the two wine glasses and he began.

'Good that your son has found the time, Engelbäät,' he said. 'Have you told him what it's about?'

'It's too delicate. I thought it would be best if you . . .'

'Let's have a toast first!' Adenauer had a glass of water in front of him, and drank their health.

The Raths raised their glasses and drank. The wine was far too sweet for Gereon's liking, but his father's lips curved appreciatively. 'A really nice drop, this, Konrad.'

'I know what you like, Engelbäät!' Their host placed his water in front of him and cleared his throat. 'So, let's get to the point . . . It's an unpleasant business . . . most unpleasant . . .'

'The police deal almost exclusively with unpleasant business,' said Rath.

'Please, young Rath! Let's forget about the police. As I said, this is a private meeting.'

'Let the mayor explain, Gereon!'

It hadn't taken five minutes for his father to catapult him back to the bad old days. Gereon, the cheeky young fool who'd be better off keeping his mouth shut when the adults had important matters to discuss.

'Your father, Herr Rath, is helping me in a particularly delicate matter, and I must say it's rather handy that the Rath family is also represented here in Berlin . . .' That's how easy it was for the Cologne crowd to catch up with you, even in the middle of the imperial capital. 'To cut a long story short, I am being blackmailed.'

'Our lord mayor is receiving anonymous letters,' Engelbert Rath whispered.

The Indian nodded. 'Someone is threatening—how shall I put it?—to make certain information public that the public has no business knowing. And which could drag the good name of Adenauer through the mud.'

'What kind of information?'

'Information that could spell the end of my political existence if the Nazis get their hands on it, or the Communists.'

'I'd need to know a little more than that. If you want me to help you, you'll have to tell me what it's about.'

'Glanzstoff shares,' Adenauer said.

'Shares in American Glanzstoff, the rayon plant,' Engelbert Rath explained.

'I've got loads of them,' Adenauer said. 'Absolutely loads. Worth millions . . . At least, they were worth millions when I bought them two years ago. My entire fortune's invested in them, and more besides. A loan from Deutsche Bank . . .'

'I see,' said Rath, 'and the share price has been falling through the floor since October.'

'It went through the floor some time ago. I'd never have thought it could slip so far, had always hoped things would pick up again. But these last few months . . . In short, my debts with the bank are now greater than the market value of my shares. Significantly greater . . .'

'In other words, you're ruined,' Rath said, pleased to register the look of displeasure on his father's face. 'How do they mean to blackmail you when you've already hit rock bottom?'

'I've got friends at the bank who are willing to help me. I just don't want it to be shouted from the rooftops.'

'And that's precisely what these anonymous letters are threatening to do . . .'

'My opponents have been waiting for an opportunity just like this, both the left and the right, and it's been handed to them on a plate. What a time for it to happen!'

'Why haven't you passed the case on to the police?'

'You know yourself that not all officers can be trusted. Something like this needs to be dealt with discreetly. By experienced police officers, but not by the police.'

Rath nodded. 'What makes you think *I* can help you? My father is far more experienced when it comes to police work.'

'The letters are from Berlin, I'm certain of it. And not just because up till now they've only been sent to my Berlin office. The blackmailer is in the city somewhere. Take a look yourself . . .' He fetched a small bundle of papers from the inside pocket of his jacket and passed one of the pages to Rath.

Red-coloured pencil. Big block capitals. Crooked letters but legible nonetheless. It looked almost like a little home-made placard.

FORD STAYS IN BERLIN, it said, OR ADENAUER GOES TO JAIL!

'What's that supposed to mean?' he asked.

'That's the fee,' the mayor said. 'The blackmailer doesn't want money, it's something else he's after. He wants to save the Ford plant at Westhafen.'

'The car factory?'

'Only I'm afraid its days are already numbered. There's nothing more to be done.'

'I don't know much about that, you're going to have to explain.'

'Ford is relocating to Cologne,' Adenauer said. 'Everything's signed, and we'll be laying the groundwork in Riehl later this year. Europe's most state-of-the-art car factory will make Berlin's seem old in comparison. Then it'll be goodnight, Westhafen.'

'And that's what the blackmailer's hoping to avoid?'

Adenauer nodded. 'It would appear so. Only he's picked the wrong man. No Adenauer allows himself to be blackmailed! Besides, even if I wanted to, there's nothing I can do. The same goes for the Mayor of Berlin.'

'Herr Böß has his own problems at the moment,' Gereon said.

'Tell me about it! The only person who can do anything is Henry Ford, who won't let a single car roll off the production line in Berlin once things are up and running in Riehl. I can say that much for certain.'

'There'll be even more unemployed people in Berlin.'

Adenauer shrugged his shoulders. 'What do you want me to do? Hundreds of jobs will be created in Cologne instead. That's how it goes sometimes, it's the way of the world, and blackmailing people isn't about to change that!'

'Even so, that doesn't mean whoever's blackmailing you can't still do some damage, and that's what you'd like me to prevent.'

'Quick on the uptake, your son,' Adenauer said to Engelbert Rath.

Rath felt as he had when his mother praised her son's school grades to assorted friends over coffee. 'How do you know the blackmailer really has the information he's threatening you with?' he asked.

'See for yourself.' Adenauer passed him another sheet of paper. 'This is the second page from the first letter.'

This letter didn't look like a placard; there was a lot more text too. Typewritten, again in red. *Wouldn't it be unfortunate if the world were to hear what was discussed in passing at the Deutsche Bank's supervisory board meeting by board members Adenauer and Blüthgen, as well as Bank Director Brüning?*

'What's that supposed to mean?'

'It means somebody knows exactly what's going on,' Adenauer said. 'I want you to find out who it is, and make it clear that it's *him* rather than me who will be facing jail time, if so much as a single word of these confidential discussions is leaked!'

'How do you suppose I do that? I'm a police officer . . .'

'Precisely, you know the best way to handle a thing like this. You won't regret it, young man. I still have a good relationship with your commissioner. My word counts for something with Zörgiebel, believe me. Your father had already made chief inspector by your age. It's time you followed in his footsteps.'

'The interior ministry has issued a moratorium on promotions . . .'

'Because Prussia must save, but there are always exceptions. Even in times like these, outstanding candidates can be rewarded.'

Engelbert Rath nodded in agreement. 'Chief Inspector Gereon Rath—it has a nice ring to it,' he said, and raised his wine glass. 'To the next chief inspector in the Rath family!'

Gereon raised his glass and smiled, but only sipped at the sweet liquid. Chief Inspector didn't sound too bad at all, and he wouldn't have that twit Böhm telling him what to do.

'Inspector Rath?'

The waiter's voice only served to remind him of his current rank. The man's gaze surveyed the group briefly before ruling out its two older members and alighting on Gereon. 'Telephone for you, Herr Rath.'

It was Czerwinski. They had finally caught Glaser. The lighting technician had come home that evening. All they'd had to do was pick him up.

'He's all nicely wrapped up and waiting for you at Alex,' the detective said. 'Thought you might like to have a little chat with him tonight. Your girlfriend was kind enough to tell us where you were. I hope we're not interrupting anything.'

Rath was about to have a go at the fat lump for his lack of respect, but chose to hold back. Czerwinski had done a good job, and it wasn't often you could say that. 'I'll be with you shortly,' he said.

'I'm afraid duty calls,' he said as he returned to the table with his hat and coat.

He offered Adenauer his hand. 'Many thanks for inviting me here, Herr Mayor,' he said.

'Take the letters with you.' Adenauer passed him the bundle across the table.

'Well, my boy,' said Engelbert Rath, standing to say goodbye to his son. The police director attempted something approaching a hug but was forced to admit defeat. Otherwise so commanding, Engelbert Rath could only offer his son an awkward handshake. 'Take care. Can you find your own way out? I still have matters to discuss with the mayor.'

'It's OK, Father.' Rath cleared his throat. 'Will we see each other tomorrow?'

The police director's face froze. 'Mother . . . we . . .' he stammered. 'Well . . . I promised your mother I wouldn't leave her too long. I'm taking the night train.'

'Not staying in Berlin a moment longer than necessary—is that right, gents?'

The remark was supposed to disguise his disappointment, but somehow he didn't get it quite right. As much as his father's unannounced visit had angered him, he was equally hurt that Engelbert Rath—in the middle of Carnival—had only come to Berlin to do his old friend Konrad a favour. But then, he knew his father, what else should he expect?

'Well, safe trip home then,' he said and made for the exit without looking round, descending the steps into the rain. Outside, he took a deep breath before returning to the car. He spent the next few minutes sitting behind the wheel observing Wilhelmplatz at night. Apart from a few pedestrians emerging from the underground, and the two uniformed officers in front of the hotel, the square was completely empty. The city's nightlife was happening elsewhere.

Rath couldn't remember having made any promises to Adenauer, but he felt the weight of the letters in his inside pocket, and knew he had an assignment that could help him make Chief Inspector.

His mind turned to Kathi, waiting for him at Luisenufer, and he was glad he could still head out to Alex. Hopefully she'd be asleep when he got home. He started the engine and drove off. It would do him good to spend a little time focusing on someone else's life. What kind of man was this Glaser? he wondered.

In the meantime he must have realised that running wasn't a solution, especially now, awaiting interrogation in the Castle. You couldn't escape guilt like that, someone's death. No matter how far you ran, no matter how quickly; nobody knew that better than Gereon Rath. It was a burden you carried with you for the rest of your life.

Behind the construction fences at Alexanderplatz, the police headquarters rose dark into the night sky. *Red Castle* was the name Berliners gave to the mighty brick building, which had turned out bigger than the City Palace. Unlike the palace, however, it still had a function. His colleagues simply called their workplace *Castle*, a name that was reassuring somehow, and fitting too, even if Rath's former stamping ground in Cologne appeared far more medieval than its Berlin counterpart. The façade actually invoked the Florentine Renaissance, but somehow the Prussians even managed to turn the building's delicate motifs into a forbidding stronghold.

Rath parked the Buick in the atrium, where a riot squad was just getting into a car. Once in the stairwell, however, he was on his own again. The endless corridors on the first floor were deserted, but brought to life now and again by the faint echoes of steps, voices or slamming doors. In Homicide, only the late shift was still present, an inspector and an assistant detective: Brenner, one of Böhm's bootlickers, and Lange, the new man from Hannover, who had been transferred to the Castle a few weeks back.

'Evening,' Rath greeted his colleagues. 'Where are Czerwinski and Henning?'

'I sent them home,' Brenner said.

'What makes you think you can give orders to my people?' Rath snapped.

'What do you mean, your people? I'm in charge of the late shift, and as far as I know neither of them are on it. We're to avoid unnecessary overtime. Orders from above.'

'They're both part of *my* team, and they've just brought in a suspect. I hope you haven't sent him home too.'

'Don't panic, Inspector,' Brenner grinned. 'Your package is sitting all nicely wrapped in custody.'

'Then what are you waiting for, Detective?'

'Waiting for?'

'Get your arse in gear and make sure my man is ready for questioning in five minutes at the most!'

Brenner reached for the receiver.

At the door Rath turned round once more. 'And another thing, Detective,' he said, friendly once more, 'if you ever give orders to my people again I will kick up such a fuss that not even Chief Inspector Böhm will be able to help you. Clear?'

'I wouldn't talk so big if I were you,' Brenner grumbled, before putting the call through.

Rath had to walk a few paces along the corridor to get to his office. Somewhat removed from the other rooms in A Division, it had been the only one available when he first joined Homicide. It was pretty cold. The heating was on low, so he kept his coat on for the time being. Taking a seat in the outer office, at his secretary's desk, he leafed through the personal file on Glaser, which Czerwinski had left alongside the man's papers. The dates tallied with those from his passport.

Barely ten minutes later, there was a knock at the door and a guard pushed a pale, intimidated-looking man into the room. 'Here he is, Inspector.'

Rath posted the guard outside and examined the suspect. Glaser had halted by the door and was looking about him uncertainly. Perhaps it was no bad thing that he'd been left to stew in custody. He smelled ripe.

'Take a seat,' Rath said, leafing through the papers. Glaser shuffled forward and sat down. Rath said suddenly and without looking up, 'Your name is Peter Glaser . . .'

'Yes.'

'Born 25th September 1902.'

'Yes.'

'Resident at Röntgenstrasse 10 in Charlottenburg.'

'Yes.'

'Since November 1st 1929 you've been working as a lighting technician at La Belle Film Production in Marien . . .'

'Pardon me?' All of a sudden the man, who up until now had been hunched in his chair like a limp dishrag, sat up straight.

'Nothing about you being hard of hearing in the file.'

'That's because I'm not.'

'I asked where you work.'

'No, you didn't.' His voice sounded as if he had just woken up. 'You read the file and told me where I'm *supposed* to work. Something to do with film, but it isn't true.'

'Then why is your name in this file?'

Glaser shrugged his shoulders and gave Rath a belligerent look. 'You'll have to ask whoever drew it up. My personal file is with Siemens & Halske. I'm an electrician at the Elmowerk.'

'The what?'

'Can't you keep up?' Glaser was beginning to get the upper hand. He had even stopped shivering, despite the cold. 'I work for Siemens! At the Elektromotorenwerk, the electric motor plant. I'd just got back from my shift when your colleagues grabbed me right outside the door to my flat, handcuffs, pistol, the lot. I just hope my neighbours didn't see. That Knauf next door is a nosy bat.'

Rath looked at Glaser's passport. The man in the photo and the man in front of him were the same, no doubt about it.

'Got the wrong man?' Glaser asked.

Rath snapped the document shut. 'We'll soon have this sorted.'

That *soon* turned out to be optimistic. Rath offered the increasingly unruly Glaser hot tea until, finally, after three-quarters of an hour that dragged interminably, the guard pushed a thoroughly dishevelled-looking Heinrich Bellmann through the door. On the telephone, Bellmann hadn't given an entirely sober impression, and now brought the smell of alcohol with him.

'Good evening, Inspector,' he said. 'I didn't realise you work in the middle of the night too.'

'Please, have a seat.' Rath offered him a chair by the desk.

'Please excuse my condition, I had a little too much . . . it's not normally my way . . . but Betty's death . . . I'm only human after all!'

'Don't you want to say hello to my guest?'

'A pleasure.' Bellmann stretched his right hand across the desk towards Glaser. 'Bellmann.'

'Glaser,' said the other as he shook the producer's hand.

'You don't know this man?' Rath asked.

'Should I?' Bellmann asked.

'This is Peter Glaser.'

'Pardon me?'

'Your lighting technician.'

'Nonsense!'

'Did you bring the photo I asked for?'

Bellmann reached inside his jacket. 'It's from the Christmas party,' he said, hunching his heavy shoulders apologetically.

The photo showed a good-looking man holding a punch glass, smiling cheerfully into the camera with his arm around a woman. Rath had never seen the man before, but the woman was Betty Winter. Alarm bells started to ring quietly, but insistently.

'Here,' Bellmann said, tapping the photo, 'that's Glaser. He got on well with Betty, especially that night.' He shook his head. 'I still can't believe it. That she's no longer with us, I mean.'

The whole time Peter Glaser had been eyeing the photo curiously. By now he was craning his neck, eyes almost popping out of his head. 'I don't believe it,' he said. 'That's bloody Felix! What's he doing next to Betty Winter?'

The matter was soon resolved. Bellmann's missing lighting technician was called Felix Krempin, and he had obviously used the identity of his unsuspecting friend, Peter Glaser, to sign up with La Belle Film Production. In reality, Krempin worked as a production manager at Montana Film.

No sooner had Glaser mentioned the name Montana than Bellmann hit the roof, going on about espionage, sabotage and worse. 'Those criminals! I should have known! They'll stop at nothing! Not even murder!'

Rath called for the guard to accompany Bellmann outside. They could still hear him through the closed door as Rath began a quick-fire interview of Peter Glaser about his friend, Felix Krempin.

'Thanks for your help,' Rath said, by way of goodbye. 'It seems your friend has played a nasty trick on you—and on us too.'

A trick wasn't how Bellmann saw it. He had calmed down by the time he re-entered the office, but wasn't about to retract his accusations. At least his suspicions could now be substantiated. He claimed that La Belle had frequently had trouble with Montana, with some disputes even going to court. Plagiarism was the least of it; it was a question of poaching artists, sabotaging premieres and all kinds of other dirty tricks. Similar accusations, 'all of them rather far-fetched', as the producer would have it, had also been made against Bellmann by Montana, resulting in the La Belle owner being 'hauled in front of a judge' on several occasions. A long list, therefore, to which could now be added sabotage of filming and the murder of the incensed Heinrich Bellmann's most important actress.

Murder as the ultimate means of sabotage seemed unlikely to Rath, but he could understand the film producer's rage. There had to be a reason why Krempin had signed on at La Belle under a false name.

Rath was deathly tired but his hunter's instinct had been wakened. He would sound Montana out first thing tomorrow before Böhm could call him off.

The search for Krempin had already begun by the time Rath returned to Homicide, though Brenner and Lange had since departed. Instead there was a fat man sitting at the desk, engrossed in the files.

'Superintendent Gennat!'

The fat man looked up. 'Rath! What are you still doing here? Don't get your hopes up! You're not getting my bed. I need it myself!'

Buddha kept a bed in the box room next to his office, which in truth was more like a living room.

'Nice to see you again, Sir,' Rath said. 'Just back from Düsseldorf?'

Gennat nodded. 'Somehow the way from the station always leads straight to Alex. Funny, isn't it? I should have got married, then this wouldn't happen.'

'Perhaps it would. Are you making any progress?'

'Don't ask! You wouldn't believe how much information we've gathered, or how many tip-offs we've received from the Düsseldorf public. We now have a pretty clear idea how each murder was committed, but even that hasn't brought us any closer.'

Gennat took a *B.Z.* from his leather bag and unfolded the paper. 'I see you've been busy too,' he said and placed the newspaper on the table in front of Rath. 'I bought it in the station just now. Can you explain this to me?'

Rath stared at the paper. A special edition of *B.Z. am Mittag* with a headline in bold on the front page.

DEATH IN FILM STUDIO! BETTY WINTER STRUCK DEAD BY SPOTLIGHT! SABOTAGE?

Alongside the story were two photos, a perfect portrait of Betty Winter and a slightly blurred image which showed Gereon Rath against the backdrop of a film studio. In the background you could even make out part of the covered corpse—assuming you knew it was there in the first place.

'There isn't much to explain,' he said. 'An actress died and her producer wanted to make the headlines. The body wasn't even cold before he called a press conference.'

'And you helped him. Or is there some other reason you're quoted here?'

'The pack had already smelt blood. I had all journalists removed from the crime scene immediately, but the police can't prevent anyone from holding a press conference. Detective Gräf and I took part to maintain control, and to ensure speculation didn't run wild.'

'Well, you did a great job, I must say.'

Rath skimmed the text and saw that Bellmann's sabotage theory had been reported at length, yet he had said nothing about it at the press conference. Clearly the journalist was aware of the running battle with Montana—even if there was no mention of the studio by name. Rath swallowed hard when he realised that his own pronouncements had been so skilfully woven into the text that it appeared as if police officially supported the sabotage theory.

'I didn't authorise any of this,' he said.

Gennat nodded. 'That's OK, Rath, no one's saying you did. You have to be damn careful when dealing with the big city press. Their reporters can be very useful, but don't harbour any illusions about keeping them under control.'

'I'd be happy just to keep them off my back.'

'Don't take it so hard,' Gennat said. 'Tell me in your own words what happened in that film studio. Betty Winter isn't just anybody, you know. Böhm only jotted something down about a fatal accident he'd entrusted to you.'

Rath gave a concise report, right up to the bogus lighting technician. 'The false name, allied to his flight, makes the man highly suspicious,' he said. 'In the meantime everything points to sabotage. Perhaps Betty Winter wasn't meant to die, but it looks as if someone intended to cause her serious harm, and whoever it was, they were at least willing to entertain the possibility of her death. Right now it looks as if Felix Krempin is our man.'

Gennat nodded. 'Highly plausible, but be sure you don't draw any hasty conclusions. You've come a cropper like that before.'

'Mistakes are there to be learned from, Sir.'

'Where did you get that from? Is that what they teach you at police academy these days?'

'My father, Sir.'

'A shrewd man, your father. Policeman, isn't he?'

Rath nodded. 'Police director.'

'Then heed his advice and don't give too much away to the press. Better to share your knowledge with us at A Division.'

Gennat gazed at him sternly. Rath knew that Buddha respected him, but that he had no truck with high-handedness.

'How long are you staying in Berlin, Sir?'

'Until Wednesday. Düsseldorf is unbearable at the moment anyway. Carnival. Zörgiebel might see the attraction in cheering *Helau*, but it's not my thing at all.'

'The commissioner is from Mainz,' Rath said.

'And you? You're a Rhinelander too, aren't you?'

'Cologner,' Rath said. 'We say *Alaaf* instead of *Helau*, but I'm more than happy to do without all the fuss this year. It's more civilised in these parts.'

'There are plenty of Fasching balls in Berlin this weekend, if you should feel homesick.'

The telephone rang and, before Rath could respond, Gennat picked up.

'Yes,' Buddha nodded. 'Inspector Rath is still here. Just a moment.' He handed him the receiver. 'The search unit,' he said. 'It looks as if your suspect really has gone to ground.'

7

Saturday 1st March 1930

Deathly tired, Rath finally dragged himself up the stairs at Luisenufer. With Gennat's blessing he had intensified the search for the fugitive Krempin and, tomorrow, every police station in Berlin would receive a picture of the man. ED were still in the lab, duplicating a cutting of Bellmann's Christmas party photo. Felix Krempin had disappeared. Whatever motive there might have been to drop a heavy spotlight on a dainty actress, the production manager clearly had it.

In this light, Bellmann's suspicions were plausible, even if his priority was most likely making trouble for Montana Film. Rath glanced at the time: half past twelve. He wouldn't get much sleep now, as he wanted to be at Montana as early as possible tomorrow, ready for action. His keys were in his hand when he remembered that Kathi would be waiting for him.

Suddenly time was frozen.

He couldn't get into bed as if nothing had happened. For a moment he considered turning on his heel, driving out to Schlesisches Tor and spending the night on Gräf's sofa. Instead he cursed his own cowardice and turned the key in the lock, surprised at how loud it was. He pulled the door quietly shut and crept through the hall without turning on the light. Closing the living room door behind him, he groped towards the chair, reaching for the switch on the standard lamp. One click and it cast its dim light around the room. He laid his hat and coat over the second chair. She had cleared away the glasses, but the bottle of cognac was still on the table. Rath fetched a new glass from the cupboard, sat in his chair and poured.

You're such a fool, he thought, creeping around like a burglar, like a stranger in your own home. He washed the thought down with cognac and poured another. He wouldn't go through to her until he'd had enough.

Hazy and blurred in the warm, yellow island of light gleaming in the window pane, he lifted the glass to his reflection. The only company he could stand right now. 'Cheers!' he said drowsily . . .

He gave a start; had he been asleep or merely nodded off? His mouth tasted like a wrung-out cleaning rag and his glass was on the carpet next to the chair. Luckily he had drained it already.

Only now did he realise how much he must have had to drink. He needed a glass of water. In the kitchen he fetched a glass from the cupboard and held it under the tap, allowing the cold water to pour over his hands. It felt good. He drank and held the glass under the tap again.

He didn't see the note until he was heading back to the door. Lying in the middle of the table was a little sheet of paper from the spiral-bound notebook she used to make her shopping lists.

Sorry, darling, he read, and felt his stomach cramping at the words . . .

but I just couldn't stand it any longer. I feel so alone in this flat when you're not here. It really isn't easy loving a policeman, but I've almost got used to it. Almost. Seems like today just wasn't meant to be. I've called for a taxi and gone to my sister, she needs someone to comfort.

We'll see each other at the ball tomorrow. I'll try to be at yours by half past six, then we could go together.

With love
Kathi.

P.S. There's some stew left on the stove. Remember it tastes best when it's hot.

Rath placed the note back on the table.

On the one hand, he felt relief. On the other, now that he knew she was no longer in the flat, he was overcome by a loneliness that pained him almost physically. He was freezing, even though she had left the heating on. Only moments ago he had been trying to avoid her, seeking refuge in cognac, and would've sooner wished her in hell. Now he felt her absence like a stabbing pain to the heart.

At least he could go to bed, but was that what he really wanted? All of a sudden, he felt choked by a dreadful fear. The night wasn't over yet; it had only just begun.

He went back into the living room, put on a Coleman Hawkins record and opened the bottle again.

8

He stares at the headline and tries to tell himself they are only letters. Bold, black letters on cheap paper.

DEATH IN FILM STUDIO! BETTY WINTER STRUCK DEAD BY SPOTLIGHT!

They are only letters.

Letters are not reality.

Just a day later and he'd know they were lying. Death would no longer be able to claim her, not anymore, because she'd already be immortal.

He lets the paper drop. The smell of fresh coffee drifts towards him, suddenly seeming less real than the letters in the paper, than what the letters in the paper are telling him; it intensifies the feeling of impotence, an impotence he hasn't felt for years.

She has been wrested from him.

'Would Master like anything else?'

Albert is standing there, just as he has always stood there, even in those grim, chill years he would sooner erase from his life.

Albert is always there, has always been there. Every day, every single one.

The day the world . . .

On the day the world withdraws from his life, Albert stands at the window, closing the room's heavy velvet green curtains. It is growing dark, only the dim gaslight remains, and the concerned faces, the stern faces, that look at him as if they mean to pin him down with their gaze, pin him down forever in this room.

They have caught him.

In the larder.

What were they thinking? What did they expect from a fifteen-year-old boy tormented by hunger and reduced to skin and bones in one of the city's wealthiest homes—whose kitchen alone employs six staff? Whose larder can compete with those of the most expensive restaurants?

He's been at it for weeks. He knew when the kitchen would be empty and the coast would be clear. Stomach rumbling, he would stand in front of all the delicacies and pick tentatively at things he wasn't allowed to eat.

At sweet things.

It doesn't matter how much he eats, he won't get fat, that's the way it's been ever since he's been afflicted by this disease.

And yet they realised.

Father realised and laid a devious trap for his son.

The shame of standing in the larder under their gaze, mouth smeared red, the bottle of juice in his hand. If only they were reproachful, but they are merely disappointed.

He's just a child, Richard, Mother says. She has tears in her eyes.

We have to protect him from himself, Father says. Otherwise he'll never grow up.

The servants are silent.

Albert closes the heavy door, the key turns loudly in the lock, and it is done. His imprisonment has begun; the world is now on the outside.

True, they still let him out, but only under supervision, two minders constantly at his side. No, he can't accept that.

He bows to his fate.

Accepts that he can no longer have friends.

No longer find love in this world.

Fifteen years in which a dark curtain settles over everything.

Don't let it! Create your own reality!

Free from pain, free from hunger, free from disease.

'Would Master like anything else?'

Albert is the only constant in his life, the only enduring presence. He shakes his head and the old servant leaves the room in silence.

He folds the paper, as he always does.

For a brief moment, he would like to be another person, in another world, like on those long evenings in front of the screen; but reality won't allow it, not this time.

Perhaps it is just a dream? But who decides what is dream, what reality?

The pain bores its way into his heart, dream or reality, for a long time it has made no difference.

Betty Winter struck dead by spotlight.

And then, in big letters, he sees that one word, framed by a question mark.

SABOTAGE?

His pain transforms into rage, into rage that knows no bounds. He reaches for the carefully folded newspaper and tears it, rips it into smaller and smaller pieces that swirl around him like oversized snowflakes.

Who has done this to him?

Who?

He loved her, damn it!

9

The Montana office was located at the expensive end of Kantstrasse. The blonde woman who had let him in indicated with a wave of the hand and a chilly glance that he should take a seat in one of the modern leather chairs in front of her desk, with no choice but to listen while she prattled into the telephone.

'. . . but of course you can view our sound films with American devices; although you *are* then obliged to pay a small licensing fee, which you will naturally . . .'

The caller finally managed to get a word in. The blonde listened open-mouthed, waiting for her opportunity and—snap—let fly once more.

'But of course! We'll have the copies sent over to you with the paperwork, all you have to do is sign, that's no problem; the rest is done automatically, I'll see that the necessary steps are taken. We'll be in touch, goodbye!'

She hung up and smiled at Rath. 'What can I do for you?'

'I'd like to speak to your managing director.'

'Can I ask what it's about?'

Rath took out his badge. 'CID.'

'Missing Persons?'

'No, Homicide.'

She raised her eyebrows. 'I'm afraid Herr Oppenberg hasn't arrived yet.'

'When are you expecting him?'

'Could be a while. At the moment he heads to the shoot first thing, as there's so much to do there. The schedule has to be changed daily since dear Fräulein Franck . . .'

'Where's it being filmed?' Rath interrupted, before she could build up a head of steam.

'In Neubabelsberg. But you can't go out there now.'

'I have a car.'

'They're sound film recordings, no one's allowed to interrupt.'

'The police are.'

'Perhaps *I* can help you.'

'I need to speak to your boss in person,' he said. 'Where will I find him in Babelsberg?'

'Near Ufa headquarters. In the great hall. North studio. Right next to the Tonkreuz, the sound stage.'

'Does Montana belong to Ufa?'

She laughed. 'Heaven forbid! But the great Ufa have been so gracious as to let out their studios. Now that Pommer has finished shooting the new Jannings film, there are a few of them empty. But, as I said, you mustn't interrupt.'

'No doubt you'll be so kind as to telephone ahead. That way I won't be interrupting anything.'

She didn't like it, but she smiled as she reached for the telephone. 'Perhaps Herr Oppenberg will be able to spare five minutes. But I can't promise anything.'

Rath stood up from the chair, put on his hat and tipped it briefly. 'Tell Herr Oppenberg I'll be there in half an hour.'

Folding down the side window to feel the wind on his face, Rath let the breeze blow life back into his tired bones. He had barely slept, having had too much to drink. Still, when his alarm sounded he had felt something akin to relief, because it had been one of those nights. One of those nights when he was frightened of sleep. Because he knew the dreams would return. The dreams that haunted him time and time again. There were weeks when he almost forgot, nights when he achieved a deep, peaceful sleep, before they returned, mercilessly and surely as the seasons. He always knew when the time had come because he felt so on edge and couldn't, didn't want to sleep. He only had to close his eyes to see them: the demons that persecuted him, dead people, people he knew, people he had known. People pale as corpses, with bullet holes in their chests, empty eye sockets and flaps of skin hanging from their bodies like moth-eaten cloaks. Time and time again he awoke with sweat on his brow, before trying to take his mind off things, by reading, by sipping from the bottle, but at some point he would fall asleep and be at their mercy. As much as the dead persecuted and pursued him, so did the living seem to flee his presence. Whenever he woke, heart beating and pyjamas drenched in sweat, he was grateful, even if he felt a thousand times more exhausted. Only with a cold shower and a strong cup of coffee could he revive his spirits.

The blonde secretary had mentioned the name Oppenberg. He had given no indication of how much it had startled him.

Manfred Oppenberg. The man who had dragged him to an illegal nightclub at Ostbahnhof less than a year before. The film producer with the nymphomaniac companion. The night when everything had veered off course, by whose end there would be another dead man to haunt his dreams.

At least he was alone. To avoid Böhm, who must by now have realised what a spectacular case he had handed to Rath, he hadn't put in an appearance at Alex this morning. Instead he had wakened his people early and briefed them by telephone from his living room chair, sending Henning and Czerwinski to Marienfelde to question the rest of Bellmann's staff, from the producer to the toilet attendant. Gräf he had sent to Dr Schwartz in Hannoversche Strasse. He wasn't about to go there himself, not after last night. The image of a disfigured Betty Winter lying on the autopsy table . . . Rath wouldn't have been able to stand the smell of blood and disinfectant and worse, to say nothing of Dr Schwartz's humour.

He felt good, despite his fatigue, and he worked best alone. He thought of Gennat's words: *better to share your knowledge with us.*

Later.

Driving down Kaiserallee he stepped on the gas. The traffic became slightly heavier at Reichsstrasse but the further out of town the road extended, the quicker his progress. As the city frayed into the countryside Berlin seemed almost idyllic, even on a dismal day like this, with raindrops pounding on the roof of the car. He turned left off Reichsstrasse, reaching Neubabelsberg via Kohlhasenbrück.

He parked the Buick on Stahnsdorfer Strasse and looked around. The entrance to the studio lot was flanked by two gatehouses with a porter's office and a barricade. It was noticeably larger than Terra Studios in Marienfelde. A uniformed doorman took a close look at the passport photo on his identification.

Rath asked for directions.

The doorman pointed into the lot. 'Past the glasshouse and through the workshops and you'll come to the great hall. That's where Montana are filming.'

'The great hall?'

'You can't miss it.'

The studio building behind the gate was glazed, like its counterpart in Marienfelde. Beyond it was a line of huts, and for a moment Rath was distracted by hammering sounds and the screech of a circular saw until, suddenly, he found himself in the narrow bazaar of a Middle Eastern city, set in the Brandenburg winter landscape. It was like a scene from the Arabian nights. He stepped back into the open through the great portal of a mosque and gazed at its unplastered rear side. A plain wooden construction was the only thing preventing it from caving in. He had veered off course somewhat, but understood now what the doorman had meant. In the plain brick hall behind the huts, there was enough space for a Zeppelin.

The hall seemed tantalisingly close, but he still needed time to find it. At last he came upon a new building, whose windowless brick walls towered into the sky.

'Is this the great hall?' Rath asked a Prussian fusilier from the Seven Years' War, who was leaning against the wall with a cigarette hanging from his mouth.

'See a greater one? An extra too, are you?'

'I need to get to Montana.'

'Round the corner, a big door, you can't miss it. The north studio.'

You can't miss it seemed to be the line around here, only this time it was true. The steel sliding door was so enormous that the normal-sized door in its front looked like a cat flap. It opened with a slight squeak and Rath stepped inside.

Behind the cat flap a uniformed guard said, 'You can't just march in here! They're filming.'

'That's why I'm here.'

The guard was wearing the same fantasy uniform as the doorman. 'Sound film recording,' he said and gestured towards the steel door. Above it in black letters was the word: MITTELHALLE II N. A red lamp burned alongside. 'We can't just have people bursting in here.'

'I'd like to speak to Herr Oppenberg.'

'In the middle of filming?'

A busybody in uniform. 'How about you just go through that door and ask?'

'If you don't give me a name, I won't know who to say is here.'

'Rath. CID.'

The guard stood to attention. 'Why didn't you say so? You don't look like a pi . . . like a police officer. One moment please.'

The red lamp went out, the guard disappeared through the door and, for a moment, Rath wondered whether he shouldn't follow. Instead he waited patiently until the guard returned and held the door open. Behind it was a silver-haired man with his back turned, issuing instructions.

'. . . then why don't you carry on with scene thirty-nine? We need to make sure we use the time, even if it means making more changes. So, get to work: scene thirty-nine, Schröder's workshop, Baron Suez and Schröder. Czerny can put on a change of clothes. Half an hour! When I'm back, I want to get cracking.'

Oppenberg was surprised to see him. 'My dear friend,' he said as he shook Rath's hand. 'How can I be of service?'

Don't let him take you in, Rath told himself. 'There's been a murder,' he said. Oppenberg's smile turned icy.

'Vivian? Has she . . . ?'

Vivian. Oppenberg's pretty companion in Venuskeller.

'I'm looking for your production manager,' Rath said, as friendly as a head waiter who hasn't received a tip. 'Felix Krempin.'

'Who is it that's been murdered?'

'Don't you read the papers? Betty Winter.'

'Wasn't that an accident? I thought you were here about Vivian.'

'Why would I be?'

The producer threw a sidelong glance at the guard and took Rath to one side. 'Let's go somewhere we can talk in private. It'll be quieter back-stage, in make-up.'

Oppenberg led him into a dark, windowless room with film posters hanging on the wall; a giant mirror framed by light bulbs stretched across its entire long side.

'I'm afraid I can't offer you anything to drink,' Oppenberg said. 'I'd have preferred to meet you in my office, but at the moment I'm hardly out of the studio. We have to change the whole schedule, and they can't manage without me. If you don't take care of things yourself, nothing gets done. Hold on though,' he said, 'I do have a little something.'

He took a flat silver case from his jacket pocket. For a moment, Rath was afraid he might offer him cocaine, but when he snapped the lid open he revealed only neatly arranged, virgin white cigarettes.

'Thank you,' Rath said. 'It's been two months . . .'

'New Year's resolution? You don't mind if I do?'

Rath shook his head.

'So tell me,' Oppenberg continued, lighting a cigarette, 'if it isn't about the missing person I reported to your colleagues the day before yesterday, why are you here?'

'Missing person?'

'Vivian's gone. Didn't I say? We started filming on Monday and she's been missing ever since. That's why things are so chaotic around here.'

The young woman whose tentacles Rath had only just escaped in Venuskeller. It was no surprise she'd walked out on a man like Oppenberg. 'I'm afraid I have to disappoint you there,' he said, 'but I'm here about a Felix Krempin. He does work for you, doesn't he?'

Oppenberg betrayed neither curiosity nor surprise, let alone any sense of having been caught out.

'It's my turn to disappoint you,' Oppenberg said. 'Yes, Krempin was my production manager, but he resigned three, maybe four months ago. No idea what he's been doing since. I haven't had any professional dealings with him.'

'Does that go for La Belle Film too?'

'Bellmann? I don't have much to do with the man.'

Rath decided to go all out. 'Allow me to speak candidly, Herr Oppenberg. You smuggled Felix Krempin into your rival's studio under a false name, and there he triggered the accident which cost Betty Winter her life.'

'Is that what Bellmann told you? I wouldn't believe everything he says; the man has too much imagination.'

'Don't play the innocent with me. Your Krempin is a saboteur.'

'He isn't *my* Krempin, Herr Rath. Felix Krempin is a free agent who changed his employer. Now, if you'll allow me to speak candidly . . .'

Oppenberg was out of his shell and building up a head of steam. 'You shouldn't be carrying on like this given my previous generosity. Your superiors won't be pleased to hear that you snort cocaine, even if you were off duty at the time.' He stubbed out a cigarette that wasn't even half-smoked.

'Cocaine I got from you.'

'I can live with my vices,' Oppenberg said, 'and perhaps you can live with yours. But the commissioner really doesn't approve of that sort of thing.'

'You mean to blackmail me?'

'I just want to be friends again, and I'll co-operate so long as you promise not to use any information I provide against me.'

'That's a promise I can't make. Our friendship stops at murder.'

'This isn't about murder.' Oppenberg lit another cigarette and took a long drag. 'OK, Felix Krempin *was* working for me at Bellmann's, but it was never about sabotage or murder. Nothing of the kind!'

'I'm listening.'

'Our industry is going through seismic change. To survive, we need to shoot talkies, and that's an expensive business. Very few production companies are as well off as Ufa. Most are small, creative enterprises lurching from one production to the next.'

'Like yours.'

'Making a talkie is infinitely more complicated and expensive than shooting a conventional film, and now we come to the point. I don't think much of Bellmann but I have to say he churns them out as cheap as anyone. I sent Felix to have a look round, uncover a few production secrets and exploit them for Montana. That's all.' Oppenberg took another drag. 'Perhaps I shouldn't have provoked him. I accused him of not being careful enough with money.'

'So, it is about espionage.'

'It isn't exactly kosher, but then, my dear Rath, nor does it stretch the limits of our friendship.'

'Why are you helping me? Your employee is a fugitive murder suspect . . .'

'Precisely! I'm looking for him myself. I don't know what happened at Bellmann's but I can tell you one thing: Felix Krempin is no murderer. Nor was he instructed to sabotage the shoot, let alone injure or kill anyone.'

'Why should I believe you?'

'Why should I lie? Especially when I know I have nothing to fear from you, my friend.'

'I'm not your friend.'

'Business associate, then.'

'This isn't business, this is blackmail.'

'If you think it's so important, we can always do business for real. Come and work for me. I pay well.'

'I won't be falsifying any results for your sake.'

'I'm talking about a completely normal assignment, one that would have most private detectives licking their fingers.'

'I'm not sure I understand . . .'

'Vivian. Help me find her.'

'That's a case for my colleagues at Missing Persons.'

'They've barely lifted a finger.'

'They'll have their reasons. Are you sure Vivian hasn't simply left you?'

'Do you want to work for me?'

'If I'm to work for you, then I need to be able to ask questions. How can you be sure she hasn't simply upped sticks?'

'Because she isn't stupid. The new film is tailor-made for her. *Vom Blitz getroffen*, her first feature-length sound film, will be her breakthrough. Your colleagues didn't get it, but I thought *you* would show more understanding.'

Rath could understand his colleagues. An old crank refused to accept that a youthful beauty had simply upped sticks and left. But why shouldn't he do Oppenberg a favour and snoop around a little? Perhaps he could use him to get to Krempin. 'So, you've been filming since Monday?'

'Correct. Tuesday would've been her first day on set, and she didn't appear.'

'Didn't you go look for her yourself?'

'Of course.'

'And?'

'We've looked everywhere, checked out all her relatives and acquaintances, all the bars and restaurants she frequents. Nothing. No one's seen her since she went into the mountains.'

'She went away?'

'After the last shoot. She loves skiing.'

'Perhaps she's broken a leg and is holed up in a hospital somewhere.'

'If that was the case we'd have heard long ago. She's hardly unknown.'

'Where did she go?'

'No idea.' Oppenberg shrugged his shoulders. 'Vivian doesn't like people controlling her.'

'How do you go about filming without your lead actress?'

'We've altered the schedule. Heidtmann's shooting the scenes she isn't in first.'

'Then everything's as it should be.'

'All very well for you to say! We keep having to make changes to the set. Do you know how much that costs in time *and* money? We've just about reached our limit. Vivian's in pretty much every scene of this film. We have to finish sometime and every day I can't shoot costs me a fortune!'

'In other words: you want me to let you know whether you need a new lead actress . . .'

'No.' Oppenberg looked at him seriously. 'I want you to bring my lead actress back.'

10

The blonde secretary was on the telephone again when Rath returned to Kantstrasse. Krempin's personal file lay on her desk and he wondered if she had removed any pages. He still wasn't sure he could trust Oppenberg, but at least he had learned a great deal about Krempin, the film obsessive who had enthusiastically taken up the challenge of sound.

It had been his idea, Oppenberg said, to get to the bottom of Bellmann's production secrets. He had last seen him a week before, but Krempin hadn't been able to tell him much, and there had been no mention of sabotage. Rath couldn't help thinking of Bellmann's photo of Krempin next to Betty Winter. Had the handsome Krempin made a hobby of picking up film stars? Perhaps he had absconded with Vivian Franck and gone to ground. If so, Rath could imagine the pair not wanting to show their faces to their erstwhile employer.

The secretary looked a little surprised when Rath took Krempin's file from the desk and sat in one of the leather chairs, but didn't break her flow of words. He looked through the papers. Nothing unusual. Krempin had a gift for technology. He had worked for Oppenberg as a lighting technician and cameraman before becoming a production manager. That had lasted until December 1929, when he was dismissed. From then on there was no apparent link between the two men. Whether that was true, or whether Oppenberg had just asked for the entry to be made, Rath couldn't say, but the ink was dry and the blonde, who had finally hung up, was giving nothing away. Krempin would surely hold dated termination of employment papers.

'Is there something else I can do for you?' the secretary asked, more curious than friendly.

'I have to make a telephone call for a minute or two. I hope you can manage without it that long.'

'Why not? I've got other things to do.' She passed the black telephone across the desk and turned to her typewriter. Clearly a screenplay had to be copied.

Rath was put through to Hannoversche Strasse, but Gräf had already left. He reached the detective at his desk.

'Back already? So what did the doctor tell you?'

'Tasteless jokes.'

Rath could imagine the liberties the pathologist would have taken with the young detective. Novitiates in the hallowed Halls of Death had to take Schwartz's litmus test, irrespective of whether they were students or police recruits.

'He could've just given me the report. It was finished ages ago. Instead . . . I feel sick thinking about it.'

'No doubt he'll have said something about the cause of death too . . .'

'He confirmed what we already suspected: cardiac arrest through electric shock. She'd have survived the burns and breakages—but she'd have paid a high price.'

'To look like Max Schreck?'

'Worse. Betty Winter would've been confined to a wheelchair, most likely for the rest of her life. The spotlight struck her spine.'

'Shit.'

'She could've just as easily been killed. Dr Schwartz says it was a matter of centimetres. If the spotlight had hit her head.'

'She was lucky.' The words slipped out before he knew what he was saying.

'You're just like Dr Schwartz,' Gräf said. 'With respect, I find your cynicism inappropriate. We're talking about a tragic death here.'

'It's all my years of service. You'll have reached that point when you no longer feel sick visiting the morgue.'

'Thanks, but I'd rather keep puking. When are you coming back, Gereon? Böhm's longing to see you.'

'Sure, because he wants us off the case.'

'He just doesn't want you *leading* it.'

'You know exactly what that means: we do all the legwork and he takes the glory . . .'

'On the subject of legwork: Henning and Czerwinski are still with the film lot. Taking their time as usual.'

'Keep holding the fort.'

'What should I tell Böhm?'

'That I'm staying on Krempin's heels.'

'How long do you mean to keep that up?'

'As long as Böhm can't call me off, we still have the case. With a bit of luck, we'll solve it too.'

'And who'll be taking all the glory then?'

'How selfish do you think I am? Already forgotten who you owe your promotion to?'

Gräf fell silent.

'Come on! It's not too much to ask, is it? I'm this close to Krempin. I might even catch him today. Don't worry about all the paperwork. Whatever you don't manage, we'll take care of on Monday. If Böhm wants to help us then, he can be my guest!'

'And you'll pick up the bill in the Dreieck on Monday night.'

'We might have something to celebrate by then. I'll call you around one. Böhm'll be in the canteen then, Voss too.'

He hung up and pushed the telephone over to Oppenberg's blonde. She didn't look up from typing.

'Thank you,' he said. The typewriter continued to hammer away.

'Can I ask you a few questions?'

The hammering stopped. 'I don't know. Can you?'

Was she flirting with him, or having a go? Even after nearly a year, Rath still couldn't quite fathom the way Berliners communicated.

He smiled. 'A few questions about Vivian Franck?'

A shrug of the shoulders. 'Far as I'm concerned . . .'

'How long have you known Fräulein Franck?'

'Since she's been under contract with us, about two and a half years.'

'Is she reliable?'

'Professionally yes. In private . . . well.'

'She isn't devoted to Manfred Oppenberg?'

She shrugged. 'Best ask Rudi, he knows her almost as well as the boss. Perhaps even better, if you know what I mean.'

'Rudi?'

'Czerny. Our youthful hero. Didn't you see him? He's filming out in Babelsberg too.'

'Perhaps you can give me his address. And a photo.'

'You wouldn't believe what I can do,' she said, looking at him without even the slightest trace of a smile, and noted the address on letter-headed Montana writing paper.

Rudolf Czerny lived in Charlottenburg, like his missing colleague Vivian Franck. First, however, Rath drove to Guerickestrasse, hoping to find Felix Krempin before he started snooping on Manfred Oppenberg's behalf. Krempin lived a few blocks away from his friend Peter Glaser in northern Charlottenburg. A green Opel was parked on the other side of the street. Rath came to a halt behind it, climbed out, and knocked on the window.

'Afternoon, Mertens,' Rath said. 'Anything doing?'

'After noon is about right, Inspector,' said the man in the driver's seat. 'The only thing happening is Grabowski's stomach getting louder and louder.'

'Nothing suspicious?'

Mertens shook his head. 'A few wary glances at most. The residents must think we're a couple of queers. Wouldn't surprise me if our colleagues from Vice paid us a visit.'

'Then stop gazing at me so adoringly,' Grabowski said from the passenger seat.

Rath grinned. The atmosphere in the car seemed good, even though a stake-out was one of the most boring aspects of police work. Mertens and Grabowski had been entrusted to him by Gennat, two recruits fresh from police academy in Eiche. Anyone who wasn't part of Wilhelm Böhm's circle was all right by Rath, and they both seemed like decent sorts.

'There's an Aschinger over on Berliner Strasse,' he said. 'Why don't you take half an hour for lunch and warm yourselves up. I'll hold the fort.'

The two men climbed out. Rath knew he had just collected a few points. A boss who looked after his colleagues and didn't mind getting his hands dirty? That didn't happen often at the Castle.

'Should we get something for you too, Sir?'

'Not necessary, thank you.'

The two of them set off. Rath sat behind the wheel of the Buick until they disappeared round the corner. Then he went over and entered the house. No one in the stairwell. Rath didn't have much experience with the skeleton key and needed time to pick the lock. Once in, he pulled the door shut quietly. His colleagues had been in the flat last night to make sure Krempin wasn't fast asleep or lying dead on the sofa, but Rath wanted to see for himself without having to wait for a search warrant.

The flat didn't tell him much. A typical bachelor apartment, simple and clean, perhaps a little cleaner than most. The bed was made and the table cleared. Nothing suggested a crazy getaway. More likely a housekeeper came by regularly. Oppenberg seemed to have paid the man well, judging by the record player in the living room. Rath whistled through his teeth when he recognised the model. He'd have liked to borrow a few of the records. There was even a telephone on the desk.

The shelves contained almost exclusively technical books: specialist literature on electrotechnics and photography, some on engineering science too, but few novels. On the desk a typewriter sat gathering dust. Alongside it lay a soldering clamp as well as a few boxes containing little screwdrivers and similar tools, a few electronic replacement parts, switches, some tubes and fuses. Rath read the warning on the tube packaging. FOR THE PURPOSES OF SOUND FILMS PLEASE ONLY USE TUBES (AMPLIFIER, RECTIFIER AND PRE-AMP TUBES) THAT CARRY THE KLANGFILM LOGO ON THE TUBE AND PACKAGING. THE USE OF OTHER TUBES IS DANGEROUS AND MAY LEAD TO MALFUNCTION. THE USE OF OTHER TUBES IS ALSO FORBIDDEN FOR PATENTING REASONS.

Rath looked inside the wardrobe. Most of the hangers swung empty on the rail and the dresser drawers were all but cleared. Krempin had calmly packed his things before disappearing. So, either he had made exceptionally good use of the time upon fleeing the studio, or he had everything ready in advance.

The biggest unknown was when Krempin had left the studio.

Rath gave a start. Not the doorbell. The telephone!

He hesitated in front of the black appliance as it rattled away. Before reaching for the receiver he took a handkerchief from his jacket. The last thing he needed was to leave fingerprints on a murder suspect's telephone.

'Yes?' There was no response, but Rath could hear someone breathing. 'Who's there please?'

Again, no response. For another second or two he heard nothing apart from that same gentle breathing. Then a click.

He continued looking around the flat but found nothing more of note, and ten minutes later was back in the car. Mertens and Grabowski were still away, so hadn't registered his little trip.

Who had called? At first Rath feared it might have been one of the officers searching for Krempin, except they knew the flat was being shadowed and that it was pointless to call. Besides, a police officer would have identified himself to provoke a response from the other party. He was growing restless.

Previously, at least, he had been able to smoke during all those interminable hours spent in flats and cars, but then he had gone and given up. What a bright idea. He thought he had seen Grabowski with a carton of Muratti Forever as the latter made off with Mertens.

Where had the pair got to? They'd been gone almost half an hour, and he still had two addresses to visit. Just then he saw Grabowksi's winter coat in the rear-view mirror and climbed out of the car.

11

Vivian Frank's apartment was even more modern than Oppenberg's office. Three rooms with a roof garden overlooked the Kaiserdamm, and an enormous bed under a champagne-coloured satin quilt that was reflected to infinity by two mirrors. Rath felt more at ease in the comparatively small living room, whose panoramic window looked out onto the Funkturm, the radio tower.

The furniture betrayed the taste of Manfred Oppenberg: simple, modern, elegant—and expensive. Fine woods, lots of leather and chrome, no scroll. Vivian Franck hadn't furnished the flat herself, nor, most likely, had she paid for it. The woman Manfred Oppenberg called *Angel* couldn't have earned so much through her films already. So, perhaps she came from a wealthy family. She certainly carried herself like a spoilt young lady. Was she a fallen princess for whom Manfred Oppenberg provided the last vestige of luxury? What else could tie her to such an old man? The promise of making her immortal on-screen?

The apartment was as polished and arranged as a film set. Only the big glass ashtray on the low, wooden table and the discreet house bar betrayed any hint of vice.

Rath searched every cupboard and drawer without locating any cocaine. He realised the thought of the white powder was almost giving him cravings. He couldn't help thinking of Vivian Franck, of her bored face, those dead eyes that only began to sparkle once she had taken a dose. He had sworn not to touch the stuff again.

Apart from the bedroom, the apartment didn't give much away about its owner's habits, although he had noticed a few empty clothes hangers in the wardrobe. Oppenberg had already told him that a dozen or so items of clothing were missing along with two suitcases and a travel bag.

Where had Vivian Franck gone, and why hadn't she returned?

He locked the door twice and took the lift downstairs. The concierge in the marble reception hall looked so old he might have been on duty since the days of Old Fritz. He only started talking when he recognised the Prussian CID badge.

'So, Herr Oppenberg did go to the police after all,' he said, removing his glasses. 'About time too. He called here at least twenty times a day to ask after that Franck.'

'When did you last see Frau Franck?'

The narrow shoulders shrugged. 'Just as she was leaving.'

'Can you be a little more precise?'

'Must be three, four weeks since she asked for a taxi. The driver had a bit of a struggle with her cases, took a while to get them in the car.'

'And then?'

'Then he got in and drove off.'

Rath smiled. 'Where did they go?'

'No idea. To some station, I'd say. Or the airport. Wherever you go with big suitcases.'

'She didn't say anything?'

'To me? That Franck's never even *looked* at me in the two years she's lived here. Normal mortals don't exist for her.'

'Did you notice anything else?'

'Nope.'

'After that you never saw her again?'

'Nope.' The concierge considered. 'Well, that is, I did, once . . .'

'Where?'

'. . . in *Verrucht*, her latest film.' This seemed to be a great joke.

Rath moved towards the exit with the concierge's bleating laughter in his ears. Suddenly, it stopped. 'Wait!'

Rath turned at the door. 'I've had my fill of jokes.'

'No, no more jokes. Seriously, there was something the day she left.'

'What?'

'Someone called around midday and asked for her, it was nothing special, but . . .'

'Who?'

'He didn't give his name, but I recognised him all the same.'

'Who?'

'He never called otherwise, always came in person. A very *personable* fellow, no doubt . . .'

The concierge winked, slowly getting on Rath's nerves.

'Who?'

'I don't know his name but I recognised his voice. Even though he must have called from the train station—there was loads of noise.'

Rath took the photo Oppenberg's secretary had looked out for him from his pocket, and laid it on the counter.

'Was it this man?'

The concierge took one look at the glossy print of a smiling Rudi Czerny and could barely contain himself. 'Hats off!' he said. 'The Prussian police are on the ball! Who'd have thought it?'

Rudolf Czerny's flat was nearby on Reichskanzlerplatz. He wasn't home, of course, as he was still filming in Babelsberg, but Rath visited precisely *because* he knew Czerny was still filming. All the same, he rang the bell three times and knocked loudly to be certain no one was at home. He was slowly getting the hang of the skeleton key that Bruno Wolter, his first boss in Berlin, had shown him how to use. At first he had resisted, but he had to admit it was a useful tool.

Rudolf Czerny lived more modestly than his lover, but then he wasn't kept by Manfred Oppenberg.

Rath rummaged through the flat, taking care not to upset the disorder. He didn't know exactly what he was looking for, perhaps some evidence of the affair with Vivian Franck, perhaps some indication of her whereabouts. It was perfectly possible she'd made herself scarce. And Czerny? Was he holding the fort until he could join her, or had she left him in the lurch like her benefactor Manfred Oppenberg? If what the concierge had said was true, then she had left without him three weeks ago—or he without her.

There were brochures on the living room table advertising holidays in the Swiss Alps. Freshly washed ski equipment hung in the wardrobe. Czerny had clearly been in the mountains himself. Finally, Rath found a towel with the words *Hotel Schatzalp, Davos* embroidered on the edge. Rudolf Czerny seemed to collect his holiday souvenirs from hotel supplies.

Rath gazed out of the window onto the wide expanse of Reichskanzler-platz and the Funkturm. Daylight was fading. The first neon signs were lighting up. He decided to wait and telephoned the station, getting Gräf on the line.

'Weren't you going to call at one?'

'I've had my hands full. Has Böhm been in touch?'

'At five-minute intervals. He's probably about to come over because the line's busy.'

'Listen, I know it's the end of the day, but there's something important you need to do.'

'Hmm?'

'At just on five, there's the Wessel funeral. Böhm's dead Nazi. At the Nikolai Cemetery.'

'Yes?'

'Go over there and take a look.'

'What the hell?'

'Böhm forced it on us.'

'Since when do you take his orders so seriously?'

'One of us has to go, and I can't get away from here. I'll tell you more on Monday morning.'

'Aye aye, Sir.'

Rath didn't get the chance to wish Gräf a good weekend before he hung up. His Saturday evening was ruined, but then he, Rath, wasn't crouched in a strange, cold apartment for his own amusement.

Perhaps it was the word 'amusement', but suddenly he found himself thinking of the ball at the Resi, for which he still had no costume. He had missed the chance to back out, and Kathi had moved heaven and earth to get tickets. If Czerny didn't appear soon, they wouldn't be able to arrive together.

Still, Kathi would understand, just like she always understood. He was on duty, simple as that. All he had to do was find a halfway decent costume and see to it that he didn't show at the Resi too late.

Czerny put him out of his misery at just after half past five. Rath was sitting in one of the comfy chairs when he heard the key in the lock. He remained seated to give the actor a suitably theatrical reception. The light in the hall went on and, from the safety of the dimly lit living room, Rath looked through the crack to see a small, slim man hanging a toffee-coloured coat and brown hat on the hallstand.

The living room door opened and a hand turned the light on. Rath was now visible, but Czerny hadn't seen him and continued reading a script as he groped his way towards the bar. *Vom Blitz getroffen,* Rath read on the cover sheet.

'Good evening, Herr Czerny.'

The actor gave a start. 'How did you get into my apartment?' He didn't sound intimidated: if anything, there was a hint of aggression. The man knew how to look after himself. Rath would have to be on his guard.

'Through the door,' he said and showed his police ID. 'I just wanted to ask a few questions.'

'But first you had to scare me half to death? Is breaking and entering part of the job these days? I'd call it trespassing.'

'I'm not here on behalf of the police. In this instance, we share the same employer . . .'

'I'm an actor . . .'

'. . . and you work for Manfred Oppenberg?'

Czerny nodded.

'Me too. At least for the time being.'

'What's that supposed to mean?'

'Your boss wants me to return his lead actress . . .' Czerny didn't say anything when Rath hesitated, but it was clear he would have liked nothing more than to shout out Vivian's name. '. . . your lover.'

Czerny turned pale, as if Rath had pronounced his death sentence. 'That's why Oppenberg sent you. Because I'm sleeping with Vivian. I only saw him half an hour ago. Why doesn't he say it to my face?'

'Herr Oppenberg understands that now and then Vivian keeps younger lovers . . .'

'Now and then.' Czerny smiled sourly. 'Is that what he told you? Oh yes, our producer fancies himself in the role of liberal gentleman. But believe me, his liberality has its limits. Of course he would never begrudge *her* a little on the side—as long as she remains his toy. But he would have no hesitation in putting *me* on the street if I were to so much as *touch* her more often than it says in the script.'

'Still, that's precisely what you did, isn't it?'

'That's not the point.'

'Don't worry. There's no need for Herr Oppenberg to hear anything of this. So long as you co-operate I see no reason why . . .'

'How very kind of you,' Czerny said, 'but I won't be blackmailed. Besides, I'm not the only one who Vivian . . .'

'I know,' Rath said, 'I've made her acquaintance too.'

Rath watched the man's jealousy surge. There was no reason to tell the actor that he had actually resisted Vivian's advances. Czerny went red before exploding.

'No one really knows Vivian!' The words came tumbling out. 'Everyone thinks they do, but no one knows who she is, the way she thinks, how she . . .'

'Except you,' Rath interrupted.

Czerny quietened down. 'I thought I did,' he said. 'I've seen sides to her that no one else has seen, that no one else would believe, that no one would even dare write into her scripts. And that's the whole problem: most people confuse her with her films!'

'What about you?'

'I loved her. I know it's a cliché and naïve too, but that's how it was.'

'Was?'

'I waited for her at Anhalter Bahnhof, suitcase packed, but she never came. We were to go to Davos for two carefree weeks in the snow. I've never felt so lousy.'

'Why don't you get us something to drink and take a seat? Then you can tell me what happened in your own time.'

Czerny seemed to be getting used to Rath's presence. He fetched two glasses of water and a bottle of whisky from the cupboard. 'I need a drink,' he said as he poured.

'Thanks, but I'd rather have water.'

Czerny went into the kitchen and returned with a jug. 'Please, help yourself,' he said and sat down.

'So you went to Switzerland without her?'

'Everything was booked. When she didn't appear and I couldn't get hold of her anywhere, I took the next train. I knew from her concierge that she'd got into the taxi with her cases and thought, maybe, she'd taken another train and was already there, or would be coming later.'

'But she never did?'

Czerny shook his head. 'I haven't seen or heard anything from Vivian in nearly four weeks.'

'Weren't you worried?'

'At some point you have to face the truth. After three or four days waiting in the snow, I accepted that Vivian had given me the boot, plain and simple.'

'If that's true then you're not the only one. She must have given Manfred Oppenberg the boot too. Only he doesn't want to believe it.'

'Not turning up to the shoot like that, it just isn't her. Vivian's more reliable than you think.'

'Professionally, at least.'

'I know very few people as hard-working as her.'

'So why skive off a film Oppenberg's making purely with her future in mind? To avoid running into you and her benefactor? It makes no sense, putting her career at risk like that!'

'She isn't risking anything. *Vom Blitz getroffen* is her second sound film. She's already proved in *Verrucht* that she isn't one of those old divas who are afraid talkies will reveal their speech impediments and acting limitations.'

'Where do you think she is now?'

Czerny shrugged his shoulders. 'Search me!'

'Just tell me everything you know, and everything you think you know.'

'There was . . . well, she told me a little while ago that she had met someone.'

'A lover.'

'No, she wouldn't have told me that. A producer.'

'You mean Vivian might've been unfaithful to Oppenberg where it really hurts?'

'More than if she'd have run off with a young lover anyway. He's invested a load of money in her and is expecting it to start paying off soon.'

'Why would she want to leave?'

'Because the grass is always greener.'

'Oppenberg doesn't seem to have taken that possibility into account.'

'He still has her under contract. She can't just get out of it like that.'

'Nevertheless, you think it's possible.'

'If she's somewhere no German lawyer can reach her . . .'

'In Hollywood . . .'

'Her English is good enough.'

Rath nodded thoughtfully and took a sip of water.

'What do you think?' Czerny poured himself another whisky. 'Can you find her?'

'Maybe. Where did she go after she got into that taxi?'

'Not Anhalter Bahnhof anyway.'

'Then we need to ask the taxi driver. Do you have the telephone number for Vivian's apartment?'

'Yes, but . . .'

'Call it. I need to speak to the concierge.'

Soon Rath was speaking to the old man from the marble foyer. He seemed to have a good memory. 'The taxi Frau Franck drove off in?' he said.

'Must have been on the eighth of February,' Rath offered.

'Are you sure? Wait a moment, I'll take a quick look.' Rath heard a hollow thump as the receiver banged against the counter, followed by the rustling of paper. 'So, here we are. You can always count on your old Panske, eh?'

Rath tried not to lose patience. 'You made some notes, did you?'

'Certainly did. I ordered the car at nine, and half an hour later it was outside the door.'

'Can you remember the driver?'

'Not exactly, but I do know he wasn't the strongest. And those heavy cases to boot! Poor guy!'

The lady in the taxi office was less forthcoming. 'Of course we can find out,' she said, 'as long as you know the exact time and address. But how do I know you're really from the police? Can I call you back at the station?'

'I'm out in the field right now.'

'Then you'll have to come here. Belle-Alliance-Strasse sixteen.'

'If you could look everything out for me, I'll come by in person.'

'You could be anyone.'

'I have a police ID.'

'Come by, identify yourself, and I'll see what I can do.'

'Looks good,' Rath said to Czerny. 'I think we'll find him.'

'Can you keep me up to date? I mean, if you hear anything?'

'That still doesn't solve my biggest problem. I'm invited to a Fasching ball tonight. Any idea where I can get hold of a costume at this hour?'

Czerny looked surprised for a moment, then grinned. 'It'll mean going back out to Babelsberg.'

12

'Well, if it isn't the Captain of Köpenick! Are you here to confiscate the box office?'

The man at the entrance was clearly a joker. Perhaps that's why he was wearing lederhosen and a sailor's cap.

'There should be a ticket for me,' Rath said.

'Yes, Sir!' The joker stood upright and saluted. 'Can you take a look, Lissy?' he called to the tinsel angel sitting behind the box office. The angel didn't have to search long before passing the ticket to the Bavarian who tore it in half and gave a stub to Rath. 'You're late,' he said.

'I'm aware of that.'

'Don't worry, there are still plenty of ladies here.' The Bavarian sailor winked.

'I have a date.'

'Well then, in you go.'

The air was heavy with cigarette smoke. Thin rays of light flitted through the grey-blue haze from dozens of rotating mirrored globes, their flecks gliding over walls and the heads of guests. The place was full to bursting. The babble of voices almost drowned out the music. They had even hired a singer to perform the latest hits. A few guests were singing along, arm in arm, swaying at their tables, but most weren't even listening. They were busy talking, dancing or canoodling. Imaginative costumes were few and far between: there were any number of pirates or fiery Spaniards running around, a few sailors, a few cowboys and not many Indians. Most had simply donned a colourful hat or a discreet half-mask, while the women were wearing as little as possible.

Rath knew the Resi as a slightly bourgeois marriage bureau, but today the stiffs seemed intent on exploring the wild side. Moving through the rows to his table he felt rather old. The Prussian captain's uniform, borrowed from the Babelsberg costume fund, constricted his body like a corset and made him so stiff it felt as if he had swallowed a walking stick. What's more, the sabre dangling by his legs kept getting caught on tables, chairs and people. It was a good thing the evening was already more than halfway over. It was nearly half past ten.

He took another look at his ticket. Table 28, right by the bar. Kathi wasn't there, only a smooching couple oblivious to everything around them. Rath checked the teeming bodies on the dance floor and eventually made out two gypsy girls, neither of whom was Kathi.

He sat by the smooching couple, who still seemed not to have noticed him. At some point Kathi would show up. Having to spend a little time waiting for her would help ease his guilty conscience. He ordered a bottle of Mosel-Riesling and two glasses, the only drink they could agree on. Even at New Year that had been his undoing.

She still hadn't turned up when the waiter brought the wine. Was she sitting at another table watching, about to call or send a message by pneumatic delivery tube? You could do all that here at the Resi. It was a Mecca for shy types, and people who 'needed all the help they could get,' as Gräf had said after learning that Czerwinski was a regular. The super cautious could even exchange photos via delivery tube before agreeing to a first dance.

The waiter placed the glasses on the table and poured. Rath held his hand flat over Kathi's glass. The waiter placed the bottle in an ice bucket and disappeared. In the meantime, the smooching couple had taken a breather. She stood up, smoothed down her crinkled harem costume and took her leave. The man gazed after her with a satisfied grin, straightening the colourful sequined hat on his head. Another one who needed all the help he could get, Rath thought. He raised his glass to the lipstick-smudged face and the man reciprocated with his flat beer.

'Your health, Captain. Since when have you been here? Didn't realise I'd been detained!'

'Just arrived.'

'An optimist, are you?' The man gestured towards the empty glass. 'Laying the bait . . .'

'I have a date,' Rath said, now finding the man disagreeable. 'But there doesn't seem to be much going on at the moment.'

'You should've been here an hour ago. What an atmosphere! There was a pirate sitting here cracking all sorts of jokes, standing round after round. And a gypsy girl, getting merrier by the glass, lovely bir . . .'

'A gypsy girl?'

The man hesitated, until the penny dropped. 'I see. The gypsy's with you.' He laughed out loud. 'No offence, but you're a bit late.'

'I know.'

'Too late, if I may say so. I fear you won't be seeing your gypsy again tonight. Cleared off about half an hour ago with the pirate, together with another couple. Probably wanted to make a night of it somewhere else.'

Rath had reckoned with all sorts of possibilities, but not this. Kathi had stood him up. How cheap could you get?! The news cut him to the quick, despite everything, and in this stupid uniform he felt more out of place than ever.

'Come on, friend!' His neighbour clapped him on the shoulder. 'Don't take it so hard. There are enough girls here. And table telephones. That's how I met mine.'

'That's not why I'm here.'

'All right, all right! You North Germans are so uptight.'

The harem lady returned to escort her beau onto the dance floor. Rath would've liked to ask old Sequin Hat where Kathi and her companion had got to, but it was too late now. He shouldn't have snapped at the man.

He felt no desire to go chasing after her and, if this was how he finally got rid of Kathi, so be it. He could definitely drink better when she wasn't there, much better. He took the wine from the ice bucket and went to the bar where there was also a table telephone and delivery tube. He poured himself another glass and waved the cigarette girl over. 'A six-pack of Overstolz, please.'

'We only sell ten-packs.'

'That's fine, and a lighter too.'

She fished the pack deftly from her sales tray. 'Fifty pfennigs,' she said.

Rath pressed a mark into her hand. 'Keep the change,' he said. Her thanks came in the form of a dazzling smile, which cheered him up straightaway. Old Sequin Hat might be a creep, but he was right about one thing. There were plenty more fish in the sea. He tore open the pack and stuck a cigarette in his mouth, trying to be as casual as possible, but his hands were shaking with excitement, likewise when he lit the match. He had resisted all day, and his defeat felt all the better for it.

Yes, he wanted to smoke again! Fuck all those non-smokers! Fuck Kathi!

As he took the first drag, he felt the nicotine like a hammer blow, pleasing, slightly painful; a wave that spread out from his lungs to his whole body. He felt almost as he had at twelve when he had pinched a couple of his brother Anno's cigarettes and smoked them with his pals on their building site hideout in Klettenberg. All four had ended up crouched by an excavation, puking like world champions. Paul, who handled it best of all, had helped him home. 'I think Gereon has given himself an upset stomach, Frau Rath. What did he have for lunch?' His mother's concerned face. Father wasn't home; he'd have seen straight through them. On Paul's recommendation, he had attempted to combat the nicotine smell with sorrel—which had only made him vomit again.

It seemed scarcely credible that he had started smoking only a few years later. For that he had the Prussian military to thank.

He took a careful drag on his cigarette; he had to get used to smoking again first. Still, he had time. He would get good and tanked up, have a little think, at least while that was still possible, then get a taxi home. The right amount of alcohol would banish the demons and rock him peacefully to sleep.

He stubbed the cigarette out and waved the barman over, ordered a cognac and had the bottle of wine cleared away. A good day all in all: he had avoided Böhm and made significant strides in the Winter case. Once they got their hands on Krempin, which was only a matter of time, the rest would take care of itself. With Oppenberg onside, he was closer to Felix Krempin than the rest of the search. Yes, everything was going just fine.

It even looked as if he'd managed to get rid of Kathi, at least for the night.

Rath drank the cognac and ordered another. The barman placed a fresh glass on the counter, and in the same instant there was a ringing noise and a little light came on. Something had arrived at pneumatic delivery tube 51. Everyone stared eagerly at the package, but Rath wasn't interested in who had sent flowers or confectionery to their beloved. He reached for his glass and drank. The barman read the note and handed Rath the little package.

'Here, Captain, it's for you.'

The glass nearly fell out of his hand. Rath took the package with a shrug and read the accompanying note. FOR THE CAPTAIN OF KÖPENICK. He looked round. The smooching couple were back at table 28, otherwise no one.

Inside was a bright green feather and a note. Rath shielded the text from prying eyes to his left and right and read.

Had a dance yet? If the Captain would like to ruffle a few feathers ...

'Where's it from?' he asked the barman.

He pointed towards the other end of the bar. 'Table fifty-two.'

Rath looked across but there were too many people standing in the low light. He pocketed the letter and green feather, took his cognac and moved to the dance floor, where it was busier than Potsdamer Platz at five in the afternoon.

He saw her straightaway. A bright green hen in a short skirt and feather boa gambolling across the dance floor. Though her legs and backside weren't bad, the woman's face was all too reminiscent of the bird she had come dressed as. Rath hid behind one of the pillars. The dancing hen still hadn't seen him.

One more cognac and then home, he told himself. Feeling halfway safe behind the pillar, he kept an eye on the dancing hen with the predilection for Royal-Prussian officers, who was no doubt just waiting for a captain to cut in on her. Then he thought he saw a face that didn't belong at all.

Nonsense, he thought, you're seeing ghosts.

But there it was again. A face under an Indian feather.

What the hell was *she* doing in a place for people who couldn't stand to be alone? Now there were two reasons to make a speedy exit, but he couldn't avert his gaze and, when he saw how she was smiling at her cowboy dance partner, the pain was so great he instantly forgot about Kathi. Charlotte Ritter.

Who was this grinning twit with the fringe who dared receive a smile from Charly?

It had been months since he had seen her. Fräulein Ritter has to concentrate on her exams, his colleagues at Alex had said, and Rath had seen it as fate's way of telling him to forget about her. Even with Kathi in bed next to him, however, he hadn't managed.

How on earth had she ended up here?

Only when he heard a familiar voice did he realise he'd been gawping at her the whole time. 'Boss? Well, there's a thing. Have they promoted you to Captain?'

Fatboy Czerwinski was standing there grinning beside him. Prison clothing hardly made him more attractive.

'I don't believe it,' said Rath. 'You? Out and about without Henning?'

'He doesn't want anything to do with Fasching.'

'I know how he feels.'

'Ha, good one!' Czerwinski nudged him in the ribs.

Rath was about to explain the difference between Fastelovend, the name for Carnival in Cologne, and Fasching, when a second prisoner emerged from the darkness carrying two beers. Detective Inspector Frank Brenner suddenly became less friendly when he recognised his colleague in the captain's uniform. Without saying a word, he passed Czerwinski a beer, and the men clinked glasses and drank.

'Will you look at that,' Rath said. 'I see you're commandeering my people after work too.'

'*Your* people! If we belong to anyone, it's Wilhelm Böhm, yourself included. I hope you're looking forward to Monday. The boss is livid!'

'I could never stand Mondays.'

'Hey!' Czerwinski gestured with his beer glass towards the dance floor. 'Isn't that Ritter over there?'

Rath didn't respond.

'It is, you know,' Brenner said. 'She makes a good Iltschi, doesn't she?'

'Iltschi's the name of Winnetou's horse, you idiot,' Rath said.

Brenner wouldn't be deterred. 'She's a hot number, that one. That arse! Tits a little small for my liking. I wonder how she is in bed.'

Rath felt the anger rising within him. It was all he could do to keep himself in check.

'Apparently she let you have a go.' Brenner was clearly determined to provoke him. 'So, how was she? Did she take your dick in her mouth?'

Rath grabbed the fatty by the collar and his beer glass fell to the ground with a wet clatter, spraying beer and shards everywhere. 'If you don't shut your fucking mouth, I will have you.' Rath's face was millimetres away from Brenner's.

'You think you're the only one that little tart's blown?'

Rath channelled all his rage into a crisp blow to Brenner's solar plexus. The detective in prisoner's clothing bent double, and Rath slammed him upright with a left hook. Czerwinski grabbed hold of his upper arm. Brenner was panting and cursing, bleeding from the nose and mouth. 'Did you learn that from your gangster friends?'

People were staring. Some had even stopped dancing, among them the Cowboy and Indian.

Charly's cute face was horrified. Hopefully she hadn't recognised him.

'It's all right,' he said to Czerwinski, tugging against his astonishingly firm grip. 'It's OK, Paul, let me go. I won't hit him again.'

Czerwinski's grip loosened, and Rath tore himself away, leaving the room without a backwards glance.

13

He has prepared everything, arranged the light, the film in the camera, laid out his tools, filled the syringe; everything is ready. As he regards the evidence of his careful preparation, he is assailed once more by a feeling of impotence, this feeling that causes his knees to buckle, to sense the void at the pit of his stomach; this strangely hollow feeling that he knows only from dreams, which allows him to glimpse his own core and—worse—realise it is empty.

It ought to have happened here.

It ought to have happened now.

If she were still alive.

The feeling of impotence remains and calls forth an image he thought he had long since cast to the bottom of the ocean, never to return to the surface. But now it emerges as he opens his eyes, spinning slowly, turning on its own axis, so that he can view it from all sides. Even with his eyes closed, he sees . . .

Even with his eyes closed, he sees Anna.

The contours of her face, her beautiful profile that is silhouetted against the bright window.

Her lips move softly, quietly.

It isn't so bad, he hears her say.

Her hand moves to stroke him, and he recoils. Sits up. Turns away.

I love you, he hears. We'll manage.

We won't manage anything.

His first words after the failure.

We won't manage anything.

He should have known. He had been hoping for a miracle, for love, for Anna whom he so endlessly desires. He underestimated the disease. It is stronger than everything else. He hasn't vanquished it. How did he ever imagine he could? He will never vanquish it. The most he can do is forget about it for a while.

The disease has destroyed him, neutered him, he is nothing, a spirit wandering ceaselessly over the earth, a sexless spirit whom no one can set free.

We'll manage, Anna says, we have time. Lots of time. I want to share my life with you.

Impossible, he says, I'm not normal. I'm not capable of being normal.

Normal? Who is? As doctors, we know that best of all.

There's no point. I'll never be able to be a real man. Never.

You're a desirable man. Do you know how much our fellow students envy me? To say nothing of all the nurses who pine after you.

She laughs. Why is she laughing?

I'm a sham, an empty shell, I'm not a man.

She tries to take him in her arms, but he pushes her away.

Her cry as she bangs her head against the bedside table. Her hand that feels blood. Her disbelief, and the tears that flood her eyes.

He didn't mean it, he never meant to hurt her, never, but he is incapable of going to her, of comforting her, of apologising; he sits there as if paralysed and just looks at her, until finally he averts his gaze.

He doesn't see her dressing, just hears the door slam as she exits the room.

Her horrified expression, her eyes staring at the blood she has wiped from her forehead . . . It will be the last time he sees her.

He doesn't return to university.

He never dates another woman.

A few days later he buys his first cinema.

He knows where he belongs now; the disease has shown him.

Paradise: a movie theatre in which a never-ending film is screening images from his dreams, complete with the voices and songs he hears in them. Sounding images that assuage his homesickness, which is really wanderlust, a yearning that has no purpose and knows no end.

14

Sunday 2nd March 1930

The demons had returned, only he hadn't recognised them at first.

He lay in bed, heart pounding, unsure of where he was until, slowly, familiar contours emerged from the darkness, the outline of his bedroom. The heavy curtains only let in a little light.

The demons had returned, but in a different guise. Even now, panting in bed with his forehead wet with sweat, staring at the ceiling, the visions were as clear as if they were on a screen. Everything had been different, but no less appalling for that.

A forest, its trees unusually tall and straight, their tops out of sight; the trunks covered in black moss and disappearing into a thick, white mist. The forest floor was lost in fog too, the trees rising from it only to become obscured again further up.

He wandered here looking for something, though he couldn't remember what until, amidst the monotony of black trunks, he had suddenly come upon red spots of colour in a sea of black and white. Someone was standing there: a woman in a red coat.

He approached her as if magnetically drawn. Her back was turned, but it had to be Kathi. It was her coat.

'Kathi,' he said. 'Good that I've found you at last. I need to talk to you.'

The woman turned slowly, as if struggling against a viscous mass. He saw the face but couldn't recognise it; its contours were fuzzy, as if her features had been left behind in the gooey matter the air had become. He saw her as if through a layer of thick paste. Something dark opened. Her mouth. She spoke and he heard Kathi's voice.

'Baumgart,' the woman said. 'What are you doing here?' It had to be Kathi. It wasn't just her voice, but her figure under the coat, her breasts, her hips that were slightly too wide.

Rath tried to contradict her, to say his own name but couldn't, nothing came out, not even a husky croak. Instead, his right arm moved. Rath saw the Kathi woman stare at his arm. He turned his head and saw the long knife in his right hand; tried to prevent the movement or at least divert it but couldn't, even though his arm was moving as slowly as a film being shown at the wrong speed.

'Let me go!' Kathi cried, for it was indeed Kathi. Her face was becoming ever clearer. The thick air was dispersing and growing more transparent. 'Help, please help!'

The knife continued on its way, slowly but with irresistible force, penetrating her chest with a repulsive squelch that seemed to go on and on. Even after the first blow it was as if the air had been taken from her lungs. Kathi's screaming died immediately, but still it wasn't over. The knife stabbed again and again, unbearably slowly, but relentlessly until, at last, he could stop. He saw the blade in his hand, now broken, and Kathi's blood-soaked body as it slid slowly down the tree trunk, covering the bark in a dark, damp red.

He wandered on through the forest until suddenly there was an electric hum somewhere overhead and spotlights came on one after the other, lighting the way. Only then did he realise he was wearing a Royal-Prussian captain's uniform. The uniform was covered in blood, but at least the knife had disappeared, filling him with an enormous sense of relief.

'Are you looking for me?' he heard a woman say.

Vivian Franck stood in front of him, just as he remembered her from *Venuskeller,* smiling the same smile she had used to try and seduce him.

'Come on, we don't have much time.' With these words she exposed her upper body, revealing her gorgeous breasts, wagged her finger at him enticingly, and twirled round.

When her back was turned, Rath saw the knife. Her pretty dance dress was soaked with blood. He recognised the butt: the same knife he had been holding moments before. He tried to follow the actress and pull it out, but couldn't move an inch and had to look on helplessly as she swayed, only to recover and take a few more steps before falling to the ground.

Black shapes, barely visible through the mist, scurried to the corpse and tore it apart, tore it in every direction. Rath tried to intervene, but it was as if his feet were nailed to the spot.

'Have no fear, they'll look after her! Everything will be all right.'

Even before he turned, he knew who had spoken. He knew her smell. Charly had returned and was leaning against a tree, smiling at him, white as snow, red as blood, black as ebony, her head tilted to one side as if mildly ashamed.

Suddenly all his worries were forgotten, his guilt and fear too.

'Everything will be all right,' she had said, and it was true. Charly was there and everything was all right.

'You're back.' He drew gradually nearer to her. She just nodded. How good she smelled!

'Do you still love me?' she asked, turning her face towards him.

He was about to reply but could only recoil in terror when he saw the grotesque face staring back. One side, hidden up until that point, was a giant scorched wound; her hair was gone and her features were unrecognisable.

That was the moment he had awoken, heart pounding and gasping for breath, her scent fading as soon as he recognised the contours of his bedroom, the images dissolving like wisps of smoke in the wind. The telephone rang.

Rath looked at the bedside table. The alarm clock had fallen and the time was impossible to read. The telephone rang again.

No, he didn't have to answer.

It rang twice more before falling silent. He sat up, his head throbbing slightly. The knuckles of his right hand were more painful. A captain's uniform lay on the chair, not as neatly folded as was customary in a Prussian barracks. He felt a shooting pain when he propped himself up using his right hand. Damn it! Gradually his memory returned. His fist in Brenner's face. He had given the arsehole a good clout.

Charly's horrified look on the dance floor. The way she had stared at him. And the cowboy next to her. Rath felt the same stabbing pain as the night before.

Damn it! It was the first time he had seen her with another man. He hadn't thought it would hit him so hard.

Their brief romance was months ago now. Why had he made such a pig's ear of it? He had gone behind her back, deceived her and taken advantage of her, without intending any of it. She hadn't been able to forgive him, just as he hadn't been able to forgive himself.

Not that that was any comfort. Quite the opposite.

In summer he had tried to win her back, and failed spectacularly. She had talked to him, been cordial, friendly even, but that didn't alter the fact that she had sent him packing for good.

Avoiding her wasn't so easy since, alongside her legal studies, Charly worked as a stenographer at Alex, in Homicide at that. Their inevitable meetings had mostly been fine: sober and businesslike. The one time they had fought had been about Wilhelm Böhm, whom Charly idolised and Rath would have sooner wished in hell.

He had watched her deal with all kinds of men at the Castle but this was different.

It was the first time he had seen her looking at a man the way she had once looked at him. The way he wanted her to look at him again.

He had to get her out of his head this instant!

His bare feet stuck to the cold hallway floor as he made his way to the bathroom, where he peed and started up the boiler, before going into the living room to put on a record. His cognac glass was still on the table. He took it into the kitchen and placed it in the sink. The kitchen clock showed half past nine. As he brewed coffee he came upon a sheet of paper: the letterhead of the Greater Berlin Taxi Owners' Alliance with the taxi driver's address, which he had placed on the kitchen table before throwing on his captain's uniform.

The uniform he had to take back!

Already two reasons to leave the house. After finishing his coffee, he returned to the bathroom, cleaned his teeth and turned on the shower. The water never got particularly warm, but it was cold enough to bring him to his senses.

The taxi driver's name was Friedhelm Ziehlke, and he lived in the shadow of the Schöneberg gasometer. It was midday by the time Rath arrived. The drive to Babelsberg took longer than anticipated, with any number of day trippers heading for the country and blocking the road when all he wanted was to return the stupid uniform.

The street in front of the Ziehlke household lay deserted. The stairwell smelled of cabbage. Rath hoofed it up to the fourth floor and rang the bell.

He had to wait a minute before a woman in a stained apron opened. The place smelled of onions and fried liver. Rath hated liver. Someone else was responsible for the cabbage odour.

The woman looked at him disapprovingly. 'What do you want?' she asked. 'We're eating.'

Rath showed his badge and her eyes widened.

'Cheeky little brat,' she hissed, 'and he told me he was at the cinema with his girl!' She turned back into the flat. 'Erich,' she cried. 'The cops are here. What've you done now?'

Rath made a placatory gesture. 'Please. I need to speak with your husband.'

'My husband?' Her eyes were popping out of her head. Before she could say anything more, a young lad of seventeen or eighteen shuffled round the corner. Hands in pockets, he gazed at Rath and his mother defiantly. 'I *was* at the cinema! What the hell is this?'

'It's OK,' the woman said, eyeing Rath suspiciously. She looked as though her worst fears had become reality. 'This gentleman wants to speak to your father.'

Erich disappeared once more.

'It's nothing bad,' Rath said. 'Just a few questions. Your husband's a taxi driver, isn't he?'

Her face brightened. 'Please come in,' she said.

Rath removed his hat as he entered. The liver smell was unbearable. The Ziehlke family was sitting at table in the spacious kitchen-cum-living-room, with three more sons sitting alongside the head of the family and Erich, the oldest of the four. Friedhelm Ziehlke was the only one with a beer.

'Friedhelm,' his wife said, 'the gentleman here is from the police and . . .'

Ziehlke pulled his braces over his shoulders and stood up. 'Is this a new police method, descending on a Sunday afternoon?'

'I apologise if it's a bad time, but this is urgent. Just a few questions, and I'll be on my way.'

'What's it about?' The man spoke with a Berlin accent.

'Can we go somewhere more . . .'

Ziehlke shrugged his shoulders, opened a door and led Rath into the bedroom. Three beds, a large one and two small ones, as well as a giant wardrobe, meant there was barely room to stand. Nevertheless, there were two chairs inside, one of which was in front of a table by the window. It didn't smell much better here than in the kitchen.

'Please sit,' Ziehlke said, showing Rath to a chair. 'It's the best I can do.'

'No, thank you.' Rath remained standing and took the piece of paper from his pocket. 'You drive taxi number two-four-eight-two?'

'Correct. Is something the matter with it?'

'No, no. It's about a passenger you picked up on the eighth of February, a famous passenger, an actress . . .'

'Well, there's plenty of them in this city!'

'Vivian Franck.'

'Old Franck! Yes, I remember. That was on the eighth?'

'I need to know where you took her.'

'Somewhere near Wilmersdorf, I think . . . But wait, I make a note of everything.'

He fetched a dark chauffeur's jacket from the wardrobe and rummaged in the inside pocket.

'Here it is!' He showed Rath a little brown notebook. 'So,' he said after leafing quickly through. '*Sonnabend.* Eighth of February, nine thirty from Charlottenburg, Kaiserdamm. Drove on till Wilmersdorf. Hohenzollerndamm. Corner of Ruhrstrasse.'

'Then?'

'Pardon me?'

'Did she make you wait? Did you go on somewhere? To a station perhaps, or the airport?'

Ziehlke shook his head. 'There was a man there, he picked her up, and then . . .'

'Someone picked her up?'

'He was standing on the corner with flowers. Looked like an actor.'

'Did you recognise the man?'

'No, never seen him.'

'What makes you think he was an actor?'

Ziehlke shrugged his shoulders. 'Because that's what he looked like. Good-looking, elegant. And Vivian Franck is an actress unless I'm mistaken.'

Rath took the photo of Rudolf Czerny from his jacket. 'Was it this man?'

'Czerny? Nah, I'd have recognised him. It was someone I haven't seen in the pictures.'

Rath put the photo back in his pocket. 'Can you remember where the pair of them went?'

'Didn't see. I went straight to the taxi rank and waited for my next fare.' He took another look inside his book. 'Reinickendorf. Not until quarter to eleven. I was waiting for ever. Stood there waiting and unwrapped my sandwiches.'

'And you didn't see Vivian Franck again. You're certain she didn't come back onto the street. Or her companion perhaps?'

'Sure did, she's on billboards everywhere. But seriously, I didn't see her again. Why do you want to know all this? Has something happened? Is it drugs? Because I don't tolerate that sort of thing in my taxi, believe me!'

Rath gave a wry smile and took his leave.

Outside on Cheruskerstrasse he lit a cigarette before getting into the car and folding the window down to get the smell out of his nose. He had despised fried liver since childhood when his mother had tormented him with it on a regular basis. It was his eldest brother Anno's favourite food but, even after he was killed in action, she continued to serve it up . . .

He started the car and drove off. There wasn't much traffic.

He parked the Buick in front of a wine dealership on Hohenzollerndamm. The junction of Ruhrstrasse seemed like a perfectly normal street corner. One end house was home to a ground-floor restaurant, the other a menswear store; the rest were solidly middle-class residences. Rath climbed out and took a look around. Who on earth could Vivian Franck have been visiting here? The plaques on the houses indicated lawyers, doctors and tax advisors, but there was no sign of any film producers. Nor did the names on the mailboxes tell him anything—but most likely film celebrities didn't give their real names. There wasn't even a travel agent where she might have collected her ticket for the crossing. The restaurant, on the other hand, was definitely unusual: Chinese. *Yangtao*, the neon sign said, whatever that might mean.

Why had Vivian Franck taken a taxi to Hohenzollerndamm on the eighth of February, and not to Anhalter Bahnhof where Rudolf Czerny was waiting for her? And what had she done after getting out of the taxi?

Showing her photo around on a Sunday when there were so few people about was unlikely to be much use. Perhaps he should ask Oppenberg if the address meant anything to him. If there was a film producer living nearby it would be a big step in the right direction.

Rath returned to the car and glanced at the time: half past one. He was getting hungry but had no appetite, and not just since his visit to the taxi driver. He slammed the heel of his hand against the wheel in rage. Damn it! When he had just about managed to forget about her.

Who the hell was this bastard! A man dressed as a cowboy, ridiculous! Probably some pompous lawyer.

He didn't want Charly in his head, but what could he do? Don't stop, keep moving. Drive, drive, drive! He started the engine with nowhere specific in mind and simply drove all over town, taking whatever turn he fancied. Somehow his route took him towards Moabit, and into Spenerstrasse where, slowly . . .

. . . he rolled past her house. What did he think, hope, fear he might see?

He took another turn around the block and pulled over on the opposite side of the road from her house, before switching the engine off and lighting a cigarette. The last in the pack. Pretty good going, considering he still called himself a non-smoker only yesterday.

He watched the front door, peering occasionally up at the windows. No one, but then he thought he saw a thin gleam of light behind one of the panes. Shouldn't he just go over and ring the bell? Then what? Start another brawl if a cowboy opened the door?

He threw the cigarette butt out of the window and started the engine.

Half an hour later, armed with a fresh carton of Overstolz, Rath climbed the stone steps of police headquarters. He had left the car in Klosterstrasse and walked to the Castle, as Böhm or one of his dogsbodies might have noticed the Buick in the atrium. The huge construction site at Alex was getting worse by the month anyway, and it was now barely possible to get through by car. Aschinger and the few other stores that, until now, had been spared demolition clustered round the station like condemned men. Rumour had it that Aschinger would be granted a home in the new building. It wasn't known what would happen to Loeser & Wolff but, for now, Rath could keep himself in cigarettes there. As long as the police commissioner smoked cigars, there was bound to be a tobacconist's at Alex.

On Sundays most units were reduced to a skeleton staff. He had hoped not to meet anyone but, at precisely the moment he emerged from the stairwell, the great glass door to Homicide opened.

'Afternoon, Lange,' Rath said, tipping his hat.

The man from Hannover was surprised. 'Inspector! You're not on weekends.'

'But you clearly are.'

Lange nodded. 'With Brenner, but he's reported sick.' Lange hummed and hawed before coming out with it. 'He mentioned . . . well . . . is it true that you . . . beat him up?'

'Let's just say I taught him a little lesson. No need to shout it from the rooftops.'

'I'm afraid someone already has.' Lange lowered his voice. 'It looks as if Brenner wants to make a big deal out of it: disciplinary proceedings. Prepare for trouble, Sir. The boss was already pissed off with you yesterday because he couldn't find you anywhere.'

'Thanks for the warning,' Rath said.

Lange nodded and went on his way.

Brenner, that back-stabber! Of course he'd run to Böhm. It had been stupid to lose his temper but Brenner had deserved it. In spite of his painful knuckles and the trouble that lay in store, Rath had the rare feeling of having done exactly the right thing.

It was cold again in his office. Perhaps he should spend more time here during normal working hours, he thought, at least then it would be heated. To avoid Böhm, he was currently out of sync with the Castle, carrying out private assignments by day and only appearing in the office after hours.

Everything he was looking for was on Gräf's desk: the report from Dr Schwartz as well as the initial analysis of the evidence secured by Kronberg's people. Gräf had been busy, even managing to get Plisch and Plum to set their interviews down on paper.

Still in hat and coat, Rath sat at Gräf's chair and opened the forensic report. He was now accustomed to how Schwartz composed his texts, and knew which parts he could skim and which parts to read more closely.

There was no doubt about the cause of death: cardiac arrest due to electric shock. No internal injuries, but severe burns to the head and shoulders, a total of five fractures to the clavicle, upper arm and ulna—as well as a spinal trauma. Had Betty Winter survived, she'd have spent the rest of her life disfigured and in a wheelchair.

Clearly, Betty Winter and Vivian Franck were cut from different cloths. There was no trace of opiates, cocaine or hashish in Winter's system, only a liver that suggested frequent alcohol consumption.

He had intended to skim the section about the contents of the deceased's stomach, but his gaze fell on a single word: *yangtao*.

An alien element, more alien than the recurring medical terminology, and yet it stirred his memory. The Chinese restaurant in Wilmersdorf, or was he confusing two Asian-sounding words? It was Chinese at any rate.

Schwartz loved to show off his general knowledge and worldliness, and here he could do both. Thus: yangtao was a fruit from China, a berry about the size of a hen's egg, with a tough, thin, brown, hairy skin, green flesh and little, hard, dark brown seeds. Satisfying and easy on the stomach, the doctor had added, which suggested he had tried yangtao himself. He had found the exotic fruit in conjunction with banal foodstuffs such as mushrooms, rice and chicken, inferring that the deceased had eaten a Chinese meal on the day of her death.

That was typical of Dr Schwartz. Instead of limiting himself to the facts of his forensic analysis, he liked to make inferences. Rath welcomed the contributions of any departments assigned to the CID, but sometimes Schwartz could be a damn nuisance. Still, as long as he only had to *read* what the doctor thought, he could put up with it.

ED officers had already examined the spotlight mounting. The technical analysis had concluded that there were no material defects. All threads were in order, and the bolt Gräf had found was intact. It must have been unscrewed by someone, and that someone was who they were looking for.

He reached for the telephone and was put through to the search unit: no trace of Krempin. A few citizens claimed to have seen him following the newspaper appeal, but so far everything had proved a dead end.

He returned his attention to the ED file. His colleagues had also taken in the deceased's clothing for analysis: the scorched silk dress, as well as her shoes, stockings and underwear. There was something uncanny about the pedantry of these Prussians. Kronberg's people had done everything to the letter. They had found blood on Betty Winter's dress (her own, naturally) and several hairs that didn't come from her (but probably from her cloakroom attendant or co-star). What insight was that supposed to provide in a case like this, a fatality that had actually been filmed?!

He reached for the interview records. Plisch and Plum had been busy. He leafed through the statements, not noticing any contradictions. Everyone who had witnessed Betty Winter's death had described it in exactly the same terms as Jo Dressler. If it really was murder then there had to be a motive, and the statements about the dead woman were more revealing. Soon Rath realised that lack of motive wasn't the problem; quite the opposite, in fact.

Betty Winter had been a regular dragon. Although those questioned had chosen their words carefully following her appalling death, reading between the lines, it was clear she hadn't had many friends amongst her colleagues. She was respected but not well liked. Others hadn't minced their words, listing all the people who hated her—always careful to except themselves, of course. It was difficult to know what to take at face value, and Rath had to keep asking himself who was trying to damage whose reputation with what remark. Quite a web of intrigue and slander was forming. He would have to take another look at Bellmann's *little family*, as the producer called it, since he couldn't rely on tracking Krempin down.

Henning had dictated a summary of the deceased's life to Erika Voss. Born Bettina Zima on July 17th 1904 in Freienwalde, she had never undergone classical training, but many colleagues testified to her natural ability. The inflation years had brought her to Berlin, where she had tried her luck in variety, achieving success in a number of revues, before landing smaller roles in stage plays. In 1925 she played in her first film, alongside Victor Meisner, who was four years her senior. It was Meisner who advanced her in film, and not Bellmann as Rath had suspected. He was already well established, above all as a hero in adventure films and crime thrillers.

With Bettina Zima at his side, or Betty Winter as she was now known, Meisner had made the leap into romantic comedy. In the last five years, the pair had filmed about a dozen pictures together, becoming one of the most popular on-screen couples—a fact that had completely escaped Rath, who couldn't bear schmaltzy love stories—as well as an item in real life, following their second film, *Fallstricke des Verlangens*. This information didn't come from La Belle circles alone. Henning had peppered the dossier with references to film and gossip magazines, clearly indulging a secret passion.

According to his research, Betty Winter and Victor Meisner, who had married in 1927 but retained their respective stage names, were regarded as the happiest couple in the industry. No doubt because they hadn't been divorced after the first three months. It looked as if Meisner was the only one for whom Betty Winter's death was a personal tragedy.

Rath had felt from the start that Bellmann's mourning for his star was purely financial.

Nevertheless, Victor Meisner, actor and husband, was missing from the list of those who had been questioned. He still hadn't returned to the studio yesterday, and it would have taken more than a miracle for Plisch and Plum to have shown some initiative and visited him at home. Still, they had managed to question everybody else in the studio, where Dressler had recommended filming despite the death of his lead actress.

Time is money, Rath recalled Bellmann's words. Or was it Oppenberg? The producer hadn't allowed his people a single day of mourning. They were probably filming now, making use of every day they had access to Terra Studios. *Time is money . . .*

He couldn't help thinking of his father's motto. *Knowledge is power.* For some people the ability to reduce everything to simple equations brought order to the world, but Rath couldn't do it and didn't want to. He was afraid he might no longer be able to see reality, and reality, after all, was what his work was about: shedding light on what had really happened, however complicated, chaotic and illogical it might sometimes be, however complicated, chaotic and illogical it usually was.

Rath glanced at the time, carefully gathered the files and returned them to their rightful place. It was time to go.

15

She can't hide the impression the surroundings are making on her. It's less the paintings on the walls and the remnants of the room's former pomp than its sheer size and incomparable view of the park and lake. She hasn't seen anything like this before. He can sense it.

Most film producers are too tight. If they receive an actress then, at most, it'll be a grimy apartment, a love nest, but never their real home, never their real life.

Albert hovers discreetly in the background, refilling their glasses when necessary and serving individual courses from the elaborate menu.

He doesn't want any other staff around him today. As always, when he has guests like her.

The enormous table just for the two of them.

He raises his glass. 'To your future, Jeanette.'

She smiles. 'To *our* future.'

'Then we are agreed?'

'You're offering a lot of money. Artistically it's also a challenge, especially now, at a time when people are only shooting talkies. How could I say no?'

It's only about the money for her. He can see in her eyes that she doesn't care about art. Albert serves the fruit salad, and she uses her dessert fork to impale a small, green piece of fruit, before carefully placing it in her mouth and making a delighted face.

'Mmmh! What's that?'

'Yangtao. You can only get it from the Chinese in Kantstrasse.'

'Very good.'

'And healthy.' He takes a forkful himself. 'You won't regret signing with me. I am financially independent and can devote myself entirely to the creation of cinematic art.'

'You don't view talkies as art?'

'How can they be?' He has said it too loud, but she is more surprised than startled. He lowers his voice. 'Sound film is destroying cinematic art. A technical fad that turns film, which has reached its artistic pinnacle, back into a spectacle, like in the beginning when it was just a fairground sensation. As an artist you must refuse to be part of it. You don't belong in the fairground!'

'Refuse? I don't know. I'd still like to make films with other people, I'm not signing an adhesion contract.'

'No one is asking you to.'

'Don't misunderstand me,' she says. 'I'm extremely grateful for the opportunity, and that you're taking me seriously as an artist. However, it doesn't mean I'm prepared to close myself off to new developments. You have to understand that. As for a fairground sensation . . . Aren't you exaggerating a little?'

He was waiting for this moment even before seeing the greed in her eyes.

'I understand you perfectly well. Of course you want to make other films. Personally, I hold your older, silent films in higher esteem, and it's that sort of film I'd like to make with you again.' He raises his glass and offers another placatory smile. He has faith in the power of his smile, and in the power of his voice. 'Forgive me for getting so worked up, but you see film . . . film is my life.'

That is only a half-truth. Without film he would be dead, would have died long ago.

The day he shattered the mirror . . .

. . . there is a crunch as his mother steps on the broken glass. She halts in the midst of a sea of glittering shards and gazes at the clouded frame, on which there are still a few sharply serrated pieces, a wreath of frozen flames. Her voice, distant and yet so near. 'What has happened?'

He doesn't respond, but stares at her out of the dead eyes he can no longer stand. He tried to banish them with the heavy tumbler, whose shards are now mixed with those of the mirror and the drops of water that glittered between them before seeping into the carpet.

He has banished his ghost forever from his room.

Mother seems to understand. She doesn't ask any more questions. The glass crunches under her feet as she makes her way towards the bed.

He must have been dreaming. He didn't notice her entering the bedroom. Yet he has been awake since five, reading. The hours according to which those outside organise their day mean nothing to him. The days mean nothing to him anymore.

What does she want from him at this hour? For him to come to breakfast? Hardly, she never fetches him to eat. She leaves that to Albert. She is never there when he wolfs down the few bites his hungry stomach can manage. Or when he takes minutes over each, waiting until his saliva has lubricated every last piece before swallowing the warm paste.

He has tried both wolfing down his food and chewing it slowly; neither can banish his hunger. His eternal hunger, the background noise that drowns out everything else in his life, this life that doesn't merit the name. He finds solace from book to book, dream to dream. It is only time he need overcome, time that consists merely of breathing, waiting and starving. Time is his enemy. He has learned that already. Only when he exists out of time can he be happy.

That is why he is angry with his mother, because she has hauled him back to the present.

He looks up, clinging to his book like a treasure she is threatening to snatch away.

Good morning, my boy. Do you know what day it is today? She gives him her hand. Your father has a surprise for you. Come on!

Too often they have lured him with promises that have turned out to be traps, but he doesn't dare contradict her.

Watch out!

She puts his shoes on for him so that he doesn't cut himself, and throws his dressing gown over him.

He follows her through several doors. His splendid prison, in which an eternal twilight reigns, is enormous. They descend the steps and enter the great hall, the vestibule in which even his mother seems tiny and lost. Her shoes click noisily over the stone floor, while his steps are so inaudible it's as if he is already as dead as he feels.

He gives a start when she throws open the cellar door, a door that is never otherwise opened. His grandfather, who made his money trading shares, built a labyrinthine medieval castle on the Wannsee, sombre Gothic, as was the fashion before the war. The cellar door is reminiscent of a dungeon. What do they have in store for him?

When she sees his hesitation, Mother smiles and takes his hand. Have no fear, she says.

She leads him down the stone staircase into the darkness. It doesn't smell mouldy, but he doesn't like the cellar all the same. He is afraid of his father, of his stick, his implacability. Does he mean to lure him into his new prison? Into a narrow, dark dungeon, the better to keep an eye on him? So that not even Mother can slip him something to ease his suffering.

Have no fear, she says again, and his fear grows.

Downstairs, she opens the door to a dark room, and a flickering beam of light. She takes him by the shoulders and pushes him through, and in the semi-darkness he recognises his father's face. That face which can no longer smile.

Happy Birthday, my boy, Mother says, taking him gingerly in her arms. Look what we have for you.

He closes his eyes. He doesn't want to be reminded that time is passing. Let them forget his birthday, let them forget the passing of time!

Over here, says Father, this is your birthday present.

He opens his eyes and hears a quiet hum in the darkness. When he sees it, all of a sudden, he knows why he must stay alive.

A bright island grows in the dark room, drawing his gaze like a magnet, seeming to absorb him into himself. Bright images, a garden flooded by sunlight, the branches of trees dancing in the wind. And happy people in this garden. He doesn't know what will happen, only that he cannot avert his gaze.

He hears them speak, hears leaves rustling in the wind, although he knows the only sound is the hum of the projector. Now he knows why it is worthwhile. Why the agony he endures merely to prolong a life full of agony could still be worthwhile.

He has found it. His new life.

16

Rath heard a ringing from the stairwell that had to be coming from his flat. He was the only person who owned a telephone in the rear building. It rang a final time as he opened the door.

After hanging up his hat and coat, he went to the living room, put on a record and sank into his chair. Coleman Hawkins's saxophone performed pirouettes, as unpredictably beautiful as a leaf in the wind. Rath closed his eyes.

Where would he be without the records from Severin? He wouldn't have lasted three weeks in this city. No matter how he tried to regain control of his messed-up life, it always went wrong. Professionally, he felt like a hamster trapped in a wheel. Would he ever make police director like his father? It seemed increasingly unlikely. And his private life? His group of friends was limited to Reinhold Gräf, with whom he occasionally got drunk in the Nasse Dreieck, and Berthold Weinert, with whom he occasionally went for dinner and to exchange information. Of his Cologne friends, Paul was the only one who hadn't turned his back on him after the fatal shooting in the Agnes quarter. His fiancée, Doris, the woman with whom he had intended to start a family, had dropped him like he had the plague.

He had seen Berlin as an opportunity to start afresh with women too, but the way things were looking he would be a bachelor forever, like Buddha. Well, as long as he didn't become like Brenner or Czerwinski, running after pneumatic delivery tubes in the Resi . . .

He lit an Overstolz. At least he could smoke again in his flat without anyone moaning. He didn't miss Kathi, not really. If she wanted to stay with that gypsy from the Resi, then why not? No, he didn't miss her one bit.

He missed Charly.

He couldn't get her horrified expression out of his mind. Had she recognised him?

So what if she had? He had ruined things anyway, completely ruined them months and months ago. Sometimes he thought his life with her might have taken a different turn, that she represented one of those rare opportunities you had to grasp with both hands. But what had he done? He had waved the opportunity goodbye with his damn lying, returned to his hamster wheel, and carried on turning.

Perhaps he had finally set something in motion after dealing Brenner that beating, but most likely in the wrong direction.

The telephone rang again. Who could it be? Kathi phoning to tell him it was over? Brenner challenging him to a duel? Or Böhm taking him off the case? He lifted the black receiver and responded with an innocuous 'Yes?'

'There you are at last! I thought you weren't coming home tonight.'

'Father?'

'Listen, my boy,' said Engelbert Rath, 'I don't have much time. Your mother and I are about to go over to the Klefischses. I'm seeing the mayor tomorrow on the parade route. What news can I give him?'

He hadn't lifted a finger in the Adenauer matter. 'It's Sunday today. The Ford plant is closed, and yesterday I didn't have any time.'

'You still haven't done anything? Do you know how pressing this matter is, boy? And how important?' Engelbert Rath was appalled. 'I'm staking my good name on ensuring the honour of our city and mayor is not besmirched.'

Why shouldn't your honour and name be a little besmirched for a change? Rath thought. 'I'll take a look at the Ford plant in the next few days,' he said dutifully. 'The blackmailer's probably around there somewhere.'

'Are you certain?'

'Who else would have an interest in keeping Ford in Berlin at all costs?'

'Maybe the blackmail is just a ruse to put us off the scent. It's in the interests of Konrad's political opponents to put one of our Party's most capable men out of action, perhaps even inflict serious harm on the Catholic cause as a whole.'

'What makes you say that?'

'How could a Ford worker, even the plant manager or managing director, get hold of such confidential information from Deutsche Bank? More likely it's someone from a completely different circle.'

'First we need to uncover the leak. If Adenauer could make a list of everyone who knows about the secret agreement between him and the bank.'

'He has already. All people of integrity.'

'Of course,' said Rath ironically. 'So you already have a list of names?'

'That's the first thing you do in a case like this.'

'How about sending it to me?!'

'I'll send it straightaway, but see to it that this matter is dealt with as quickly as possible.'

'If it really is his political opponents, how am I supposed to stop them from spilling the beans in future?'

'Once you have a name, everything will take care of itself. Everyone has their dirty secrets.'

The call ended. Rath always forgot that his father was more politician than policeman. Still, he was right about one thing: the blackmailer must have good links to Deutsche Bank. Someone must have spilled a few secrets in confidence, a conversation that had been overheard by chance or deliberately monitored.

The telephone rang again. Rath tore the receiver from the cradle. 'What is it now?'

Not his father. At the other end of the line, Rath heard only gentle breathing. Then finally a male voice. 'Inspector Rath?'

Not a voice he recognised. 'Speaking.'

'You're the inspector in charge of the Winter case, aren't you?'

'What gives you that idea?'

'It's in the paper. I . . .'

'What's this about, please?' Rath couldn't stand it when people didn't get to the point, or when they pestered him with police matters at home.

'The Winter case, as I said.' The caller cleared his throat before continuing. 'Inspector, you're looking for the wrong man.'

'Krempin, is that you?'

It took a moment for the answer to arrive. 'You have to believe me. Otherwise there's no point continuing.'

'It's good you called. You're an important witness.'

'Don't talk rubbish! I'm not a witness, I'm your chief suspect.'

The man wasn't stupid. Rath held the receiver in his hand, frantically considering how he could bring Krempin in. First, keep him on the line.

'So,' Krempin continued. 'Do you believe me?'

'You haven't told me what all this is about.'

'It's about whether you trust me, and whether I can trust you.'

'If you're innocent, you have nothing to fear. I'll do everything I can to help you.'

Krempin paused before continuing. 'I didn't kill Betty Winter, that's the most important thing. You have to believe me! It's just a series of stupid coincidences. No one meant for her to die.'

'Why did you disappear from the studio after the accident?'

'That's not what happened! I didn't leave *after* the accident; I left *before* it. I had been at home for hours when it happened.'

'How do you know when it happened?'

'From the paper, where else? How do you think I know you're the one chasing me, or that I'm being chased in the first place?'

'Are you surprised we're looking for you? Why did you just clear off like that?'

It took a moment for Krempin to answer. 'Because I'd been exposed. It had to happen sooner or later, I simply waited too long. And then the false name . . .' The man fell silent once more.

'Herr Krempin, you can tell me everything. I've spoken to Oppenberg, I know that you . . .'

'You spoke to Manfred?' There was relief in his voice, as if a weighty confession had been heard. 'Then you'll know that it was simply a question of delaying Bellmann's shoot. That's the only reason I came up with the spotlight idea. The camera's insured, he could've had it replaced. Just not that quickly. It takes a long time to deliver these new, soundproof special cameras, especially at the moment. One or two weeks' delay would've been enough. Especially now, with Vivian not here.'

Oppenberg, that rat! So he *had* lied to him! Krempin was talking about deliberate sabotage, about manipulating the lighting system to destroy the sound film camera. Too many thoughts were racing through his mind, distracting him. 'What are you trying to tell me?' Rath asked.

'That my cards are on the table. I know I've done bad things, and I want to take responsibility for them. But I'm no murderer!'

'Then why are you hiding?'

'Because you're after me.'

That sounded plausible. People wanted for murder hide. They had those damn newshounds to thank for that! 'Perhaps it was only involuntary man-slaughter. Perhaps you didn't mean for the spotlight to kill anyone. But that's what happened, and you need to face up to it.'

'I removed the wire before I left, deactivated the whole thing. Nothing else could've happened. It's a mystery to me.'

'Then come to the station and we'll talk things through.'

Krempin gave a short, bitter laugh. 'How stupid do you think I am? You'll arrest me. You don't have any other choice. That's why you have my flat under surveillance.'

'You called me once already,' Rath said. 'Yesterday, when I was in Guer-ickestrasse.'

'You have good instincts, Inspector, but don't expect me to come to Alex. I have good instincts too.'

'Then tell me what you did. How you prepared the spotlight. When . . .'

Felix Krempin hung up.

Rath kept the receiver in his hand, gave the cradle a quick tap with the side of his hand and had himself put through to the private number listed on Manfred Oppenberg's card. A maid told him that the master of the house wasn't home. She wasn't expecting him until late, as he was attending an important meeting tonight. Rath swallowed his rage for a moment and used all his charm to get the time and address.

That left him a few hours to drive back to Guerickestrasse. The green Opel was still parked outside the door, though with a different team this time. Plisch and Plum looked bored.

'What are you two doing here?' Rath asked. 'I thought you were part of my investigation team.'

'Your team doesn't exist anymore,' said Czerwinski. 'Böhm's taken it over, and proceeded to ruin our weekend. By the way, he was fuming that you were nowhere to be found.'

'I've got things to do. Besides, I'm here now.'

'You definitely can't be accused of lacking commitment.' He gave Rath an appraising look. 'What's got into you, giving Frank a bloody lip like that?'

'He provoked me.'

'He told me you started laying into him out of the blue.'

'He's lying.'

'He was pretty mad!'

'Well, did he calm down?'

'No idea. He said something like *I'll tear strips off him*, before going after you.'

'Didn't catch me though.'

'Listen, Gereon,' Czerwinski said. 'You don't have many friends in the Castle as it is, and you're not making your life any easier. Frank is livid and baying for your blood, with a good chance of getting it, given his relationship to Böhm.'

'What about my relationship to the commissioner?'

'Like I said: you're not making yourself any friends in the Castle. Between us, it'd be a good idea to show your colleagues a little more loyalty.'

Rath hunched his shoulders. 'I am loyal. I'm paying you a visit, aren't I? And look, I've even brought something for you.' He passed him the container he'd used for Kathi's reheated stew. 'Here,' he said, producing two spoons. 'Silesian lentil stew. There should still be two portions inside, if you split it fairly.'

'Sure,' Czerwinski said, 'according to rank.'

'And girth,' Henning piped up from the back seat.

'Are you just here to feed the troops?'

'No, I have an idea. Tuck in and keep an eye on things. I'll be back in a minute.'

There were two possible houses, and Rath decided on the left-hand one first, beginning on the ground floor. A grey-haired man opened and eyed him suspiciously.

'CID,' Rath said, only to be interrupted.

'I've already told you I didn't see anything! I don't spend all day staring at the house opposite.'

Rath remained friendly. 'It's about this house, not the one opposite. Have you noticed anything unusual, particularly in the last two days?'

The man looked at him from top to bottom. 'No,' he said and slammed the door.

He scarcely had any more luck in the remaining flats. Even where people were friendlier, their information was similarly vague. Nor did he find anyone he thought capable of hiding Felix Krempin.

'You think he might have taken cover in someone's flat?' a small, bespectacled man in a grey cardigan asked, a resident from the third floor. 'Save yourself the effort. No one here's stupid enough. Better to ask next door.'

Again, Rath worked his way up from the ground floor, only to receive the same answers. On the second floor was a bell that appeared to be broken. He knocked, but no one answered. He knocked again.

'You can knock as long as you like, no one will open.'

A full-faced woman was standing in the entrance to the flat opposite, her eyes alert.

'Why not?'

'No one lives there anymore.'

'Since when?'

The woman shrugged. 'The cops came about two or three weeks ago to kick the Seyfrieds out. They hadn't paid their rent for months.'

'No one's replaced them?'

'If Oppenberg wants as much for that dump as he's charging us, then I'm not surprised.'

'Oppenberg?'

'The landlord.'

Rath nodded. 'Have you noticed anything in the last few days? Was anyone in the empty flat?'

'Not that I'm aware of. Why do you ask?'

The woman looked surprised when he showed his badge. 'The man you're looking for? I don't know, but he'd have to be pretty brazen to hide opposite his own house. How's he supposed to have got in anyway?'

Rath rattled the handle, making the answer superfluous: the door wasn't locked.

The woman continued to peer over nosily. 'Thank you,' Rath said, 'you've been very helpful.'

It took her a moment to understand, then she withdrew to her flat and closed the door.

Rath entered. There was no furniture, only a telephone that had been left on the hallway floor. A series of sharp contours on the yellowing wallpaper revealed where the furniture had stood. The place smelt of cold cigarette smoke.

The living room looked directly onto the street below. When Rath looked out of the window, and leaned forward a little, he could make out the green Opel on the street corner. Across the way he was looking straight into the flat he had visited yesterday. He could even see the telephone.

In the Seyfrieds' former bedroom Rath struck gold. Krempin hadn't left much, just a few stubbed-out cigarettes in a tin. Enough for the boys from ED. It was time to disappear before things got too hectic and Wilhelm Böhm showed up in person.

He went downstairs and knocked on the car roof. Czerwinski folded down the side window.

'Enjoy it?' Rath asked.

'Thanks.' Czerwinski passed him the empty container.

'You can bring it to my office tomorrow.'

'Very tasty, by the way. Who's the cook?'

'A secret, but I'll tell you something else.' Rath leaned over so that Henning could hear too. 'If you want to score some points with your boss, call the Castle and have ED come out. Seyfried, on the third floor.'

Czerwinski's eyes practically popped out of his head.

'Krempin,' Rath said. 'I fear we've been watching the wrong side of the street.'

It wasn't easy finding a parking space at Potsdamer Platz. Rath drove past Haus Vaterland and parked under a double street sign opposite Europahaus. The old name KÖNIGGRÄTZER STRASSE had been crossed out, and its replacement housed on a snow-white sign below. STRESEMANNSTRASSE. Rath recalled his deep sadness on the dull autumn day on which news of Stresemann's death had done the rounds. Although hardly interested in politics, he felt that something had been destroyed that day, and that more had died with this man than simply the foreign minister. He had been a strict but loving father to Germany, and Rath could see no one capable of replacing him. A strong politician who loved his country, who neither spread the hollow pathos the German National People's Party used to mask their feelings of inferiority, nor behaved with the arrogance Goebbels's Nazis mistook for patriotism.

Walking back to Potsdamer Platz, he wondered what was happening in Guerickestrasse. He hadn't waited for his colleagues to arrive, simply taken leave of Plisch and Plum. Böhm would be annoyed, first because he hadn't discovered Krempin's hiding place himself, and second because Rath had slipped through his fingers again. Krempin too, the fact that they had discovered his hiding place didn't change that.

Rath knew exactly when Felix Krempin had left the flat. Yesterday, when Mertens and Grabowski had gone for food and their replacement, Detective Inspector Gereon Rath, had left his observation post to take a look around. Krempin had telephoned to make sure the street remained clear before leaving his hiding place, which had been turned into a trap thanks to the permanent lookout stationed outside the door. Even if no one else knew, Rath realised he had screwed up. He swore to rectify his error.

As he crossed the square a little BMW emerged from a parking space, creating the ideal spot for a Buick. Pschorr Haus was situated on Potsdamer Platz, and Rath had often driven past without entering the building. Cigarette smoke and the smell of beer greeted him in the dark, wood-panelled bar. He stopped a waiter balancing a tray full of beer steins and asked where today's meeting was taking place.

'You mean the movie theatre owners?'

He nodded.

'Go past the bar, and through the big door on the right. They've already started.'

'Doesn't matter,' Rath said. 'They always save the best till last.'

He opened one of the double doors and saw the backs of people's heads. Someone was speaking from the platform at the front and all were spellbound. A few heads turned when he entered, their faces ranging from curious to reproachful. He quickly closed the enormous oak doors behind him, shutting out the mishmash of voices and clinking of glasses from the bar.

With the audience's attention having returned to the speaker, he allowed his gaze to wander. He couldn't see Oppenberg anywhere.

He made his way slowly along the rows of tables, careful not to obscure anyone's view or be too conspicuous. Everyone was looking at the speaker, who was saying something about the art of film-making and how sound film was destroying that art. Sound film, in short, signified the death of cinematics. It wasn't a subject Rath was particularly interested in. He liked films the way they were, particularly when the cinema employed an orchestra and not just an organist or piano player; but these new films, in which people spoke, were a different matter. Although what was being said onstage meant little to him, he couldn't resist the effect of the slightly husky yet pleasant voice delivering the words of protest into the microphone.

The room was almost full, and he was surprised that so many cinema owners were going to the barricades against sound film. Wasn't it progress? Shouldn't they be happy? There were posters on the walls, some of which he had already seen hanging in cinema displays.

SOUND FILM IS THE DEATH OF CINEMATICS, proclaimed one. THE PICTURE PALACES DIE WHEN FILMS TALK.

Manfred Oppenberg was seated at a table in the front row, his white-haired head resting thoughtfully in his hand.

The man on the platform finished his speech and Rath made his way towards Oppenberg's table through the applause. Before he could reach him, however, the producer stood up to shake the speaker, who had just descended the platform, by the hand, only then to step onto the platform himself.

Rath would have to listen to another speech.

'Good evening!'

Rath turned round. The speaker proffered a hand. Tall and thin, in his mid-twenties at most, the type of person who enters a room and is immediately the centre of attention.

'It's good that you came, even if you are a little late. We need all the support we can get. Though I . . . I'm afraid I don't remember which movie theatre you run . . .'

'The one at Alex. I'm here to speak to Herr Oppenberg.' Rath showed his badge. 'In private,' he added.

'Then please take a seat while Herr Oppenberg is speaking,' the man said, gesturing towards a table in the second row. 'Can I get you something to drink?'

'I wouldn't say no to a beer.'

Rath sat down, gratefully accepting the beer brought to him by a waiter, and listened.

Oppenberg was defending talkies. No wonder, he was filming a number himself. He admitted that it wasn't easy making the switch to the new, expensive technology, but if you missed the boat you'd find yourself stranded at the harbour. Realising he was in danger of incurring the audience's displeasure, he skilfully changed tack.

'It goes without saying that Montana Film will continue to produce the high-quality silent films for which it is renowned,' he said. 'And that we will gladly deliver them to your theatres.' He saw no tension between sound and silent films: 'both art forms are legitimate, and both will find their audience—and their theatres.' He continued on the technical and licensing aspects of sound film, and Rath was soon lost.

'We all know that the question of whether to use optical or stylus sound is above all a patenting issue. A struggle is being waged for patents and licences, for market control and for monopolies, and it is being waged at our expense, at the expense of film-makers, theatre operators and the public.' Oppenberg took a sip of water and assessed the effect of his words. 'What pains you, gentlemen, is not knowing which technology to invest in. Believe me: I don't merely understand your despair, I share it. Why should installing technology from Western Electric preclude you from playing films made in Germany? And why should choosing Klangfilm machines mean you have to miss out on American films? Or pay high licensing fees in addition to all the costs sound film already entails. It is, and let me make this perfectly clear, an unsatisfactory state of affairs. Not just for cinema owners and for myself as a producer of motion pictures. No, above all it is unsatisfactory, indeed completely unacceptable, for those people for whose pleasure we all work tirelessly—that is, for our viewers!'

Despite isolated catcalls, the majority of cinema owners applauded courteously, if still a little warily. Oppenberg had managed to turn it around. He thanked his audience briefly and descended the platform, looking more pleased than surprised to see Rath.

'Herr Rath, what a surprise. I hope you're bringing good news!'

Before Rath could respond, the previous speaker had clasped Oppenberg's hand and was thanking him for his contribution.

'It was no more than anyone would have done, my dear Marquard,' Oppenberg said. 'We're in the same boat: cinema owners, producers, it doesn't matter!'

'I had hoped, however, that you might delve a little more closely into the artistic side of things. Shouldn't that be of greater concern to you as a film-maker?'

He really did have an impressive voice. Even when it was expressing disapproval, it sounded warm and reassuring.

Oppenberg genuinely seemed embarrassed. 'Everybody has their own opinion, Herr Marquard. For me it's a question of whether we can overcome the challenges sound film presents. That ought to be of interest to you too, with your film lab and distribution firm. We can't leave everything to Ufa.'

'For me, it's always been about the art. That's the reason I manage movie theatres. You, however, are in the happy position of being able to make films, which, sadly, is not a talent I possess.'

'Cinematics as we know it is flourishing, that is true, but I am certain that sound film can become an art form in its own right. That's what we're working towards.'

'I hope nevertheless that you continue to confer real films upon us.'

'My duty is to my public, Herr Marquard. Now if you'll excuse me, Herr Rath has come here especially to see me.'

'Rath?' Marquard raised an eyebrow. 'Aren't you investigating the death of Betty Winter?'

Rath nodded.

'The papers say her accident could have been murder. Do you have any leads?'

'It's still early days.'

Oppenberg took Rath to one side and led him to the cloakroom. 'You must have news if you're visiting me here,' he said.

'Depends. News for me, but not news for you.'

Oppenberg considered this, only for the attendant to interrupt his thoughts and pass him his heavy winter coat with fur collar, together with leather gloves and homburg.

'Let's go down to the Esplanade,' he said. 'We can speak freely there.'

Rath couldn't wait that long. 'I've spoken to Krempin,' he said, as they crossed Potsdamer Strasse.

'So you found him!'

'No, he found me. He called me.'

'Where's he hiding?'

'No idea. Not in your flat anymore, anyway.'

'Pardon me?'

'The empty flat in Guerickestrasse. In your block of flats. Don't pretend you didn't know.'

'I swear I had no idea. I own several houses in that street, including the one Felix lives in.'

'He manipulated the lighting on your behalf, in return for which you found him a hiding place.'

'I have no idea . . . really.'

'Herr Oppenberg, you've lied to me once already. I can only work with you if I know I can trust you.'

A few pedestrians turned as Rath's voice grew louder.

'Calm down,' Oppenberg said. 'Let's talk like adults, and not in the middle of the street.' He took Rath by the arm and pulled him down Bellevuestrasse. 'Come on, we'll be there in a moment. Let's have a drink. We can discuss these matters at our leisure.'

Moments later they were sitting in a recess at the Esplanade Hotel bar, waiting for the bottle of wine Manfred Oppenberg had ordered. He seemed to be known here. 'So,' he said, already looking more cheerful than he had done on the street. 'Tell me what Krempin said and why you're so worked up.'

'You lied to me! You smuggled your man into Bellmann's studio knowing full well about his sabotage plans. He was supposed to delay the shoot.'

'Delaying the shoot is not sabotage.'

'What else would you call dropping a heavy spotlight on an expensive sound film camera?'

'That was his plan?'

'Stop acting the innocent, he was there on your behalf.'

'I can assure you, I knew nothing of his plans. Felix had completely free rein. Yes, he was to delay the shoot, but how he did so was his business.'

Oppenberg shook his head. 'Felix tried everything. He even made a move on Winter, but . . .'

'And when none of that worked, he came up with the camera idea. Without telling you?'

'It was probably too late anyway. Bellmann had smelled a rat and cast everything aside, put the new adventure film with Victor Meisner completely on ice and started shooting this schmaltzy rubbish.'

'And you couldn't allow that to happen . . .'

'Our film is supposed to be out first. That's all that counts. *Vom Blitz getroffen* is a completely new departure, a divine romantic comedy, and the *divine* is meant literally. I bought the book a year ago, and had it adapted last autumn. Somehow Bellmann must have got wind of it, and now he's trying to pip me to the post with one of his sorry efforts . . . And then there's Vivian's disappearance . . . It's enough to make you despair.'

'And your despair was so great that you were prepared to risk the life of an actress. I've warned you, if you should be involved in a murder I won't be able to make any allowances.'

'Your imagination's getting the better of you. I don't know what Felix was planning, but it certainly wasn't murder.'

'Let's call it manslaughter then.'

'It's Victor Meisner you ought to be accusing, if the newspapers are to be believed.'

'Don't get confused now! Without the spotlight, this wouldn't have happened. And the lighting *was* manipulated. We know that much for certain.'

Oppenberg shook his head. 'It just isn't his way.'

'Pardon me?'

'Felix would never risk the life of another person. Whatever he figured out with the spotlight, believe me, it was perfect.'

'So perfect that Betty Winter's lying dead in the morgue?'

'I don't know why she's there.' Oppenberg shrugged his shoulders. 'That's your job.' The waiter arrived with the red wine and poured. Oppenberg raised his glass. 'I will support you as best I can.'

'Why should I believe you when you've already lied to me?' Rath asked when the waiter had withdrawn.

'I didn't lie to you. Perhaps I didn't tell you the whole truth.'

'Why didn't you say that the houses in Guerickestrasse belong to you?'

'I didn't think it was important.'

'And the empty flat? Didn't it stand to reason that Krempin would be hiding there?'

'Right under the noses of the police?'

'Fair enough,' Rath conceded. Perhaps Oppenberg was right. 'Still, in future you have to tell me *everything*, whether you think it's important or not. Otherwise this won't work. Don't go thinking you can do as you please.'

'My dear Rath, I'm sorry if I've given you the wrong impression. I will help you solve your case as best I can. As long as you keep to your side of the bargain. Have you discovered anything about Vivian's whereabouts?'

Rath was speechless at how easily Oppenberg reverted. 'Speaking of bargains, I've kept to my side more than you have to yours.'

Oppenberg reached inside his jacket pocket. 'You're right.' He counted out five twenty-mark notes on the table. 'A down payment.'

Rath gazed at the notes. He could certainly use the money; the car wasn't cheap to run, and the money he had found in his mailbox one morning in late summer had mostly gone on its purchase. Still, something inside him resisted Oppenberg, who seemed to think all problems could be solved by money. He pushed the notes back over the table. 'I think we're friends,' he said.

Oppenberg returned the money to his pocket with a shrug. 'Tell me what you have found.'

'Vivian Franck's final taxi journey,' Rath said. 'After she left her apartment.'

'On the day of her departure?'

'She was never in the mountains. She never made it to the station, even though she loaded her cases into the taxi.'

As he was speaking it occurred to him that he hadn't asked Ziehlke, the taxi driver, what had happened to her cases.

'Where did she go?'

'Wilmersdorf, Hohenzollerndamm. Does that mean anything to you? Does Vivian know anyone there? An actor, or a producer perhaps?'

Oppenberg shrugged. 'In Wilmersdorf? Not that I know of.'

'Someone picked her up. If you could put together a few photos of

Vivian's acquaintances, I could visit the taxi driver again. Perhaps he'd recognise the man.'

'No problem.'

'Good, then I'll be in touch.'

Rath left the table without finishing his glass of wine.

17

Monday 3rd March 1930

The demons had gone. Rath never knew when, but at some point they would simply vanish from his dreams as unexpectedly as they had arrived.

He had slept peacefully, but wakened early. He hit the alarm before it rang, got out of bed and, by half past six, was sitting at the kitchen table with a cup of coffee. The sound of Duke Ellington's piano rippled through from the living room. In his notebook he wrote down what he had to do that day.

It was Rosenmontag, Carnival Monday, his first in Berlin, and he was glad he had enough work. *Kölle Alaaf.* He drank a second cup of coffee and smoked a cigarette before setting off. On the way to Schöneberg he stopped at the petrol station on Yorckstrasse and filled up. By half past seven he was in Cheruskerstrasse. He had thought about whether he should call so early but, with the exception of the mother, the family had already left for the day.

'You'll have to get up earlier,' she said. 'My Friedhelm's already out and about by this time.'

He gave her his card and requested that her husband get in touch urgently. 'He should ask to be put through to this number,' he said, writing his private telephone number. 'Best after six in the evening.'

'You think we can afford a telephone? It costs twenty pfennigs at the salon downstairs. Blum, that shark!'

Rath rummaged in his pockets and pressed fifty pfennigs into her outstretched palm. 'In case you should dial the wrong number,' he said. 'But I can count on you, can't I? It's important.'

'Of course, Inspector.'

She closed the door behind her. A rough exterior doesn't necessarily hide a heart of gold, he thought, but she seemed reliable.

He didn't have any photos to show the taxi driver, but it was the suit-cases he was interested in. Ziehlke must have taken them somewhere; he certainly hadn't put them on the pavement beside Vivian Franck when she alighted from the taxi on Hohenzollerndamm.

He arrived at Marienfelde early too, but any hopes he might have had of looking for the wire Krempin had mentioned were dashed. On his last visit the place had been guarded by police officers but now, as in Babels-berg, there was just a lone watchman, this time in civilian clothing. The man placed a finger to his lips and gestured towards the red light above the door. Rath nodded. He already knew the soundproofing in this glass-house wasn't perfect.

He showed his badge, offered an Overstolz, and this time it was the guard's turn to nod. The pair smoked in silence and were still smoking when the light above the door went out.

'You can go in now, but make sure you put your cigarette out first. Fire hazard.'

Rath took another drag before treading the butt out on the concrete floor and entering. It was eerie. The scenery in the fireplace room was still there, and everything had been patched up, even the spot on the parquet where the heavy spotlight had fallen to the floor.

What confused him most though, were the two people chatting by the fireplace. The man was wearing the same outfit as Victor Meisner three days before, the woman, a green evening dress that looked exactly like the one in which Betty Winter had died. Drawing nearer, he picked up a few scraps of conversation. The two actors were speaking in English.

'Well, there's a surprise! I didn't know police officers were up and about so early.' Heinrich Bellmann stepped out from behind the line of spotlights and shook him by the hand. 'Do you have any news? Were my suspicions accurate? Did Oppenberg have a hand in it?'

'Do you know Vivian Franck?' Rath asked.

'Oppenberg's floozy? Why do you ask?'

'So you do know her. Can you tell me where she's staying?'

'Has Oppenberg told you I'm pinching his third-rate actresses? No, thanks. I don't need a slut like that Franck!'

'*Verrucht* was relatively successful . . .'

'Because she spends most of the time gambolling half-naked through the set. Betty didn't need to do that, none of my actresses do. If Oppenberg's girls are running away from him, he needn't look for them here!'

Bellmann didn't give the impression that he knew anything about Vivian Franck's whereabouts. Time to change the subject. 'Actually, I'm here for another reason,' Rath said. 'I need to speak to Herr Lüdenbach again, and take a closer look at the spotlight mounting.'

'Go up to the lighting bridges? I'm afraid that's not possible during filming.'

'Correct, which is why you won't have anything against taking a little break.'

'For how long? You know that . . .'

'. . . time is money,' Rath completed the sentence. 'That's true for me too, by the way. Where's your senior lighting technician?'

Bellmann waved Dressler over from talking to the sound engineer. 'We're taking a short break,' he said. 'The inspector would like to go back onto the lighting bridges with Lüdenbach.'

Dressler disappeared into the dark behind the spotlights. In the meantime, the two actors left the parquet and advanced curiously. 'What's going on?' the man asked in English.

'Short break,' Bellmann answered in heavily accented English, gesturing towards Rath, 'because of the Prussian police.' When he saw Rath's quizzical expression, he introduced the man. 'Keith Wilkins,' he said, in German now, 'male lead in *Thunder of Love*.'

'Nice to meet you,' Wilkins said, shaking the inspector's hand before disappearing behind the set. Rath suspected he would make use of the unexpected break to top up on cocaine.

He looked at the woman as if she were a vision from the hereafter. She was cast in an eerily similar mould to Betty Winter, only younger and prettier. He was searching for the correct English phrase when she greeted him in accent-free German.

'Eva Kröger,' she said.

Rath gazed at her, even more astonished than before.

She laughed. 'I was raised bilingual,' she explained. 'My father is a Hamburg businessman, my mother a variety artist from Boston.'

'Eva has all the makings of an international star,' Bellmann said. 'Not

with that surname, however. We're looking for something more sophisti-
cated. *Thunder of Love* is her first major film.'

'You shoot English films too?'

'*Thunder of Love* is the English version of *Liebesgewitter*,' Bellmann said.
'If you want to maintain an international presence with sound films, you
have to film several language versions. Or at least an English version for
the American and British markets. That way you're killing two birds with
one stone. Two big birds, if I may say so.'

The actress turned to accompany her colleague backstage. From behind
she was the spitting image of Betty Winter.

'We've taken her on as Betty's double.' It was as if Bellmann had read
Rath's mind. 'So that we can finish *Liebesgewitter* . . .'

'. . . as you owe it to the great Betty Winter, after all,' Rath said.

If Bellmann noticed his sarcasm, he ignored it. 'We've caught up on
the production schedule by working through the weekend. Editing starts
this afternoon. The distributors are pestering us to bring out the film earlier than planned. The cinemas are positively scrambling to get their hands
on it.' He sighed. 'If only Betty had been alive to see it!'

No doubt demand wouldn't be quite so overwhelming were it not for
the press sensation following Betty's violent death, Rath mused, but kept
his thoughts to himself.

'So, thanks to Eva Kröger, you're actually killing *three* birds with one
stone,' he said instead.

'How do you mean?'

'Well, if she passes for Betty Winter's double, then you can shoot all
original versions with her in future, and the English ones on top of that.'

'Multilingualism is just one of many advantages Eva brings,' Bellmann
said, a little peeved.

'And her fee will be lower than that of the great Winter. You really have
done well out of this.'

'I don't know what you're trying to insinuate, Inspector,' Bellmann said,
his face reddening after Rath's remark. 'But you should be aware that I have
good lawyers.'

Rath shrugged his shoulders and looked innocent. 'I'm not trying to
insinuate anything. I'm only interested in the facts. If I've miscalculated
the size of her fee, all you have to do is show me the contracts.'

'Before you go snooping around my business, you should take a look at Oppenberg.' Bellmann was now struggling to keep his anger in check. 'That Jew is free to smuggle saboteurs and murderers into my studio, while I'm treated like a common criminal!'

'Are you one of those people who view being Jewish as a crime?'

'You're putting me, the victim, in the pillory, and you're leaving the real criminals be. That's the issue here! You have superiors too, Herr Rath. There are limits to what I'm prepared to put up with.'

'I always push my limits. Sometimes I even exceed them.' At this point they were interrupted.

'You wanted to speak to me, Inspector?' The senior lighting technician, Lüdenbach, appeared beside them, glancing irritatedly at Bellmann, who was eyeing Rath like an attack dog ready to pounce. Then the producer seemed to flick a switch and bring himself back under control.

'I'll give you half an hour, Inspector,' he said. 'But if you should delay the shoot for any longer, I'll be lodging a complaint with your superiors. I really have no idea what you can still be looking for.'

'Let me worry about that,' Rath said, smiling pleasantly. 'And thank you, I appreciate your co-operation. Now if you would excuse me, I'd like to speak to Herr Lüdenbach alone.'

Rath took the technician by the shoulder and moved away. 'I see you've fixed the lighting system,' he said. 'Did you notice anything unusual?'

'How do you mean?'

'Was anything missing apart from the threaded bolt? Or was anything in the wrong place? A rod, a wire, I don't know, anything suspicious . . . ?'

'A wire?'

'Yes.'

'There was something caught in the grating. A thin wire, scarcely visible. I only noticed it when my colleagues were checking the effects lever down below. The wire ought to have triggered the thunder machine, but somehow it must have come loose and got caught, before the tension catapulted it back up onto the lighting bridges. I can't explain how it could have got there otherwise.'

'Can you show me where this switch is? And the wire?'

'You don't think . . .' Lüdenbach shook his head. 'No, no! Even if the wire hit the flood at full force, it'd never be enough to wreck the suspension. Never!'

'Just show me,' Rath said through gritted teeth. He was on the verge of losing his patience with the man again. 'Please!'

The technician led him to a wall where a big lever had been installed, one of those huge switches that were used on the railways to change tracks or set the signals.

'Max, can you come here?' Lüdenbach called backstage. A powerful man appeared wearing similar overalls to Lüdenbach. He seemed more like a butcher.

'Morning,' he said, and Rath thought he discerned the Duisburg dialect that his mother used to revert to when she was angry or drunk—neither of which happened very often.

'The inspector's interested in the wire you found in the grating yesterday. Show him everything. I need to get back to work.'

Max held out a hand once the technician had disappeared. 'Krieg,' he said.

'Pardon me?'

'That's my name. Max Krieg.'

'Very well, Herr Krieg. Perhaps you can explain this lever to me. Is this the wire?'

'Strictly speaking it's a thin wire rope.' Krieg pointed towards a cable that was connected to the lever and passed through various eyelets and coils, ultimately disappearing somewhere in the studio roof. Rath looked up but could only see the familiar labyrinth of steel catwalks and thick lengths of material.

'That's how the thunder machine is triggered,' Krieg said. 'It gets a lot of use in *Liebesgewitter*. It's a normal thunder run in which iron balls are rolled up and down wooden slats: a trick from the theatre. When the film's finished you won't be able to distinguish it from real thunder.'

'I thought things like that were recorded later.'

'Anything that needs to be added later costs time and money. Bellmann is an old theatre hand; he insists we make direct recordings wherever we can. Thunder's an easy one, but gunshots are more difficult. They overload the microphones.'

'Can you show me this thunder machine?'

The stage technician led Rath behind the scenes to a large, wooden box, which rose ten metres and almost reached the lighting bridges. Two microphones had been mounted in front of the box.

'Impressive, isn't it?' Krieg said. 'It's been going almost fifty years. From Bellmann's old theatre. It was a bit of a grind, heaving it out this way.'

Rath gave an appreciative nod. 'How does it work?'

Krieg gestured towards the top of the wooden box. 'The iron balls are inside. When you release them, it thunders.'

'And you release with the switch back there . . .'

'Correct.'

'Why isn't it next to the machine?'

'When I trigger the thunder I need to have the scene in view. The timing is essential, especially with a script like this. We're talking split seconds.'

'Why?'

'The thunder plays a decisive role. The male lead—how can I put this? It sounds a little crazy . . .'

'You wouldn't believe the kind of crazy things policemen sometimes hear.'

'Well, it isn't my idea anyway. So: Count Thorwald is actually Thor, the God of Thunder, who has fallen in love with a woman and is living amongst mortals in present-day Berlin. Naturally, this is a source of confusion. At any rate, whenever the Count—that is, Thor—shows certain feelings for this woman, the first time he speaks to her, for example, when she looks him in the eye, when she slaps him and so on, it thunders. Gets a laugh every time. And in the last scene, when they finally kiss, everyone's waiting for the thunder but it never comes. Because he's become mortal for her sake.'

'It does sound a little crazy.'

'It's a romantic comedy, with a hint of the supernatural. Bellmann believes in it, and says it's part of the new wave. That's why he wants to get *Liebesgewitter* in cinemas as quickly as possible. Before Montana brings out its Zeus story . . .'

'*Vom Blitz getroffen* is about Zeus?'

'That's what people are saying. They're both written by the same author. It's two different stories, but with the same basic idea. It's first come first served.'

'Or every man for himself, and the Devil take the hindmost.'

Krieg nodded. 'After the thing with Betty, I thought that's it, you can look for a new job. But Dressler just filmed the missing scenes with Eva. I still haven't seen the rushes, but it was uncanny how authentic she was. She could even imitate Betty's voice. It can't have been easy for poor Victor, but he's an actor and gets the job done no matter how he's feeling.'

'Meisner's back filming?'

'Yesterday.'

'Where is he today?'

'Everything's in the can, the boss has given him the day off. Doesn't he have to go to the station?'

Rath nodded. Neither Bellmann nor Oppenberg had told him the whole truth about their rivalry. 'Now show me where you found this wire.'

They had to go back up. Max Krieg was considerably heavier than the senior lighting technician, and the lighting bridges wobbled more. The stage technician squatted on the grating and pointed. 'This is roughly where the wire was stuck. Hardly visible—unless you scramble along here on all fours.'

'How did you find it?'

'It was quite simple. During filming with Victor and Eva yesterday, the effects lever jammed and the thunder wasn't triggered. That's when we re-alised it hadn't worked for Betty's final scene either. I took a look at the thunder machine and saw the wire was missing, so I traced it back from the lever to here.'

They were standing close to where the spotlight had fallen.

'How did the wire get here?'

'It will have jammed, then come loose. A taut wire like that goes a long way when it snaps. There was still a little cotter pin attached. That's where it must've snagged.'

'So the wire doesn't normally run through this grating?'

'No, it goes through a bridge a few metres away. You can't see it because of the cloths. That's where the thunder machine is.'

Rath inspected the metal grate on which they were crouched. Suddenly he hesitated. 'Then why are there eyelets on this bridge too?' He pointed to where the eyelets were attached. The effects wire ran up the wall through an almost identical set.

The stage technician gazed in astonishment. 'Shit,' he said. 'I didn't see that before!'

They continued looking and found a snatch block on one of the corners. The row of eyelets ran to the point where a hole had been made in the battery of spotlights.

'I'm not one for technology,' Rath said, 'but is it possible that . . .'

'I know what you're thinking,' Krieg said. 'Yes. The spotlight fell when it ought to have thundered.'

'Who was operating the lever?'

The technician looked crestfallen. 'I'm afraid that was me.'

18

The dial tone was already buzzing by the time Rath realised he'd left Gräf in the lurch. Too late.

'Nice of you to get in touch,' the detective said. 'Weren't you going to help us with some paperwork today?'

'Sorry, change of plan, you have to . . .'

'Have you gone mad?' Gräf hissed into the receiver. 'All hell's breaking loose here.'

Rath could picture the atmosphere at Alex. 'I had an idea this morning,' he said, 'and drove out to Marienfelde, to the studio.'

'You didn't have time to come by and share your ideas first? Böhm is beside himself. There's a briefing scheduled on the Winter case, and you're nowhere to be found. The case isn't yours anymore, Böhm's taken it over. We're part of his team now. "Fall in" is the command—only it doesn't seem to have reached you yet.'

'What I don't know won't hurt me.'

'You buttered your bread, now lie in it. Let's leave the proverbs.'

'We've come this far, and Böhm's just going to take everything away. Do you think that's right?'

'It doesn't matter whether I think it's right. I'm a detective, and Böhm's detective chief inspector. You're a detective inspector, without the *chief*.'

'Thank you, I'm familiar with the hierarchies.'

'Then start acting like it.'

'A detective issuing orders to a detective inspector? What were you saying about hierarchies?'

'This is serious, Gereon. You don't have many friends in the Castle as it is, and beating up a colleague doesn't exactly help your cause. It's high time you put in an appearance.'

'Is that story doing the rounds already?'

'What do you think?'

'Beating up is a bit strong. I clouted him a couple of times, that was all. He was asking for it.'

'I don't like that arsehole any more than you do, but hitting him is going too far. Especially in front of witnesses! You should hear what people are saying.'

'Is it Czerwinski? To think, I did him and Henning a favour yesterday.'

'No, old Fatso's actually standing up for you, even though he's a good friend of Brenner's.'

'He's just cosying up to people ranked higher than him, and there are a lot of those.'

'Don't make fun of him, you've put him in a lousy position! Why leave Brenner an open goal? The arsehole's been plotting against us from day one. Now he can tell everyone how violent you are.'

Rath couldn't think of an answer, at least not one he could share with Gräf.

'Gereon, you need to put in an appearance here. It doesn't look good.'

'I'm investigating a case.'

'You're not a private detective. We're a department. CID. Each one of us is just a little cog in the machine. We all work together, and those with the highest rank have the most authority.'

'Is that right?'

'If you're not here soon, Böhm will eat you alive. The briefing starts in ten minutes. What should I say?'

'Just tell him you have no idea where I am. But you can let him know we'll need ED out in Marienfelde again.'

'If I alert ED, I won't be able to stop Böhm coming out.'

'Let him. The main thing is you're there too. Then at least you'll know what's at stake.'

'Victor Meisner's coming here at eleven. He just rang to confirm. Actually, he wanted to get out of it, but I dug in my heels.'

'That's still two hours away. Leave him to me.'

'You're not going to wait for me at the studio?'

'I thought you wanted me back at the station.'

'I'm beginning to think you're trying to avoid *me*.'

'Don't take it personally.' Rath explained what he had found on the lighting bridge, but didn't say anything about Krempin's telephone call. Instead, he made his way back to the studio.

Heinrich Bellmann pulled a wry face when he heard that police were about to bring his studio to a standstill again.

'You'll manage,' Rath said. 'You're a quick worker, and I need to borrow your cameraman for an hour anyway.'

Twenty minutes later Rath stood beside Harald Winkler and Jo Dressler in front of a low counter in the film laboratory at Tempelhof. The director had joined them to 'look at the remaining rushes'. Both the cameraman and the director seemed glad to escape Bellmann's ill temper for a while.

They had hardly spoken on the short journey to Tempelhof, and now they stared silently at the door through which a frantic man in a white coat had disappeared with Dressler's order slip. No one was in the mood for small talk; everyone knew they were about to watch the final minutes of an actress's life, the first time Rath would see someone die on-screen for real.

The lab technician returned with ten film cans under his arm. Winkler had a quick look and pulled one from the pile. 'Must be this one,' he said.

'We need a projection room,' Dressler said, and a little later they were sitting in a small, completely darkened room together.

Rath took his seat next to the director and was lighting an Overstolz when he noticed the ashtray built in to the armrest. He was smoking almost as many cigarettes as he had before giving up. Winkler operated the projector after sending the lab assistant away. They didn't want any witnesses. The projector hummed and a beam of light shot through the dark, making the cigarette smoke seem to dance. The reel started, and a clapperboard appeared on-screen. Winkler focused the image, the board was taken away and Rath recognised Betty Winter in her silk dress. She was breathing heavily, while Victor Meisner leaned against the mantelpiece in his tux. His mouth was moving, but there was no sound.

'I thought this was a talkie,' Rath said.

'The soundtrack is on another reel,' Dressler explained. 'Light and sound are filmed and developed separately, and put together in the final cut. If you want, Harry can run them parallel.'

Rath nodded and Winkler rewound to the point where the clapperboard sounded. Then he fetched a second reel, which he loaded into a device emblazoned with the Klangfilm logo.

'Should be more or less in sync,' he said, before starting the film again.

'You need to turn it up,' Dressler said.

There was a scratch as Winkler turned a knob, then they heard Dressler's voice seemingly from a distance: *'And . . . action!'*

Betty Winter's breathing became heavier. *'Did I hear you right?'* she hissed.

Rath followed a moderately entertaining exchange between the pair, until Betty Winter said something that was too quiet for him to understand. Suddenly—Winter had already raised her hand in preparation for the slap— Rath heard Dressler shout. All movements froze, the picture went black and the clapperboard was back on-screen.

'That was the first attempt,' Dressler whispered, slouching nervously in his folding chair. 'This must be it now.'

Rath watched the same scene replayed, only this time Betty Winter portrayed her anger much more convincingly, to the extent that Rath could almost believe it was real.

The camera followed the angry Betty as she approached Victor Meisner, who stood smiling by the fireplace the whole time. Everything she said was so clear it was as if she were standing in the room.

She raised her hand again, but this time followed through. There was an audible slap and, as Meisner's head jerked back, Rath thought he heard a soft *pling*. Betty Winter closed her eyes and made a desperate face, then there was a loud crash. The shadows on her face seemed to shift and something black knocked her out of shot. There were shouts, shrill, somehow unreal, and the camera panned to a screaming Betty Winter. She was lying on the floor, the spotlight still burning bright, clouds of smoke rising where blazing glass and steel met skin, hair or silk. Then a great torrent of water struck the screaming woman. There was a sizzling noise, before everything went black.

Kept on running, my arse, Rath thought, as he turned to Winkler, who was standing by the projector. He had captured the moment as if he worked for the newsreel company.

Rath gazed at Dressler, who appeared to be thinking the same thing.

At any rate the director was slumped dejectedly in his chair, looking genuinely upset.

'End of the show,' Winkler said into the room, in which there was no noise save for the hum of the projector and the scratch of the loudspeaker. 'Do you want to watch it again?'

Rath nodded. 'Can you play it a little slower this time? From the slap, I mean.'

Winkler rewound the reel until the camera panned to Betty Winter moving towards the fireplace. Then he allowed the picture and sound to run at reduced speed. Her voice sounded strangely deep and her movements appeared stiff; indeed, it all looked faintly comical, although all three knew there was nothing comical about it.

Then came the slap but, before the hand struck Meisner's face, Rath heard the metallic noise, this time more of a *plong* than a *pling*. At this register, the slap sounded like someone's boot squelching in the mud. Betty Winter closed her eyes.

'She realises there's no thunder,' Dressler whispered. 'She does everything right and the thunder doesn't come. That's why she's looking so peeved.'

'She isn't looking at all,' Rath said, 'that's why she doesn't realise what's happening.'

The spotlight came into shot, still very fast despite the reduced speed, and Rath saw Betty Winter's face as it struck her. She couldn't even open her eyes before her face was knocked from the camera's field of view.

It took quite a while for the camera to locate her again, eyes wide open, lying on the floor screaming in a diabolical voice that was far too deep. It was unbearable. Rath was on the verge of covering his ears; Dressler had already done so. 'Turn it off, Harry!' he shouted. 'I can't take it anymore!'

Winkler shrugged. 'The inspector wants to see it.'

'It's all right, you can turn it off,' Rath said. 'I've seen enough for the time being. Shame that we can't see what Meisner's doing. The way he reacts, the way he fetches the bucket of water, and so on.'

'The reel with the countershot must be here somewhere,' Dressler said.

'Countershot?'

'Another perspective. For Meisner's dialogue. You'll see more of him on it.'

'I don't know how long Hermann left the camera running,' Winkler said.

'Let's have a look,' Rath said.

Winkler changed the reel and moments later they were watching the scene for a third time from a different perspective. This time Winkler didn't play the audio track. Victor Meisner moved his lips but remained silent, the camera on his face in a frontal close-up. A hand struck his cheek, and Meisner took a step back in shock. Then something black tore through the frame, and the actor's face contorted in horror. His upper body leaned forward and he disappeared. The camera kept filming but didn't shift focus. After a moment, the actor reappeared with a grave expression, and Rath knew he was about to tip the pail. Part of the metal bucket hove into view, then the film went black again.

'You want to see that in slow motion as well?' Winkler asked.

'Pardon me?'

'That's what we call it when the film's played slower,' Dressler explained.

Rath nodded. 'In slow motion then, please.'

The film started again and Rath tried to read Meisner's expression, the look in his eyes. What was going through his mind as he watched his wife being struck by a heavy spotlight from close quarters? After the slap, he wore an expression of surprise, probably simulated, but possibly genuine, since Winter had actually struck his cheek. Or perhaps he had recoiled instinctively after catching sight of the falling spotlight out of the corner of his eye? And his wife hadn't seen it because her eyes had been closed? If that was the case, no wonder Meisner blamed himself. Could he have saved his wife by reacting differently, removed her from harm's way with one courageous leap?

'One more time at normal speed,' Rath said.

He looked at the seconds hand on his wristwatch, waiting for the moment that Meisner disappeared to fetch the bucket. It took him barely five seconds, short-circuit decision-making in every sense.

'Good,' Rath said. 'Then if you could give me both reels, I won't take up any more of your time.'

Dressler looked at him as if he had just asked for the lead role in his next film. 'Pardon me?'

'I'll take these with me. We have projectors at Alex too.'

'But . . . I need the material,' Dressler protested. 'I need as much of Betty as I can get, even with Eva doubling for her. Despite everything, Bellmann still wants to bring the film out as soon as possible. We were hoping to start editing this afternoon.'

'Then have a copy made for yourself,' Rath said. 'This is a film lab, isn't it?'

'And who's paying?'

'The taxpayer. The Free State of Prussia will bear the costs.'

'Fine,' Dressler said. 'Can you take care of that, Harry? Tell them to be quick; it's for the police.'

The cameraman nodded, packed the two reels back in the tin and disappeared.

'Do you mind if I use the time to look at the remaining rushes?' Dressler asked.

He was just as proficient with the equipment as the cameraman. Soon more scenes flickered across the screen, all with sound. Dressler made notes, sometimes on the sound, sometimes on the picture, as Rath looked on. More scenes played out in the fireplace room. Betty Winter was very good as far as he could judge, much better than her husband, whom Rath had found equally unconvincing as a plucky detective on a previous visit to the cinema. If Meisner and Winter were a dream couple, then it was Betty Winter alone who was responsible for the 'dream'.

Suddenly Rath hesitated. The camera was filming a scene by the door. Meisner had just opened it for his wife, and they had started arguing in the door frame. Something else was puzzling Rath, though: the perspective.

The camera must have been positioned exactly where he had just seen Betty Winter hit the deck, right by the fireplace.

'What the hell is it doing there?' he asked, and for the second time that morning Dressler looked at him as though he had lost his mind. 'I mean: what's the camera doing there? Isn't that the spot where Betty Winter died? Right in front of the fireplace?'

At that moment, there was a loud peal of thunder from the loudspeakers.

19

Armed with two reels of film and a screenplay, Rath arrived at Alex at quarter to eleven. He parked the car by the railway arches and took the public entrance, where there were scarcely any officers, only civilians. In the stairwell, the unmistakeable mix of sweat, ink, blood, leather and paper, fused now and then with a little gun smoke from the range, soon returned him to the daily grind. The closer he came to the custody cells in the southern wing the greater the smell of sweat, now mixed with the stench of urine and fear. The Castle, that hulking, formidable building, that vast, complex police apparatus, had swallowed him again, suffocating the feeling of freedom he enjoyed on the streets. Böhm must still be out in Marienfelde with Gräf, but securing the evidence at the lighting bridges would take time. Rath doubted whether they would find much more than the wire and the eyelets, but at least Böhm would be kept occupied, and it wouldn't hurt to get a few clear photographs. Perhaps the technical experts would manage a reconstruction of the device that had cost Betty Winter her life.

He no longer had any doubt that it was Krempin's construction, or that the technical whizz had built it to sabotage Bellmann's shoot. He had known the moment he heard the thunder, but had asked for another explanation from Dressler and his cameraman all the same.

On Friday morning, the main camera had stood exactly where Betty Winter would die only hours later. An 'X' marked the spot on the parquet. 'That's where we positioned the camera for scene forty-nine,' Dressler had said. 'The mark was the same for Betty in scene fifty-three.'

Scene fifty-three was the one they hadn't been able to finish, and that Victor Meisner had to reshoot with Eva Kröger.

The actor was due at the station for eleven, still ten minutes away. Rath had instructed the porter to send Meisner straight to interrogation room B, which he had reserved moments before. Not the usual surroundings for a routine witness interview—the rooms were normally reserved for breaking down the real hard cases—but Rath didn't want to show his face in the corridors of A Division.

After his telephone conversation with Gräf, he had given some thought to how he might take the edge off his inevitable meeting with Böhm. The best way was with results: a comprehensive report of his findings thus far in the Winter case. That way he could let Böhm's reprimand wash over him while he pressed the file silently into the bulldog's hands. He thought about taking a typewriter home that evening, sticking a few records on and dealing with the paperwork over a glass or two of cognac, uninterrupted by colleagues and superiors.

He reached the interrogation room without meeting a single officer from A Division, or anyone else who knew him. Brenner, for example.

The rat! Using two simple blows against him like that, playing the innocent victim roughed up by a colleague. Rath really shouldn't have let himself be dragged into it. But . . . the way that arsehole had spoken about Charly—Brenner was lucky to get off so lightly.

Rath spread the items he had brought with him across the table. He sat down, reached for an ashtray and lit a cigarette. In truth, he was only interested in two or three pages: scenes fifty-three and forty-nine, the two sequences he also had on celluloid. The thunder effect was heavily marked in both, indicating exactly when it should sound. Anyone familiar with the production schedule would know who was due to be standing where and at what time.

Had Krempin made use of that knowledge and, if so, why had his construction failed in the morning but worked in the afternoon? In scene forty-nine the effects lever had triggered the thunder, meaning the wire could only have been connected with the spotlight *after* this scene. When had Krempin left the studio? The statements Plisch and Plum had gathered didn't tally. No one, at any rate, had seen him after ten, about the time Dressler filmed scene forty-nine. At that stage, the thunder had still worked; thus Krempin's construction could only have been activated after this point. So, either the technician was still in the studio and had connected the wire to the spotlight—because, despite his protests, he did have it in for Betty Winter—or someone else had discovered it and used it for their own purposes following his departure. Heinrich Bellmann, for instance. The producer had got over Winter's death quickly; indeed, it seemed to have brought him more advantages than disadvantages.

Rath would have liked to have Krempin here now, as there were any number of questions he could have asked. For Victor Meisner, on the other hand, who would arrive any minute, he couldn't think of a single one. That wasn't quite true. There was *one* question preying on his mind, but it had nothing to do with the investigation: how could anyone be so unconscionable as to reshoot with the double, the scene in which they had been forced to watch their wife die only two days before? A scene that was frivolous and funny, and completely devoid of tragedy. How could you perform a scene like that after such a calamity?

There was a knock on the door. Rath glanced at the time: five past eleven.

'Enter,' he said, and a woman poked her head through the door. It was the grey mouse who had been looking after Meisner on Friday.

'Good morning. Are you Inspector Rath?' She didn't seem to have much of a memory for faces. At least not for his. Rath nodded, and the door opened to reveal Victor Meisner, who seemed even paler than before. Dark glasses made his face appear almost white. The woman led him in by the hand as if he was a blind man being shown to his chair.

'Good morning, Herr Meisner,' Rath said. 'Good morning, Frau . . .'

'Bellmann, Cora Bellmann,' the woman said. 'If you don't mind, I'd like to be here for Herr Meisner during this difficult conversation.'

'That is a rather unusual request,' Rath said. 'But in view of the circumstances I am happy to make an exception. Perhaps I can take the opportunity to ask you a few more questions too. You're the daughter . . .'

'. . . of Heinrich Bellmann. That's correct.'

'Your father never told me . . .'

'He says I'm to learn the trade by working my way up from the bottom. He doesn't treat me any differently from the rest of his employees. Worse, if anything.'

'Please take a seat.'

She pushed a chair over to Meisner, who was gazing into thin air through his glasses, before finding a second chair for herself.

'Herr Meisner,' Rath began. 'It's very kind of you to make the effort to come here. Now, if you could please remove your glasses. I like to look the people I'm talking to in the eye.'

'As you wish.' Meisner's voice had a cracked hoarseness, as if he needed to accustom himself to speaking again. He took off the sunglasses and revealed two red-rimmed eyes with heavy bags, no longer bearing the slightest resemblance to a youthful hero. It seemed scarcely credible that he had stood before the camera with Eva Kröger in this state. In a comedy! Were actors really able to deny themselves to such an extent? Perhaps they had to, if they wanted to be successful? Or if they had an unscrupulous boss like Heinrich Bellmann?

'I would like, once more, to offer my condolences on the death of your wife, Herr Meisner . . .' Meisner looked through him as if he were made of glass. '. . . I know this isn't easy for you, but I need to ask you a few questions.'

Meisner nodded.

'How did the accident happen? Can you outline the order of events?'

The actor's eyes grew larger. The memory seemed to terrify him.

'We did the scene again,' he said at last, 'and I had the feeling that this time Dressler would go for it. It went off without a hitch, Betty was marvellous. We were already through when there was this technical issue, the thunder didn't work. I thought: it doesn't matter. Just add it later, you can do that.'

Rath was as sympathetic as a priest in the confessional.

'That's when it happened,' Meisner continued. 'The light came loose somehow, and then . . .' He broke off. 'My God! At first I didn't even know what was wrong. Only when I saw her lying there . . .'

'Why didn't you pull her away? Why did you fetch the bucket?'

'Pull her away? Impossible. And what can I say about the bucket? I don't know myself why I fetched it. At that moment, I wasn't thinking about anything save for perhaps, my God, Betty is burning! When I think about how she screamed! The bucket was backstage. There's one every few metres. The boss always stressed how important they are; we have a fire drill once a month. I just grabbed the nearest one. My God, her screams! I only have to close my eyes and I hear them again.'

Meisner closed his eyes and, gradually, Rath began to sense that the grieving widower was just another role for him; that his whole life was comprised of a series of different roles.

'How was it with Eva Kröger?' he asked.

'Pardon me?' Meisner opened his eyes again.

'You filmed the scene again with her. How was that for you?'

Cora Bellmann interjected. 'How dare you?' she said, rising from her chair. 'Do you have any idea what Victor's been through in the past few days? What he's still going through, and here you are reproaching him for his professionalism? He's an actor. Actors are expected to block out their private lives when they play a role.'

Meisner pulled her down onto her chair. 'Leave it, Cora. The inspector's right. I don't know who it was in front of the camera yesterday, some robot reciting a text, but it certainly wasn't me.'

A robot reciting a text. Business as usual, Rath thought, remembering Meisner's last adventure film. 'How are you coping with the death of your wife?'

'Not a day goes by that I don't wish I could turn back time, the way you rewind a film, and bring her back to life.' He faltered. 'My God, how I miss her.' He grimaced and began weeping silently.

Rath looked at him helplessly.

'I'm a murderer, Inspector!' Meisner screamed suddenly, his chair clattering against the floor as he rose. 'I killed my own wife!' He pressed his wrists together and held them out towards Rath. 'I killed Betty, I'm responsible for her death, I alone. Arrest me!'

'Calm down! No one here's blaming you for anything, nor should you be blaming yourself. Someone manipulated the spotlight so that it fell on her, and that same someone intended for her to die, or at the very least entertained the possibility of her death.'

'What does that change? Without me, she'd still be alive!'

'. . . and lying in the Charité with life-threatening injuries. If you're to be charged with anything,' Rath said, receiving an angry glare from Cora Bellmann, 'then it'll be for causing death by negligence. But no judge in Berlin is going to convict a grieving widower for that.'

'She's dead,' Meisner screamed. 'Don't you understand? She's dead and I killed her. I don't give a damn what any judge says!'

He buried his face in his hands and turned towards Cora Bellmann, who took him in her arms. She petted him and whispered something in his ear, as if comforting a nervous racehorse. At that moment Rath was glad he wasn't alone with Meisner: anything was preferable to a despairing widower on the verge of breakdown.

Meisner sobbed silently into his hands, and from time to time his body shook violently. Cora Bellmann looked at Rath as if to say: nice job, Inspector!

'I think it's better if you leave now,' Rath said. In the doorway Cora Bellmann cast him a final, reproachful glance. She had put the actor's sunglasses back on, probably so that no one on Alexanderplatz would recognise him, and for a moment Rath thought that if the pair of them were just a little more shabbily dressed they could earn a heap of money on Weidendammer Bridge, selling matchsticks or shoelaces, or by simply holding out a hat. He shook his head. These film types were hard as nails in front of the camera, and soft as putty in real life.

There was a telephone on the wall, and Rath asked to be put through to Erika Voss. She started on the same theme as Gräf.

'Inspector, what luck! Where are you? DCI Böhm has asked after you a hundred ti . . .'

'Erika, would you be so kind as to bring the Betty Winter file up to date by this afternoon, I'd like to . . .'

'The file is with DCI Böhm. Inspector, I . . .'

'Then get it back.'

'DCI Böhm is leading the investigation now, Inspector. You need to come to the station urgently. Superintendent Gennat has also been asking for you, Fräulein Steiner was even here in person and . . .'

'Hello? Hello?' said Rath.

'Inspector?'

'What's that? The connection's terrible. Can you hear me? Hello?' He hammered the cradle with his index finger and hung up.

The vultures were circling overhead, and their orbit was growing smaller. He couldn't show his face in the office for the moment, typewriter or not, and it was only a matter of time before someone found out who had booked interrogation room B until one o'clock.

Rath packed his things and decided to consider any further matters at Aschinger, in the branch at Leipziger Strasse. The risk of running into a colleague there was considerably lower than at Alex.

He didn't encounter anyone in the corridors, but almost collided with

Brenner in the atrium, managing to duck behind a police vehicle in the nick of time. A few uniformed officers he didn't know gazed curiously in his direction and he made a placatory gesture with his hands. Brenner was limping and wore his arm in a sling. Rath was already intrigued by the certificates he was planning to use against him. Brenner often skived off, which suggested the man had an unusually easy-going doctor.

Rath waited until Brenner had disappeared into the stairwell, then took the quickest route outside, got in his car and drove off.

The clientele in the Aschinger on Leipziger Strasse was different from Alex. No small-time criminals, no policemen: mostly office workers and a few journalists from the nearby newspaper quarter, and shoppers taking a break between stores. Rath felt happier knowing there was no chance of being recognised, and ordered goulash soup as he leafed through the script. The thunder effect appeared on twelve separate occasions. He compared the scene numbers with the production schedule. All thunder scenes had already been shot, and there had been no incidents, save for the last one.

'You're Inspector Rath, aren't you?' A small, familiar-looking man stood beside his table. Instinctively Rath was on guard.

'Who's asking?'

The little man placed a card next to Rath's bowl. 'Fink, *B.Z. am Mittag*. May I?'

Without waiting for a response, the man pulled up a chair and sat down. Rath continued eating his soup, now remembering him as one of those firing questions at Bellmann's press conference.

'I'm surprised,' Fink said, 'that there has been no news on the Winter case. Has it been confirmed as sabotage? Your colleagues have been pretty tight-lipped. I was referred to Inspector Böhm, but all he did was shout at me.'

'*Chief* inspector,' Rath corrected, wiping up the last remains of soup with half a bread roll.

'He's the one leading the investigation?'

'There's always someone in charge,' Rath said, 'it's the others who do the work.'

'I knew I was talking to the right man.' Fink seemed genuinely pleased. 'You've issued a warrant. Does that mean you know who the murderer is?'

'Let's not rush to condemn. We're looking for an important witness. I can tell you one thing for sure: Betty Winter's death was no accident. Anything else would be speculation, and I'd sooner leave that to you.'

'I'd sooner have facts.'

'I'm afraid there's nothing new.'

'Does Betty's death have anything to do with the script in your hand?' Fink pointed to the screenplay. *Liebesgewitter*. That's the name of her final film, isn't it? Does it contain the key to her murder?'

'Just routine.' It was the only cliché Rath could think of.

Fink looked Rath in the eye a moment too long and a shade too aggressively, before standing up. 'You have my card,' he said. 'Call me when you know more. You won't regret it.'

Rath had heard that phrase suspiciously often recently, and couldn't help thinking that someday he just might. He pocketed the card, even though he knew he wouldn't be calling Stefan Fink.

The clock in the dark, smoky restaurant showed shortly before one. Rath lit a cigarette and ordered a coffee. Now all he needed was a typewriter. It was too loud in Aschinger, so he gathered a few coins once he had finished his coffee and started looking for a public telephone. He found one on Dönhoffplatz, just next to Tietz. He knew the number of his old digs by heart. The operator put him through.

'Behnke,' a woman's voice said.

'Herr Weinert, please,' said Rath.

'Who's there, please?'

'A friend of Herr Weinert's.'

There was a click, and Rath could just see the receiver being placed on the little telephone table. He wondered if Elisabeth Behnke had recognised his voice, but it didn't matter. The main thing was that she fetched Weinert to the telephone.

The journalist came on the line with a careful 'Yes?'

'Gereon here.'

'Oh, so it's you who's acting so mysteriously. I might have known. Old Behnke's dying of curiosity. I told her something about anonymous sources.'

'That's kind of true. At least sometimes.'

'Have you got something then? I could use a big story, preferably an exclusive. The rent's already due.'

'I'll see what I can do.'

'Aren't you on this Betty Winter story? That would be something.'

'Are you interested in that?'

'I'm interested in anything people are talking about.'

'I don't have much for you. Actually, I'm calling about something else.'

'Do you want to move back in?'

'*Nit för Kooche.*'

'Pardon me?'

'That was Cologne dialect. Not if you paid me.' Before Rath could continue, a heavy CLICK-CLACK by his ear made him start. Someone was pounding on the glass pane, not Böhm, not Brenner, but a woman. A grim-looking Fury, who might, perhaps, have been young and beautiful during the Kaiser's reign, was banging on the cabin glass with the point of her umbrella, gesturing to the sign above the telephone that stated unequivocally: KEEP IT BRIEF, BE CONSIDERATE OF THOSE WAITING. Rath gave the dragon a nod and a placatory wave of the hand.

'Gereon?'

'Let me cut to the chase: I need your typewriter.'

'Is there anything of mine you *don't* want? I need that typewriter for work. Without it, I'll starve.'

'I don't want to buy it. Just to borrow it for a day.'

'When?'

'Today.'

'Don't you have any typewriters at Alex? Or have you been barred from the station?'

'Something like that.'

Weinert considered for a moment. 'I'll make a suggestion,' he said finally. 'My typewriter for your car.'

He could manage without the Buick for the rest of the day. True, he had been intending to drive out to Westhafen to visit the Ford plant, but that could wait so long as they hadn't sent him the list of names from Cologne. Outside, the woman knocked on the glass once more. 'OK,' he said, 'but I need it back early tomorrow morning.'

'Wonderful! Then at least I've got a security against the typewriter.'

'I'll pick you up at Wittenbergplatz.'

'And I'm supposed to just tuck the typewriter under my arm, am I?'

'It's only one station with the train.'

Weinert laughed. 'Might be better anyway. Old Behnke's in such a good mood at the moment. I don't want to jeopardise that by your coming here.'

The dragon knocked again. He hung up before opening the door with a jolt and showing the woman his badge. 'Do you know what it means to obstruct a criminal investigation?' he shouted, without warning. 'I could take you down to the station!'

She gave a start. 'But officer! I had no way of knowing. If you need to make another call, please go ahead.'

Rath made a serious face and said: 'Fine, let's leave it at that. But in future, you should treat the work of police with a little more respect.'

'Of course! Of course!' The woman clasped her umbrella and handbag to her breast and made an immediate about-turn, no doubt glad to have narrowly escaped arrest.

20

Weinert was on time. Standing outside the underground station at Witten-bergplatz, he was difficult to miss despite the crowd, since he was the only one with a typewriter under his arm. The passers-by were unperturbed. Sometimes Rath thought that a five-legged, three-metre giant strolling across Tauentzienstrasse would elicit nothing more than a slightly raised eyebrow from a seasoned Berliner—provided, of course, that he was moving quickly enough. The only type of person who made an immediately negative impression on Berliners in the mad rush of their city was the astonished provincial, pausing to gawp at something and constantly running the risk of being steamrolled. The city showed its new arrivals no mercy, that much Rath had experienced himself; either they were consumed and ingested by the great organism within a matter of weeks, or they were spewed out.

He turned onto Tauentzienstrasse, paused at the red light at KaDeWe and tooted. At least a dozen people turned to look before Weinert recog-nised the car and started towards it. No sooner had he settled into the pas-senger seat than Rath stepped on the gas.

'Hello, my precious,' Weinert said, stroking the dashboard. 'I hope he's treating you well.'

'If I'd known I'd be tearing a relationship apart . . .'

'If you knew how many tears I've cried.'

'You seem to be more faithful to cars than women.'

'Could be.' Weinert shrugged his shoulders. 'On the other hand: I've never sold a woman.'

Rath wore a dutiful, slightly wry grin. 'Do you regret it?' he asked. 'I thought I'd done you a favour.'

A few weeks before Christmas Weinert had lost a lot of money on the stock market, and his position as editor shortly afterwards. Rath had given himself the car as a Christmas present, in so doing helping his friend, who urgently needed cash, out of a jam. It had also enabled him to spend a portion of the five thousand marks he had found in his mailbox one late summer's day.

'I'm happy, at any rate, that *you* have the Buick and that I can still see it from time to time.' Weinert held tight as Rath took the bend at Bülow-bogen at top speed. 'What do you need a typewriter for anyway?'

'I'm taking a little work home.'

'Is it that time again? Can't you show your face at the station?'

Weinert was brighter than he looked. 'You work from home too,' Rath said.

'Yes, because I was too expensive for my publisher. Now I deliver more stories for less money, and they don't even have to pay my heating costs.'

'Times are hard.'

'You're telling me? That's why I'm hoping we can rekindle our working relationship.' He gestured behind the seat, to where two film cans were clattering alongside the typewriter. 'Is that part of your case?'

'Evidence. Winter's death on celluloid.'

'They filmed it?'

'It happened during the shoot.'

'Come on then, spill.'

'We'll do it like we always do. I tell you everything I know, but you wait until I've given the green light before publishing.'

'I can live with that.'

'And you make sure my name appears in the right places, without making it seem like I'm the one who told you everything.'

'It isn't my first time.'

When they arrived at Wassertorplatz Rath parked the Buick directly outside the Nasse Dreieck. 'Fancy a beer?' he asked.

Weinert nodded and a few moments later they were sitting at the counter. They were the only patrons at this hour, and Rath suspected they had his status as a regular to thank for the fact that Schorsch, the landlord, had served them at all. He hadn't even taken all the chairs down, and the boiler hadn't been on for long. Fortunately the pub wasn't very big and it would soon warm up.

Rath had taken his things out of the car, and placed the typewriter, film reels and script one after the other onto the counter. Schorsch gave the items no more than a sideways glance, placing two beers and two shorts in front of the early birds, before returning to polishing glasses. The men toasted, drank the shorts and washed them down with beer.

'Strange place,' Weinert said, 'do you come here a lot?'

Rath nodded. 'Since I moved. By the way, did you know that Zille, the illustrator, used to come here regularly?'

'Well, not anymore, I guess.' Weinert raised his glass. 'God rest his soul.'

'Do you know a journalist called Fink?' Rath asked. 'From *B.Z. am Mittag*.'

'Has he been trying to pump you for information?' Weinert shook his head. 'Be careful. You won't be able to make the same sort of arrangement with him as you can with me. A real hard-nosed type. Sensation before truth.'

'I thought that was all journalists' motto.'

Weinert laughed. 'You should revise your opinion on our profession. With the exception of Stefan Fink, perhaps. So, who has Betty Winter on their conscience?'

'I haven't got that far yet, but there's lots of news. See what you make of it.'

Rath told Weinert everything that he intended to present to Böhm in written form the next morning. The only thing he omitted were Felix Krempin's telephone calls, but he didn't want to tell anyone about them, not even his colleagues at the Castle.

Weinert listened attentively. 'So what are you doing with the script?' he asked.

'It says in which scenes the thunder effect was to be triggered. The murderer deliberately chose a scene in which Winter was standing under the spotlight.'

Weinert took the script in his hand and gazed at it thoughtfully. 'An innocent script as timeline for a murder?'

'Actually it would be the *production schedule* that determined the timeline. But in essence, you're right.'

The journalist hesitated when he read the name on the title page. 'One of Heyer's scripts.' He nodded appreciatively. 'He isn't the worst.'

'You know him?'

'Willi Heyer used to be a journalist. We met once; I needed a few technical hints for my first film.'

'You write film scripts?'

'You've got to look out for number one. I haven't sold any yet, but there are few lying on producers' desks, awaiting discovery. The problem is, if you don't have a name then no one reads your script; and you don't *get* a name until one of your scripts makes it onto the screen. It's a vicious circle.'

'I could introduce you to a couple of producers,' Rath said.

'Seriously?'

'I'm not in Bellmann's good books at the moment, but I might be able to persuade Manfred Oppenberg. And if Oppenberg wants you, Bellmann will probably be keen on you too.'

'Sounds good,' Weinert said.

'If you could introduce me to this Heyer in return?'

'Why? Because you think he writes scripts you can use to kill people?'

'Not intentionally, anyway. I'm hoping he might be able to provide some of the background to Bellmann and Oppenberg's rivalry.'

Weinert nodded. 'I'll see what I can do,' he said. 'It's on me.' Weinert snapped his fingers for Schorsch, a habit that the Dreieck landlord couldn't stand, but the journalist was too euphoric to notice.

Rath only had to cross the intersection to get home. A few minutes later, with the script, production schedule and film reels balancing on the heavy typewriter, he negotiated the courtyard at Luisenufer. When he entered the rear building, he discovered he had post. First he had to unload his things at the flat. With great difficulty, he managed to fish the keys out of his coat pocket and open the door.

He unpacked the typewriter and film paraphernalia on the kitchen table, went straight back downstairs and opened his mailbox. Two letters without stamps caught his eye; they reminded him of the envelope containing the five thousand marks last September. He opened the first while still in the stairwell. It wasn't money, but glossy prints showing grinning male faces. So, Oppenberg had taken care of the photos. There was a fifty-mark note in the envelope, evidence of the producer's guilty conscience.

The second letter was more official. Rath opened it in the kitchen, recognising the police letterhead.

It was from Böhm!

Since it appears impossible to reach you through the normal channels, we are taking the unusual step of advising you in writing that the investigation into the death of Betty Winter has passed into the hands of Detective Chief Inspector Wilhelm Böhm with immediate effect. Please report to the right-hand signatory without delay upon receipt of this letter.

The right-hand signatory was Wilhelm Böhm. The left-hand side had been signed by Ernst Gennat. So, the bulldog had snitched to Buddha.

Gennat had expressly warned him about going it alone, but did Rath really have anything to reproach himself for? He had kept Gräf, Czerwinski and Henning busy; as well as initiating the search and calling in Forensics and ED. The fact that Böhm was too stupid to reach him was hardly his problem. Gereon Rath wasn't one of those police bureaucrats who sat around on their fat arses waiting to be put out to pasture. No, he was out there, on the street. The truth could only be uncovered there, on the ground where crime took place, rather than between two file covers.

Rath flung Böhm's letter in the wastepaper basket, hung his coat and hat on the stand, went into the living room to put on a record, found some paper in the dresser drawer, fetched the open bottle of cognac from the cupboard, and returned to the kitchen where he inserted the first sheet into the typewriter.

Progress was slow initially; he couldn't help thinking of Charly. Was she worth all the trouble he had landed himself in with Brenner?

Of course she was worth it. She was worth a whole lot more too, whatever the consequences. Rath banished the thought of her with another sip of cognac and got back to his report.

He hammered the letters word by word onto the paper. Gradually he gained momentum. They wouldn't be able to bite his head off tomorrow. Böhm would have to acknowledge that Detective Inspector Rath had done a good job—or rather that Rath's *team* had done a good job; which was how he'd have to present it. He had fetched ED to Guerickestrasse yesterday and back out to Terra Film today. Hardly the work of someone who was going it alone!

The telephone rang a few times; he let it ring.

The stack of crumpled paper on the floor grew as the bottle of cognac became emptier. He needed the entire afternoon and evening, pausing only to change the record and for a light supper. He felt halfway at peace with himself by the time he laid the final sheet on top of the, by now, considerable mound of papers. The bottle of cognac was empty. Something told him he wouldn't be having any nightmares tonight either.

21

Tuesday 4th March 1930

Rath had set the alarm for early but it was the telephone that startled him out of sleep. Who the hell was calling at quarter to six? Whoever it was, they were persistent. He got up, determined to give the caller a piece of his mind only to find it was someone he had to be friendly to.

'You wanted to speak to me urgently, my wife said?'

'Herr Ziehlke! Good of you to call!' Rath didn't sound quite as cheery as he would have liked. 'If a little early.'

'I couldn't get hold of you yesterday, chief. So, Friedhelm, I thought, try again before your shift begins. The cops are on the ball.'

'Ever ready,' Rath said, yawning silently.

'At least here in the garage we have a telephone. Once I'm on the move, it'll be trickier. What can I do for the boys in blue?'

'Could you come to the station later today? I'd like to show you a few photos. You might recognise the man who picked up Vivian Franck.'

'How about twelve? Or, better, make it half past, in case I have to drive across town to get to Alex.'

'Half past twelve is perfect. I'll buy you lunch at Aschinger.'

'Thanks.'

'Ah, Herr Ziehlke . . . there is one thing I haven't asked yet. When you drove Frau Franck that day, what did you do with her luggage? I'm sure you didn't just leave all those suitcases on the pavement beside her on Hohenzollerndamm?'

'We'd already got rid of the luggage. From Kaiserdamm we went first to Bahnhof Zoo, where I had to wrestle with her cases again, and only then did we go on to Wilmersdorf.'

'Where did you take the suitcases? To check them in for a train journey?'

'I just delivered them to left luggage.'

'Do you know what number Fräulein Franck had?'

'Well, you've a nerve!' Ziehlke gave a dry laugh that sounded like something had gone down the wrong way. 'If I could remember that I'd be a variety performer, not a taxi driver!'

'See you later. Have a good day at work.'

'You, too.'

Rath hung up and considered for a moment. Why not, he said to himself and asked to be put through. To his surprise, it only took a few seconds for someone to pick up.

'Behnke.'

'Herr Weinert, please.'

'You again? Didn't you call yesterday?' Rath remained silent. 'I'm afraid Herr Weinert is still in bed.'

'Then wake him up, please. It's important.'

It was unlikely that the landlady would catch Weinert with one of his girls, since he normally sent them home in the middle of the night when she was too drunk to notice. Still, there was no harm, Rath thought, in a little schadenfreude.

Weinert seemed genuinely dozy, announcing himself with a 'Yes?' that sounded more like a yawn.

'We need to rearrange.'

'Gereon?'

'Are you crazy, shouting my name like that? Do you want to make yourself unpopular with Behnke?'

'What are you doing getting me out of bed in the middle of the night?'

'You mean early in the morning. Your landlady is up and about anyway.'

'She wasn't as late as me yesterday.'

'I'm calling about the car. What do you think about returning it half an hour later than agreed . . .'

'Great, that way I can have a lie-in!'

'. . . and not to me. We'll meet at Bahnhof Zoo, that's nearer for you.'

'No problem. You'll bring the typewriter?'

'I wasn't planning on dragging it through the underground. Can I bring it round later? Tonight?'

'This is my livelihood we're talking about. If I can take it on the train, then so can you. Otherwise, get a taxi.'

At half past seven Rath was standing at the Bahnhof Zoo left-luggage of-fice with a jet black Remington tucked under his arm alongside a brown briefcase. He felt pretty stupid, especially when the man at the counter asked if he wanted to leave the typewriter in the checkroom.

'Taking our favourite pet for a walk, are we? You should buy a lead.'

Rath didn't blink. 'I need some information,' he said, putting the type-writer down to reveal his badge.

'Well, what do you know! CID have mobile offices these days, do they? And the crooks? Give 'em a piggyback when you catch them, do you?'

'You should be a variety performer . . .'

'That's what my Ilse always says.'

'. . . but save your jokes for your audition at the Wintergarten.'

'All right, all right. Is humour against the law now too?'

Rath showed the man a photo of Vivian Franck. 'Do you remember this woman?'

'Who wouldn't?' The little eyes behind the counter twinkled. 'Saw her in *Verrucht*. Divine! Vivian Franck, isn't it?'

'She must have checked in several large items of luggage about three weeks ago. On the eighth of February to be precise, around ten in the morn-ing. Have the items been collected?'

'That's a lot of questions at once,' the baggage porter said in his thick Berlin accent. 'A Sunday, wasn't it? I wasn't on that day, but I can take a look and see what I can find. It's rare for something to be left that long.'

'If you could.'

'Might take a moment, though.'

'Fine, as far as I'm concerned.'

'As far as you're concerned perhaps, but what about my customers? I don't get any help till ten.'

'I'll take care of things here, you go and look.'

'You do have a typewriter,' the baggage porter said, 'which ought to make filling out forms easier.' He paused, perhaps wondering if he could think of a better joke, before disappearing behind a door that led to a windowless, neon-lit room. After five minutes he returned without any cases, but with a stack of index cards which he laid on the counter.

'So, this is everything that's been here longer than two weeks. Let's have a look.'

He leafed through the pile and, amazingly, found what he was searching for.

'Here it is. Eighth of February. Three items, checked at nine forty-five. Number three-seven-zero-seven. Pretty expensive to redeem by now.'

'Can I take a look?'

The man put on his most officious face. 'Either you have number three-seven-zero-seven or a court order, or everything stays where it is. Rules is rules.'

'And if you were to take a quick look and report back . . .'

'That's even more illegal! Do you think we fiddle about with our customers' luggage? Don't worry, Inspector, if there was a corpse inside we'd smell it.'

Rath took his leave politely and sat down in the station restaurant with a stack of newspapers. At least the waiter didn't comment on the typewriter. It wasn't very busy. Most Berliners didn't have time for coffee at eight o'clock.

The sun rose behind the bare trees of the zoo. It promised to be another fine day. Rath leafed through the papers. The Wessel funeral had been accompanied by one or two unpleasant scenes on the fringes of the cortège. Nothing more serious had occurred, though the Communists had done their best to provoke the Nazis. Thanks to Gräf, he hadn't needed to be there. He mustn't forget to show his partner a little appreciation; the detective had had to carry the can for him on a number of occasions over the last few days.

The resignation of Interior Minister Grzesinski was no longer much of a story; instead the headlines were dominated by speculation about a possible government crisis. Was the Great Coalition not quite as stable as Rath senior, the old centrist, maintained? Not all those in the Centre got on as well with the Social Democrats as Police Director Engelbert Rath, who had them to thank for much of his career.

Speculation was the order of the day in the Winter case too, with the papers relying in the main on Bellmann's sabotage theories. They were careful not to mention Oppenberg by name, even though Rath felt sure Bellmann would have gone to great lengths to spell out the identity of his hated rival to any journalist who'd listen, no doubt while whispering: 'But you didn't get this from me.' One way or another, the rumours were running wild. No wonder, given that there was nothing new from the station. Böhm had been unable, or unwilling, to tell journalists anything they didn't already know and didn't come off well in the articles. Rath registered with satisfaction that the majority of crime reporters had written *Inspector Böhm* although they must surely have been aware of his rank. That would make the bulldog very angry.

Gradually the time came. Rath finished his cup. He gave only a small tip, as the waiter could help himself to the coffee left in the pot.

Weinert was on time; the clock in the station forecourt showed half past eight as the Buick pulled up alongside a bus stop sign. He left the engine running and climbed into the passenger seat while Rath got behind the wheel.

'Where to?' Rath asked.

'Nürnberger Strasse, then you'll be rid of me.'

Rath stayed in the car outside Weinert's apartment. Looking at the entrance to the next door house, he remembered how he and Charly had once hidden there from Elisabeth Behnke. It seemed so long ago.

22

He arrived at the Castle shortly after nine carrying a brown leather brief-case, feeling like an insurance salesman. Normally he didn't bring anything to work apart from hat, coat and service weapon.

Erika Voss was expecting him. 'There you are! Inspector, you'll never believe what's happening here! DCI Böhm . . .'

'Then call him and tell him I'm here. Actually, wait a moment, I still have to file some things.'

'You've got a nerve!'

'As a matter of fact, I do. Is Gräf here yet?'

'Already come and gone. Nine o'clock briefing in the small conference room. For all those working on the Winter ca . . .'

'Henning and Czerwinski?'

'Böhm's detailed them for surveillance duty in Guerickestrasse.'

'You're well informed.'

'Someone has to hold things together here, Inspector.' She gave a wry grin under her blonde fringe.

'Speaking of holding things together. You can start with this.' He took the report he had typed on Weinert's machine from the briefcase. She nodded dutifully, rummaged for a new file in the drawer and reached for the big black punch.

'Any other documents on the Winter case?' he asked, as she wedged the paper under the punch.

She shook her head. 'Gräf took them all with him.'

'Then the report will have to do.' Rath returned the file to his briefcase. 'Now, into the lion's den.'

'Good luck, Inspector,' she said compassionately. In all the months they had worked together, Erika Voss had never offered him so much encouragement; he was almost touched.

Carrying the leather case he at least felt somewhat armed, as he entered the small conference room. The briefing had been going for twenty minutes and the air was thick with smoke. He resisted the temptation to reach for his carton of Overstolz, and met any curious glances with a nod. A few colleagues whispered to each other when they saw him.

He sat next to Gräf. 'Good morning,' he said.

'Gereon, damn it!' Gräf hissed. There was trouble in the air.

Up on the podium, Kronberg from ED was going through yesterday's findings. Böhm stood listening with arms folded, and when he darted a glance at Rath he seemed to gaze right through him.

'. . . manually removed, so that by now the spotlight is attached to a single bolt, which, itself having been loosened, is being held in place by a cotter pin alone,' Kronberg droned. The crime scene man was reading aloud from a sheet of paper. One or two colleagues couldn't help but yawn. 'Now, if, using the abovementioned lever and the wire cable attached to it, one were to remove the cotter pin from the bolt, the bolt would consequently come loose, causing the spotlight, now deprived of support, to fall. This appears to have occurred on the eighth of February this year, the intention clearly being to cause death or serious injury to the actress Bettina Winter.'

Rath was continually astonished at the formulations of the Prussian police. It wasn't just them, however: the whole of the Prussian civil service would have been capable of describing a person's agonising death as though it were a technical process, a physics experiment in school.

Kronberg gazed at the assembled company over the rim of his glasses, probably to make sure that every last person in the room had given up trying to follow his report. 'Based on the positioning of this construction, it seems reasonable to assume that . . .'

'How about you leave the assumptions to us, my dear Kronberg?!' Clearly Kronberg hadn't managed to lull Böhm to sleep. The bulldog had been paying attention. The ED man looked slightly aggrieved, but didn't dare protest. Instead he cleared the way for the DCI.

'Many thanks, Herr Kronberg.' Böhm could make a 'thank you' sound like an insult. 'Inspector Rath?' he continued. 'I thought I saw you come in just now?' The room fell silent, like a classroom after the teacher has asked who left the wet sponge on his chair. Everyone turned to look at Rath. 'Ah, there you are. Would you be so kind as to come to the podium and tell us about your recent work in the Winter case?'

Rath moved towards the front, taking the report from his leather case as he went. 'Good morning, gentlemen,' he said. 'Good morning, Detective Chief Inspector.' He lifted the file in the air. 'I have taken the liberty of summarising my findings in a report, which I . . .'

'Get to the point!'

Böhm was glaring at him, his eyes like two frozen glass marbles. Very well, Rath thought, the whole nine yards it is.

'Herr Kronberg has already told you a thing or two about the device that *I* discovered yesterday in Terra Studios,' he said, taking the screenplay and production schedule from the brown case. 'Here I have the time frame according to which the . . . saboteur, as I will call him for now, proceeded. The script and production schedule for *Liebesgewitter*, Betty Winter's final film.'

He looked across the group. Curious faces, tense silence. He outlined his theory: that Krempin had devised the wire construction to release the spotlight and destroy the film camera, but had been exposed. He had therefore neutralised the device at the last minute and left the studio in a hurry. Someone else must have reconnected it.

Böhm actually let him finish. 'Where did you get such a fanciful idea?' he asked.

'I thought I made that abundantly clear. Scene forty-nine was filmed just before eleven o'clock in the morning; the effects lever was still working and triggered the thunder. On the afternoon of that same day, however, while shooting scene fifty-three, the same lever loosened the one bolt still holding the spotlight in place—the mechanism that Kronberg just described. It can't have been Felix Krempin because by eleven o'clock he was no longer in the studio.'

'What gives you that idea?'

'The eyewitnesses Lüdenbach and Krieg. Supported by others who last saw him in the studio around ten.'

'Perhaps you haven't heard, Inspector. Since there were a number of conflicting witness statements, we decided to question all parties a little more thoroughly. If you had arrived on time you would have heard all this, but I will repeat it once more for your sake: three witnesses now concede that Felix Krempin could still have been in the studio around twelve. That is to say at the time when everything had already been arranged for the afternoon shoot. Where does that leave your little theory?'

Rath stood there like a star pupil who had just spectacularly failed an important exam, and was now being paraded in front of his gloating classmates by the disappointed teacher.

Böhm turned to face his assembled colleagues. 'Gentlemen, you know what you have to do,' he said. 'To work!'

The silence was broken by loud crashes and a low muttering as the room slowly emptied. Rath packed his things and was about to leave too when Böhm held him back. 'Where are you going?'

'To work.'

'What work? Have I given you an assignment?'

Rath looked the bulldog in the eye. He wasn't about to kowtow to Böhm.

'You can hand me your report,' Böhm said, 'and then you are temporarily relieved of all duties on the Winter case.'

Rath bit his tongue and handed Böhm the file. 'What should I do instead, Detective Chief Inspector, Sir?'

'Go to your desk. You'll find everything there.'

Rath saw what Böhm meant by *everything* when he entered his office. There was a stack of files on his desk. 'What am I supposed to do with these?' he asked his secretary.

Erika Voss shrugged her shoulders. 'Fräulein Steiner just brought them. With greetings from DCI Böhm, was all she said.'

According to Böhm's instructions he was to prepare the Wessel case, chaotic and disordered as it was, for the public prosecutor. It was the first time Böhm had actually entrusted him with the case—save for the ridiculous order to attend the funeral, and it was exactly the kind of work Rath despised: a mindless chore, painstaking and monotonous. A punishment.

There was a knock, and Erika Voss poked her nosy head through the door. 'Coffee?'

'No, thank you,' he said. 'Where's Gräf got to? He was at the briefing just now.'

'He's gone to Grunewald with Lange, to scour the allotments. Böhm seems to think Krempin's hiding there.'

Böhm had expressly requested that Rath tack on a report about the Wessel funeral, a report that only Gräf could write, since it was he who had been at the cemetery on Saturday.

'If he calls, put him through to me right away. See if you can reach him while he's out and about.'

'I wouldn't get your hopes up, Inspector, not if he's as hard to get hold of as you've been in the last few days,' Erika Voss said, and closed the door.

Rath sorted the papers into stacks of various heights: witness statements, reports, crime scene descriptions, crime scene photos, medical reports, technical reports, evidence logs, summaries, possible conclusions. At one the telephone rang. He was hoping for Gräf but was disappointed. It was Erika Voss, who once again had been too lazy to leave her desk.

'There's a Herr Ziehlke here to see you.'

He had completely forgotten. 'Send him in,' he said, and moments later there was a knock.

Friedhelm Ziehlke had taken off his hat and was kneading it in his hands. 'Here I am, Inspector,' he said. 'Nice place you've got.'

Rath was about to offer the taxi driver a seat, but there was a pile of statements on the visitor's chair. 'Why don't we go out?' he said. 'Fancy a beer at Aschinger?'

'I'm still on duty, but I wouldn't say no to a Bratwurst.'

It was noisy at Alex. The steam hammer was still driving supporting irons into the ground, although the underground was supposedly as good as finished. Everywhere you looked construction hoardings blocked the view. Rath had the feeling that they moved every day so that you had to negotiate a new labyrinth each time you wanted to cross the square.

'Haven't been here for a long time,' Ziehlke said. 'Every halfway sensible taxi driver avoids Alexanderplatz.'

Whatever else was being torn down at Alex, Aschinger remained. The old building was scheduled for demolition, but a number of little placards revealed that the restaurant would find a home in one of the new buildings. An Alex without Aschinger was something Rath couldn't imagine. Half the station ate their lunch or drank their after-work beer here.

As always at lunchtime, it was full to bursting. Rath ordered a Bierwurst with potato salad for Ziehlke, and a Sinalco to drink. For himself he ordered Rinderbraten and potato dumplings with a glass of Selters mineral water. At least the man didn't want fried liver.

'Nice of you to invite me,' Ziehlke said, and began to cut up his Bierwurst. 'I'm here to look at photos then?'

'First let's eat.' Rath got stuck into his beef. 'But yes, I'd like you to take a close look at each picture for the man who picked up Vivian Franck.'

'Why are you looking for her anyway?' Ziehlke asked between mouthfuls of potato salad. 'You still haven't told me that.'

'Because she's missing,' Rath said.

After the waiter had cleared their plates, Rath fetched Oppenberg's envelope from his bag. There were nearly twenty portraits, not just of actors, but of other men Oppenberg deemed capable of meeting with Vivian in secret. Among them was Felix Krempin, though the photo was better than Bellmann's Christmas party snap. Ziehlke examined each image thoroughly, hesitating on just two occasions, firstly over Krempin, before realising that he recognised him from the paper. 'He's the one you're looking for, isn't he?' The second time it was a dark-haired actor, but eventually he ruled him out too. 'No, that's not him. A similar type, that's all.'

Rath thanked Ziehlke. 'If you see the man anywhere, be it on a billboard, in your taxi, or on the street, call me immediately. Any time of day.'

Before returning to the Castle, Rath found a telephone box from which to call Oppenberg, and managed to wangle an invitation to dinner from his secretary.

Erika Voss still wasn't back from her break when Rath sat down at his desk and set about the stack of papers. It was a curious case, this Wessel business, and the Nazis had exploited it to the full: a landlady calls in a few Communist friends to give a defaulting tenant a beating. The situation escalates, and the SA Sturmführer gets a bullet in the face at the door. Conveniently enough the killer, Ali Höhler, is the former pimp of the whore with whom this Wessel now resides.

The bullet had made Wessel a martyr for the Nazi movement, but he was an unlikely saint: a young priest's son who had jolted the SA in Friedrichshain into action, only to fall in love with a prostitute and start shamefully neglecting his SA. Goebbels didn't care. For Berlin's top Nazi, the Sturmführer made the perfect martyr. Nevertheless, it was fortunate that Wessel had finally succumbed to his injuries, otherwise the model Nazi might yet have resigned from the NSDAP. In the last few months, he seemed to have lost all interest in politics. There were even whisperings that he had started playing pimp for his beloved, though such rumours had just as likely come from Communist circles.

A coarse ringing sound interrupted his thoughts. The telephone on Erika Voss's desk. Perhaps it was Gräf. Rath took the call on his own line. 'Yes?'

'Am I speaking with Detective Inspector Rath's office? A Division?' a woman's voice asked.

'You're speaking with Rath himself. With whom do I have the pleasure?'

'Greulich, Dr Weiss's office. The deputy commissioner wishes to speak to you in half an hour, Inspector.'

'What's it about?'

'Dr Weiss will tell you that himself.'

Rath was surprised. Until now he had only seen the Vipoprä, as Zörgiebel's deputy was known in the Castle, from afar, and had barely exchanged a word. What could Dr Weiss, undoubtedly one of the best criminal investigators in Berlin, want with little old Inspector Gereon Rath? Had Böhm lodged a complaint? Rath smelled trouble. He would have preferred it to be Zörgiebel, one of his father's old friends, but the police commissioner had disappeared to Mainz for the carnival period.

He spent the next half-hour thinking, before leaving Erika Voss, who still hadn't returned from her break, a note, and making his way over.

Frau Greulich was very brightly dressed. 'Your colleagues are waiting,' she said, and Rath wondered why she had used the plural. She lifted the receiver and dialled a number. 'Herr Rath is here,' she said. And then to Rath: 'Please go on through.'

Rath went on through.

Dr Bernhard Weiss sat behind a large desk covered in files, his eyes alert behind thick spectacles. The man exuded a natural authority that made Rath nervous. He knew how to deal with Zörgiebel, but the deputy seemed to be of a different calibre: definitely nobody's fool. He was more reassured by the presence of the second man. Ernst Gennat. As long as Buddha was there, things couldn't get too bad.

'Good morning, gentlemen,' he said, shaking the men's hands in order of rank.

'Sit down, please,' Weiss said, a little chilly. No friendly *please take a seat. Sit down* sounded more like something a teacher would say.

Rath sat in an armchair next to Gennat. For a moment silence reigned, as the noise of the typewriter penetrated quietly and somehow soothingly through the padded door. 'Good that you could come at such short notice, Inspector,' Weiss began the conversation. 'It concerns a delicate matter.'

Almost a year ago someone had accused Rath of murder; back then it was Gennat who had showed up. He had used a similar turn of phrase.

Weiss looked him in the eye. 'How would you describe your relationship with Detective Inspector Frank Brenner?'

So, Brenner had made a big deal of their little quarrel. 'Not exactly friendly,' Rath said. 'More collegial?'

'I have received an internal complaint,' Weiss continued. 'Inspector Brenner claims that you struck him several times without cause last Saturday night in the Residenz-Casino. What do you say to that?'

'I did strike Herr Brenner, Sir, but not without cause.'

'What reason can there be to strike a colleague in public? You do know that we should be mindful of our institution's reputation at all times.'

'No one knew we were police officers,' Rath said. 'It was a masked ball and we were both in fancy dress.'

'That doesn't answer my question.'

'There was a reason, Sir, but a private one. Inspector Brenner violated a woman's honour.'

'A woman's honour?'

'A mutual acquaintance.'

'Inspector, the age where one fought a duel over a woman is over, thank God. Don't you think your reaction was a little over the top?'

'I warned Herr Brenner—I asked him to stop.'

'Stop what?'

'He said some very coarse things, revolting in fact. I wouldn't like to repeat them here, Sir.'

'Who is the woman in question?'

'I'm afraid I can't tell you that either.'

'Why not?'

'With respect, it is none of your concern. My quarrel with DI Brenner was a private matter.'

'If a police officer strikes someone, be it a colleague or a civilian, it is anything but a private matter!'

Weiss was shouting.

'I apologise, Sir, I didn't mean it like that. Nonetheless, I don't want to drag the woman in question into this.'

'I didn't mean to offend you, Inspector,' said Weiss, more conciliatory. 'It's simply a question of naming possible witnesses who in case of doubt might testify on your behalf. Inspector Brenner has named Detective Czerwinski, who appears to have witnessed the incident.'

'What does Czerwinski say?'

'We still haven't questioned him.'

'It was a minor difference of opinion between colleagues—I'm not sure it needs to be described as an incident.'

'Don't talk it down, Rath. Inspector Brenner toyed with the idea of bringing charges against you and instituting disciplinary proceedings. Luckily for you, I was able to persuade him that it made more sense for us to deal with it internally. What do you think will happen if the press gets wind of this?'

'So why isn't Brenner here? We could shake each other by the hand and the matter would be forgotten. That's how I'd deal with it.'

'Inspector Brenner is currently unable to work on account of his injuries,' Weiss said, still in his ultra-matter-of-fact tone.

Rath swallowed hard. There was no way he had beaten the fatty up that badly. Perhaps he had fallen awkwardly? He couldn't help thinking of the arm in the sling. 'I'm sorry to hear that,' he said.

'So you should be.' Weiss gazed at him seriously, making Rath feel like a flagellate under a microscope. 'Do you often lose your temper?'

'What do you mean, Sir?'

'I think my question was clear. Do you have your temper under control?'

Was that an allusion to his past? Rath wasn't sure how much he knew about what had happened in Cologne. Still, that didn't have anything to do with his temper, he couldn't mean that.

'Of course, Sir. I am always conscious of my responsibilities as a police officer.'

'Except for this one occasion, clearly.'

'Yes, Sir.'

'Good, then please see to it that nothing like this happens again. I'd like your report of the incident on my desk tomorrow.'

'Yes, Sir.' Rath thought he was dismissed. He rose from his chair, casting a sidelong glance at Gennat who had remained silent throughout.

'Wait a minute, Inspector,' Weiss said, 'we're not finished with you yet!' Rath sat back down.

'We'd like to hear your opinion on this,' said the deputy, placing the latest edition of *B.Z. am Mittag* on the table. Rath didn't recognise the article, only the name in the author byline: Stefan Fink.

He skimmed the article. Fink had dredged up the old rumours and coaxed a few conspiracy theories out of Bellmann, but had nevertheless managed to quote Detective Inspector Gereon Rath in all the crucial places.

> *Police are still searching for a fugitive lighting technician. 'Betty Winter's death was no accident,' Detective Inspector Gereon Rath revealed to our paper. Does that make the technician a murder suspect? Inspector Rath spoke of an 'important witness', but it wouldn't be the first time police have used this circumlocution to lull a potential suspect into a false sense of security. So, where do police stand? When will they finally arrest the killer walking among us? Detective Chief Inspector Wilhelm Böhm, the officer leading the investigation, was unable to provide an answer. Rath had this to say: 'there's always someone in charge, it's the rest of us who do the work.'*

Shit! That rat! 'I have already informed Superintendent Gennat that I don't set any great store by appearing in these newspaper articles.'

Buddha remained silent, although he appeared less friendly than normal.

'What I mean,' Rath said, 'is that I am being quoted against my will here.'

'Then you don't know this Fink? You've never met him?'

Weiss had done his research.

"Met' is the wrong word. He approached me and tried to pump me for information, but I refused.'

'That's not how it appears in the article. Did he just pluck all this out of thin air?'

'He's taken it out of context, anyway.' Rath realised he had to be careful. Weiss would have already telephoned the paper. 'Fink is a muckraker. He doesn't care about truth, only sensationalism and pillorying police officers who refuse to co-operate. DCI Böhm doesn't exactly come out of it well either!'

'Thanks to your comment, Inspector!' Weiss grew louder again. 'Thanks to your comment. How dare you pass judgement on your department and your superiors? And to the press at that!'

'That's not what happened!'

'You maintain that you didn't say it?'

'If I did it was in a completely different context. In no way did Herr Fink make it clear that he was intending to quote me in his paper.'

Weiss dissected him with a look.

'It's lucky for you that I know this Fink,' he said. 'And you're right: he is an unscrupulous representative of his guild. Otherwise, I would find it hard to believe you.' Weiss leaned forward. 'You still have a lot to learn about dealing with the big city press. Rash comments can lead to fatal consequences, as you can see. We, as police, need the press, but don't be fooled into thinking you can toy with it. It's the press that toys with you.'

'What should I do, Sir? Demand right of reply?'

'That would only make matters worse. Leave things as they are. I just want you to be more careful in future, so that this sort of thing doesn't happen again.' Weiss rose from his chair. 'And naturally,' he said, 'you should apologise to Chief Inspector Böhm.'

Rath and Gennat made their way back to A Division together. Rath was unable to bear the silence. 'When are you going back to Düsseldorf, Sir?'

'As soon as I've sorted out this mess. Don't try and smooth things over, Rath. I'm furious with you. But let's not discuss it in the corridor.'

That was all Gennat said the whole way back to Homicide, a way that seemed to stretch interminably. At last they reached Gennat's office, where Buddha told Trudchen Steiner, his long-serving secretary, that he didn't want to be disturbed.

He didn't let his ill temper show in front of his secretary, but nevertheless turned down her offer of coffee and cake, at which point Steiner cast Rath a sympathetic glance. Even serious criminals were offered cake in Gennat's office.

Buddha closed the door and sat at his desk, directing Rath to the seat in front which was normally reserved for condemned men, and spent a long time staring at him in silence. Not reproachfully, more enquiringly. It was an unpleasant feeling to find oneself under his gaze, the gaze of a teacher wondering how on earth his favourite student has botched his exams.

'I don't understand you,' Gennat said. 'Why do you have to be such a fool?'

'I'm sorry about Brenner, but it wasn't as bad as it sounded. His incapacity for work . . .'

'Forget about Brenner! That was Dr Weiss's axe to grind.'

'Then I'm not quite sure what you mean, Sir.'

'Stop pretending. We spoke about it only days ago. The fact that you're a part of A Division, not a lone hand; that you should share your knowledge.'

'With respect, Sir, that's exactly what I did. I asked Henning and Czerwinski to alert colleagues about Krempin's hideout the day before yesterday. As for the wire in Terra Studios yesterday—I notified Detective Gräf immediately by telephone and requested assistance so that . . .'

'. . . you were no longer present when Böhm arrived on the scene.'

'What am I supposed to say to that? I provide DCI Böhm with a decisive breakthrough, and he has nothing better to do than complain about me to his superiors.'

'No one's lodged a complaint. Luckily for you, DCI Böhm is a loyal colleague. Loyal to his department and loyal to each and every one of his team, no matter how defiant they might be.'

'I assume you're talking about me, Sir.'

'Don't start quibbling!' Gennat had only raised his voice slightly, but Rath sensed it would be wise to bite his tongue. 'This is about your conception of loyalty, and your conception of police work in general.' Gennat leaned forward. 'The police force is a complex organism in which many small parts act together to create a whole. It's an organism that works very well, by the way. That's the reason we have hierarchies, and that's the reason you should do what you're told. The best thing for you is to be amicable and respectful towards both your superiors and your subordinates. There is no place for high-handedness, petty jealousies and rivalries in my department. Do I make myself clear?'

Rath nodded. 'I understand how important these things are, Sir, but sometimes in the heat of the moment . . .'

'The heat of the moment! Stop talking such nonsense! You made yourself scarce because you guessed that Böhm was about to take over the investigation! You wanted to make it impossible for him to bring you back into line. But you must have known it would end like this. If you had just gone about your business as normal, Böhm would have allowed you to operate as part of his team, if not necessarily as leader. Now you're on the outside.'

'With respect, Sir, DCI Böhm is making a mistake. I'm responsible for most of the findings in this case, and it would make more sense if . . .'

'DCI Böhm is your superior,' Gennat interrupted. 'And if he puts you on toilet-cleaning duty, that's his business!' Now Buddha really was shouting, something that happened so rarely he surprised even himself. He returned to his customary, paternal tone. 'Kindly do as your superiors ask. Clear?' Rath fell silent. 'Do I make myself *clear*?'

Rath nodded, beginning to understand why so many people softened under this gaze, confessing to the most serious crimes.

'Your high-handedness got you into this predicament.'

'Yes, Sir.'

'Stop grovelling and start changing your behaviour. Böhm isn't going anywhere for a few years, and you'd better get used to it. This isn't the first time I've said this to you.'

'No.'

'Then for God's sake take it to heart. We all have to work together. There's no room for personal animosities. You certainly can't hold it against Böhm that he hasn't become your best friend. I have no wish to dredge up the past . . .'

'With respect, Sir, it's DCI Böhm who's blurring the line between personal and professional. Since he took over from you, he's been putting the squeeze on me . . .'

'Don't start complaining! Police work can be boring and damned exhausting at the same time, so unspectacular that not a single paper is interested in it. But that's not something you should be worried about. Just take care of the tasks you've been allocated, no matter how monotonous, and people here will start taking notice. In your case it might even be helpful to draw *less* attention to yourself.' Gennat's tone was more placatory now. 'You're a good detective, Rath. But show that you are part of the force too, and—I don't need any more meetings with Dr Weiss. I've got better things to do than take care of brawling officers.'

'Yes, Sir.' Rath made one final attempt. 'I apologise for the trouble I've caused you. Nevertheless, I would ask you to support my reinstatement on the Winter investigation. I am, with respect, the officer most familiar with the details of the case.'

'I'm not about to tell Böhm how to deploy his officers. We can't just drop everything because the press has pounced on a celebrity case. Take care of the task Böhm has given you, and apologise to him. You heard what Dr Weiss said.' With that, he began sorting papers, not deigning to cast even a glance in Rath's direction.

23

Gräf still hadn't been in contact and couldn't be reached. 'He's out,' said Erika Voss, who had reappeared in the meantime. According to her, Gräf wasn't expected until the next briefing, early tomorrow morning. Böhm wasn't in the office either. Erika Voss shrugged her shoulders apologetically.

'Then make an appointment with his secretary, ask him to call back—anything,' Rath said. 'I need to speak to the DCI today.' Slamming the door to his office, he sat behind his desk. He felt like sweeping the mound of papers to the floor, but restrained himself and smoked an Overstolz. As soon as he had stubbed it out, he reached for the receiver. 'Erika, please go to ED and search for anything Kronberg and his colleagues have collected on a man named Höhler, Albert.'

That would occupy her for a while, and spare her the temptation of listening to his telephone calls. After he heard the door close, he checked to see if Voss had gone and picked up the telephone. The first thing he did was ask to be put through to the editorial office at *B.Z. am Mittag*.

'Herr Fink is popular with the police today,' the editorial secretary said before putting him through. So Weiss *had* called.

'Inspector Rath!' The reporter sounded pleased. 'Have you decided to tell me a little more?'

Rath went on the attack. 'What were you thinking?' he shouted. 'Why the hell did you put all that in your paper?'

'It's only what you told me. The thing is, Inspector, you and your colleagues think you can foil us with your silence, but that is a mistake. If I want to write a story, I write it. If you try to stint on detail, then I cobble together from whatever you have provided, intentionally or otherwise, and infer the rest. Provide me with more comprehensive information and you'll have, firstly, more control over the report and, secondly, a new friend.'

'You think I'm looking for a friend?'

'As I said, you won't regret it.'

'But I *will* regret it if I don't speak to you. Is that what you're saying?'

'Your detective chief inspector comes off far worse . . .'

'You quoted me against my will!'

'You knew you were talking to a reporter.'

'But not that you would write what I told you!'

'Really? That's my job.'

'Nothing could be further from my mind than to publicly denounce a colleague.'

'Then don't do it.' The swine had an answer for everything. 'You should have told me your remarks were confidential. I keep agreements like that.'

'We never made any agreement.'

'You see why we should have?'

'I had, and have, nothing to say to you. And yet at Alex, people think I'm your informant. How do you explain that?'

'If that's the case, you might as well be.'

'Pardon me?'

'You might as well be my informant. I mean, if people already think you are. Work with me and I promise . . .'

Rath hung up. He was in luck with the next number he dialled. Weinert had his coat on, but was still at home.

'Cut to the chase,' the journalist said, 'they're pining for me over at *Tageblatt*. The Great Coalition crisis needs to be analysed.'

'Do you think you might be able to pitch a second story?'

'Is this the green light for the Winter story?'

'Yes, but with one qualification. It would be good if my name didn't appear too often, since I'm no longer responsible for the case.'

'I have to give a few names. A few police sources. One, at least.'

'DCI Böhm is leading the investigation.'

'He's not saying anything.'

'Then I'll give you someone's private number. He's sick at the moment, but is usually part of Böhm's team.'

'Does he know the case? If he's sick, I mean.'

'Ask the right questions and you'll get your answer. I don't have to tell you how to do your job.'

'Give me the number and I'll try. While we're on the subject: I've arranged a meeting for you. With Heyer.'

'Who?'

'Willi Heyer. The screenwriter. Tomorrow at one in the Romanisches Café.'

'With all those would-be celebrities?'

'I'll be there too.'

'Well, no offence intended.'

'It's OK, it contains the highest density of unsuccessful authors in the country. As well as a few successful ones.'

There was a knock and Erika Voss poked her head around the door.

'Back from ED already?' Rath asked, covering the mouthpiece with his hands. 'I said I didn't want to be disturbed.'

'It's DCI Böhm! He can speak with you now but doesn't have much time. You'll have to hurry.'

Gräf and Lange were loitering around Böhm's office when Rath entered. The DCI didn't look up from the file he was studying. 'You wanted to speak to me?' he said.

'Yes, Sir,' Rath said, 'but I thought we might be able to speak in priv . . .'

'I don't keep secrets from my colleagues and don't have much time. What's this about?'

'I wanted to apologise, Sir.'

The words came out with great difficulty. Rath's whole body resisted as he uttered them, but he had to see it through. Weiss and Gennat had both told him to apologise to Böhm, and it was an order he couldn't disregard.

Böhm still hadn't looked at him.

Gräf moved towards the door, clearly embarrassed at watching his former boss eat humble pie. Rath signalled that Gräf should give him a call.

'Where are you going?' Böhm barked.

Gräf gave a start. 'I thought . . .'

'Don't think, get to work.'

'Yes, Sir.' Gräf returned to the map on which he and Lange had circled and shaded various areas with the aid of a compass. Rath recognised Grunewald. Erika Voss was right: they were clearly looking for Krempin in the southwest.

'Do you have anything else to say to me, Inspector?' Böhm asked. 'Or was that it?'

'I apologise for the fact that I expressed myself ambiguously to a reporter so that the impression arose that I was . . .'

'What language was that? Don't make your sentences so complicated that you can't finish them.'

Böhm looked at him for the first time. 'What's the latest with the Wessel file? Is your report finished?'

So Böhm knew. 'Detective Gräf is composing the report on the Wessel funeral. I assigned the task to him and . . .'

'You disregarded my orders.'

'In no way did I disregard your orders, Sir. I did, however, assign Detective Gräf to carry them out.'

'Herr Rath, if you are ever to become a proper member of this department, then you must stop shirking your responsibilities.' Rath sensed it would be wise to remain silent. 'That means,' Böhm continued, 'carrying out the orders you have been issued. *Personally.* It also means ensuring that your colleagues and superiors have as much information as you do—and the press.'

Rath swallowed his anger. The bulldog was using the opportunity to humiliate him, deliberately ignoring his outstretched hand.

'Do I make myself clear?'

'Yes, Sir! It's just . . . the Winter case . . .'

'Concentrate on the Wessel case. It's not my fault you didn't attend the funeral. Detective Gräf won't be able to write any reports for the time being—so you'll just have to wait.'

Rath feverishly considered whether he should say something more about the Winter case. The bulldog couldn't just get rid of him like that, not when he was the one pulling all the strings.

'What are you still doing here?' Böhm said. 'I thought I had made myself clear.'

'Yes, Sir.'

'Well, don't just stand there. On your way.'

That was that. Böhm returned to his file, leaving Rath standing like a schoolboy and Gräf and Lange looking at their map of the Grunewald. Rath could have slammed the door in anger but managed to control himself. The best way to confront a humiliation of this kind was simply to ignore it.

'I take it that's an order too, Sir,' he said, and left the office.

24

She has fallen asleep. How peacefully she lies there and how beautifully, he thinks as he clears away the glasses, hers half-empty, his almost full. He doesn't consider himself too good for such things when Albert has his evening off. He tips the contents of both glasses into the sink, rinses them with water and dries them with a kitchen towel. Only then does he place them beside the other dirty glasses.

When he returns, she's lying exactly as before. He feels her pulse and counts. She hasn't had enough to drink. If he doesn't act now she will wake in a few minutes, but luckily he has prepared the syringe. She doesn't react as he penetrates her skin with the needle.

He carries her next door, though she is heavier than she looks, this delicate blonde angel. As he lays her on the table she seems to blink, but that could be a side effect of the injection.

He washes his hands thoroughly before beginning. Carefully he bends her neck, stretches it out until the head hangs over the edge of the table and gently slides the tube through her mouth and throat, to the glottis, watches how the metal makes her neck bulge. He adjusts the lamplight, opens his little black suitcase and lays out his tools. Before he begins he washes his hands again. He reaches for the large pair of scissors he had specially made years ago in order to . . .

In order to silence his mother's screams. He can no longer listen to that high, drawn-out sound that might once have been a laugh, a laugh that has wandered too far inside a dark forest and been transformed into a wild gurgle; a squeal that saws through the air and howls in the distance like a stray ghost.

She has gone mad. Mother has gone mad, and he has realised too late. Two human lives too late. Too late, and yet he has locked her in the same golden cage in which she kept him prisoner for years—the tower wing with its gloomy rooms and wonderful view of the lake. He has locked her in with Albert's consent, before she can do any more harm.

He expected her to fly into a rage, a mad fury, but she sits down and laughs for such a long time that her laughter no longer sounds human and he fears that her madness might be a contagion, carried by the laughter.

He has been preparing for a long time, had the scissors and tube made to order, practised the manoeuvres time and again in the anatomical institute. Now he feels secure.

She is already fast asleep when he returns, and the operation is over in minutes, a question of several precise incisions. He still keeps the surgical instruments in the same black velvet-lined case she gave him only a few years ago.

He has already prepared the iced water, which he now pours in. Her swallowing reflex kicks in, she drinks and coughs and, for a moment, he fears she is regaining consciousness, but she soon settles down again. The ice-cold water staunches the bleeding and alleviates the pain. It is less painful than tonsillitis; she will hardly feel anything when she awakes.

When the moment comes, he has already tidied. Cleaned everything he has used and packed it away, sat her back in her favourite chair by the window. Placed the carafe of iced water in front of her. She must drink, slowly and carefully so that she can learn how to swallow again, but she doesn't touch the water.

After briefly opening her eyes she continues dozing, only to sink back into sleep and wake with a start. Seeing him sitting next to her chair, her eyes fill with love. She loves him even though she knows she is his prisoner. That is the only thing she has left: blind love. That she killed for. Killed for blindly.

She sits up and tries to say something. Or scream? Or laugh? Whatever the case, nothing comes but a hoarse gurgling. She looks surprised but tries again before grabbing her throat in horror.

He has taken away her voice, that is all. Without that voice, the voice of a madwoman, she looks almost normal again, almost like before, when she was still his mother and not some old lunatic. It's for your own good, Mother, he says.

The very words she once used.

The expression of surprise yields to one of recognition, and they are almost cheerful: the eyes with which she gazes at him. She smiles and seems to understand, seems to take pleasure in the hoarse gurgling that has taken the place of her voice. The look in her eyes says: I know everything, we both know everything, only the two of us know—how funny, how *deathly* funny! And though she has no voice, she tries to start laughing again. There is a rattling, a rasping, a gurgling; spittle sprays out of her mouth, and blood.

He covers his ears and leaves and, with every step, distances himself further from her madness.

25

Oppenberg was already seated when Rath entered at half past eight. It was an exclusive restaurant and Rath felt a little out of place in his off-the-peg suit.

'I've ordered a bottle of wine,' the producer said.

'Thank you, not for me.' Rath asked for a glass of Selters.

'Your decision, my friend. Hopefully you won't be so modest when it comes to your food. That would be a sin here.'

Rath would have preferred to eat something more substantial at Aschinger, but he bowed to his fate and studied the menu.

'I'd recommend the fish,' Oppenberg said, and Rath joined him in his choice. 'You requested this meeting, which means you have news.'

'That depends. At any rate, you should get used to the idea of finding another lead actress for *Vom Blitz getroffen.*'

'Has she . . . what have you discovered? Does the taxi driver know the man who collected her?'

Rath shook his head. 'I'm afraid not. I still don't know anything for sure but, at the very least, she was forced to change her plans abruptly.'

'What makes you think that?' Oppenberg reached nervously into the bread basket.

'You remember her last taxi journey? Before she was picked up by this stranger in Wilmersdorf she had her suitcases brought to Bahnhof Zoo, to left luggage.'

'So what?'

'They're still there.'

Oppenberg had to chew longer on this piece of news than on the slice of white bread he had just spread with butter and shoved in his mouth. 'How do you explain that?'

'I can't believe she meant to leave her cases for three or four weeks in left luggage. Something unexpected must have happened.'

Oppenberg lit a cigarette, and Rath realised he hadn't been expecting bad news. The waiter brought the starters, but Oppenberg didn't touch his. Instead he continued smoking. 'Damn it!' he said. 'Are you saying I should prepare myself for the worst?'

'Not necessarily, but it doesn't bode well.'

'You've already written her off!'

'I fear, anyway, that I won't be able to carry out your assignment. I can't bring Vivian back.' Rath pushed a green banknote across the table. 'There was one picture too many in your envelope.'

Oppenberg understood and didn't hesitate long before pocketing the fifty. 'Can you see that your colleagues stop badgering me about Felix? I told your Böhm that we had parted on bad terms, but he seems to give more credence to Bellmann's claim that I put a saboteur and murderer onto him.'

Rath shrugged. 'They've taken me off the case. I can only advise you to be careful. If you want to keep your involvement in the whole thing under wraps—fine. I won't stab you in the back, but don't underestimate the police. If they start grilling your friend . . .'

'Felix has always been loyal. Besides, they need to find him before they can interrogate him.'

'Do you think it's possible he's found a new hideout in Grunewald somewhere? In the allotments, for example? Does he know anyone there who could help him?'

'Don't ask so many questions at once, otherwise I won't know which to respond to first.'

'How about the ones you know the answer to? Apparently Krempin is holed up there somewhere. My colleagues think he's a murderer, the press think he's a murderer. I'm the only one who believes he's innocent. It's better I find him, and not one of them.'

'And the accusation of sabotage? Will that go by the board if you find Felix?'

Rath shook his head. 'If he wants to be cleared of murder, he'll have to admit to his sabotage plans.'

'I hope my name can be kept out of all this.'

'That depends entirely on your friend. I don't have any influence there.'

Oppenberg stubbed his cigarette out and reached for his cutlery. 'I have a proposition,' he said. 'I'll help you track down Felix Krempin if you keep looking for Vivian.'

'If you don't just *help* but actually find Krempin, then maybe.'

'Well, if you don't stop at *searching*, but find Vivian for me.'

'I'll do my best.'

'Then it's a deal,' Oppenberg said. 'Did the photos help? Did the taxi driver recognise anyone?'

'Just Krempin, from the mugshot.' Rath took the photo of the dark-haired actor from his bag. 'He said this one was similar to the man who picked up Vivian.'

'Gregor? Vivian hardly noticed him.'

'The taxi driver only said he was similar. Do you know anyone else who looks like this? Could be a producer as well.'

Oppenberg shook his head indignantly. 'I think it's a waste of time only searching among my people. Why don't you show this taxi driver a few photos of Bellmann's lot? Perhaps it was one of them who picked her up and she's been made to stew in some hovel underground for weeks!'

'You think Bellmann abducted her to prevent you from shooting your film?'

'He's capable of it. Perhaps he paid to have her abducted. There are enough criminals in this city who would do that.'

Rath thought of Johann Marlow. He probably wouldn't let himself be roped into such a dirty job. But perhaps Dr M. would know someone who might. He must still have his number, the number that wasn't in any telephone book.

He had already polished off two beers and two shorts when Gräf arrived. The atmosphere inside the Nasse Dreieck was already sticky and the gust of fresh air that blew in with the detective did nothing to change that. Rath gave Schorsch a brief nod, and the bartender put two more glasses under the tap. Gräf took his seat beside Rath at the bar.

'You're smoking again?'

'What makes you say that?' Rath muttered, lighting an Overstolz. The bartender placed two beer glasses on the counter, along with two schnapps.

The pair clinked glasses, drained the schnapps and washed them down with beer. 'Has Böhm had his hooks in you all this time?'

Gräf shook his head. 'I had something else to do.' He took a large brown envelope from inside his coat. 'My report on the Wessel burial. You can file it tomorrow, but it's the last time I do a favour like that for you. It was more of a street fight than a funeral.'

Rath opened the envelope, pulling out a stack of folded typing paper. 'That's at least ten pages.'

'Twelve. I did it out of friendship.'

'I don't know what to say.' Rath pocketed the envelope.

'I can think of something.'

'All right, all right.' Rath laughed. 'The drinks are on me.'

'Lucky, given how thirsty I am,' Gräf said.

'Thanks to your help, I should be through with my punishment tomorrow.'

'You think Böhm's going to let you back on the Winter case? I wouldn't get your hopes up.'

Rath shrugged. 'If he doesn't, you can keep me up to date.'

Gräf tilted his head to one side. 'You're not planning on going it alone?'

'I just want to know how everything's progressing. It was our case, and we were doing pretty well until Böhm interfered. And now? Is he making you scour the allotments in Grunewald?'

'Work like that needs to be done. Need I remind you that when I was working for you, my main jobs were to sit in the office and fob Böhm off. And if I were to track down our prime suspect . . . I certainly wouldn't object.'

'You think Krempin meant to kill Winter?'

'Why else would he make himself invisible?'

'Because *everyone* thinks he meant to kill Winter: the police, Bellmann, the entire big city press, and with it half of Berlin.'

'We should never have let Bellmann go through with that stupid press conference.'

'He would have got his conspiracy theories out there one way or another. Besides, he's not entirely wrong. Only Krempin is no murderer.'

Rath went through the theory he had only been able to sketch in the most cursory fashion that morning at briefing.

'And you believe this Oppenberg?' Gräf asked.

Rath shrugged his shoulders. 'No less than Bellmann. The pair of them are desperate because a crafty screenwriter sold them the same story twice, and whichever film comes out first could be vital for each firm's survival.'

'They're shooting the same film? I don't think the author is allowed to do that. There must be a clause in his contract which prevents him from selling the story to other parties.'

'I'll know more tomorrow after I meet with him.'

'I'm starting to wonder who's keeping who up to date!'

'I'll tell you what I find out, and you can start collecting points for your next promotion. You just have to make sure Böhm doesn't take all the credit himself.'

Gräf shook his head. 'You're incorrigible, Gereon,' he said, raising his glass. 'Only bearable under the influence.'

26

Wednesday 5th March 1930

Ash Wednesday arrived under ash-grey skies. Rath turned over, buried his head in the pillow and closed his eyes—and he didn't even have a hang-over.

Sometimes he wished he could just skip a day. Open his eyes after quarter of an hour to a new dawn and all his problems solved. He wished for that now, but when he opened his eyes the alarm clock had barely advanced by seven minutes. The day still lay ahead, and behind the dark outline of the roofs the same ash-grey sky remained. The fifth of March. He had felt it coming, the way a storm is foretold by oppressive humidity.

Staying in bed was pointless. He got up, thinking: Let's get it over with, and shuffled wearily into the kitchen to put on water for coffee, then into the bathroom. Before using the toilet, he splashed cold water onto his face and turned on the boiler. Perhaps he'd be in luck and get through the day without being reminded of the date. No one in the Castle knew, apart from the grey figures in Personnel who handled his file.

Back in the kitchen, still half-asleep, he poured the now boiling water into the Melitta filter. Coffee dripped into the little porcelain pot and its smell comforted him. There was one consolation: things could hardly be worse than last year, when he hadn't even left the house.

Only a year ago, but already that time was so remote, so foreign, as to feel like someone else's life, like someone else's nightmare. With his face in all the papers he had stolen through town like a beaten dog, hat pulled over his forehead. When, that is, he had dared to venture outside at all.

His parents, whose spacious Klettenberg house he had crawled back to and remained at after Ash Wednesday because he couldn't bear the carnival rumpus on the Cologne Ring, had behaved as if everything was normal.

No, as if everything had been like it was before, when they all lived under the same roof. When they were still a family. Back then, before the war.

Mother had baked a cake, as she did each year for her children, and for Gereon it was always hazelnut cake. It was waiting on the breakfast table when he came downstairs, with Mother smiling expectantly. Father, of course, had long since left for the station. You had to be up early to bid Engelbert Rath good morning. The good son didn't show his distaste when she planted a congratulatory kiss on his cheek and passed him the first rustling package. He dutifully opened his presents: a packet of cigars from Father, a hand-knitted scarf from Mother. Like every year, although he didn't smoke cigars and never wore the woollens—except when he held the new present up against the mirror and said *Lovely!* He could never bring himself to tell Mother the truth, and Father certainly not, even as a child. Under Severin's knowing gaze he had simply mumbled *Lovely*, whatever she pressed into his hand. That day, however, he was on his own. Even his sister Ursula wasn't expected until the afternoon . . . but then she had to cancel because her stupid husband let her down, and she was stuck with the kids. It seemed fitting given how the day would pan out. No one had been in touch, not Doris, who had broken off their engagement, nor any of the boys, most of whom he had known since school. After the first article about the shoot-out in the Agnes quarter they no longer kept up with their monthly round of skat. Not even a telephone call. That's it, he thought, the rest of the world has forgotten about you.

He was just coming to terms with all this when Paul came by in the evening and, for the first time in many weeks, Gereon dared to venture outside for more than half an hour. Paul, the only one from the skat group who had kept faith, shoved him into a waiting taxi and took him out to Rudolfplatz where they roamed the Ring, Cologne's nightclub district. Moving from one bar to another they got good and drunk, the first time since the fatal shooting. He was still grateful to Paul for dragging him from his dark pit back into the light of day. To some extent the evening drinking session made up for the day gone by. Perhaps that was the only way to celebrate a birthday, by getting hammered enough to forget why you were drinking in the first place.

Rath went into the living room and put on a record. He lit a cigarette, drank his coffee and listened to the music in peace. How to begin the day? By sorting the Wessel file or by writing the report for Dr Weiss? What an enticing prospect! He decided to treat himself to breakfast at Josty in honour of the occasion, and went back into the bathroom to shave. 'Happy Birthday,' he said to his reflection, and began lathering his face.

Half an hour later he was sitting at a table with a view of Potsdamer Platz, a copy of *Tageblatt* in his hand, watching the grey sky gradually brighten over Leipziger Strasse. Weinert had written his article about the latest developments in the Winter case—in spite of the government crisis, to which he had devoted considerably more column inches. However, it wasn't the article Rath had been expecting. With each line he grew more enraged. He folded the paper, took it into the mahogany-panelled telephone booth and called Nürnberger Strasse. Weinert answered, sounding rather drowsy.

'What the hell is this?' Rath asked without a word of greeting.

'Give a guy a chance to wake up before you start abusing him.'

'Abusing you? Look what you've written?'

'What was I supposed to do? I called this Brenner, like you told me to, but he had a completely different perspective from you on all the main points. Besides, there was a press conference. The news that this lighting technician is wanted for murder isn't only in *Tageblatt.*'

'I explained to you that the murderer most likely only took advantage of Krempin's design, and that he must have known the production schedule and script . . .'

'Gereon, you don't have to tell me all that again! If the police issue an official statement I have to adhere to it, and they're saying that Felix Krempin is being urgently sought in connection with the Winter case—they're even offering a reward! If you read my article more closely, you'll realise that *Tageblatt* is the only paper that presents its readers with an alternative sequence of events.'

'You sound like your chief editor,' Rath said. He unfolded his paper and read:

'The theory is not shared by all officers, however. According to our source, the fugitive Felix Krempin could be a thwarted saboteur, whose infernal machine was used by someone else to kill Betty Winter.

Further insights are to be expected only once Krempin is found and makes a statement.

Spectacular stuff!'

'Sorry if you don't like it, Gereon, but there wasn't much else to say. You waited too long; your story wasn't an exclusive anymore. Besides, it was you who told me that I shouldn't mention your name.'

'That *would* have capped it!'

'You spoke to him didn't you, Gereon?'

'Pardon me?'

'You spoke to Krempin, admit it!'

'Why do you want to know?'

'I have no idea what your connection is to this man, but if he's innocent and wants to talk I would listen. As well as guaranteeing him one hundred percent anonymity and complete discretion. Is he really holed up in an allotment somewhere in Grunewald?'

'You overestimate me. I have no idea where he's hiding.'

'I just wanted to let you know. He can trust me. Tell him the next time you speak to him.'

'See you at lunchtime.' Rath hung up.

He didn't make it into the Castle until about nine, only to find the office deserted. Had Böhm stood Erika Voss down too? Rath got straight to work, filing the twelve pages of Gräf's report with the rest of the reports on the Wessel funeral, which, among other things, he had requested from the political police. Böhm wanted the case to be treated as a straight murder, and everything political ignored—which was nigh on impossible given the reports on the victim's burial. The Nazis had turned it into a kind of state funeral, and the Communists had disrupted it by denouncing the victim as a pimp. Reading Gräf's report, Rath thought he discerned a certain sympathy for the Nazis at having to endure the abuse of the Red mob. They had conferred martyrdom on the dead man, while the Reds derided him as a ponce.

Rath took less than an hour to log everything, but, having finished, felt no desire to run straight to Böhm with the files. Better to wait until Voss got in and assign the task to her. He made a start on Weiss's report. It wasn't so easy to put his quarrel with Brenner into words, he discovered, as he searched for the most neutral way to phrase things. He could hardly write:

Detective Inspector Brenner grievously insulted my erstwhile lover, homicide stenographer Charlotte Ritter, with the result that I saw myself obliged to restore the lady's honour, but not without first having warned the detective against continuing with his affronts. When, however, Brenner refused to see reason and persisted with his slander, I was left with no choice but to prevent him by force.

He wrote the sentences anyway, as something to build on and edit until it was close enough to the truth without exposing Charly.

There was a knock on the door. Rath cursed his secretary. Did he have to take care of everything himself? He shouted, 'Enter!'

Erika Voss came in, eyes fixed guiltily on the floor, said hello and hung her coat on the stand.

'What's all this? Why are you knocking? And why are you only here now?'

'I'm sorry, Inspector, but—I . . .'

'Lucky for you you're usually on time,' Rath said.

She lowered her gaze again, a shy gesture that didn't at all suit her cheeky Berlin demeanour, and sat at her desk.

'Then see to it that I'm not disturbed in the next hour,' Rath said and closed the door.

He heard her telephoning quietly, most likely her sister again, but didn't take her to task. Barely five minutes later, there was another knock.

Rath reacted brusquely. 'What is it?'

The door remained closed, there was another knock. He lost patience, ran to the door and tore it open.

'Did I not clearly say that I didn't want to be . . .'

Pop! A champagne cork ricocheted off the lampshade with a metallic clang and hit the wall before coming to rest between the wastepaper basket and the desk.

The champagne bottle fizzed wildly as Reinhold Gräf endeavoured to collect the jet of liquid in a number of glasses. Next to him stood a beaming Erika Voss, and behind, looking a little embarrassed, Plisch and Plum. They began to sing. A reluctant four-voice choir gave him a birthday serenade. Their intonation wasn't exactly secure, but they sang with heart.

Rath hated displays like this, especially on his birthday, but on this occasion he was touched that they had taken the time and effort.

Reinhold Gräf stepped forward, two champagne glasses in his hand. 'Happy Birthday,' he said, holding one out to Rath, who toasted all four of them.

Erika Voss dropped a curtsey. 'Congratulations, Inspector.'

'All the best from us, Gereon,' Czerwinski said, raising his glass at the same time as Henning.

They drank. The stuff was sticky sweet, but goodwill was all that counted here. 'I'm flabbergasted,' he said. 'How did you know?'

'Simple detective work,' Gräf said.

'My sister works in Personnel,' Erika Voss said.

'You've got the right date, anyway. Your sister didn't let you down.'

'We thought you were keeping your birthday quiet because you didn't want to buy any drinks,' Gräf said. 'But you won't get away with that here!'

'I might have known,' Rath said, feigning remorse.

'But first here's something from us, Inspector!' Erika Voss fetched a bright red package from the depths of her drawer and passed it to him. 'From all of us.'

Rath tore the red paper to reveal a metal cigarette lighter and case. Normally he smoked straight from the packet, but it wouldn't hurt to have something more stylish. For occasions like yesterday evening, for example.

'Thank you,' he said. 'Word got around quickly that I was smoking again!'

'A development we wish to encourage,' Gräf said. 'You're less irritable when you smoke.'

'Well, you'll be shot of me in a moment anyway—except for Fräulein Voss. How come you're here in the first place? Don't you have to scrape and bow to Böhm?'

'We were all here anyway,' Henning said. 'We're assuming, of course, that you won't tell Böhm where we went after the briefing.'

'There was another briefing today?'

Gräf shrugged. 'Böhm has one every day now. He wants to bring the Winter case to a quick resolution.'

'I heard he's even offering a reward for Krempin.'

Czerwinski nodded. 'If we find him, the case is solved. If we don't, it looks ominous.'

'Does that mean no one's conducting enquiries anymore? That you're all just looking for poor Krempin?'

'How do you mean, poor?' Czerwinski hunched his shoulders. 'If he hadn't killed anyone, no one would be chasing after him.'

'Good luck,' Rath said. 'Finding Krempin, I mean. Perhaps you'll catch the murderer at some point too.'

'You're pretty much on your own with that theory, Gereon,' Gräf said. 'Most of us think it was Krempin.'

'That's why he's hiding. He knows he's got no chance against all your prejudices.'

'We'll get him,' Czerwinski said. 'Then the truth will be revealed.'

The three CID officers were gradually becoming restless. 'Time to go,' Rath said. 'I don't want to be responsible for you getting into trouble with Böhm.'

A short time later, he was sitting at his desk tinkering with his report. 'Your sister, Fräulein Voss?' he asked his secretary, 'does she have access to doctor's notes and certificates, things like that?'

'Could do. I'd have to ask.'

'If you would, but discreetly please. I'd need to know what kind of injuries Detective Brenner has.'

'Why? I'm not sure if I'm allowed.'

'I'd like to apologise. I'm sorry about what I did to him. I never intended it.'

She looked at him sceptically.

'I'd only need a quick look, that would be enough. I just want to know how he's doing.'

'I'll ask Franzi, but I'm not making any promises.'

27

The porter was sitting in his lodge behind the revolving door.

'I have a meeting,' Rath said, wondering which name would make the greater impression, 'with Herr Heyer . . .' the porter furrowed his brow '. . . and Herr Weinert.'

'I'm afraid I don't know these gentlemen,' the porter said, 'but you could take a look among the non-swimmers.' He gestured towards the big room to the right of the entrance, which was full to bursting. Rath took off his hat and coat and looked around at not so many writers as onlookers trying to catch a glimpse of writers. That was his impression. Weinert was nowhere to be seen, and if one of the figures sitting at the tables chatting, reading the papers or simply staring into space was Willi Heyer, or if he was one of the many more scribbling in their notebooks, Rath couldn't say.

He looked for a table on the glazed veranda, which was mostly populated by tourists hoping to do some celebrity spotting. Rath ordered a coffee and requested a copy of *Tageblatt* from the newspaper waiter. It was very pleasant in this glass case; the view of Berlin life as it raged around the stoic mass of the Gedächtniskirche was spectacular. The coffee was good too, and even came with a glass of water. Rath smoked a cigarette with his coffee, leafed through the newspaper and waited.

At shortly after one, Berthold Weinert entered the glass case together with a lean, tallish man who couldn't have been much older than thirty, but whose hair was already thinning. He wore thick glasses and hadn't shaved for at least two days. Weinert saw Rath, showed his companion to the table and made the introductions.

'You write screenplays?' Rath asked.

'And you put murderers behind bars,' Heyer replied. 'Berthold told me about your work. Perhaps I can ask for your advice next time I'm writing a crime film.'

'It wouldn't hurt. The crime thrillers I've seen have precious little to do with real police work.'

The men took their seats at table. Weinert ordered a glass of Bordeaux, Heyer a vodka Martini. Rath sipped on his coffee, a little envious of the others' drinks. He offered Heyer a cigarette but Weinert, the dedicated non-smoker, wasn't afforded a look at Rath's new case.

'Let's cut to the chase,' he said, while lighting Heyer's cigarette. 'You sold the same story twice. Is that normal in your line of work?' Not a good start, Rath noted, realising he had touched a sore point.

'I don't know what's normal in this line of work,' Heyer said. 'It seems normal, at any rate, to take a story from an author and pass it on to a complete stranger.'

'You'll have to elaborate there,' Rath said.

'Gladly.' Heyer drew greedily on his Overstolz. 'I've been working with Oppenberg's Montana for a long time, and we always got on well until I sold him my Zeus story.'

'Didn't he pay?'

'He paid well, in fact, and on time, as always. The problem is that he bought the script about a year ago and wanted to turn it into a conventional silent film. However, as sometimes happens in the film industry, the project stalled, others were brought forward, and things kept getting in the way. Then finally something huge got in the way.'

Heyer paused theatrically, as the waiter served the drinks.

'Talkies,' the author continued. 'Oppenberg decided to turn my film into a talkie, but in order to do so the script had to be rewritten. A silent film manuscript has very little dialogue, and if it does, it needs to fit on an intertitle.' Heyer took another drag on his cigarette. 'Sound film is different; there, dialogue is far more important.'

'Let me guess,' Rath said. 'Oppenberg didn't pay you for the additional work.'

'Worse,' Heyer said, 'he had the dialogue written by someone else. To crown it all, he even changed the title. *Vom Blitz getroffen*—how poetic. Ha!'

'What's your script called then?'

'*Olympische Spiele*. You get it? Zeus, the Olympian, is playing games with the mortals . . .' Heyer aided his explanation by frantically waving his hands.

'And you can just do that, can you?' Rath asked. 'Turn a script into a completely different film?'

'Oppenberg bought my script, it belongs to him. He can do whatever he chooses with it. At least the story hasn't changed.' Heyer took a deep drag on his cigarette. 'But for some reason Oppenberg must have thought I couldn't write dialogue. Anyway, he left it with someone else, some snotty little theatre upstart. And the worst thing? It's his name that'll be appearing in the opening credits. All I'll have to show for my creative efforts is that fair but fickle phrase: *based on an idea by Willi Heyer.*'

'Haven't you spoken to Oppenberg about it?'

'Spoken? I've crawled on my knees, but in vain. The man is hard as nails. All my demands came up against a brick wall. Oppenberg showed me what screenplay authors are worth in this business: nothing.' Heyer stubbed his cigarette out. 'That's when I got really angry, and thought: I'll show him I can write dialogue. So, I transferred my Zeus story to the Nordic pantheon and offered it to Bellmann. With talking characters.'

'*Liebesgewitter* with Thor, the God of Thunder, instead of Zeus, the Olympian . . .' Rath nodded. 'And Bellmann went for it straightaway?'

Heyer grinned. 'Of course. He takes any chance he can get to hurt Oppenberg, the old anti-Semite. I have to say, I don't particularly like Bellmann. Give me Oppenberg a thousand times over, both as producer and as a person, but in this case I made no allowances for that! I'm still hoping that *Liebesgewitter* will be a massive success and *Vom Blitz getroffen* comes a cropper. Then Oppenberg will realise who writes the better dialogue, and how important a good script is for a successful film: a thousand times more important with talkies.'

'Unfortunately, Bellmann's leading actress didn't survive the shoot.'

'I doubt that'll harm the film's chances of success,' said Weinert, sipping his wine. 'Quite the opposite. Bellmann is using the attention her death has caused. The title has been mentioned in almost every newspaper article, even made headlines.'

'Death as a means of propaganda,' Rath said.

'You could see it like that,' Heyer said. 'Do you really think that Bellmann's behind it? That he paid this technician to kill Betty Winter?'

'If he wanted her to die, then he didn't pay anyone. He did it himself,'

Rath said. 'Felix Krempin might have devised the mechanism, but some-one else triggered it. Someone who knew the script.'

Weinert nodded in agreement. 'I can't see Bellmann being that someone. Even if he's an arsehole, he has his limits, and Betty Winter is one of them. His best actress! Now he only has Meisner, whose best days are behind him.'

'Bellmann has already appointed Winter's successor,' Rath said. 'Eva Kröger. Heard of her?'

Heyer shook his head. 'Must be new.'

'She still needs a stage name,' Rath said. 'Perhaps you can think of one, and sell it to Bellmann.'

'He won't pay for that. Anyone can think of a name. I don't think they're protected by law.'

'And a story?' Rath asked. 'Can you really sell a story twice? Isn't that open to a legal challenge?'

'The lawyers are currently arguing that, but it looks bad for Oppenberg because I sold him a silent film manuscript, and Bellmann a talkie. That's what Bellmann told me a few days ago. They're completely different things, in terms of the number of pages alone. Besides, it was stupid of Oppenberg to change the title. The way things look, the race will be decided at the box office and not in the courtroom.'

'Do you know Vivian Franck?' Rath asked, changing tack.

Heyer nodded. 'I've written a few films for her, though not her latest. Oppenberg got *Verrucht* from the same amateur who ruined my script.'

'You know that she has disappeared?'

'There are a few rumours going around.'

'What kind of rumours?'

'In the industry,' Heyer said, 'people are saying that Franck was going to leave Oppenberg and change producers. Even move across the pond.'

'Across the pond?'

'America, to Hollywood.'

'Is her English good enough?'

'No idea.' The author shrugged. 'If they want her, it must be. Unlike Jannings. They gave him an award and then sent him on his way.'

'The great Jannings, a victim of sound film?'

'If you like. We'll soon see if the best actor in Hollywood can still hold his own here in Germany. The new Jannings film is out shortly.'

'I know,' Rath said. 'If Vivian Franck really is in Hollywood, then why doesn't anyone know?'

'She doesn't have to tell everyone. If she makes the big time, we'll all hear about it, and if she's a flop . . . well, who knows what she'll say?'

'You don't think it's possible that something might have happened to her? Did she really have no enemies, people wanting to harm her, or out for her blood?'

'That's a bit much. No one's out for her blood, even if she is a spoilt little madam who's always bullying her entourage. Then again, she's isn't the only one in this business.'

'If you had to find Vivian Franck, where would you look?'

'Me?' Heyer gave it a moment's thought. 'I'd book a passage on the *Bremen*.'

28

Erika Voss had good news. 'My sister will help you, Inspector, but she says you owe her one.'

'I always show my appreciation when someone does me a good turn, you know that.'

'Hmm,' his secretary said, grinning. 'Just go up to the third floor and give Franzi back the book she lent you, and while you're at it take a look at the open file on her desk.' She pressed an old, well-thumbed book into his hand. A crime novel.

'You should work for the secret service, Fräulein Voss. You have real conspiratorial qualities.'

'Only too happy to place them at your disposal, Inspector. Whenever you need them.'

Franziska Voss wasn't hard to find. She had the same blonde fringe as her younger sister, but was a little more full-figured. At the other desk sat an old bag, staring through her glasses at a sheet of paper in her typewriter, as if trying to bore holes in it.

'Ah, Inspector,' Franziska Voss said, as he passed her the book. Either she had looked at the photo in his personal file, or her sister had provided a good description. 'That's very kind of you. Did you enjoy it?'

'Very exciting,' he said.

'Wait a moment,' she said. 'I've got something else for you.' She fetched her bag and began rummaging inside. 'It must be here somewhere,' she said as she gradually emptied and repacked the contents. Rath cast his eye over the file that lay open on the desk, at the top of which was a medical form attesting that Detective Inspector Frank Brenner had sustained a number of serious injuries. The doctor had diagnosed a fractured ulna, in addition to a concussion of the brain, two missing teeth and a broken nose.

'There it is!' Franziska Voss closed her bag noisily. Rath made a mental note of the doctor's name and address, somewhere out in Reinickendorf, and gave her a friendly smile. She pressed something into his hand.

'Lipstick?' he said. 'What am I supposed to do with that?'

Even the office dragon looked sourly up from her typewriter.

Franziska Voss laughed. 'Not for you! For Erika.'

Rath took his leave. It was the first time he'd brought lipstick back to the office for his secretary. 'There were a couple of calls for you just now,' she said. 'A man and a woman.'

'What did they want?'

'They didn't say. They'll call back. I said you'd be here in a few minutes.'

Rath sat down at his desk, lit a cigarette and immersed himself in his thoughts. Who could it be? More well-wishers?

His trip to Personnel had been worth it. As he had suspected, Brenner had really gone to town. The doctor must owe Frank Brenner a favour. He skimmed his report for Dr Weiss once more. He could make a fair copy now he no longer needed to be careful what he said; soon it would be Brenner who had some explaining to do. He typed it himself as communications with superiors were none of Erika Voss's concern. He proceeded as carefully as possible, checking each key twice before striking down, and finished after about half an hour. It read pretty well, without a single typing error.

Putting the duplicates to one side, he folded the sheets and sealed them in an envelope. He lit another cigarette, and sent Erika Voss upstairs with the letter. No sooner had she left than the telephone rang.

'Congratulations, Inspector,' a female voice said. Rath almost choked on cigarette smoke.

'Forgive me for not singing,' the voice said, 'but that was never one of my strong points.'

He still didn't know how to respond. Fortunately, she carried on speaking. 'Had a look in your desk yet? A little hint: bottom drawer.'

Rath wedged the receiver against his shoulder and looked inside at a delightfully wrapped package, flat and square-shaped with a bow on top.

'Speechless?'

He had to clear his throat before he could say anything. 'I really wasn't expecting that. You were in my office?'

'At lunchtime when you were out. Have you opened it?'

'One minute.' He loosened the bow to reveal a record. An American import, cut only half a year before.

'I don't believe it. How did you get hold of it?'

'There are lots of things you can get hold of in Berlin.'

'I didn't realise you knew my taste in music so well.'

'I know a lot about you. We used to listen to music together from time to time. Or had you forgotten?'

Or course not. He hadn't forgotten anything, not a single thing. No matter how hard he tried.

'We haven't seen each other for ages,' he said, realising in the same instant how uninspired that was. And that it was a lie.

'We just about managed it *Sonnabend* in the Resi.'

'Pardon me?'

'It was you who sent Brenner to the floor, wasn't it?'

'Word's got around to you too?'

'I just saw Brenner lying there and heard later that you were the one who did it. Could it be that you were wearing a captain's uniform? Then I might even have seen you.'

'Guilty on all counts, your Honour. Even in the matter of the captain's uniform.'

'I didn't think you were the sort who got into fights at Fasching parties.'

'Neither did I, but I'd have given Brenner a good clout at a Christmas party or a funeral too if necessary.'

Suddenly her voice sounded more serious than before. 'Why in God's name did you do it? Did he insult you? Offend your male pride or some rubbish like that?'

I'd rather die than tell you the truth, Charly.

'I can't explain,' he said. 'Just that the arsehole was positively begging for it.'

'There are few people more deserving of a punch in the face than Frank Brenner,' she said, 'but you can't just go around beating up your colleagues.'

'That's what Gennat and Weiss said too.'

'It's gone to the Vipoprä already?'

'Zörgiebel might have been more understanding, but he's away on holiday.'

'You need to keep your anger under control, Gereon.'

'There's just too much of it.' It was supposed to be a joke but the words betrayed his state of mind.

'How are you?' he asked quickly, to distract from himself, and as he uttered the harmless cliché he realised just how much she still affected him. He was anything but indifferent to how she was.

Charly began telling him about herself, and there was a lot to tell: her exams, long hours spent in the library, the envy and lack of understanding on the part of her male colleagues. 'I'm afraid the legal faculty is overrun with reactionary idiots,' she said. 'And these are the same fools who will be representing our constitutional state in future. Goodnight, Germany! I'd like to know how many of my classmates are Nazis.'

'It's fashionable to be a Nazi,' Rath said. 'But so what?—fashions come and go.'

'Only that politics is a little more important than a new pattern on the catwalk.' She paused. 'I'd like to see you again, Gereon,' she said at last. It sounded almost affectionate, but perhaps he was just hearing what he wanted to hear. There was a little puppy dog inside him that came running, tail wagging, at the sound of her voice, at even the slightest kindness she showed; a little puppy dog ready to fulfil her every desire, and abase itself completely. He hated this little puppy dog and shooed it away by recalling their final fight, which had been fierce. She had been ready to belt him one, but instead she had simply beaten her little fist on the table and walked out. That was a long time ago, a few weeks before Christmas. He hadn't seen her since, until the Fasching ball at the Resi.

He tried a casual laugh but only partially succeeded. 'Only if you can guarantee it won't end up in a fight.'

'You know what, Gereon? Fighting with you is still my favourite pastime.'

He was barely responsive after hanging up, hardly noticing that Erika Voss had returned or taking in what she said. She closed the door and left him in peace. He couldn't think straight; his mind kept returning to Charly. He had been ready for anything, but not for her getting back in touch. Now they even had a date. The telephone interrupted his thoughts. 'Rath, CID.'

'Likewise.' Only one man answered the telephone like that. 'Congratulations, my boy,' said Engelbert Rath. 'I hope I'm not disturbing.'

'Only slightly.'

'I just wanted to offer my congratulations, on behalf of your mother too. You know how she doesn't like speaking on the telephone.'

'Thank you.'

'How are things in Berlin? Karl tells me the Communists are making trouble again?'

Karl. Police Director Engelbert Rath spent more time telephoning Berlin Police Commissioner Karl Zörgiebel, whom he knew from Cologne days, than he did his own son.

'Dörrzwiebel's back from Mainz?' Gereon said. 'There's been absolutely no sign of him here at the Castle.'

'Stop using that unspeakable nickname.'

The commissioner was known as 'Dörrzwiebel' on account of his dessicated onion-like complexion.

'As far as I know the Communists have simply called on workers to strike, and Zörgiebel's forbidden it again. He doesn't seem to have learned anything from last year.'

The police had upheld Zörgiebel's May demonstration ban at the cost of more than thirty fatalities.

'Karl knows what he's doing, you have to act quickly against the Communists.'

'It isn't our job.'

'Let's put politics to one side,' Engelbert Rath said. 'I don't want to fight with you. How are things going otherwise? Made any progress?'

'Pardon me?'

'Any leads? Have you taken a look at the factory?'

'I've had too much on my plate, and there's not much I can do without a list of names.'

'That should have arrived long ago, together with our card.'

'I'll take a look in the mailbox.'

Engelbert Rath cleared his throat. 'Gereon, I'm not sure you're taking this assignment seriously enough. If you want to make chief inspector you have to work for it. Something like that doesn't get handed to you on a plate.'

'You should know.'

'And so should you! This isn't just about a promotion. The mayor is trusting us to help him out of a tricky situation. If you betray that trust, you'll be dragging the good name of Rath through the mud.'

'But *your* name above all.'

'Start taking this more seriously and see that it's done.'

'Aye aye, Sir!'

Rath hung up. His father was right, but he didn't have to admit it just yet. He reached for his hat and coat and said goodbye to Erika Voss. There was nothing more he could do in the office anyway.

29

Westhafen was more or less on the way to Reinickendorf, meaning Rath could kill two birds with one stone. A metal sign on the brick façade announced that the Ford Motor Company manufactured their automobiles in a warehouse on the quayside. He parked the Buick out front by the admin building since he didn't want to roll up in a rival product.

Large, wooden crates were being loaded by crane and stacked next to the shop, at the other end of which dozens of spotless Ford A models were lined up, all of them painted red-black. Bruno, his first boss here in Berlin, had driven one just like it. A few men were hanging around outside the shop, turning eagerly as an iron door opened and a man in grey workers' overalls appeared on the loading platform.

'We could use two auto locksmiths for the next shift!' he shouted.

Four men peeled away from the group and stood next to Rath, who was already on the platform steps.

The foreman made his choice. Paying no attention to a man in a suit waving his engineering diploma, he instead gestured towards a powerfully built worker in a boiler suit and a small, nimble-looking man in a thin jacket. 'You,' he said. 'And you.'

The pair climbed the steps, while the other two returned to the group of unemployed. Rath followed them up the stairs.

'I'm sorry,' the foreman said, 'but we only need two.'

The two workers eyed Rath suspiciously. He flashed his badge. 'CID,' he said. 'I need to have a look around your plant.'

'What's this about?' the foreman asked, but before Rath could answer he shouted at the two unemployed men. 'Are you here to work or stare? Go inside and report to Section D. You'll be briefed there.'

The smaller man opened his mouth but his partner pulled him through the door before he could speak. Probably for the best, if they didn't want to lose the work, Rath thought.

'So,' the foreman said, 'what's this all about?'

'I can't tell you anything about the background to the investigation, but I can assure you that I will respect any trade secrets. You can tell me as much as you would any journalist.'

'It's only management that speaks with journalists.'

'I'm certain that you can help me, Herr . . .'

'Bahlke, shift supervisor.'

'Then, Herr Bahlke, let me have a quick look around. Explain to me roughly how everything works, and I'll be on my way. Five minutes.'

Bahlke yielded. 'Come with me,' he said. 'But there isn't much to see.'

There was a hellish din in the shop. 'It's best if we go up here,' Bahlke shouted over the noise, and pointed towards a steel staircase. The stairs led up to a room with an overview of the shop. 'The shift supervisor's office,' Bahlke said. 'You get a view of everything from up here. You need it too.'

Rath gazed beneath him. A caravan of half-finished vehicles moved at a snail's pace through the shop and workers were everywhere assembling parts. At each station the frame of the car grew: steering, seats, wheels, and finally the engine and body, which arrived from above, floating down into the chassis to make the finished product, a Ford Model A.

'Sixty cars a day,' Bahlke said proudly. 'Individual parts come from over-seas and we assemble them here, using the American conveyor belt sys-tem.' He pointed to a station along the line where a red-haired man was showing the two new recruits how to fit the engines. The bodies were al-ready approaching from above. 'You see the site of the marriage? Section D is where the body is fitted to the chassis, just after the engine has been in-stalled.'

The red-haired man looked up at precisely the moment Bahlke pointed at him. Even from here Rath could see the worker grow wide-eyed and set to work with renewed vigour. Standing up here was like being in a display case on the Ku'damm. Every worker could see them through the great glass window, and they all realised they were being watched. It kept the workers on the go, along with the relentless march of the conveyor belt.

'Impressive,' Rath said. 'What happens if someone needs the toilet?'

'Then he works his way forward. For longer breaks, he organises a stand-in, which is deducted from his wage. You only get paid for the work you do.'

'Do you always recruit your workers like that?'

Bahlke shook his head. 'Most of them applied the usual way, but there are more and more awaiting their chance outside. We pay well, and the more work you do, the more you make. No one pays as well as Ford. No sign of the financial crisis here. I'm telling you: in five years' time the Berlin Ford plant will be as big as Siemens!'

This man has no idea what's coming, Rath thought. The blackmailer was not only well informed about the state of Adenauer's finances; he also had exclusive knowledge of Ford's move to the Rhine. *Knowledge is power.* Rath couldn't help thinking of his father's motto. It sounded like an instruction manual for blackmailers. 'Who's to say you're not picking up criminals when you take men straight from the streets without papers?'

'I see how they work first. If I'm satisfied, they take their papers to Personnel. Why do you ask? You're not looking for criminals here, are you, just because the prison's around the corner?'

'Don't worry, I'm not looking for anyone who's escaped from Plötzensee. I'm interested in any possible link between your workers and Deutsche Bank. Who might have a connection?'

'There are almost three hundred people working here. How am I supposed to know that? Your best bet would be the people in the wages office, not the workers here.'

Rath nodded. 'Can you tell me how to get there?'

'You see that door?' Bahlke pointed across the hall to a steel door behind the engine assembly. 'Go through there to Admin, and ask for Personnel. Oh, what the hell? I'll take you myself.'

The red-haired assembly man seemed to think the shift supervisor was pointing at him again. Rath could see him getting more and more nervous, as if he thought he was about to get the sack. They descended the stairs until, suddenly, a loud horn sounded, drowning out the factory din.

'What's that?' Rath shouted in the shift supervisor's ear. 'Fire alarm?'

'No. It means someone hasn't completed their work on time and is causing a hold-up.'

'Leaving their workplace without getting a stand-in.'

Bahlke shrugged. 'Or just dawdling.' The horn sounded a second time and the assembly line ground to a halt. 'Shit!' He dashed off.

Rath tried to keep up. Stopping at the first station he reached, Bahlke snapped at a worker tightening padded seats. 'What's going on? Which idiot turned off the conveyor belt?'

The worker shrugged his shoulders. 'I think there are problems on the marriage line.'

Chaos reigned in Section D. The four men, whose task it was to lower the bodies onto the chassis, were exchanging furious words with the two new recruits. There was no sign of the red-haired man who was supposed to be training them.

'What's going on here?' Bahlke yelled. 'Are you crazy? Who stopped the line?'

'I did,' a giant of a man said, positioning himself legs apart in front of them. 'The engine's crooked as a dog's hind leg and there are umpteen screws missing. I'm not putting a body on that. Why don't you ask the two recruits why the belt isn't running?'

The small man in the thin jacket didn't wait to be asked. 'We've barely been here ten minutes, boss,' he said. 'Toni said hello, showed us two manoeuvres, then buggered off without saying where he was going. What chance do we have? On top of that, I have to deal with this gorilla tearing into me.'

'I'll give you gorilla, you squirt,' the giant said.

'Cut it out, Kurt, and leave the new boys in peace. Where's Toni gone? He can't just drop everything like that.'

'He just ran off,' the little man said.

'Is he sick or something? It's not like him; hardly even takes a piss to make sure he gets his piece rate.'

The new recruits shrugged.

Rath thought the time was right to take his leave. He left the assembly hall and went up to Personnel to ask for a list of all factory employees. Upon comparing it to the Cologne list he might, with luck, stumble across an identical surname or some other anomaly that would enable him to establish a connection between Ford and Deutsche Bank. Then he'd have the blackmailer hook, line and sinker.

A simple list of names; it was a modest enough request, Rath thought, but the goateed man behind the desk was of a different opinion. 'Do you know how much work that would mean? We have almost three hundred people.'

'Listen, I could force this, but then I'd be taking the original files with me and turning your office inside out.'

Goatee Beard swallowed. 'Very well,' he said. 'You'll get your list. I could have it finished by next week, I think.'

'I'll be back tomorrow morning to collect it.' The man was about to protest, but Rath cut him off. 'And if you don't have anything for me, I'll be back with a search warrant, and you won't be able to use your office for the rest of the day. I'd factor in two days to tidy up, just so you're aware of the alternatives.'

The man nodded as Rath took his leave, stopping at the doorway. 'A little tip,' he said. 'Get down to it right away, and you'll be finished quicker.'

There was still a group of jobseekers standing outside the brick building when he left. It might be better than the dole, Rath thought, but there was no future here, however tempting the wages might be. This was a stopgap, not so much an automobile factory as an assembly shop in a storage facility that no one else wanted to rent. No wonder Ford were looking elsewhere.

Three hundred people in Berlin would lose their jobs, but hundreds more would find work in Cologne; and from somewhere inside this building someone was trying to prevent it.

From Westhafen it wasn't far to Reinickendorf. The receptionist was just about to close the practice, but Rath told her it was an emergency and showed her his police badge. 'I'm a friend of Frank Brenner's,' he said.

'In that case, please wait a moment.'

She went to the back, returning after a short while. 'The doctor's about to make a house call, but he'll fit you in.'

'Thank you.'

'Please take a seat in the waiting room, though I'm afraid I'll have to leave you. He hasn't approved any overtime.'

'What a shame,' he said. She smiled coquettishly back and waved goodbye with her fingertips.

He looked around at pictures of battleships on the walls, a portrait of Admiral Tirpitz with his imposing, forked beard, and was pondering where Brenner might have served when the milk-glass door to the waiting room swung open. A man with a doctor's case and a greying full beard stormed in, almost tripping over Rath's legs. 'Good afternoon,' he said. 'Roswitha didn't give me your name. Have we met before?'

'I don't think so.'

'But you are a friend of Brenner's?'

'A colleague more than a friend,' Rath said, and showed his badge. 'We both work in Homicide.'

Dr Borghausen stared at Rath's identification as it dawned on him who he might have here. Rath could see the hatches being battened down. It won't save you from capsizing, he thought.

'I see,' the doctor said. His voice was quiet and decidedly frosty. 'What can I do for you? Surgery ended some time ago.'

'I just have a few questions.'

'You're the policeman who beat up Frank, aren't you? What do you want?'

'You ought to be a detective,' Rath said. 'The thing is, seeing as I was present when Herr Brenner sustained the injuries that have unfortunately led to his being declared unfit for duty, I wouldn't mind comparing our experiences a little. You call him by his first name . . .'

'Frank Brenner is an old friend. We served together.'

'Then it must be his old war injuries that have surfaced again.'

'I don't understand.'

'I doubt whether the certificate you issued would stand up to medical review.' The doctor grew red. Time to check your blood pressure, Rath thought.

'You mean to blackmail a Prussian doctor?' Borghausen choked.

'I'd like to give this Prussian doctor a choice regarding his future. Go to jail with licence revoked, possibly to return one day as a corpse-washer, or continue as a respected doctor who might have fallen foul of an old friend over a silly incident, but is otherwise very happy.'

Behind the doctor's eyes the wheels were turning. 'How do you know about the certificate?' he asked.

'I'm a detective, and perhaps a little harder-working than Herr Brenner.'

'You know that you're not authorised to see such certificates?'

'Who says I've seen anything?'

The doctor took a deep breath. 'If I'm not mistaken,' he said, at pains to remain calm, 'Frank has decided not to pursue disciplinary proceedings—luckily for you. Which means that there will be no need for a medical review.'

'It's good of Herr Brenner to rely on defamation of character alone,' Rath said. 'But perhaps *I'll* insist that disciplinary proceedings are brought against me.'

'Why would you?'

'To bring the truth to light. Detective Inspector Frank Brenner has been submitting bogus certificates.'

'Are you implying that *I've* been issuing bogus certificates?' Dr Borghausen turned a glowing violet above his white collar. The man really ought to do something about his blood pressure.

'I'm not implying anything,' Rath said, still calm and friendly. 'I'm merely advancing a theory, as detectives are wont to do. Perhaps Brenner submitted a forged certificate after deceiving his old friend Dr Borghausen.' Rath now had the doctor's undivided attention. 'Let's suppose that you are in the habit of placing a few blank, signed certificates in the charming Roswitha's desk so that she can take care of such matters for you? The thing is—and you know this because you keep an exact count of these blank certificates—only today you realised that a few forms, or perhaps just one, I'll leave that to your imagination, had been stolen. The first thing you do is report the matter to the police, and the local station sends someone round. This officer asks you for the time frame in which the theft might have taken place. You give a time during which, among other patients, Frank Brenner was seen at your practice. And things take their course without any damage resulting to you.'

Rath sensed that this was a straw Dr Borghausen might just grasp.

'If you'll excuse me, I have a house call to make,' the doctor said. 'And then I must go to the police—to report a theft.'

Rath came home to a surprise he hadn't in the least been expecting. In the centre of a lovingly laid dining table a birthday cake stood regally on a pristine white tablecloth, flanked by two candlesticks. Kathi was standing by the table. She must have heard him in the stairwell as the candles were already lit. 'Happy Birthday, Gereon,' she said and smiled.

He almost felt a little sorry for her, and for a moment would have liked nothing more than to take her in his arms. At the same time, he felt angry, his anger growing the longer he stared at the cake and the flickering candles.

What was she thinking just turning up like this, after she had stood him up? After he had begun to forget about her! Why was she making it so hard? 'Still here, I see,' he said bluntly.

Her smile faded, and her face crumpled up like a paper bag.

'Where have you been these last few days?' he demanded. 'You vanish without a word, and then reappear as if nothing has happened.'

'You mustn't be angry! It was nothing. I . . .'

'I'm not angry. I'm just wondering what these games are about. Walking out on me, not getting in touch for days, and then turning up again out of the blue.'

'No games, Gereon. We're free to live our own lives. You said so yourself.'

That was true, but only to warn her not to expect too much from him. Yet those cold words hadn't driven her away; quite the opposite. 'Of course they're games,' he said. 'Why invite me to a costume ball only to go and disappear on me?'

'Oh Gereon! You kept saying you were coming, and then you didn't. I thought you'd stood me up again.'

'So that's why you left with another man?'

'It's not what you think. Herbert . . .'

'I don't care what his name is!'

'Gereon, don't get so worked up. You mustn't be jealous, I . . .'

'I'm not jealous. You're right: we're free to live our own lives. This thing is over, I've come to realise that in the last few days.'

She gazed at him disbelievingly, her lower lip gradually starting to tremble.

'What thing? You mean our love? Is that a *thing* to you?' Tears flooded her eyes. 'Is it something to just throw away?'

Someone has to be the arsehole, he thought. Might as well be me. 'Did you really think I'd let myself be treated this way?' he shouted. 'Take your cake and scram! Go to this Herbert, go to your sister, go to hell!'

It was like a bad film: The Betrayed Lover. He was a rotten actor, truly rotten, and rotten was how he felt.

'It's your birthday cake, I . . .'

'I don't want your damned cake!'

Behind the tears her eyes flashed. 'It's *your damned cake*! I made it for you, whether you like it or not!'

She opened the door and made for the hallway, silently retrieving her coat from the stand. Suddenly she began shaking, and the tears started again. He could hardly bear to watch but had to resist the urge to go over and comfort her. He went to the window and looked outside.

Listening to her gathering her things from the bathroom, his heart nearly broke. It took an eternity for the front door to click shut. Her steps echoed on the stairs, and he watched her red coat glow in the murky gas-light of the courtyard before disappearing through the gate for the final time.

He had a lump in his throat. Why did she have to come back? Why hadn't she spared him that scene? Perhaps him behaving like an arsehole had made things easier for her, but he didn't really believe that.

His birthday candles were still lit. He blew them out and took the cake from the table, resisting the temptation to hurl it against the wall. Instead, he placed it in the cupboard, before overturning a chair and kicking the dresser. He couldn't stand it any longer in the flat, so he fetched the bottle of cognac from the living room, threw on his hat and coat and went out into the stairwell. He didn't meet anyone on the way up. The only people who lived here were the Liebigs but they went to bed early; the Steinrück flat still stood empty.

It was cold in the attic. Rath took a swig of cognac before opening the skylight and climbing outside. Liebig's doves cooed quietly as he sat on the narrow ridge beside the dovecote. He hadn't been here since October. Strangely, he experienced none of the giddiness that usually seized him when he ventured too high. Perhaps it was because the precipice was a few metres away and he couldn't see the ground. From here he could make out the house fronts at the other end of the large playground which the city council had built in a filled harbour basin. To the left, the slender dome of Sankt Michael rose as a dark shadow into the night sky.

Up here he could breathe freely, drink and gaze out over the roofs of the city. Kathi was out there somewhere now, on the way to her sister. All roads seemed to lead away from him. In truth it had always been that way.

He had never been able to hold onto anyone, nor had he ever wanted to—except for one.

Cheers, Charly, he thought, and raised the bottle. To solitude! Because that's what it all boils down to in the end. For you, for me, for every one of us.

He drank and gazed into the night. Gereon Rath, you sentimental arsehole, he thought. Time to stop feeling sorry for yourself.

30

Thursday 6th March 1930

The murder wagon raced westwards across Leipziger Strasse. None of the four occupants spoke a word.

Rath gazed out of the window, immersed in his thoughts, which now no longer concerned Charly. He had been expecting a quiet day at the Castle, with time to collect the list of Ford employees from Westhafen, but news came in during the morning briefing: a female corpse had been found in a disused old cinema in Wilmersdorf. Böhm quickly halted proceedings, before issuing instructions and forming a new homicide team on the spot.

Alfons Henning sat behind the wheel with Christel Temme, the stenographer, alongside him. The padded rear seat was reserved for the two most senior members of the team: Inspector Gereon Rath and its leader, Detective Chief Inspector Wilhelm Böhm.

Rath was still racking his brains over Böhm's decision to hand the Winter case over to Gräf, a detective, rather than himself, a detective inspector. It seemed that Böhm meant to keep him off the case at all costs, perhaps as punishment for his insubordination. It was certainly true that the closer together they worked, the better Böhm could keep him in check. In the car, he had the unpleasant feeling of being watched, even though Böhm hadn't so much as glanced at him. He had been silent the whole journey and nobody else had dared open their mouth.

The Luxor looked run-down and dirty, as if nobody had cleaned the strip lights or electric bulbs on the façade for years.

Böhm and Rath greeted the uniformed officer at the door silently as they entered, while the stenographer uttered a shy 'good morning'. Henning took the camera from the boot of the car. A second officer led them down past rows of seats to the screen.

Despite all the lights being on, even on the artificial firmament, the auditorium was still dark and gloomy. A few people from ED were clambering between the pipes of the organ, which looked as miserable as the cinema itself. The musty smell inside the room intensified the impression of decay.

'Up there,' the officer said, gesturing towards a steep, wooden staircase. 'I don't need to see it again.'

The staircase led inside the organ where the smell was abominable, and the higher they climbed, the worse it got. Rath let Böhm lead, following with a handkerchief held to his nose. Christel Temme remained below with her writing pad.

The corpse lay on a service platform beside the battered organ pipes, which an ED man with a mask over his mouth was dusting for fingerprints. Next to the pipes were a glockenspiel, a drum, a rainstick and even a miniature version of Bellmann's thunder machine. The body took up most of the space between the organ pipes and the back wall. There wasn't much room left on the platform, so that the ED man, who didn't seem to mind the smell, had to be careful where he stood.

Rath recognised her the moment he saw her face.

Shit, he thought involuntarily. Now you can tell Oppenberg what's become of her. No Hollywood star. Vivian Franck's dead eyes stared out of a perfectly made-up face that appeared to have been done up for a shoot; the glittering dress might have come from a film fund.

Rath remembered her lust for life and felt sick looking at what was left of her. He pulled himself together and decided to look instead at the organ pipes that rose like metallic stalagmites. The last thing he needed was to pass out in front of Böhm.

'Doctor here yet?' Böhm asked the ED man. Even the bulldog was having trouble breathing. The ED man gestured with his head towards the back.

They found the pathologist at a small table in an adjoining room. Dr Schwartz sat in hat and coat, making notes in his little red book. He glanced at Böhm and Rath as they entered, before reassuming his indifferent, slightly cynical expression. Two men stood behind him, and by the look on their faces neither had quite got to grips with the situation. The first, a gaunt figure, was kneading his hat in his hands nervously, blinking in embarrassment out of a pale face, while the second was mildly overweight and blushing grimly under his light-coloured felt hat.

'Morning, Doctor,' Böhm said. 'Now that's what I call hard-working. What can you say about the cause of death?'

'Not much.' Schwartz said. 'The only certainty is that the woman is dead. No external agencies, at least not at first glance, but I haven't turned the corpse yet. Didn't want to tread on your toes.'

'How long has she been dead?'

'Based on the degree of decomposition, I'd say three to four weeks. But it could be longer.'

Böhm nodded. 'Smells about right. Strange that she wasn't found earlier.'

'No one's been in here for weeks,' the gaunt man chipped in. It sounded apologetic.

'Who are you?' Böhm asked.

'Riedel, the broker. We're looking for new tenants, and today was the first visit with an interested party. I was showing Herr Strelow here the premises . . . we were just wondering about the smell, and then on inspecting the organ . . .'

'It had to be Vivian Franck,' said Strelow, shaking his head. 'That was a real shock.'

'Do you know the woman?' Böhm asked. Which suggested that *he* didn't.

'Not personally. But I saw her in *Verrucht*!'

'A film actress?' Böhm mumbled. 'That fits.'

'I was going to open the Luxor with her new sound film,' Strelow said.

'*Vom Blitz getroffen?*' The words slipped out before Rath had a chance to think.

Strelow nodded, but Böhm looked at him disapprovingly. 'You're well informed,' he said. 'No doubt you spend too much time in the cinema. Do you know the film?'

'It doesn't exist yet,' Rath said. 'They were about to film it.'

'Her most expensive production to date,' Strelow added. 'Her first full-length talkie. Eagerly anticipated by the whole industry.'

'Well, nothing will come of it now,' Böhm said.

'Do you still need me?' Dr Schwartz asked in his calm, sonorous voice as he pocketed his notebook. 'If you want to question the witnesses, perhaps I could apply myself to the remains.'

'It's yours, as soon as Henning has everything in the can,' Böhm said.

No sooner had the doctor taken his leave than Böhm turned the space into an interrogation room, questioning the broker and cinema owner separately. Rath he told to stand aside, but it was unclear whether his purpose was to act as a doorman or a heavy, or something else entirely. Böhm assigned Christel Temme the remaining place at the little table.

The two men didn't have much to say, apart from the fact that they had found the body. There were no contradictions in their statements. The broker explained that the Luxor had been out of commission since the start of the year because its former owner had taken it to the brink of ruin. Now, thanks to a progressively minded cinema enthusiast—he pointed to the door behind which Strelow was waiting—they were using an opportune moment to convert it into an ultramodern sound film cinema. As for who might have brought the body here, Riedel had no idea. There were no signs of a break-in. Böhm had then asked the broker for a list of everyone who had a key to the Luxor.

While Böhm questioned the two men, Rath immersed himself in his thoughts. The intersection where Vivian Franck had been picked up by a stranger almost four weeks ago was only a few streets away. Had she gone willingly to that ominous stranger waiting by the roadside?

'Inspector!' Böhm's voice startled him. For the first time since that morning, when he had fetched him to his team with a brusque 'Rath, you're coming too!' the DCI had addressed him.

'Inspector, please check whether the woman has any relatives in the city who might be able to identify her.'

'Now?'

'When do you think? We're investigating a murder.'

'But I'd need to go back to the station . . .'

Böhm was unmoved. 'And when you've finished that, you can deliver news of her death. Take Lange from the Winter team if you like. He's the right man for a job like that.'

'How am I supposed to get to Alex without a car?'

'Do I look like your chauffeur?'

For the first time in a long while Rath was obliged to take the underground. He was annoyed: Why had Böhm brought him along, only to make him hang around for three-quarters of an hour and then send him back to the Castle? The journey from Fehrbelliner Platz to Alex took about half an hour, but at least he didn't have to change. It was his old route, past Nürnberger Platz, and he couldn't help thinking back to his first few weeks in Berlin, and a journey he had made with Charly. He gazed past his reflection into the darkness and tried to order his thoughts, carried as they were by the rattle and judder of the train.

Vivian Franck was dead.

His private assignment had become an official case.

It would be better if Böhm didn't learn of his connection to Oppenberg. Somehow he had to sell the groundwork he had carried out privately as freshly acquired and, if possible, collect a few rewards for his endeavour. He had to speak to Oppenberg and the taxi driver as quickly as possible and weave them into the official investigation, but hadn't managed to get hold of either from the underground station. Oppenberg was back in Babelsberg, while Ziehlke was out and about with his taxi. At least he had been able to keep Erika Voss busy with a few tasks.

By the time he arrived in his office, she had already discovered that Vivian Franck had no relatives in Berlin. Rath was growing to appreciate his secretary more and more. True, she didn't display a lot of initiative, but any tasks he assigned her, she carried out with care and attention. The documents from the passport office revealed that the dead actress came from Breslau. Erika Voss had already called the local station and was waiting for further information on the Franck family.

The way things looked, the person Vivian Franck was closest to in Berlin was also the person Rath intended to see next: Manfred Oppenberg.

Before setting out on the long journey towards Babelsberg, he tried the taxi office again, but there was still no sign of Ziehlke. No sooner had he hung up than Erika Voss popped her head in. 'Assistant Detective Lange is here for you.'

The new man from Hannover was standing behind the secretary. 'Inspector Rath,' he said, 'DCI Böhm said I should place myself at your disposal.'

Böhm wasn't leaving anything to chance. Rath liked the new man, but even if he didn't know it himself, Lange was being used as a spy. Still, what were police hierarchies for?

'Perfect timing, Lange,' Rath said. 'You can hold the fort here. I need someone to establish contact with our colleagues in Breslau, where Vivian Franck's family lives. Fräulein Voss is waiting for them to call back but isn't authorised to issue our colleagues with instructions.' He gestured towards Gräf's abandoned desk. 'Please take a seat in the meantime—I have an appointment. And if you would like a coffee. Fräulein Voss . . .'

The secretary smiled. 'Make yourself at home, Herr Lange,' she said.

Rath took the AVUS to Babelsberg, as he didn't have a moment to lose. WANNSEE TEN KILOMETRES proclaimed big letters by the tollhouse. The fun only cost a mark. He flogged the Buick mercilessly over the arrow-straight track, but it was already almost twelve when he reached the group of studios at Neubabelsberg. This time he didn't park on Stahnsdorfer Strasse but drove the car directly onto the site. The porter opened the gate when he saw the police badge. The oriental city in which Rath had lost his bearings scarcely a week ago had been stripped down to a shell, and he could already make out the great hall from the gatekeeper's lodge. He drove the car up as far as the door. Security let him in straightaway.

The set looked similar to that of *Liebesgewitter*: a drawing room, perhaps a little more elegantly and tastefully furnished than Bellmann's. On the parquet Rudolf Czerny was rehearsing with a woman who bore a vague resemblance to Vivian Franck. Bellmann had done a better job when he replaced Betty Winter with Eva Kröger, Rath thought. Since he couldn't find Oppenberg anywhere, he waited dutifully until Czerny had finished rehearsing. The actor recognised him and came over.

'Herr Rath,' he said, shaking his hand. 'What brings you here? Have you found a lead on Vivian?'

'That depends,' Rath said. 'I'd like to discuss it with Herr Oppenberg.'

'I'm afraid you're too late. Our producer has just left us for a few hours.'

'I hope he hasn't gone to his office; they're the ones who sent me here!'

'No, he's been invited to a lunch, can't be too far away, I think. But wait . . .' Czerny looked around enquiringly. 'Silvia,' he called. 'Can you come here for a moment?'

A lively brunette with a clipboard under her arm hurried over. She was mid-twenties at most, with a severely knotted hairstyle that failed to disguise a pretty face.

'Silvia, can you tell Herr Rath here where the boss is this afternoon?'

She looked Rath up and down before answering. 'The invitation is from an important business partner.'

'Which business partner, and what restaurant will I find them in?'

Again she hesitated a little before answering. 'Not a restaurant,' she said. 'Herr Marquard likes to entertain his guests at home. He has a kitchen to rival the best in Berlin.'

'Marquard, the cinema owner?'

She seemed surprised that he knew the name. 'He runs his cinemas purely as a hobby. Well, that's not quite true—he also owns a film lab and a big distribution firm. One of the largest of the independents. Important if you want to stand up to the all-powerful Ufa.'

'Like Montana?'

'And many other smaller firms. Marquard is fighting on our side against Ufa.'

'And against talkies.'

'He's not interested in money. For him, it's about the art. He isn't the only one who views sound film as an attack on cinematics. He believes that smaller firms should focus on silent film, especially as Ufa is throwing everything it has behind talkies.'

'But Herr Oppenberg sees things differently.'

'Exactly. Everyone here at Montana sees it differently. Talkies might cost a vast amount of money—hiring the recording equipment from Tobis is expensive enough alone! But Oppenberg says if we don't keep up we might as well pack it in, and I fear he's right.'

Rath nodded. 'And that's why he's meeting Herr Marquard today?'

'He hopes, above all, to persuade him to open up his distribution company to talkies. We had to distribute *Verrucht* through another company, and even though the film did well enough, it was by no means a financial success. That has to change with our second talkie. My personal view is that at some point Herr Marquard will have to acknowledge that sound film has just as much artistic potential as silent. Only he mustn't take too long over it. We need him to help us fight Ufa.'

Rath nodded. 'Even so, I'm going to have to interrupt this important meeting.'

She appeared almost scandalised. 'A meal in a private residence! I don't think you can just go barging in. Herr Oppenberg . . .'

'Leave Herr Oppenberg to me. He'll want to see me, trust me.'

'If you say so.' Silvia fished out the address of a villa on the Wannsee.

Rath needed less than quarter of an hour. He parked the Buick on a quiet street lined with trees. Behind the trees was a huge building with countless nooks and crannies, oriels and turrets, crowned by an immense keep; a huge castle villa—built according to the Middle Ages model, if not always stylistically accurate. Rath hadn't seen anything like it outside of the Middle Rhine. In this English-style park, however, the crenellated structure appeared more like a haunted castle that had been magically transported from Sussex to the sand of the Brandenburg March.

The name MARQUARD was all that stood on the highly polished brass plate. Rath pushed the bell. While he waited, he couldn't help thinking of the eloquent opponent of sound film whom he had met in Pschorr Haus. So, this was how the cinema owner and film distributor Marquard lived.

He's not interested in money. True, Rath thought, anyone who lived like this didn't have to be *interested* in money, they simply *had* it. The heavy oak door opened and a white-haired servant surveyed the uninvited guest.

'Can I help you?' he asked in a scratchy voice that sounded as if it was rarely used. Must be at least eighty, Rath thought.

'I'd like to speak to Herr Oppenberg,' he said politely. 'I was told . . .'

'I'm afraid I cannot disturb the gentlemen while they are dining.'

Rath showed the old man his card. 'Tell Herr Oppenberg it's about Vivian Franck, and please ask Herr Marquard to excuse the interruption.'

The servant raised an eyebrow over Rath's identification before turning silently away.

He returned five minutes later. 'If you could wait in the vestibule,' he said, stepping invitingly to the side. 'Herr Oppenberg will be with you presently.'

Rath entered a hall that was as high as a house and seemed as if it had been built for the latest *Nibelung* film. At any moment he expected to see Kriemhild, princess of Burgundy, descending the stairs.

Great double-leaf doors led from the hall into another part of the massive building. Only a small, dark oak door seemed out of place and, being more like the entrance to a castle dungeon, probably led down to the cellar. Rath realised he had taken off his hat, a reflex that must have been triggered by the sacred atmosphere of the room and its immense ribbed vault. There he stood, the grey felt hat in humbly clasped hands, examining the knight's armour and the huge oil paintings on the walls that glorified the darkest episodes from the Middle Ages. He heard steps on the stairs and turned around.

It wasn't Kriemhild but Manfred Oppenberg, his face filled with fearful anticipation. Things couldn't bode well if Rath had driven specially out to Wannsee to interrupt a business lunch.

'I'm sorry to disturb you now of all times, Herr Oppenberg.'

'It doesn't matter,' Oppenberg said. He gestured towards the front door. 'Let's go to the park. I think I need some fresh air.'

As they stood outside on the half landing, Oppenberg nervously patted his jacket pockets. 'You don't happen to have any cigarettes on you?' he asked. 'Mine are on the table upstairs . . .'

Rath took out his new case and Oppenberg helped himself. 'Thank you,' he said, as Rath struck a match. The cigarette in his hand was shaking slightly. Oppenberg inhaled deeply. 'I'll need it.'

'Me too,' Rath said, lighting an Overstolz. Gradually they made their away along the gravel path, down to the lake. Rath waited a moment before speaking.

'I'm very sorry, Herr Oppenberg,' he began at last, and watched Manfred Oppenberg stiffen in his elegant suit, 'but we've found Vivian Franck.' Oppenberg didn't say anything, nor did he take another drag on his cigarette. Slowly the colour drained from his face. 'Homicide are now conducting an official investigation. I wanted to come myself to tell you in person . . . I'm truly sorry.'

Oppenberg pointed to a bench on the side of the path.

'I need to sit down,' he said. 'Even if I've been expecting to receive news like this since our last conversation.' They sat and Oppenberg gazed silently towards the silver grey shimmer behind the trees. 'Tell me what happened.'

Rath described where and how they had found Vivian Franck's corpse.

Oppenberg listened in composed silence for a moment and then spoke so quietly that his words were scarcely audible. 'Find the man who did this, Herr Rath. Find him and I will reward you handsomely!'

'Catching killers is what I do,' Rath said. 'And it's the Free State of Prussia that pays me, not you.'

'Nevertheless—a little reward couldn't hurt.'

Rath shrugged. 'In a case like this—I don't know. This is no ordinary crime, no ordinary murder. Perhaps it was just an accident: a drugs accident, and her companion disposed of the body. Anything's possible.'

Oppenberg shook his head indignantly. 'No, not an accident! Did you investigate my suspicion that Bellmann had hired someone from the underworld . . . ?'

'My contact is asking around,' Rath lied. 'Do you really think Bellmann is capable of something like that? Of ordering a murder?'

'That scoundrel's capable of anything. Any crime.'

'He feels the same about you.'

'Of course, slander is one of his specialities. I had nothing to do with Betty Winter's death. How many times must I tell you?' Oppenberg stubbed out his cigarette. 'Two film producers killing each other's actresses? Doesn't that sound ridiculous?'

'You're the one who set me on that track. We'll see how ridiculous it is. Have you any enemies apart from Bellmann? Did Vivian Franck? Enemies capable of something like this?'

Oppenberg considered for a moment. 'For all her popularity, I'm certain she didn't just have friends. That's how things are in this profession. The public only sees the adulation, it sees nothing of the jealousy.' He gazed briefly at the lake before continuing. 'But enemies who would do something like this? Not in the industry, at any rate. Perhaps you should take a look at the local SA's membership list, those thugs. Maybe you'll find the killer there.'

'You're saying the Nazis would kill an actress because she works for a Jew?'

'She didn't just work for a Jew. Vivian is . . . was a Jew herself. Not a particularly devout one, but those idiots don't care whether we visit the synagogue or not. For them it's about our *race*. As if we were dogs or horses, not people.'

'You think the Nazis would do something like that? At a time when they'd sooner present themselves as victims?'

'I don't know what to think,' Oppenberg said, 'except the Nazis are no victims!'

Rath tossed his cigarette into the nearest shrub and stood up. 'Herr Oppenberg,' he said. 'There's something unpleasant I still have to ask of you. I need you to identify Vivian's corpse.' Oppenberg nodded. 'I don't want to take up any more of your time. You're in the middle of an important meeting . . .'

The producer stood up as if in slow motion. 'It all seems so ridiculous now,' he said. 'What am I fighting for now that Vivian is dead? Talkies were *her* future. Marquard liked Vivian, worshipped her, even. She was my best argument to give up his outmoded resistance and finally invest in sound. And now?'

'But you're still shooting. I was in the studio just now.'

'Yes, we're shooting,' Oppenberg sighed, 'but the new actress is a catastrophe! At least, if you keep picturing how Vivian would have played the scene.'

The castle towers of the Marquard villa loomed threateningly over the bleak, wintry park. Behind one of the tower windows, Rath noticed a white figure watching them. At first he thought it was the old servant, but it must have been someone else—unless he had exchanged his black suit for something lighter.

Slowly they made their way back to the house.

'Marquard isn't just my distributor,' Oppenberg said. 'He's also one of my most important donors. You can see how rich he is, but he simply doesn't want to acknowledge that his beloved silent film is dead, and that we will die with it if we don't change. Perhaps he can afford that, but I can't!'

Marquard was waiting for them outside the house. Once more, Rath marvelled at the man's warm, pleasant voice. 'It's you, Inspector,' he said, proffering a hand, 'I thought I recognised the name when Albert gave me your card.'

'Please excuse the interruption,' Rath said, 'but you may now continue your meeting.'

'Clearly you haven't brought good news. What has happened?'

'Let's go inside,' Oppenberg said, 'I'd rather not tell you out here.'

The two men disappeared inside the house, Marquard taking Oppenberg by the arm. Rath gazed after them, until Albert, the servant, closed the door, casting him a final, contemptuous glance. Although it might have looked like friendship that bound them, in reality the two men were nothing more than business partners. If Marquard hadn't been willing to focus on talkies when Vivian Franck was alive, what chance did Oppenberg have of persuading him now?

Rath took the AVUS for the return journey too, more on a whim than because of any time pressure. It was fun to drive the Buick at full speed, even if he had to rein himself in upon rejoining the city traffic. There was a telephone booth level with the Städtische Oper on Bismarckstrasse, where Rath tried the taxi office again. At last he got Friedhelm Ziehlke on the line. He told him whose body they had found, and summoned him to the Castle.

Just after half past one Rath stepped out of his car in the atrium feeling very pleased with himself. *Fortune favours the brave!* was another one of his father's sayings. The Oppenberg problem was ticked off, and soon the Ziehlke problem would be too. After lunch, the taxi driver's statements would officially find their way into the new Vivian Franck file. Now it was time to see what his colleagues in Breslau had found.

When Rath entered his office, however, Lange was no longer sitting at Gräf's desk. 'He's with Böhm,' Erika Voss said, 'and they're expecting you, I was told to say.'

Rath went over. Böhm had just returned to the Castle, with everyone gathered around his desk like it was the campfire of an Indian chief: Henning, Christel Temme and Lange, who gave Rath an apologetic shrug as he entered the room.

'There he is, the prodigal son,' Böhm said. 'Why didn't you take Herr Lange with you as I requested?'

Rath cleared his throat. Why did he always have to justify himself in front of Böhm? 'Vivian Franck has no relatives in Berlin,' he said. 'Her family lives in Breslau, which is why Herr Lange . . .'

'So why didn't you go to Breslau?'

'Pardon me?'

'Why are you and Lange not in Breslau informing the relatives of the murder victim?'

'It seemed a little excessive, Sir. Assistant Detective Lange was to ask our colleagues in Breslau for assistance. I thought that in the wake of the Interior Ministry's saving measures . . .'

'You shouldn't think! You should do as you're told.'

'As far as thinking is concerned, Sir—with respect, I must beg to differ.'

'Don't get fresh with me, Inspector.'

'A trip to Breslau is unnecessary because it is highly doubtful whether any family members will come to her funeral, let alone to identify the body.'

'What makes you say that?'

'Vivian Franck had fallen out with all her relatives. Her father is a respected Breslau rabbi—and Vivian—well, she was the black sheep, so to speak, whom no one mentions at family gatherings.'

'That may be,' Böhm said, 'but death changes many things.'

'Contact with Breslau has been established, so we'll see,' Rath said. 'As a precaution, however, I have asked Franck's producer to identify the body. He was also privately involved with her. He can be at the morgue at three.'

'All right,' Böhm snarled. 'Let's leave it at that.'

'If he identifies the actress beyond any doubt, we could arrange a press conference for this afternoon.'

'Pardon me?' Böhm looked as if Rath had just made an indecent proposal. 'Get that thought out of your head, and that goes for everyone in this room. I don't want to read anything about this case in the press for the time being! Another dead actress, the second inside a week! It's possible that the press will uncover more connections.'

'But the two fatalities have nothing to do with each other,' Lange objected. 'Nothing at all, except that they're both actresses.'

'The hacks aren't interested in that,' Böhm said, and Lange blushed. 'No press conference, no press release, and I don't want anyone in this room leaking anything. Not until we have closed the Franck file and can say to Berliners that there is *no* serial killer at large in their city.'

Everyone fell silent, examining their shoes or fingernails.

'I've something to add, Sir!' Rath ventured, despite Böhm's ill temper.

'What is it?'

'I've been able to trace a witness, the taxi driver who picked up Vivian

Franck when she left her flat with a few suitcases. That was . . .' Rath leafed through his notebook even though he knew the date by heart, '. . . on the eighth of February.'

'How did you find all that out so quickly?' Böhm sounded suspicious.

'Just a few calls, Sir. The concierge in Franck's block of flats, then the taxi office. Herr Oppenberg gave me the . . .'

'Who?'

'Manfred Oppenberg. Vivian Franck's producer, whom I visited in order to . . .'

'Isn't that the man we've already questioned as part of the Winter case? Felix Krempin's former employer, who claims to know nothing?'

'That's him. He was kind enough to give me the telephone numbers . . .'

'You shouldn't be associating with people who are possible suspects in a murder enquiry!' Böhm barked.

'Oppenberg is suspected of murder?'

'He certainly isn't out of the woods if his former employee has committed murder. As for the Vivian Franck case, he's a suspect just like anyone else connected to the deceased. That goes without saying, even if you have clearly made friends with him already. If you carry on like this, I'll have you withdrawn from the case on the grounds of bias.'

'I haven't made friends with him, I've been investigating! When I have a piece of information, I pursue it, instead of wedging it between two folders and letting it go mouldy!'

Henning and Lange hunched even further over their files. Christel Temme wrote something on her pad, although no one was dictating. For a moment the only sound was the scratching of her pen. Böhm took a deep breath.

'Don't get ahead of yourself, young man!' he said. 'I'm still the one who assigns the tasks! Where would we be if everyone simply worked for themselves? Investigative work has to be co-ordinated, and *that* is precisely what you still have to learn. How to work with other people!'

Rath had to let a lot of air out of his lungs before continuing. 'What task have you assigned me then, Sir?' he asked.

'You're coming with me to the morgue,' Böhm decided. 'That way you won't get any stupid ideas. You might as well postpone lunch. Better to see Dr Schwartz on an empty stomach.'

Damn it! 'I can't. I have to take care of Herr Ziehlke. He's arriving at the station any minute.'

'Who?' the DCI barked.

'Friedhelm Ziehlke. The taxi driver I was speaking about just now.'

Böhm glanced at his watch and waved him away. 'Herr Lange can deal with that. You're coming with me!'

Dr Schwartz had worked quickly, eager to be rid of bodies like Vivian Franck's. It was still lying there, however, when Rath and Böhm entered the autopsy room in the cellar of the morgue. Schwartz was washing his hands when they arrived, an activity he engaged in with unusual frequency. He greeted his visitors with a brief nod in the mirror.

'Well I never,' he said, without turning around, 'Messrs Böhm and Rath. You've been inseparable lately!'

Böhm gave an involuntary grunt.

'Good that you could come so quickly,' Schwarz continued, greeting the police officers with a freshly washed handshake, before leading them to the marble table. Rath couldn't help but swallow when he saw what death had done to such a beautiful woman. Her face looked more dead than at the crime scene, not that it fazed the doctor. 'Should we get something to eat afterwards?' he asked.

'No time,' Böhm said, 'there's someone coming to identify the corpse at three. So, whenever you're ready.'

'In short, this is one of the strangest corpses you've ever entrusted me.' Schwartz produced a pencil and pointed towards the dead face. 'She was heavily made up. We had to give her a good wash. Don't worry: ED took a few samples of the make-up beforehand. Without wishing to pre-empt Kronberg, I'd say theatre make-up, or rather, film make-up. She was done up for a shoot.'

There wasn't much left of it now. Vivian Franck's face looked like most four-week-old corpses, pale and blotchy, a little deformed in places, finger-nails yellow and a little too long.

'And now we come to the strangest part.' Schwartz pointed his pencil towards her throat. 'Her film career was finished before she died. Acting's a tough job without vocal cords, I should think.'

'Pardon me?' Böhm said.

'Someone cut out her vocal cords.'

'And that's how she died?'

Schwartz shook his head. 'You don't die from having your vocal cords cut. Though you are right about one thing: this was done to her ante-mortem. I took a look at the incision under the microscope. It must have been carried out shortly before she died.'

'Her death having being caused by?' Böhm asked.

'That question isn't always so easy to answer, my dear Böhm; and some-times it can't be answered at all.' Schwartz could make even Böhm seem like an impertinent student.

'I wonder what the meaning of it all is,' Böhm said. 'Why maim a per-son like this?'

'Torture?' Rath ventured, receiving two disapproving glances.

Schwartz shook his head. 'That doesn't fit. It's as painful as having ton-sillitis, perhaps less so. If it wasn't an accident during an operation—and complete removal would seem to go against that—then the person who did this meant to humiliate her, I think. Or to prevent her from crying out.'

'Did she suffer a painful death?' Rath asked, reintroducing the subject a little more diplomatically than Böhm.

'No idea.'

'What do you mean, no idea?' Böhm asked. 'That you still don't know?'

'I found an injection site in her skin, probably from a hypodermic needle. It must have been administered shortly before she died.'

'And?'

Schwartz shrugged. 'So far we have found no sign whatsoever of poi-son,' he said. 'If that remains the case, I would say that she died a natural death. Perhaps she just couldn't bear no longer having a voice.'

'Don't forget drugs,' Rath said. 'Perhaps that's what she died of.'

'For me they come under poison, no need to mention them specifically.'

Böhm shook his head thoughtfully. 'Does that mean what we have here might not even be murder?'

Schwartz shrugged. 'Or a very skilful one.'

31

The pathologist disappeared for a late lunch while Rath waited for Oppenberg with Böhm and Schwartz's assistant. He appeared promptly at three, as subdued as Rath had ever seen him. The body had been covered; all the assistant had to do was expose the head and show Oppenberg the pale, blotchy face. A brief nod and he signed. His expression was inscrutable but his silence said everything.

Rath hated moments like these. What could be worse than identifying the body of someone close to you? Perhaps standing alongside and having to watch. He always felt strangely responsible. As once upon a time he had been.

The corpse of a madman had lain on an autopsy table, his life ended by a bullet from Rath's service revolver. He would never forget the stony face of the father who had come to identify the body: Alexander LeClerk, one of the most important newspaper publishers in Cologne. Nor would he forget the gaze that bore through him like the beam of an X-ray, much less the devastating press campaign that followed, that changed his life and forced him to relocate to Berlin.

Still, there was no reproach in Oppenberg's gaze, just silent humility, the acceptance of one's powerlessness against the raging of arbitrary, meaningless fate. There was something else in those eyes though: deep sorrow. Oppenberg seemed to have genuinely loved Vivian Franck. She wasn't just an investment that had to pay off, as Betty Winter appeared to have been for Heinrich Bellmann.

Rath noticed that Böhm was eyeing Oppenberg suspiciously. He had a few questions still to ask. 'Did Fräulein Franck have any problems with her voice?'

'Not at all!' Oppenberg seemed surprised. His gaze flitted briefly to Rath, before realighting on Böhm. 'There was scarcely a film actress of her generation more predestined for sound film than Vivian Franck!'

'Then she didn't undergo a procedure recently on her vocal cords . . .'

'Not that I'm aware of. Why should she have?'

'Shortly before her death, her vocal cords must have been cut out,' Böhm said. 'Can you explain how that happened?'

'Her vocal cords were removed?' Oppenberg's calm voice was mixed with horror. Again his gaze darted towards Rath.

Böhm nodded. 'A failed operation would be one explanation. Against that is the fact that they weren't simply cut, but completely removed. Besides, her doctor knows nothing about it.'

'Did they . . . did they torture her?'

'Hard to say, but no, she probably wasn't in pain.'

'What does that matter if they took her voice away? Don't you think that's torture enough for an actress?' Suddenly Oppenberg was shouting, 'That crook! What devil did Bellmann unleash on her, poor girl?'

Not so clumsy after all, the bulldog: he had actually managed to break down the producer's reserve. For a moment Rath feared Oppenberg might forget himself and reveal his special relationship to Gereon Rath.

'Those are some serious accusations you're making,' Böhm said. 'Do you have any basis for them?'

'You only have to read the newspaper to know that he'll use any means he can to destroy me.'

'Bellmann at least makes a case for your smuggling a saboteur onto his shoot,' and with that Böhm had arrived at the Winter case and pushed Oppenberg into a corner.

Oppenberg cast Rath another brief glance, but soon had himself back under control.

'I can make just as strong a case for Bellmann having abducted my lead actress in order to sabotage *my* shoot. She's been missing for weeks!' He had decided to go on the attack. 'Before you adopt the untenable assumptions of my rival, you could ask your colleagues from Missing Persons why they did nothing. Perhaps Vivian would still be alive if they had begun their search in good time!'

'You think your actress was abducted?'

'She never set out on the holiday she'd planned. Instead of going to the train station three weeks ago there was a stranger waiting for her, in Wilmersdorf somewhere. No doubt that's where you found the corpse too.'

Oppenberg had said too much; Rath had no choice but to intervene. 'Why didn't you tell us all that just now, Herr Oppenberg?'

The producer played along. 'Quite simple,' he said. 'You never asked me.'

'But *I'm* asking you now,' Böhm said. 'How do you know all this?'

'I engaged the services of a private investigator, since your colleagues in Missing Persons did nothing.'

Rath began to sweat.

'You put a watch on your lover because you were jealous?' Böhm was really going for it now. 'Caught her unawares and then killed her?'

Oppenberg shook his head. 'Stop talking nonsense! If I really was the type of man who kills out of jealousy, then I might have killed her lover, but not Vivian. You're on the wrong track, my good man, I'm not about to kill my best actress.'

Böhm backed down. The missing vocal cords, if they were indeed the work of the killer, didn't tally with a murder committed out of jealousy. He had wanted to break down Oppenberg's reserve, and he had managed. 'You understand that you must continue to remain at our disposal,' Böhm said.

'I will support you in any way I can, if you and your young colleague just find Vivian's killer. What kind of devil does something like that? Taking an actress's voice?'

Böhm shrugged. 'If we knew that we'd have our killer.'

The meeting with Oppenberg had been relatively painless, but Rath was relieved when they could finally leave the morgue, having already said good-bye to Oppenberg.

Böhm seemed positively cheerful as he opened the door to Hannoversche Strasse, and they emerged from that unprepossessing brick building that housed more of the dead than living. 'I don't mean to boast,' he said, 'but did you see how much you can learn from just a brief conversation? The same witness *you* interviewed three or four hours ago, when he said no more about this private investigator than he did about the stranger in Wilmersdorf.'

'What are you trying to say?'

'Don't be offended, Inspector!' Böhm looked Rath in the eye. 'That wasn't meant as a criticism of your interrogation methods, but you should understand that your colleagues can get results too. Even your superiors.'

Only now, in the fresh air, did Rath realise how hungry he was. It was almost four o'clock.

Böhm seemed to read his mind. 'We won't get anything in the canteen now,' he said. 'We'll make a stop at Aschinger. My treat.'

Rath was speechless. What had he done to deserve this? Was it a thank-you for allowing Böhm to dispense advice without interruption? Less than quarter of an hour later, they were sitting together at a dimly lit corner table, breathing in the fug of beer and studying the menu.

'Try the rump steak,' the DCI said cheerfully. 'With chips. I can recommend it.'

Rath decided to do his unexpectedly jovial boss a favour and ordered the steak, although he felt more like schnitzel. They even allowed themselves a glass of beer, on duty at that! The man wasn't nearly as Prussian as he looked. Böhm raised his glass. '*Zum Wohl*,' he said, and drank. Rath did likewise. If anyone from A Division could see them now: raising a glass to each other over a beer!

Böhm set his glass down and for a time there was an awkward silence before he cleared his throat and began to speak. 'Time we had a little heart-to-heart, Rath,' he said. 'I want to be open with you. I don't like the way you operate and never have, but you are part of my division and that means we have to get along.' The waiter brought the food and Böhm tucked the serviette into his collar. 'Bon appétit.'

'Thank you for inviting me,' Rath said.

He was confused. What did Böhm want from him? *Time we had a little heart-to-heart.*

For a while they ate in silence. Eventually Böhm took up the thread again. 'If we are to get along with one another you need to change certain aspects of your behaviour.'

'I don't know what you . . .'

'I am prepared to show some goodwill!'

'But I . . .'

'But you need to do something too! It's time to show you are part of this police force. Start doing as you're told. Work with and not against your colleagues. And above all,' he said, 'play with an open hand!'

'Sir . . .'

'Do I make myself clear?'

'I'd like . . .'

'Have I made myself clear?'

'Yes, Sir.'

'Good.' Böhm pushed his plate to the side. 'Stick to what I've told you and we'll . . . well, perhaps we won't be friends exactly, but we'll get along just fine.'

Rath nodded silently. The bulldog was actually offering him a peace pipe. It must have been Gennat's idea; there was no other way to explain this discussion, which in reality had been more of an address.

Böhm waved the waiter over and asked for the bill.

Outside they were greeted by all the noise and chaos Alexanderplatz had to offer at four in the afternoon. On the other side of the road, in front of the station, a paper boy was proclaiming the day's news. 'Second actress dead! Second actress dead! Murderer strikes again!'

Böhm marched silently over, fished a few coins from his pocket and pressed them into the boy's hand, taking a *B.Z.* from the pile in return. The headline was even worse.

ANOTHER DEAD ACTRESS! IS THERE A SERIAL KILLER ON THE LOOSE IN BERLIN?

Böhm walked on without looking up from his newspaper. He came to a halt at the tram stop and slumped onto a bench. A quick sidelong glance at Rath was enough to suggest that he had a good idea whom to thank for this unwanted media coverage. Rath had had his suspicions the moment he heard the paper boy, and when he saw which newspaper it was he also knew who had written the article. Stefan Fink. He sat next to Böhm and tried to catch a glimpse.

The front page featured a photo of Vivian Franck in all her glory. Alongside it, a little smaller, was Felix Krempin's mugshot and below it, smaller still, an up-to-date photo showing the dilapidated façade of the Luxor cinema. The murder wagon was still parked outside, which could only mean that Strelow had alarmed the press while Böhm was still in the cinema. No wonder the bulldog was riled.

The cinema owner was of the same mind as Heinrich Bellmann: headlines at all costs. Media coverage was bound to have a positive effect on business one way or another.

Strelow had provided the information readily, even the meagre details Dr Schwartz had passed on to the DCI in the cinema. Böhm should never have spoken to the pathologist in the presence of the two civilians, despite how little Schwartz had given away. Rath felt a certain sense of satisfaction now that Böhm knew how it felt to be at the mercy of these ink-slingers.

The article Stefan Fink had written was as bad as it could get, above all on account of that one term: serial killer.

It was the *one* phrase Böhm had wanted to avoid. The fact that it was a completely far-fetched theory, that there was neither any evidence of a sexual crime, nor any similarity between the victims' causes of death, didn't matter to the journalist. The victims were actresses and Krempin had known both, so that had to be enough. The hunt for the fugitive would now take on hysterical proportions.

Still, perhaps it would help them finally capture the man and resolve the Winter case. Gennat's reports on the infamous Düsseldorf murders had stated that the series of murders, but above all the press reports, had triggered fully-fledged *psychoses* amongst elements of the population.

When Rath and Böhm returned to the Castle the article was the only topic of conversation and, for the time being, no one was interested in the results of the autopsy. *B.Z. am Mittag* was the only paper that had carried the story, but it was only a matter of time before the others would be singing in chorus, first the evening editions, with the rest joining in tomorrow morning.

In fact, the first journalists had called when Rath and Böhm were on their way to the morgue, meaning that copies of *B.Z.* had already reached the editorial offices of its rivals still damp with printer's ink. Lange and Henning had gamely held the fort, pleading ignorance to all callers. Not that it would be of much use; the story was simply too juicy not to be written. Besides, there was still Strelow to provide ready information. Böhm tried to reach the new leaseholder of the Luxor Cinema, but was put off by a secretary who had the riot act read to her in return.

The next few days would be spent fielding calls and issuing denials. Rath wondered if he should exploit his connection to Weinert so that there would be at least one press voice to query the serial killer line.

Fink's headline had thrown Böhm completely off course. He seemed all at sea as Lange reported on his conversation with the taxi driver, and Henning on the search of the Franck apartment. Fortunately, Christel Temme was taking everything down, her pen scratching across the pad at the merest cough or slip of the tongue. Only when he was reporting on the results from the morgue did Böhm appear a little more focused. He included Oppenberg's latest statements, which partially corresponded to those of the taxi driver.

'We need this private investigator,' he said. 'Rath, see if you can squeeze whatever information he gave Oppenberg out of him.' Then he allocated the remainder of the tasks for the next few days, once again urging his men not to provide any more information to the press. 'Best of all, say nothing.'

Rath very much doubted whether that was the best method, but it was Böhm who had the final say—which was more or less what he had explained at Aschinger. In any case, one day spent with Rath seemed to have been enough for him. He had assigned Rath a new partner: Andreas Lange. Together with the assistant detective Rath was to investigate the stranger whom Vivian Franck had gone so willingly to—and who was most likely her killer, or at least the man who had led her to him.

In the corridor, Lange took him to one side. 'Sir, could I speak to you privately?'

'Let's go into my office,' said Rath, wondering what he had on his mind. Erika Voss had already finished for the evening so they could leave the connecting door open. Rath sat at his desk and offered Lange Gräf's chair. 'So,' he said. 'What can I do for you?'

'Well . . . this Ziehlke . . . the taxi driver . . . he told me you'd already questioned him . . .'

'I telephoned him this morning.'

'He says he spoke to an Inspector Rath a few days ago. He even had lunch with him on one occasion.'

'He says that?'

'Yes, that's what he says.'

'Fine. I'll tell you something now in confidence. And you're not to snitch on me to Böhm.'

'As long as you haven't killed anyone,' Lange said.

'I took on a private assignment without running it by our bosses first.'

'Then you're the private investigator Böhm just spoke about?'

'A favour to a friend, not for money.'

'I don't want to tell you what to do, Sir, but in your position, I'd inform the person leading the investigation. Your client is a murder suspect. That's a conflict of interest.'

'I have my reasons,' Rath said. 'First: I was tasked with finding Vivian Franck, and now we've found her. Second: I don't want to be kicked off another investigation team for a matter that's long since been resolved. That would be the second time inside of a week and my fragile personality couldn't cope with it.'

'Like I said, I don't want to tell you what to do. But if the matter's exposed it will be on *your* head, not mine.' Lange looked serious. 'I won't . . . snitch . . . on you. I don't know a thing.'

'On that note,' Rath said, stretching out a hand, 'here's to a successful partnership.'

Bahnhof Zoo was busy at this time of day. There was a new baggage porter behind the left luggage counter, a taciturn Prussian, unlike the previous joker. Rath showed his badge. 'We're here to collect Vivian Franck's luggage.'

The man had read about the actress's death in the papers.

'How did you know we'd find her bags here?' Lange asked once he had disappeared.

'The taxi driver,' Rath said, and Lange nodded.

The baggage porter returned, wheeling two large suitcases and a travel bag and placing them in front of Rath and Lange on the floor. They packed everything onto a luggage trolley and wheeled it to Rath's Buick, where they struggled to fit it all in. They could only manage the heaviest suitcase as a pair, wedging the second in the dickey seat, while Lange was forced to take the travel bag on his lap. Rath could imagine how Friedhelm Ziehlke must have cursed that day.

It was even more of an effort dragging the luggage upstairs once they reached the Castle. ED was based a floor above A Division. Kronberg's men were still working when they pushed the heavy luggage through the door. 'What's all this?' Kronberg asked.

'Items of luggage,' Rath said, short of breath. 'The last Vivian Franck ever checked in.'

Kronberg called two forensic officers over. 'Can you get it open, Schmidthaber?' he asked the younger of the pair. The man nodded. 'Good, then go and fetch your tools. Before that let's see if we can secure any fingerprints. Perhaps we'll be in luck.'

They only found a few prints, and Rath doubted whether they would be much use after all those weeks moving back and forth in left luggage. At length Schmidthaber, the key expert, began fiddling with the locks with a special bunch of skeleton keys. It didn't take him long.

There was nothing unusual about Vivian Franck's luggage—if you discounted the profusion of high-quality underwear that Kronberg's officers had a wonderful time noting down. Apart from that, the outfits were suitable for many types of occasion and weather conditions, not just for snow in the mountains. Rath was astonished at how many smart evening dresses Vivian Franck owned. She hadn't packed them for Davos, more likely for Hollywood. They didn't find any drugs. Having seen enough, Rath took his leave.

'Take a close look,' he said in the doorway, 'perhaps you'll find something. And no matter what, make sure you let DCI Böhm know.'

It was already late when he arrived home, having driven Lange back to Schönhauser Allee. His mailbox was overflowing. He hadn't opened it since Sunday, and there were a number of bills, as well as a letter from his parents. As he was leafing through the pile a postcard fell to the floor, its picture showing Cologne Cathedral.

Rath picked up the card and turned it over. When he saw who had written it, he read it then and there.

Many happy returns, Sir!
    Attached a little slice of home for life in the Far East.
    I hope you're looking after yourself.

We missed you at Carnival, just as we did last year.

I'd never have thought it possible, but without you it's only half as much fun.

One of these days, if my schedule allows, I'm going to catch a train and brave the wrong side of the Rhine to visit you Mongols in the East.

Don't say I haven't warned you!

Your friend
Paul

Rath grinned. Paul must have written the card in the aftermath of Rosenmontag. Was he serious about coming to Berlin? Until now no one from Cologne had visited save for his father and Mayor Adenauer.

He opened the door, went into the living room with the pile of letters and put on a record. Once he had removed his hat and coat, he made himself comfortable and looked through the rest of the post.

He put the bills to one side and opened the letter from Cologne. Father was just as thrifty as he had been during the war. From the envelope fell not just a birthday card written in his mother's fine hand, but a typewritten list of names. Adenauer's list of secret holders. The possible blackmailer—or an accomplice. After all that, he hadn't managed to get out to Ford today to collect the list from Personnel. It was too late now, but tomorrow he could set off a little earlier and make a detour via Moabit.

He skimmed the list of names from Cologne. None meant anything to him. There was no Bahlke or any others that he recognised. It was no good, he needed the Ford list to compare. The telephone rang. It was Gräf. 'Congratulations on getting your own case,' he said.

'Thanks. But it feels more like Böhm is passing the buck.' There wasn't much else to say. They still hadn't found Krempin and the *B.Z.* headline had thrown a spanner in the works for the Winter team as well. Fink's serial killer theory had produced another half dozen false leads. 'Without Krempin, we won't get anywhere,' Gräf concluded. 'And we're not getting anything out of this Oppenberg either.'

'I don't think he has anything to do with the death of Betty Winter.'

'You'll admit it's strange that one of his actresses has copped it. Bellmann taking revenge?'

'Franck was already dead while Winter was still romping around her film sets.'

'Hmm. The other way around then?'

'Oppenberg only heard today that his actress was dead. He reckons Bellmann's behind it. I think the two of them are good at making accusations against one another and creating suspicion.'

Rath hung up, gazing at the black telephone for a long time before picking up the receiver again. He had been putting off making this call, but it had to be today. Now it was officially his case, why shouldn't he make use of a few unofficial channels? He hadn't dialled the number that wasn't in any telephone book for a long time. One ring was all it took.

'Yes,' said a deep voice.

Rath had never heard the man say a word, but felt almost certain he was speaking to Marlow's Chinaman.

'Rath here,' he said, before clearing his throat. 'I need to speak to Herr Marlow.'

'He's busy. What's it about?'

'I can only discuss that with Herr Marlow himself.'

'Give me your number. We'll call back.'

It really was as easy as that. Rath was astonished, thinking back to the first time he had tried to make contact with Berlin's craftiest gangster. He placed the telephone on the living room table and stood up to turn the record: Coleman Hawkins. The telephone rang before the piece was over.

'That was quick!'

A cough. 'Inspector Rath?'

That wasn't Marlow!

The music had ceased, and the needle kept striking the end of the groove, making a crackling sound. All of a sudden, Rath was wide awake. 'Herr Krempin? Good of you to call. Have you thought about what I said?'

'If you're asking me to hand myself in, then I'm hanging up.' Clearly he had seen the headlines.

'*You* called *me*,' Rath said. 'I'm just wondering why.'

'Because I wanted to speak to you.'

'Why me? I'm one of the people chasing you.'

'But the only one who doesn't think I'm a killer.'

It sounded as if Oppenberg had spoken to him. 'It's good to know you trust me but, as a police officer, I can only advise that you give yourself up. Tell us what you know, and the truth will come out.'

Krempin laughed bitterly down the line. 'I don't think you're quite as naïve as you sound, Inspector. If I come to the station, they'll pounce on me: the press, the whole public. Do you seriously think the police can still conduct an impartial investigation? They're not even doing it now! They're hunting me, and that's all.'

'And you mean to confide in one of your pursuers?'

'I want you to know what happened in the studio the day Betty Winter died. Then you'll know that I don't have her on my conscience.'

'Then tell your story, perhaps it will help me after all.'

'Not on the telephone. We have to meet.'

'Aren't you worried that I'll have our meeting point surrounded by a hundred officers?'

'If you do that you'll never hear from me again. You won't get me that easily.'

'I'm not about to give you up. But what do you suppose is going to happen? You tell me your version of events and everything will be well and good?'

'You'll find Betty's killer, and people will stop hunting me.'

'I'm honoured by your trust but what if I don't? How long are you planning to hide then? I can't help you on my own. It would be good if someone else . . .'

'You're the only officer I'll speak to.'

'I'm talking about a journalist.'

Rath thought he might hang up. 'You're not serious,' he said.

'You can only fight public opinion with published opinion. I'm friends with a newspaper reporter who will listen to you. He's one hundred percent reliable. Then it'll be your version of events in the paper. How does that sound?'

This time the silence lasted a little longer. 'If you try and pull a fast one, this is the last time we speak.'

'Don't worry, I won't risk it.' Rath took a pencil from his jacket and rummaged for a piece of paper. 'So, where do you want to meet? An isolated clearing in Tegel Forest, no doubt.'

'Not a clearing. The Funkturm. In the restaurant. Bring your journalist, but no one else. Tomorrow at one.'

'I'll be there,' Rath said. 'How will I recognise you? I'm sure you look different from your mugshots.'

'I'll recognise you. Just make sure you're on time.'

32

Friday 7th March 1930

The sound didn't surprise him; he had set his alarm for earlier than usual. But it wasn't his alarm, it was the telephone! Rath switched on the light and glanced at the time: just before five. He rolled out of bed and walked barefoot across the cold floor into the living room. The telephone rang stubbornly. It could only be the Castle. Please, he thought, not another corpse.

'Rath,' he said, trying to sound awake, ready for Böhm's voice, or some colleague on standby duty.

'The boss can speak to you now,' said a deep, sonorous voice. Marlow's Chinaman.

Rath was immediately awake. 'Thank you,' he mumbled.

'Inspector!' Rath recognised the voice of Johann Marlow despite not having heard it in over a year. 'Long time, no see. Except for in the papers, of course. Good that you haven't forgotten an old friend.'

'Let's say business associate. Nice of you to call back. I had forgotten that you don't go to bed until this time.'

Marlow laughed. 'You're right, I was just finishing when I saw you on my call list. Now I'm curious as to why you're back in touch after such a long time.'

'I have a favour to ask.'

'Anytime. I have already offered you a small token of my appreciation, but I realise that I am still in your debt.'

The five thousand marks in a brown envelope, which Rath had found in his mailbox last September. He had guessed where the money was from, but spent it all the same. What else was he supposed to do? Drive out east and stuff it back in Marlow's jacket pocket?

'It concerns Vivian Franck,' Rath said, outlining the case before telling Marlow what hadn't been in the paper, above all the suspicion that someone from the underworld might have kidnapped and tortured the actress on somebody else's behalf. The removal of the vocal cords as a message to Oppenberg: we have destroyed your great sound film hope.

'You want me to ask around, see if anyone has been doing these vile things in exchange for cash?' Marlow asked.

'If that someone also has a key to the Luxor Cinema in Wilmersdorf, then we have a firm lead.'

'I know a few people who'll open just about any door for you without having the right key; but no one who'd take out someone's vocal cords. For your sake, I'll look into it. Can we meet tomorrow evening?'

'I have a date.'

'Come to the Plaza, I'll get you tickets. Surely your companion will be able to spare you for five minutes. Half past nine, in the foyer, during the interval.'

After speaking to Marlow he hadn't gone back to bed, but taken breakfast and set off. It was still dark enough for headlights, and it was a long drive out to Westhafen. Although he wasn't happy to be back in touch with the gangster boss, Marlow was the best person to ask for information about the underworld. He had links to several of the Ringvereine, and was just as well, if not better, connected to the most important divisions at police headquarters.

Passing through Moabit, Rath stopped in Spenerstrasse again. On the other side of the road, behind the windows of her flat, a light was already on. She was probably having breakfast with Greta. With Greta rather than somebody else, he hoped. His heart was devoured by a jealousy so strong he had to light a cigarette to calm himself before continuing on his way. Ten minutes later he was rolling across Westhafenstrasse towards the harbour.

The clock tower by the admin building showed quarter to eight, but the harbour was already humming with activity, the Ford plant too. Even at this hour a few unemployed men were loitering hopefully outside the entrance. He parked the Buick directly under the Ford advertising hoarding.

Goatee Beard from Personnel was unpacking his briefcase when Rath entered the office. 'Weren't you supposed to come by yesterday?' the man grumbled, passing several pages of names across the table. 'I needn't have hurried.'

'More haste, less speed,' Rath said.

He skimmed the lists in the car: over two hundred names complete with address and date of birth, details of training and start date. There were huge numbers of unskilled workers engaged here. No wonder there were queues of unemployed outside. Only four names appeared on both these and the Adenauer list: two Müllers, a Schröder and a Krüger. However, there was only one Anton. Anton Schmieder, trained car mechanic, had been with Ford for two years. It had to be the red-haired assembly worker whom Bahlke had called Toni. Why would a man like that leave his workplace on the spur of the moment? Perhaps after hearing that a police officer was speaking to the foreman? Rath noted the address.

He arrived at the morning briefing at nine sharp, ahead of Lange. Vivian Franck's luggage was on the podium in front of the blackboard, which Böhm sometimes used to make notes or scrawl arrows and geometric figures that no one understood. He had laid out the contents of the suitcases on a long line of tables and was talking quietly to Kronberg. When he stepped onto the lectern, conversation in the room gradually ceased. At the last moment Lange scurried through the door, gazing around searchingly before sitting next to Rath.

Böhm praised the newcomer for having found the luggage together with Rath. Although Lange was keeping a low profile, the DCI probably thought the whole thing had been his idea, since the assistant detective had been the one to interrogate the taxi driver.

The luggage hadn't yielded any significant insights, except that Vivian Franck must have had both good taste and a lot of money. Böhm was hoping for more from the list of names provided by the broker, which contained all those who possessed a key to the Luxor Cinema.

Nor had the bulldog forgotten the task he had assigned to Rath. 'Have you found that private detective yet?'

'I was going to look into it today,' Rath lied, casting a sidelong glance at Lange, who didn't bat an eyelash.

Surprisingly, the Winter team, which hadn't made any progress for days, had made a little headway: Gräf and his squad had taken up Krempin's trail again in Grunewald, in whose allotments the previous search had been concentrated. Gräf and Czerwinski had found cigarette butts in an abandoned summer house, the same kind Rath had uncovered in the empty flat on Guerickestrasse.

Unfortunately, Krempin was already gone by the time the police got there. The man never seemed to stay in the one place for any length of time. Would he be at the Funkturm this lunchtime? Rath still wasn't entirely sure, but he had asked Weinert to come along and the journalist had needed no second invitation. Rath could barely concentrate on the briefing. He hadn't told anyone about the meeting save for Weinert, and he intended to keep his word.

The morning passed uneventfully. At least Böhm hadn't assigned them any of the key owners. He and Lange were to continue looking into the stranger at Wilmersdorf.

The police sketch artist was already waiting in the office when they emerged from the briefing. Erika Voss was making him coffee and seemed very interested in the man's artistic skills.

'What sort of thing do you usually paint?'

'I draw,' the man said. 'Mostly in the courtroom, rather than for the police.'

'Do you do it for pleasure too?'

'Only to pass the time.'

'What do you paint then?'

'I draw. Cityscapes or street scenes mostly. Sketching from life.'

'I see,' Erika Voss said, pouring hot water into the filter. Perhaps cityscapes weren't her thing.

'The witness should be here any moment,' Rath said, hanging up his hat and coat. 'Have you drawn a portrait from your imagination before? From another person's testimony?'

'It can work,' the sketch artist said. 'It depends on how good your witness is at describing things.'

Friedhelm Ziehlke provided a clear answer when he arrived shortly afterwards. The sketch artist had to keep pressing him every five seconds, aided by Lange, who tried again and again to jog his memory. Ziehlke wasn't even sure about the man's hair colour, remembering only that it was 'kind of dark'. After quarter of an hour, the sketch artist had discarded five sheets of paper.

Rath doubted whether they would be able to identify the stranger from Wilmersdorf using this method, but at least it provided a pretext to keep Lange in the office. Rath took him to one side.

'You hold the fort until old Zille here is finished,' he said. 'I'll use the time to head out to Wilmersdorf. Perhaps something will occur to me there.' Lange nodded and gave a forced smile, saying nothing. 'Give the taxi driver until one. If we don't have anything half-decent by then, send him home, and go and get something to eat with the artist and Fräulein Voss.'

There was still more than an hour until his meeting. Before making for the car, Rath looked for a free telephone booth at Alex.

Charly wasn't home, only her friend Greta. If he had got her on the line, he might have tried to postpone, but he couldn't call off like this, not through another person and over the telephone. He asked Greta to tell Charly that he would pick her up at half past seven.

Next he called the editorial office and asked for Weinert. 'I can give you a ride in half an hour,' he said. 'That way, at least we'll be on time. The last thing we want is to get stuck in traffic.'

Rath used the time to eat a little something at Aschinger before driving to Kochstrasse. Weinert was waiting outside the editorial building, a black umbrella wedged under his arm, seeming more nervous than usual.

They still had quarter of an hour when Rath parked the Buick in Masurenallee. It was quiet at the base of the Funkturm. There was no trade fair taking place, and the weather wasn't exactly enticing. Weinert let Rath under his umbrella when it began to drizzle. They had to pay entry before entering the lift, just like everywhere in this city where there were too many tourists, and by five to one had managed to locate a window seat in the Funkturm restaurant. The waiter looked a little peeved when Rath only ordered a glass of Selters and Weinert a coffee.

'We're waiting for someone,' Rath explained when the drinks came. Not that it was going to be a lavish midday meal, but the waiter didn't have to know that.

What would Krempin tell them, and would he even come? Rath hadn't told a soul about the meeting, with the exception of Weinert. Any one of his colleagues would have used the opportunity to intervene, and no doubt that was what Krempin meant to find out. The man was here somewhere checking the lie of the land; indeed, had probably been doing so for quite some time, making sure that Rath and Weinert really were on their own.

They sat at the table in silence, sipping their drinks. Rath lit an Overstolz. He was growing impatient. They had been sitting for ten minutes now. Had Krempin got cold feet, or had he taken some harmless passers-by for police officers and fled?

Outside, the rain fell in fine droplets over the roof edge and into the depths below. The weather wasn't getting any better, but he could still just about make out the spire of Charlottenburg Town Hall. The view didn't extend any further over the sea of houses, which disappeared into the dull haze.

A noise made him start. A loud bang, directly above their table. As if a large fist had struck the roof of the restaurant. The bang was followed by a clatter, scraping noises, as if something was sliding across the roof, and for a moment Rath's heart stood still. For a fraction of a second he was gazing straight into Felix Krempin's wide-open eyes on the other side of the window pane!

A dream, was his first thought.

Not a dream! He had really seen it. He lunged forward, his chair crashing to the ground. Weinert gazed at him in astonishment and a woman issued a brief, sharp cry. Rath turned and looked into horrified faces. Everyone had stopped what they were doing and stood rooted to the spot.

The waiter's voice cut through the silence. 'My God, somebody just jumped!'

Rath lay on the wide balustrade so that he could see down as far as possible through the sloping pane. There *was* someone lying there. The first onlookers were cautiously approaching the lifeless corpse on the exhibition grounds below. Rath looked at Weinert and the pair dashed to the lift which, predictably enough, wasn't on the restaurant floor. A queue had already formed outside the doors.

'This could take forever,' Weinert said. They took the stairs at full speed, but it was still some time before they reached the bottom.

A handful of onlookers had formed an uneven circle around the body and were keeping a respectful distance, attracted and repelled in equal measure by the shattered corpse. Rath and Weinert pushed towards the front, and Rath recognised the tilted face of the dead man instantly. He gave Weinert a nod, and the journalist understood.

'Weinert, *Tageblatt*,' he said, approaching the bystanders with his pad at the ready. Instinctively, they stood back. 'Did anyone see how it happened?'

A few people understood the question as an invitation to leave, but a stocky man in a grey uniform replied. Rath recognised the Cerberus to whom they had paid their entry fee.

'He'll have jumped, won't he? Wouldn't be the first! About time they stopped letting 'em up on the viewing platform, or built a high railing so they can't climb over.'

Rath examined the corpse. It was Krempin, no doubt about it, heavily made up with his hair bleached light blond and his nose lengthened with a piece of wax. Apart from that, he was wearing a false moustache, which had come loose on impact and was now hanging by a shred. His face was unscathed save for a graze on the right cheek, but his unnaturally contorted limbs were a nasty sight. A pool of blood was growing under the body. Rath felt his carotid artery all the same.

Nothing, the man was dead.

A thought flashed through Rath's mind. Better if your colleagues don't find you here. 'I need to get out of here,' he said to Weinert. 'You call the police.'

Weinert nodded and Rath took his leave. In the meantime, the lift must have reached the bottom floor, as a whole load of people he recognised from the restaurant came towards him. Even the lift attendant had left his post. Rath gazed up at the steel framework of the Funkturm. The viewing platform, from which Krempin must have plunged first onto the restaurant roof and then onto the surface of the courtyard, was easily a hundred and fifty metres. Seeing the abandoned lift Rath climbed in and, this time, went past the restaurant to the top.

He couldn't believe that Krempin had jumped. Someone must have pushed him. Betty Winter's killer, hoping to prevent Krempin from incriminating him, or from helping the police pick up his trail. But how did he know about their meeting?

Surely Krempin hadn't confided in him. Or perhaps he had? Had the person whom Felix Krempin trusted most turned out to be his killer? The face of Manfred Oppenberg flashed through Rath's mind.

The glazed viewing platform was deserted when he emerged from the lift. To get to the highest point he needed to climb another set of stairs. Suddenly he was standing in the open air.

Although it was no longer raining, there was a strong wind. Definitely not the weather for observation platforms. The parapet was fairly high, but it would be easy enough to scale, or to pull someone's legs from underneath them and throw them over.

He leaned over the railing and gazed below. Krempin's fall had left its mark on the roof of the restaurant. He felt dizzy. If someone grabbed his feet now, he would be done for. He stepped back and looked around. There was no one up here.

He inspected the railing more closely. If Krempin hadn't jumped, where was the man who pushed him? He would hardly have taken the lift. Perhaps Rath could still catch him. He hastened down the steel stairs. He had found it easier with Weinert a moment ago, but it didn't help that he was now a hundred metres further up.

Don't think about it! Just keep moving!

He tried to look down without his knees trembling, but it still wasn't clear if there was anyone moving below. Every so often he thought he saw patches of colour flitting past, but couldn't be sure. He continued to stumble down the steps until, all of a sudden, he saw something that seemed out of place in the steel framework. At first he thought it was an animal cowering in the supporting beams, but when he looked a little closer he realised what it was.

A toupee.

Had Krempin lost part of his disguise when he fell? Hardly—he had coloured his hair. Besides, whatever was being ruffled by the wind was only a hairpiece, rather than a full-blown wig. Someone had lost their toupee. Either a tourist who'd leaned too far over the railing, or a man who'd had it torn from his head.

The hairpiece was too far away to reach and, just as Rath was considering whether he was staring at a crucial piece of evidence, it was seized by a gust of wind and carried off, sailing slowly towards the ground, pirouetting further and further away before landing in a dense shrub.

When he reached the foot of the Funkturm the first uniformed officers were already on the scene. One of them was questioning Weinert—or perhaps Weinert was questioning the police officer, Rath couldn't be exactly sure. Had the journalist struck lucky during his search for an eyewitness? At any rate, Berthold Weinert had his exclusive, even if it wasn't the one he had been expecting.

Time to leave, before CID arrived and, with it, the prospect of familiar faces. Rath stole away from the exhibition grounds and tried to locate the shrub where the hairpiece had landed. Now wasn't the right time; he would have to come back. He still wasn't sure how he was going to explain it all to Böhm, but he'd think of something. At any rate, the DCI couldn't get wind of the fact that Gereon Rath had been intending to meet a fugitive murder suspect without having first informed the police.

Not a moment too soon he reclaimed his seat in the Buick to see the murder wagon shooting along from the direction of Kantstrasse. Rath slipped down and waited until the black vehicle had turned onto the exhibition grounds.

33

Lange and a few others were holding the fort. Otherwise, nearly all of Homicide had flown the nest. One of the uniformed officers Weinert had alerted must have recognised the dead man and reported back to Alex, as Böhm had driven to the exhibition grounds himself. Erika Voss passed on the news before Lange could say anything. Rath pretended to be surprised.

'Krempin? Are you sure?' he asked.

'Looks that way. Seems like he jumped from the Funkturm.'

'Suicide? Has that been confirmed?'

'I'm just telling you what everyone's saying.'

'What else could it be?' Lange asked.

'Murder,' said Rath.

'Who would want to kill Krempin?'

'Half of Berlin, I'd say. Since the whole world's decided he's a serial killer.'

'That makes suicide just as likely. Imagine your picture's in all the papers and the whole city's hounding you—how long can any one person stand it?'

'If he's got a good hiding place, I'd say quite a while. Until now, Krempin always had a good hiding place.'

'Yes, but Gräf and his men were closing in on him all the time.'

'By the way, Inspector,' Erika Voss said. 'Frau Kling called. You have an appointment with the commissioner.' She looked down at her pad. 'Monday, three o'clock.'

'What's it about?'

'She didn't say. You'll have it confirmed in writing. She just wanted to arrange the appointment.'

Rath nodded. 'What's the latest with our case?' he asked Lange. 'Did our artist produce anything worthwhile?'

Lange handed him a drawing of a gloomy-looking man who bore no resemblance whatsoever to the actor Ziehlke had picked out from Oppenberg's collection of photos. If anything he looked like . . .

'Lange, that could just as well be you!'

'That's what Fräulein Voss thinks, but it wasn't me, I swear!'

'I hope you have an alibi,' Rath said sternly, before breaking into a laugh.

'If you ask me, that taxi driver would be incapable of giving a recognisable description of someone with three eyes and two noses.'

'Perhaps it's our sketch artist who's not up to the job.'

'I don't think it's his fault. He did what that Ziehlke told him, as far as possible. It's just that our witness kept contradicting himself.'

'Doesn't look like the sketch is going to be much help then.'

'No,' Erika Voss said. 'If we go to the press, poor Lange will be denounced and arrested by tomorrow morning.'

Lange was about to throw the picture in the wastepaper basket when Rath stopped him. 'Leave it! Perhaps we might be able to use it after all.'

Lange hunched his shoulders. 'If you think so. How about you? Did you find anything out?'

Rath described his trip to the corner of Hohenzollerndamm on Sunday. The Chinese restaurant, the menswear store, the wine dealership.

'Not very fruitful then,' said Lange.

'No,' Rath said. 'And yet that corner is precisely where we need to start. That's where she met our stranger. Roll the drawing up and fetch your coat. We're heading there now.'

'With this picture?'

'First we'll show people the picture of Vivian Franck. We'll canvass the shops, and if that doesn't yield anything, the flats too. Perhaps someone saw her. Perhaps even together with our phantom.'

The salespeople in the menswear store only knew Vivian Franck from the screen.

'Women don't often shop here,' said one. 'Or did old Franck play for the other team?' The sketch didn't yield any results either, just confused glances at Lange.

It was a similar story in the wine dealership, only the owner spared them the stupid remarks and, indeed, was rather taciturn for a Berliner.

The Chinese restaurant was still closed, but after they knocked loudly against the roller shutters someone opened. The man who poked his head through the door didn't speak a word of German, but understood the two police IDs well enough. He bowed and bade them enter. Inside it smelled of beer and exotic spices; they were preparing for an onslaught of guests and things were suitably chaotic. Nevertheless, the whole team looked patiently at the picture of Vivian Franck.

The Chinese didn't appear to go to the cinema; Rath and Lange received only shakes of the head. Nor did anyone recognise the stranger. The manager was the only one who spoke German. Rath pointed towards a green fruit with brown skin that a kitchen hand was currently slicing in two. 'Yangtao?' he asked.

'Yangtao!' the manager said, smiling broadly. The fact that Rath recognised the fruit seemed to impress him. 'Very good. Want to try?'

The bright green flesh was juicy and sour and didn't taste bad at all. So that was what Betty Winter had eaten just before her death.

'Good for health,' the manager said.

Rath rummaged in his pockets, eventually finding the photo he was looking for. He didn't know why, but suddenly he felt feverishly excited. A thousand intangible thoughts raced through his mind, as always when he spotted something, some lead, some connection that he still couldn't quite make sense of. He showed the Chinese the high-resolution print of Betty Winter. 'Do you know this woman? Was she ever here?'

To his surprise the man nodded. 'Yes,' he said. 'Nice lady. Liked yangtao a lot.'

Rath stared stubbornly at the traffic, immersed in his thoughts.

'How strange,' Lange said. 'There we are conducting a fruitless investigation into the Franck case, and we stumble upon a restaurant where Betty Winter used to eat.'

Rath's head was spinning with ideas. The two dead actresses had worked for rival producers, which was enough for Fink to cook up his nonsense about a serial killer, and now there was a second, more puzzling, connection: Betty Winter had eaten in the restaurant outside which Vivian Franck had been met by her suspected killer. It could be coincidence, but against that was a tingling sensation in his veins, and a hollow feeling in his stomach. He was onto something, he could feel it, even if he still didn't know quite what.

It was already late and he didn't want to go back to the station, where they would only run the risk of Böhm saddling them with overtime, or asking about Oppenberg's private detective. He set Lange down at Gleisdreieck to catch the Prenzlauer Berg train, and drove home. If he wanted to pick up Charly promptly at half past seven he'd have to get his glad rags on sharpish.

At home he started up the boiler and showered. As the water ran down his neck, he couldn't help thinking about Krempin plunging to his death before his eyes.

What would Böhm say about the case at briefing tomorrow? And how would Oppenberg take the news of his friend's death? Had the producer pushed him himself, out of fear that Krempin might implicate him? It was hard to imagine how someone with a heart condition like Oppenberg could make it down all those steps, but who else could have known that Krempin was at the Funkturm? And that he meant to use the viewing platform as a lookout before going to his secret meeting in the restaurant? Rath wondered whether Oppenberg could have sent someone to silence Krempin.

Tomorrow he'd have to start looking for the toupee; it was possible that it belonged to the murderer. If, indeed, there was a murderer. His instincts said yes, and they had served him well enough in the past.

When the water grew cold he climbed out of the shower. He was getting nervous. Thoughts of Charly banished all others from his mind. Soon he would be seeing her. Going out with her. For the first time in more than half a year. He didn't want to think about how their last evening together had ended in a huge fight.

34

The neon letters on the Plaza façade burned brighter than the dim gaslights around Küstriner Platz. Rath found a space near the entrance and parked the Buick. Charly smiled when she realised where he was taking her. He hadn't revealed their destination even as they journeyed ever deeper into the forbidding Stralau quarter.

Rath was relieved, she seemed to like variety theatre. He didn't have happy memories of the Plaza, and not just because of the indifferent programme with which the theatre had opened the year before. The complex had been built inside the station concourse of the former Ostbahnhof, whose goods station, in contrast to the passenger terminus, was still in use. It was here, in an unprepossessing warehouse, that Johann Marlow had his office: a room seemingly lifted straight from an English country house, complete with fireplace. It was less than a year since he had met Marlow here for the first time, the secret ruler of the Berlin underworld, the only Berlin underworld kingpin yet to see prison from the inside. Rath often thought about that night, which had ended with a dead man who, to this day, still haunted his dreams.

He didn't want to have to go through anything like that again, but Charly made him feel like a different man. Not the man from that night, but the Gereon Rath currently strolling across Küstriner Platz with a beautiful woman at his side.

As they entered the foyer he gazed round instinctively. Marlow probably wasn't here, but was almost certainly having him watched. Rath didn't see any familiar faces, but then he didn't know all of Marlow's people. Not by a long shot.

'Are you looking for someone?' Charly asked.

'Just the box office. Ah, there it is.'

They took their places at the back of the queue. Rath was a trifle nervous, but when he gave his name to the cashier it transpired that Marlow had set aside two box tickets for him.

Charly was astonished, but Rath behaved as if acquiring box seats for Charlotte Ritter was the least he could do. Hopefully, the programme would be better than last year. In truth, he was no fan of variety theatre but Charly seemed to like the idea. In the cloakroom queue, she recounted how she had once been at the Wintergarten with her family to celebrate the end of her school exams. 'The first student in the family.'

Although Plaza wasn't quite as glamorous as the Wintergarten, box seats weren't exactly cheap. Gradually they advanced towards the cloakroom attendant. Rath wanted to take Charly's coat, but she refused. 'If you want to play the gentleman I can think of better ways.'

'Such as?'

'All in good time.'

'Very well. A gentleman never tells.'

'We'll see about that.' At last it came to their turn. 'What's the latest news at the Castle?' she asked.

Rath told her about Krempin's death, neglecting to mention that he had been an eyewitness.

'You think he couldn't cope with the pressure? A murder on his conscience, the whole city looking for him?'

'I was in Wilmersdorf almost all day working on the Vivian Franck case. Let's see what Böhm says at briefing tomorrow morning.'

'I do miss it sometimes,' she said. 'I'll be glad when I have these stupid finals behind me.'

'Will you come back to Alex?'

'Even if I didn't enjoy the work, I'd still come back. Out of necessity. A girl's got to live.'

'And it's that easy? You can come back whenever it suits you?'

'That's what Böhm promised, and he's a man you can rely on.'

Rath said nothing. There'd have only been trouble otherwise. There was always trouble when they discussed Böhm.

Both of the other seats in their box remained empty. Marlow really had pulled out all the stops. Even if he didn't actually own the theatre he obviously held considerable sway. The view from up here was outstanding.

'Strange,' Charly said as she peeped over the balustrade, watching the stalls fill. 'Looks like it'll just be the two of us. Tell me you didn't arrange this? Book a whole box to seduce a defenceless girl!'

'Certainly did,' he said and laughed. 'You know me.'

'Quite.'

She looked at him with her dark eyes. He couldn't avert his gaze, but she didn't look away either.

Oh God, he thought, drawing gradually closer to her suddenly ever-so-serious face. He felt her breath and closed his eyes, tasting her soft lips as she surrendered to him open-mouthed and he took off and flew and flew, before landing, after what seemed like half an eternity, back in the box.

They gazed at each other as if they had awoken from a dream. 'God, I've missed you!' he said, stroking her cheek.

'I don't know if this is a good idea, Gereon,' she said.

'You mustn't think I wanted this—that is, of course I wanted it, I mean, you mustn't think I planned it . . . that I'm only going out with you to . . .'

She pressed a finger to his lips with a soft 'shhhhhhhh' and smiled, revealing her dimple.

'Don't talk so much,' she said, kissing him again. It took them some time to realise the bill had long since begun.

'This is all wrong,' Rath said. 'Normally you watch the show together, eat and drink something, maybe go dancing, and only *then* do you kiss. On the way home, just before you decide who's sleeping where.'

'Then we need to rearrange ourselves,' she said. 'The tickets must have cost a fortune and we've barely seen half the show.'

'What do you mean, barely half? I haven't seen anything at all.'

'That's even worse.'

'So where do we go from here?'

'How about we watch and applaud? Then we'll see.'

'Rearrange ourselves it is.'

She looked on at the show, and he looked on at her looking on at the show, which was better than last year's. Less glamour, perhaps, but more to laugh about, and people who lived in this part of town needed that. Rath didn't get a single one of the punchlines but laughed along with Charly and the rest in all the right places. How he loved seeing her laugh.

The closer the interval came, the more he found himself thinking about Marlow. He still didn't know how he would steal himself away without Charly noticing.

At length the curtain fell for the interval, and she linked arms with him as they went downstairs to the foyer. Rath could see neither Marlow nor Liang anywhere in the crowd but knew that Dr M. would keep his appointment. He wouldn't have taken care of the tickets otherwise.

'What are you looking for this time?' Charly asked.

'I'm just wondering if we can still get a seat at the bar.'

But it was hopeless. They were all taken.

'That ought to answer your question,' Charly said. 'Now what?'

'I'll get us something to drink all the same.'

'Then do your gentlemanly duty. I need to go to the little girls' room anyway.'

She started towards the toilets. When she had gone a few steps, however, she turned around.

'Food as well,' she called to him. 'I could eat a horse.'

Once she was out of sight Rath looked again for Marlow, but he was at neither the bar nor one of the little tables, and Rath could scarcely imagine him standing in line for sticky champagne.

'Inspector Rath?'

It was a slim man in a fitted suit. He wore no dinner jacket and looked more like a businessman than a theatregoer.

'That's me,' Rath said.

'Herr Marlow sends his apologies. He's running a little late.'

Rath couldn't remember having seen the man in Marlow's entourage before. 'But he still wants to meet?'

'Of course.'

'Listen, I've got company here. There's no need for the lady to know I have a meeting, or who it's with. I'm sure that's in accordance with Herr Marlow's wishes too.'

'Herr Marlow sets great store by discretion.'

'Now, if you'll excuse me, I have to order food, as well as something to drink.'

'It would be Herr Marlow's honour. I'll have something sent up.'

The man disappeared before Rath could say anything. He was about to call after him when he saw Charly's green dress. It seemed the queue for the Ladies was shorter than that for the bar.

'Who was that?' she asked.

'The man just then? Someone from the house.'

'He didn't look like a waiter.'

'He wasn't. It's taking far too long to get a drink, so I complained.'

Rath took his place at the back of the queue for the bar but when he finally got hold of two glasses of champagne the interval was almost over. He raised his shoulders as he handed Charly a glass, and she smiled at him.

'Let's go then,' he said. They clinked glasses and drank, before making their way hurriedly back to their seats, losing some of the champagne in the process.

'What a shame,' she said. 'We won't get anything else for over an hour.'

'Next time I'll get a bottle.'

The first act had already started by the time they returned to their seats. A man in a turban speaking in Saxon dialect was telling people how old they were and what job they had despite having his eyes blindfolded, while his assistant moved around the stalls holding up the identity papers of their victims. The Saxon fakir was taking his bow when there was a polite knock and two friendly waiters wheeled in a large trolley. Charly's eyes widened in delight as they laid out the spoils: half a dozen bowls and plates, and a bottle of champagne enthroned, centre stage, in a cooler.

'So that's what you were discussing. And there was I thinking a glass of champagne was all I'd be getting.'

Praise be to Marlow, Rath thought. 'I hope it's to your liking.'

Marlow's errand boy had put together a nice mix, just the thing for a cosy evening alone with a hungry woman. There were lovingly prepared canapés, roast beef, smoked salmon, a cheese plate, devilled eggs and even a little caviar.

Charly really did seem to be hungry, loading her plate in a most unlady-like manner. Rath was a little more restrained, though pleased at her appetite. He had just poured them another glass of champagne when there was a second knock. The man in the grey suit poked his head around the door. 'Everything to your satisfaction?'

'Yes, thank you,' Rath said, and Charly nodded with her mouth full.

The man leaned towards Rath and whispered: 'Herr Marlow will see you now.' Given the orchestra in the background, there was no chance Charly could've picked up the name.

'Telephone,' Rath said, apologetically. 'The Castle. You know how it is.'

'Well, let's hope it's not an operation.'

'Statistically speaking, A Division's death quota has already been achieved this week.'

Rath followed the suit downstairs. A single patron sat at the deserted bar, a powerful yet lithe-seeming man in an elegant dinner jacket who had just lit a cigar and was sipping occasionally at his whisky, gazing absently into the mirror in front of him. Still, Rath was certain nothing in this room escaped those eyes. Johann Marlow hadn't even brought his Chinese shadow, so safe did he feel here. It was almost as if he took a drink at the bar most days after work. Rath sat on the stool beside him.

'Good evening, Inspector. I hope you haven't been too bored.'

'I've been very well looked after.' Rath took his new cigarette case from his pocket and lit an Overstolz. 'I'm afraid I can't leave my companion for very long; she thinks I'm taking a call from the station.'

'We'll be finished by the time you've smoked your cigarette.'

'What have you discovered?'

'There *was* a case where an actress was abducted on behalf of the competition. A man named Steger was responsible, a piece of shit from the Nordpiraten, together with a friend. They kept the poor woman hidden in a cellar for two weeks and had their fun with her. She was no good for film after that, a nervous wreck. They even made a few cuts to her face for good measure.'

'There are some lousy bastards out there.'

'A thing like that goes against the code of honour. The Nordpiraten ended up cancelling this Steger's membership, even though he's a passable safe-breaker. The pressure from the other Ringvereine was simply too great. Since then, the guy's had to make do on his own.'

'Doesn't sound like he's the one. Vivian Franck only had her vocal cords cut. Her face was intact when she was found, made up in fact. And she wasn't raped.'

'You're right, it wasn't him. My people have already paid him a little visit. If he was the one you'd have been able to take him back to Alex all nicely wrapped.'

'Hardly. I'm here privately.'

'Nevertheless, I'm sorry I couldn't help you this time.'

'You've helped me more than enough already.'

'Come now, Inspector. I'm indebted to you, just as you are to me. You just don't want to admit it. I can understand why you don't want to be seen with me in public, but don't worry, that's not going to happen.'

'That's me reassured. You mean you won't be visiting me tomorrow in my office?'

'I have never once tried to tap your professional connections for my own ends . . .'

'You wouldn't get anywhere if you did.'

'. . . but I live by the motto that one hand washes the other. The time will come when I ask for a favour, and you won't turn me down.' Marlow's voice was suddenly cold.

'Don't be so sure. I certainly won't be divulging any police secrets.'

'Inspector, don't pretend you don't have any skeletons in your closet. Or should I say: encased in concrete!'

Rath felt as if Marlow had rammed his fist into his stomach. 'I'm afraid I don't follow.'

'No? Allow me to be more plain.' Marlow blew a cloud of smoke across the bar. 'I know it was you who killed Josef Wilczek.'

Rath tried not to betray any emotion. 'Why are you being so friendly to me if I eliminated one of your men?'

'Luckily for you, only two people know about it, otherwise I'd have had *no choice* but to take action. I can't allow someone to gun down one of my men and get away with it, even a police officer.'

'I didn't gun anyone down; someone's been talking nonsense.'

'I have something else for you. My people came across something that might be of interest. Deutsche Kraft have got their paws on a film company. It's called Borussia and is based over at Weissensee.'

'Thanks, but right now I'm not interested in whether a Ringverein is involved in the film industry.'

'Oh, I think you will be,' Marlow said sharply. 'Pass the tip on to your colleagues. There's bound to be something in it for you. Otherwise Kraft wouldn't be involved.'

'We'll see.' Rath took a final draw on his cigarette and stubbed it out. 'Time to go. Thanks for your help.'

'Anytime,' Marlow smiled.

There was no escort for the return journey. The suit remained at the bar. As he climbed the steps, Rath could feel his body slowly relaxing.

Marlow knew.

Someone had seen how Josef Wilczek had died. Rath recalled the beer bottle shattering against the courtyard paving, and the window that had slammed shut after the shot was fired from his service weapon. In the Stralau quarter no one went to the police with information like that. They went to Johann Marlow, who knew how to make capital from it. *Pass the tip on to your colleagues.* That was an order, not a good turn. Dr M. wanted to pull one over on the competition.

Rath cursed the day he had met Johann Marlow. Suddenly tonight, with all its fake lustre, seemed worthless, poisoned and dirty: the box seats, the food, the champagne.

At least Charly hadn't noticed anything. 'Well?' she asked. He had been away less than ten minutes.

'Lange,' he said. 'Nothing important.' The assistant detective from Hannover was the only person in A Division Charly didn't know. 'I had to remind him that he needn't call me about every last thing.'

'What do you mean, *nothing important*?' She could be damn stubborn.

'About the duty roster.' He waved a hand dismissively. 'Completely unimportant. Come on, we've spoken too much about work already this evening.'

'Let's talk about us then.'

'How about a drink first?' he said, filling their glasses again before drinking her health.

'With a proper toast!' She raised her glass. 'Let's drink to the fact that we've been together for more than two hours without having a single fight.'

They managed not to fight for the rest of the evening too, but the magic had passed and Rath was no longer entirely there. While she followed what was happening onstage, clearly enjoying the box seats, he couldn't tear his thoughts away from the conversation with Marlow. He was still in shock that someone knew, and that it was Marlow of all people.

He had felt that he was being watched during the struggle with Wilczek, but there was no way his face had been visible in the dark rear courtyard. Absolutely no way! Someone had seen the fatal shot and the body being buried in the concrete, and then told Marlow, who must have figured out the rest. Because he had discovered in the meantime that Wilczek had followed the inspector from Ostbahnhof that evening.

Charly turned to face him. 'Hello, anyone there?'

'Sorry, I've just got so much on my mind . . .'

'Me too.' She smiled and her dimple finally hauled him back to the present. 'Today was something of a surprise, wasn't it?'

'You can say that again.' He tried a smile too, but didn't manage half as well. 'Come on, let's go to the car.'

'Can you still drive?'

'All the better after a glass or two.'

She linked her arm in his again and they descended the stairs in silence, mingling with the other three thousand leaving the theatre.

When they emerged onto Küstriner Platz, the parking lot was bedlam. Some cars had had their wheels removed and were now resting on bricks, looking like clumsy insects on spindly little legs. They moved along the row, passing one wheelless car after another.

'That's all we need,' Rath said, but the tyre thieves hadn't made it as far as the Buick. They had stopped at the car next to it, a Horch. This time, however, they had taken only the rear wheels and jacked up the bumper.

'They must have been interrupted,' Charly said. 'A patrol probably.'

Rath shook his head and gestured towards the square. 'The police don't have much say in this quarter. There must be another reason.'

He persuaded himself it was coincidence that the car thieves had stopped exactly in front of his Buick, but his gut told him that he had Johann Marlow's protective hand to thank for not having to take the train home.

On the journey west both were immersed in their own thoughts. Only an hour before, Rath would have done anything to prevent the evening from ending so soon, but now all he wanted was to be alone in the silence of his flat with Coleman Hawkins and a glass of cognac. He drove her straight to Spenerstrasse and accompanied her to the door, not knowing how he should say goodbye. 'So, what now?' he asked.

She shrugged.

'Sunday's supposed to be nice. We could take a drive out to the country-side if you like.' She nodded. 'I could pick you up in the car. Then perhaps we could . . .'

This time she didn't press a finger to his lips to silence him. She kissed him.

35

Saturday 8th March 1930

He awoke at five in the morning, heart pumping, staring at the ceiling, but it wasn't Charly who had kept him from sleeping. It was the dead Josef Wilczek haunting his dreams, and Felix Krempin gazing at him through the window glass of the Funkturm restaurant with those rigid, terrified eyes.

Rath couldn't sleep, and didn't want to. He decided to pay the exhibition grounds another visit before heading out to Alex.

In the first light of dawn the Funkturm was even more imposing. Someone must have given the area a good scrub, as the bloodstain Felix Krempin had left on the concrete was now scarcely visible. The pay booth was still closed and there wasn't a soul on the grounds.

The shrub was a good distance from the Funkturm and hadn't been searched by ED. Its branches were full of morning dew, so that Rath's coat was soon wet and glistening, but at least they were bare. The search would have been a lot trickier in summer. He bent the branches apart with a stick, trying to locate something furry in their midst, and was on the verge of giving up when he found the toupee on the ground. Reaching with the stick he pulled it through the mud towards him and finally managed to catch hold, before picking it up gingerly and returning to the car.

When he passed the Funkturm on the way back, the lights were on in the pay booth. The exhibition grounds were coming to life and it was time for him to disappear. He threw the wet and slimy toupee, which somehow reminded him of a drowned guinea pig, onto the leather of the passenger seat, started the engine and drove off.

He got through the morning traffic on Kantstrasse quicker than expected and stopped on Savignyplatz by a telephone booth. Weinert was eating breakfast. 'How did you fare yesterday?' he asked.

'Your colleagues kept asking if I knew the man who was with me by the corpse. The one who went back up the Funkturm.'

'You didn't, of course.'

'Several witnesses saw you, Gereon.'

'Still, the fact remains: I wasn't at the Funkturm. A detective inspector meeting with a murder suspect in secret—how do you think that looks?'

'Just as lousy as a journalist meeting with an alleged killer. Especially when he uses the occasion to jump to his death.'

'Are you going to write it up?'

'I don't know. As long as your lot don't broadcast the fact that the Funkturm suicide was Felix Krempin, the other papers won't carry anything. A suicide report at most. First I need to think about how I sell the fact that I was there to my boss.'

'As coincidence.'

'He isn't stupid.'

'I'd rather you didn't write everything you know. If people think Krempin flung himself from the Funkturm out of guilt, they'll also think he killed Betty Winter and Vivian Franck, and that is total nonsense. Krempin didn't commit suicide.'

'Are you sure? Your colleagues seem to think he did.'

'He didn't agree to meet us, only to plunge to his death before our eyes!'

'He wouldn't be the first.'

'Someone pushed him, and that same someone lost something that I found.'

'Don't keep me in suspense.'

'A toupee.'

'Pardon?'

'A hairpiece, a toupee, you know.'

'You're serious? That's your evidence?'

'There was someone else on the viewing platform when Krempin fell. He exited via the stairs while I was in the lift. I went after him but he had too big a start. Did you see anyone emerge from the Funkturm after the others?'

'Only you. But you don't wear a wig, do you?'

'Leave the jokes, this is serious. Someone up there pushed Felix Krempin, and if I find *him* I find Betty Winter's killer too. I'm certain of that.'

'Then good luck. I'll help as best I can, but you'll need to supply more facts.'

'Officially I'm off the case, but perhaps you can help me. Could you find out who made this hairpiece, and where it was bought?'

'You made off with the toupee?'

'Yes, this morning. It looks a little worse for wear. More something for forensics than your follicles.'

'If there's a story in it, I can always try my luck. I'll be over your way later, why don't we meet? In that Nasse Viereck . . .'

'. . . Dreieck.'

'Right. Around nine?'

'Sounds good.'

Rath hung up and returned to his car. The toupee on the passenger seat still looked like a drowned guinea pig, albeit one that had half-dried in the sun. He stuck it in the glove compartment and drove to the Castle on time. His coat had more or less dried by the time he climbed the steps to A Division but, before entering the conference room, he gave his hands a thorough wash and removed a few traces of mud from his clothes.

Böhm had asked both teams to attend morning briefing again. It was only in the eyes of the press that the Winter and Franck cases were linked, but that was why it was so important for both groups to know exactly what was going on. Today, the focus was on the death of Felix Krempin. Böhm started to reconstruct the fatal fall as Rath entered the room. At most he was a minute late, but it was enough to elicit an angry glance. Rath listened, for once not having to feign interest.

According to Forensics, Felix Krempin had plunged almost a hundred metres from the railings on the north side of the viewing platform onto the roof of the restaurant. He was most likely killed on impact, and would not have felt his body slide across the surface of the roof and thud into the concrete slabs at the foot of the Funkturm.

'The man was heavily made up, had bleached his hair and was wearing a false moustache,' Böhm said, 'but we have nevertheless been able to identify the deceased beyond any doubt as Felix Krempin.'

'Case closed,' Czerwinski said. 'And the Free State of Prussia gets to save on prison costs as well.'

'Despite the wishes of Herr Czerwinski here,' Böhm continued, and the laughter that had accompanied Czerwinski's outburst evaporated, 'we will not be discontinuing our investigation.' Czerwinski mumbled something into his beard.

Böhm announced that Kronberg would make a full report. A few officers yawned as a preventive measure. ED had been on the roof and managed to locate both the exact point of impact and the trail the body had left on the roofing felt. They had also taken photos, some of which Kronberg would presently show. Before they could hear what else would make up Kronberg's monotone report, however, the door swung open and Kleinschmidt, a colleague from Missing Persons, burst in.

Böhm didn't grumble. He had asked to be notified at once of any missing actresses, and that was exactly what Kleinschmidt was doing. The missing woman's name was Jeanette Fastré. She hadn't turned up to the premiere of her new film yesterday evening, and her producer had notified police this morning.

'She's not at home; we've already checked. Nobody's opening, but there's a dog barking behind the door.'

'And that's why you haven't gone in?'

'With respect, Sir, the flat might still be of interest to Forensics. It was *you* who asked *us* for help.'

'OK,' Böhm said, 'I'll send two of my men out.' He looked around. 'Rath, Lange,' he barked, 'take a look at this Fastré's flat, and make sure the press doesn't get wind of it. Report back immediately upon return.'

Rath would have preferred to listen to Kronberg, but clearly Böhm meant to punish him for not being present yesterday when news of Krempin's death reached Alex. The DCI was passing the buck. If anything about this case should make the papers, they'd have a scapegoat in Gereon Rath. That was the real reason Böhm wanted all cases with missing actresses on his desk. Not because he imagined a serial killer to be at work, but because he didn't want to provide the press with any further ammunition for their theory.

Rath and Lange left the conference room like pupils condemned to sweep the schoolyard. At least now the bulldog couldn't ask him about Oppenberg's sleuth. Rath still hadn't managed to think of a credible story.

Jeanette Fastré lived in Friedenau, a little away from Kaiserallee. Two officers from Missing Persons were sitting in their car outside the door.

Rath, who had made out the green Opel straightaway, went over and knocked on the windscreen.

'You can go back to the station,' he said, showing his identification. 'Homicide are taking over.'

'Kleinschmidt didn't say anything about that,' the driver said.

'No, but *I* did. Go to the canteen and take your morning break. What floor does this Fastré live on?'

'You can find that out for yourself.' Before Rath could reply, the car screeched away. He jumped back, to make sure the rear mudguard didn't graze him.

'What an arsehole!'

'You could have been a little more diplomatic,' said Lange.

The actress's name wasn't amongst those on the mailboxes. They had to ask the caretaker. 'Vanhaelen, second floor,' he said. 'Are the cops asking for her on the hour now?'

'Do you have a key to the flat?'

'Why?' The accent was local.

'So I can pick your nose with it. Why do you think?'

'You are obliged to assist police in such matters,' Lange said. 'Or risk prosecution.'

The caretaker mumbled something that sounded like 'give me a moment,' before disappearing into the flat.

'Sir, I don't want to interfere,' Lange said while the man was away, 'but if you can't shake off your bad mood, perhaps you should leave the talking to me.'

Rath couldn't help but grin. 'Perhaps you're right.' He thanked the caretaker politely when he returned with the keys. The man gazed after them with a shake of the head as they climbed the steps.

It wasn't until they reached the stairwell on the third floor that they heard the dog, not just barking but yelping and whimpering. As they approached it began to scratch from the inside. *Vanhaelen*, it said next to the door. That was all.

'Do you know anything about dogs?' Rath asked. Lange shook his head.

The scraping increased as the key turned in the lock.

'I was, more or less, raised in a dog pound,' Rath said, as he unlocked the door. 'My father has had German shepherds ever since I can remember.'

'I've got two cats at home,' said Lange.

'Then just pray you don't smell too strongly of them, and that the dog behind that door isn't too big.' Lange swallowed and reached for his service weapon. 'Don't start spraying bullets everywhere,' Rath said. 'Leave the beast to me.'

With that he opened the door, slowly and carefully. Lange followed and the barking grew louder until it was replaced by a low but menacing growl. Lange started, but the attack didn't materialise.

Rath opened the door completely, revealing the author of these menacing sounds: a black ball of wool that growled vehemently while at the same time wagging its stumpy tail and slowly retreating from the intruders.

'It's just a puppy,' Rath said. 'The poor thing seems to be completely beside itself.'

'My God, it stinks in here,' Lange said, holding his nose.

'There was a butcher's downstairs. See if you can fetch a few pfennigs of offal.' Lange looked at him as if Rath was asking him to sell his grandmother. 'Come on! The poor thing's starved. I'll pay you the money back.'

Lange disappeared while Rath tried to console the dog, which made a sudden sally, darting between his legs into the next room. He followed it in.

The flat was as elegant as a film set, but stank like a kennel that hadn't been cleaned for weeks. There was dog mess everywhere and little puddles that polluted the air with their stench. The scratch marks weren't confined to the door. Rath found a drinking bowl in the kitchen, which he filled with water. The dog must be about to die of thirst, if, that is, it hadn't drunk from the toilet—but it was too small for that. On the living room table was a glass bowl full of mouldy fruit, which the animal had nibbled at. No more than that; it was too much of a carnivore.

Rath placed the bowl on the tiled floor of the bathroom and withdrew slowly, keeping his movements as steady as possible. The dog, which had been staring at him the whole time, darted back and forth from a respectful distance. Half-crazy with thirst but still fearful, it waited until he had left the bathroom before drinking the water.

Amidst all the slurping and splashing noises, Rath continued to look around. He tried to sniff out the smell of decay among the dog stench, scanning every room, ready to stumble upon Jeanette Fastré's corpse at any moment. Fortunately, he was out of luck: keeping a *third* dead actress under wraps would be next to impossible.

As he finished scanning the rooms the doorbell rang. He took care that the dog couldn't escape before opening to Lange, who was carrying a large paper bag through which blood was seeping. He made a disgusted face. 'Give it here. I'll see that the beast is fed.'

The dog had stayed in the bathroom but, when it smelled the meat, it ventured out a little. Rath placed some of the offal in a food bowl from the kitchen. The dog dashed out of the bathroom, beside itself with hunger, time and time again making little advances, jumping to the bowl before withdrawing again, a strange dance that didn't end until Rath placed it next to the empty drinking bowl on the floor. This time the dog started eating before Rath could take his hands away. He stroked the animal as it ate, and refilled the drinking bowl.

'You're being nicer to dogs than people today,' Lange said.

'What makes you think it's just today?'

'I didn't mean to offend you. Did you find anything?'

Rath shook his head. 'A load of dog mess, but no woman, neither dead nor alive. No trace of a struggle either. Anything that looks that way was probably caused by the dog.'

'What do we tell Böhm?'

'Either that a completely unscrupulous woman is neglecting her dog while she does a runner, or that we're dealing with something more serious. People who get themselves a puppy but decide that they don't want it anymore might abandon it in the woods. They don't leave it alone in their flat. You can see where that leads.'

'I can smell where that leads.'

The dog barked. Rath looked to find the bowl empty and the animal gazing up at him, head to one side and tail wagging.

'Well then, Greedy Guts,' he said. 'There's more, but only a little. We don't want you upsetting your stomach.' He refilled the bowl and the dog started eating straightaway.

'Let's get back,' said Lange. 'I think the flat's best left to Forensics. Perhaps they'll find something.'

Rath nodded as he watched the dog. 'It's a nice image,' he said. 'Kronberg's people packing dog turds into little bags.'

'Surely ED aren't going to be as meticulous as that. There hasn't been a murder.'

'You don't know Kronberg.'

'Not as well as you do.' Lange went to the front door.

'Where are you going?' Rath asked.

'Alex, of course.'

'We'll come too.'

'Surely you don't mean to take the dog?'

'I certainly do.'

'In the car?'

'He's not going to be sick.'

Lange made a disgusted face.

There was a lead on the coatstand. Rath attached it to the dog's collar and it followed them eagerly down the stairs.

When they returned the key, Rath took the opportunity to give the caretaker a piece of his mind. 'There's a dog barking here for days and you don't do anything about it?'

'Listen here! Firstly, the cur wasn't barking any more than usual. Secondly, I can't just go wandering into every flat. I only have the key for emergencies. For the cleaning lady when someone's on holiday, that sort of thing.'

'You don't regard a dog that's practically dying of hunger and thirst as an emergency?'

'I couldn't have known that Fastré was letting it starve to death!'

'You should pay a little more attention to what's going on around you, my man,' Rath said. 'There have been more people jailed for negligence than you might imagine.'

Erika Voss was thrilled when Rath returned with the little black ball of wool on its lead. 'Isn't he sweet?' she said.

'I take it you mean the dog,' Rath said, and Lange blushed.

The secretary didn't seem to notice; she only had eyes for the dog.

'Be careful, he's not very clean,' Rath said, as she stroked the shaggy, matted fur.

'Where did you find the poor little thing?'

'He was cooped up in a flat for days. He's already eaten. I think he needs a bath. Do you think you could take care of that?'

'Leave it to me, Inspector. I have an idea.'

'You could ask the canine unit if they have space for a puppy. I don't think he's even a year old.'

'All in good time. I'll give him a bath first, then make him a little basket so that he can sleep. He's obviously exhausted.'

She took the filthy little dog in her arms. 'Little rascal! Mummy will get you all cleaned up,' she said, as she disappeared through the door.

Rath gazed after her, shaking his head. His secretary, in whom he had so little confidence initially, continued to surprise him. 'Let's report to Böhm,' he said to Lange.

'What are we going to say to him?'

'We'll tell him what we saw. That the flat looked like it had been left in a hurry.'

'But that doesn't mean Fastré's lying dead in some cinema.'

'No, but it wouldn't be such a bad idea to check all disused cinemas in the city.'

They encountered a couple of civilians whispering excitedly to one another in the corridor on the way to the DCI's office: a fat man in a striped suit accompanied by a rake-thin woman in a yellow rain jacket. The fat man looked up, and for a moment his gaze met that of the inspector.

There was a flicker of recognition, but Rath couldn't quite place him. It was only when they reached the Homicide office that he realised the fat man had been at the Funkturm yesterday afternoon. He was one of Böhm's witnesses. Hopefully there weren't any more sitting behind the door. As a precaution, he entered the office a little behind Lange. It was like a waiting room, but he didn't see any other familiar faces.

Böhm was in the middle of an interrogation, so they had to wait. No one paid them any notice. A missing actress was of no interest at that moment; Felix Krempin's fatal leap was far more spectacular. For Rath too. He would have liked very much to know what was said at briefing that morning, but of course Böhm had sent him away, probably to make it clear, once and for all, that the Winter case was no longer his.

At that moment one of the doors leading from Homicide opened and

Reinhold Gräf entered, looking harassed and handing a stack of papers to a secretary. When he saw Rath his face brightened and he went over to his old partner.

'Gereon,' he said, 'back again! How does it feel to be subcontracted to Missing Persons?'

'It's a dog's life,' Rath said. 'Do you have a moment? Coffee in the canteen?'

Gräf nodded.

Rath turned to Lange. 'Is it OK if you report to Böhm alone?'

'You're the boss,' Lange said, shrugging. 'What should I tell Böhm if he asks where you are?'

'Meaning: what I am doing? Gathering important information, of course. See you in my office at one. OK?'

'OK.'

There wasn't much happening in the canteen at this hour—the calm before the lunchtime storm. Rath and Gräf balanced their coffee cups through a sea of tables. Only two were occupied, by a group of young uniformed officers who were relaxing after an operation.

'Why shouldn't the Commies and the Nazis bash each other's heads in?' one of them asked. 'It would save us a lot of work.'

'You can't lump them all together,' another responded.

'You can. Pack 'em in a bag and start pounding. You'd strike lucky every time!'

A few officers laughed, but by no means all.

Police were still dealing with the aftermath of the Wessel funeral. In almost all workers' districts, conflict simmered between members of the red and brown proletariats.

As Rath and Gräf approached their table, conversation ceased.

'Good day to you too,' one of them said as they walked past. This time his colleagues all laughed.

Uniform had been ill-disposed towards CID ever since their chief Heimannsberg had come off second best in a long-running debate with Vipoprä Weiss, and been forced to acknowledge that Uniform was not an independent branch but subordinate to the commissioner and his deputy. Magnus Heimannsberg and his officers were therefore accountable to

Zörgiebel and Weiss's CID, a fact that was chipping away at Uniform's self-confidence.

Rath and Gräf sat down off to the side where they could talk in peace. 'Tough time to be in uniform,' Rath said.

'I wouldn't want to be in their shoes right now,' Gräf replied. 'Duty in a Communist area is enough to make you fear for your life.'

'If anything, the Nazis are worse.'

'All I'll say is they were considerably more respectful towards us at the funeral last week.'

'If you were a Jew, they'd call you Isidore. You think that's respectful?'

'But I'm not a Jew!' Gräf was outraged.

Rath had no desire to argue, and certainly not over politics. It was bad enough that such altercations were becoming more and more of an issue for police—and all because these self-styled politicians were going at each other with sticks, knives and pistols. 'How's life without me then?' he asked.

'What can I say, Gereon. I'm at the end of my tether. Without you, I just don't know how to get through the days.' He looked as if he was about to cry. Then he grinned at Rath. 'Seriously: do you think Böhm will let us work together again soon?'

'No idea.' Rath shrugged. 'Probably not until Gennat's back in charge. Böhm's even separated Plisch and Plum.'

'I heard a moment ago that Trudchen Steiner will be boosting the turn-over of local bakeries from Monday.'

'Gennat's coming back?'

'Looks that way.' Gräf stirred his coffee. 'They're not making any pro-gress in Düsseldorf, despite our help. Even the famous Gennat has had to admit defeat.'

'We need him here, old Fatso. If it's true, I'll go to him first thing on Monday and request that we be reunited.'

'That trouble you're in with Brenner, even Gennat can't help you any-more. Next stop: stacking files in Köpenick.'

Rath took a cigarette from his case and lit it. 'I've taken care of that.'

Gräf looked at him. 'You haven't done anything underhand, I hope.'

'Underhand? Not from my end. It's Brenner who's playing dirty.' He drew on his cigarette. 'Let's talk about something else. Tell me what came to light at briefing this morning.'

'That it really was Krempin who jumped.'

'I was still there at that point. Is it certain he jumped?'

'How else is he supposed to have got down there? An accident?'

'How about murder?'

'You sound just like Böhm. He's forbidden us from mentioning suicide.'

'You of all people should know why. We've worked on enough together. Only when third-party involvement has been ruled out can we speak of suicide.'

'Sure, but we always had a feeling beforehand. Whenever we thought it was suicide, that's how it turned out.'

'Then our feelings differ on this occasion.' Rath stirred his coffee even though he hadn't added sugar.

'Could be,' Gräf nodded. 'All the same, I think Böhm's taking things too far. He's still looking for Krempin's final hiding place. Well, perhaps we'll find a suicide note or something. Then there's Oppenberg. He must still be hoping to get something out of him.'

Rath stopped stirring. 'But what? The motive for the alleged suicide?'

'That's clear enough: the killer could no longer bear his guilt. On top of that you have the manhunt, the "wanted" posters.'

'Krempin was no killer, and no suicide either. Someone pushed him, and it was probably someone he knew: the same person who killed Betty Winter.'

'I had forgotten you thought Krempin was innocent. Then we need to look for this mysterious stranger.'

'Who?'

'A few witnesses have mentioned a man who was one of the first to appear beside the corpse, before vanishing without trace.'

'Not all onlookers wait like model citizens for the police to arrive.'

'True, it's strange all the same. The man went back up the Funkturm before making himself scarce.'

'Maybe he left something in the restaurant.'

Gräf shook his head. 'When the lift attendant went with the others to look at the corpse, the man took the lift to the viewing platform. He came back down on foot. The attendant had to take the stairs all the way up to the top to retrieve his lift. The car was stuck on the platform because the door was still open. He wasn't best pleased.'

'And Böhm thinks that's suspicious? Someone taking the lift?'

Gräf shrugged his shoulders. 'No idea, but he's summoned the sketch artist.'

36

Lange still wasn't back when Rath returned to the office. Instead he was greeted by Erika Voss and a fresh-smelling dog that wagged its tail like crazy as soon as he opened the door.

'He recognises you, Inspector,' the secretary said with delight. 'I think he likes you.'

'I'm good with dogs,' Rath said. 'It's one of my inestimable virtues.' He bent over and let it lick his hands. 'But he was happy to go with you too. What did they say at the canine unit?'

'They weren't too keen, but I was persistent.'

'And?'

'They're sending someone to pick him up.'

'Good. Lange still not back from Böhm?' She shook her head. 'Anything from Forensics?' Another shake of the head. 'Did you get the producer's address from Missing Persons?'

Erika Voss nodded and passed him a piece of paper. 'I've got the list here.'

He looked at a few names along with addresses and telephone numbers.

'See if a woman resembling Jean Fastré has been admitted to any of the city's hospitals in the last few days.'

The secretary reached for the receiver, and Rath went into the back room. The dog followed him to his desk, sat down on its hind legs and watched its new friend curiously.

'Well now, sonny,' Rath said. 'If you think I'm going to play with you or take you walkies, then I must disappoint. There's an expert coming to do all that.'

The dog stuck its tongue out in response and started panting. It looked as if it was smiling. Rath reached for the telephone.

'Berolina Film Production. How can I help?' a woman's voice said.

'Rath, CID. You can fetch your boss to the telephone.'

'I can put you through.'

'Or that.'

'It's lucky you caught him. Herr Grunwald is very busy.'

There was a clicking noise, and shortly thereafter a man who sounded like he didn't have much time. 'You reported the actress Jean Fastré as missing this morning?' Rath said.

'That's right,' Grunwald said. 'Have you found something?'

'Only that she hasn't been in her flat for days, and that she wasn't intending on being away so long.'

'Has something happened to her?'

'Difficult to say. We're currently checking the hospitals.'

The dog seemed bored. It saw the wastepaper basket, sniffed, and made to put one of its paws on it.

'Off!' Rath cried, and the dog gave a start.

'Pardon me?' Grunwald said.

'Sorry, I wasn't talking to you,' Rath said. 'I've got a dog here. We found it in the flat. Did Frau Fastré have a dog?'

'Yes, a Bouvier called Kirie.'

'Strange name.'

'French. Stands for: *la petite qui rit*, the little girl who laughs. It was sent over from Belgium. We had to forbid her from bringing the damn thing to the shoot as it spent the whole time yapping. You can't have that with a talkie. Once upon a time we might have turned a blind eye.' He gave a brief laugh. 'There are few noisier things on earth than making a silent film.'

'So, what? She just left the dog at home when she had to go to a shoot?'

'No idea. All I know is she came to the shoot, and the dog didn't.'

'But leaving the dog alone for a few days would be unusual?'

'I'm afraid I don't know a lot about my actresses. We have a professional relationship, not a private one. What I do know is that she didn't appear at the premiere of her new film yesterday, and that's not like her at all.'

'When did you last see Frau Fastré?'

'A week ago, perhaps.'

'And it was certain that she would come to the premiere?'

'Of course! That's what the viewers expect, and Jeanette always enjoyed such occasions. She never missed them, which is why we're so concerned.'

He paused and his voice grew softer. 'She's crazy about driving. What if . . . she was out in the country somewhere . . . an accident . . . ?'

'Didn't you try her house yesterday evening?'

'Your colleagues have already asked me that. Of course I did! We telephoned her flat, then the concierge and, when he said he hadn't seen her for a few days, we began to wonder and reported it to the police.'

'Leave it!'

The dog had stood both its front paws on the filing shelves, the lower base of which was tilting forward alarmingly, along with the lever arch files.

'I hope you're talking to the dog again, Inspector.'

'Can you give me the names of a few people who know Frau Fastré a little better? Those who are closest to her here in Berlin?'

'Difficult. Like I say, I don't know a lot about her. She spent time with her family in Belgium whenever she could. She's from Malmedy.'

'Could she be there now?'

'We've called, but I've told your colleagues all this before.'

Rath thanked him and hung up. He hadn't learned a lot, but at least he now knew what the dog was called. There was a knock, and a gaunt officer with a boozer's nose came in.

'Word is you've gone to the dogs, Inspector.'

'Looks that way.'

'Then I'll take the beastie off you, shall I? We still have room at the pound.'

The officer took a step towards Kirie, who was sniffing the rubber plant that stood next to the window in the corner.

'Come to Daddy,' the man said, bending down. She eyed him suspiciously and, when he stepped forward, started growling and retreated into the corner. 'What's his name then?'

'Kirie. And he's a she.'

The officer tried his luck again. 'Come along now, Kirie, *chérie*, come along!'

Kirie was immune to the charms of the Prussian police, however. Her growling grew more threatening, then she gave a few short, firm barks.

'If you're not willing, then I'll use force,' the officer said, making a determined lunge. Kirie effected a sidestep, the lunge came to nothing and the officer wound up on the floor.

'Treat her with care, she's a pedigree and certainly not cheap. She belongs to a film actress.'

'A pedigree?' The officer picked himself up from the floor. 'I've never seen a dog like it.'

'She's a Bouvier. From Belgium, like her mistress.'

'She's acting like she's still mad at the Prussians for The Great War.'

'We can trick her,' Rath said. 'She likes me.'

He reached for the lead on the desk and leaned towards the floor. 'Come along, Kirie,' he said, and the dog came running to nudge its wet nose against him, wanting to play. He attached the lead. 'So,' he said to the officer, handing him the leather pull strap. 'All yours.'

'Much obliged. Shall we, then?'

The dog realised what was happening. No sooner had the lead changed hands than she began to bark and strain against the harness.

'Boy, she's a strong one,' said the officer, who was having great difficulty hauling her to the door. Erika Voss came in.

'What's going on here?' she asked. 'The poor thing, what on earth are you doing?'

'I know her kind,' the officer said, his boozer's nose now glistening. 'She'll calm down once we get her to the pound.'

'You brute! Say something, Inspector.'

'But Fräulein Voss! The man is only doing his job.'

'His job? It's cruelty to animals, that's what it is.'

'I don't have to stand here and take this!' said the officer.

'You heard me, cruelty to animals!'

'Fräulein Voss!'

'Now listen to me, young lady! I'm doing you a favour here. If you don't want me to—then be my guest. I've better ways to spend my time!' With that, he passed the lead to a startled Erika Voss and moved towards the door. 'Good day!'

He almost collided with Andreas Lange on the way out. 'Who was that?' the assistant detective asked.

'A colleague from the canine unit, whom Fräulein Voss has just succeeded in scaring off,' Rath said.

The secretary looked a little sheepish. 'I'm sorry, Inspector, but you saw how the man was treating him, poor thing.'

'He's a she, and her name is Kirie.'

'A *lady* dog! That's how she knew not to go with a wretch like that.'

'So what are we going to do with her now?' Rath asked.

'Simple,' the secretary said. 'One of us takes her home.'

'I'm not taking her,' Lange said. 'Impossible! I've got . . .'

'. . . two cats in your flat. I know,' Rath said. 'Perhaps you can help us out then, Fräulein Voss. After all, you're the one who got us into this.'

'I'd love to, but pets aren't allowed where I live.'

Rath looked at his two colleagues as they stood with lowered eyes, and at the shaggy black dog training its innocent, shining gaze on him. When Kirie tilted her head to one side and seemed to smile, his resistance was broken.

'Fine,' he said. 'I'll take her. But only until her mistress turns up.' A smile flitted across the face of Erika Voss. 'I'll be charging the food costs to the Free State of Prussia. And you, Fräulein Voss, will see to it that Prussia pays.'

'With pleasure, Inspector.'

Erika Voss disappeared back to the outer office, leaving the two CID men alone. Lange sat down at Gräf's desk. 'It's dog eat dog in here,' he said.

'You're at least the twenty-seventh person to make a joke about dogs today.'

'I just hope you won't be bringing her to the office.'

'Right now it's the weekend. Hopefully Kirie's mistress will have turned up again by Monday.'

'You don't really think that, do you?'

Rath fell silent. 'No,' he said finally and shook his head. 'Not from the way it looked in the flat.'

'That's what I said to Böhm. He was extremely annoyed that you weren't there, by the way.'

'What did you tell him?'

'That you were hard at work, of course.'

'Doing what, exactly?'

'Combing the area around Fastré's flat, trying to ascertain who saw her last. The usual.'

'And that's precisely what we're going to do now. I've already spoken to the producer. It wasn't very fruitful, but we do have a list of names, drawn up by Missing Persons this morning. People who were close to her in'the city, and some who had more intimate dealings. We'll canvass them systematically: when and where did you last see Frau Fastré? The usual questions.'

'I'm afraid something has happened to her.'

'So am I, Lange, but that won't spare us the grunt work. Does Böhm think there's a link to the Franck case?'

'No.' Lange shook his head. 'At least, he's hoping there isn't. If the press get any more fuel for their serial killer theory he's afraid there'll be hysteria in Berlin, worse than Düsseldorf even.'

'If people want to get hysterical, then that's what they'll do. Not even Gennat was able to prevent it.'

'DCI Böhm impressed upon me that we should proceed as discreetly as possible. On no account should anything be leaked.'

'Easier said than done. That doesn't just depend on us—Böhm should know that by now. What does he think of our suggestion to search all disused cinemas in the city?'

'Not much. Too costly, and above all too hasty, he says, no need to throw the cat amongst the pigeons. We shouldn't be looking for possible links to the Franck case. On the contrary, we should be trying to locate evidence which shows there are entirely logical explanations for Fastré's disappearance.'

Rath gave an angry shake of the head. 'Lange, my man, I'm afraid I didn't hear a word of that. Before we set to work on our list, I'll telephone the search unit and ask them to find out which cinemas are no longer in use. That way, local stations can carry out the checks. That shouldn't be too costly, should it? And if the press don't hear of it, there won't be any pigeons to throw the cat amongst.'

'Böhm will kill us.'

'Don't worry about that. If anyone's for the chop, it'll be me.'

37

She is exhausted. It's no use anymore. He has to end it.

How many days has she been here now? He doesn't know.

What time is it? Morning again? Afternoon? Evening? What does it matter?

Time no longer exists; it has been banished from this room where daylight does not enter, this room which does not depend on the course of the sun.

How beautiful she is. He gives her a final jab, and she looks at him with an expression of profound gratitude. She has not only grown used to it, she positively longs for it. Soon she will be summoning her final reserves.

Since he has taken her false voice, a certain intimacy has grown between them. She has overcome the shock quicker than the first, whom he could only film on one occasion before setting free.

She has submitted completely to her fate and entrusted herself to his care, as if she knows he will grant her immortality. Even though he hasn't spoken to her since. Not a single word. He doesn't want to sully these silent, angel-like beings with the sound of his own imperfect voice.

He places the glass in front of her, as he has each time in the preceding hours, closes the door and takes his position behind the camera. She knows that he is watching her through the screen. She probably knows he is filming her too, even if the whirr of the camera can't reach her. The room is soundproof.

She gazes into the black screen as if she knows he is standing behind the thick glass and yet she sees only herself, in all her perfect beauty.

He gets some wonderful scenes again, even if the exhaustion is now writ large on her face. She gazes directly into the lens, as if she knows where to look.

One of those images he will never forget, for which he needs no camera because it is forever burned into his memory, her eyes, her gaze . . .

Her gaze that day at the Christmas table . . . The way Mother places her cutlery to one side and dabs her mouth with the serviette before speaking. He ought to have known it then, the moment she asks her question, her voice warm and solicitous, her eyes ever so cold.

Richard, are you not well?

Don't worry, darling, a little dizzy spell. You've only just given me a jab; I'll be fine in a moment.

Perhaps you should go and lie down, says the warm voice beneath the cold eyes.

Certainly not . . .

Should I give you another jab?

Father waves her away, but soon it becomes worse. There is sweat on his forehead, he starts to speak incoherently. Before dessert, Albert and Mother carry him to the sofa in the library where it is quiet and dark. They have to support him, so weak is he suddenly, this powerful, old man with the biblical beard.

When they look in on him quarter of an hour later, he is no longer moving. Dr Schlüter is called, but the senior medical officer can only pronounce the death of his old friend. Richard Marquard, head of a vast financial empire, is dead, deceased on Christmas Eve 1925, before the exchange of gifts.

At the time he attached no significance to the glance Dr Schlüter cast his mother. He took if for sympathy, for compassion, and not for love.

He believes Mother's tears. Because he still doesn't know she has gone mad.

When he checks his insulin ampoules a few days later, he is surprised there are so few; he had thought he could get by for longer. But he thinks nothing of it. Dr Schlüter will get him more.

After the death of his father, the senior medical officer comes by more and more often to comfort them. Mother is grateful, but soon it becomes too much for her; all too often the doctor disrupts the togetherness of mother and son.

Her tears soon dry.

She is happy when she is alone with her son. And he is glad he can console her about the death of her husband.

Then Dr Schlüter dies too. Only a few months after Father, on the same sofa.

This time the results are clear: death from hypoglycaemia. For some years, the senior medical officer had been suffering from mild, age-related diabetes, which he treated with small doses of insulin to continue eating and drinking normally. It is inexplicable that the experienced physician should have administered himself the incorrect dose.

Once again there are insulin ampoules missing from the cupboard, and the memory of Christmas Eve returns with a vengeance. He is standing next to his dead father again, and this time sees clearly how Dr Schlüter takes the syringe and smells the hypodermic needle. Sees the brief moment of shock, of horror in the doctor's eyes as his gaze flits to that of Mother.

He knew! The doctor knew!

And yet he covered for her.

Why?

Now he is lying there himself, dying a miserable death from too much insulin. And there are only two people who know the truth.

Mother and son.

And now? What is he to do with her? With a murderer in the house? He cannot give her up to the police; she is the only person he has left.

Why did you do it? he asks after Dr Schlüter's funeral, when they are back alone in the house.

Because you are my son and I love you.

She smiles blissfully as she says it. At last she has her son to herself.

Father had it coming for a long time, she says. Have you forgotten how he tormented you?

And Dr Schlüter?

What do they want from me, all these men? It's you alone that I love! Come to me, my boy! No one will torment you anymore.

You are mad. He doesn't say anything else. Just these three words.

She smiles blissfully. My darling boy.

And when he locks her up, when she is locked up by her own son, she laughs her laugh for the first time, that unbearable squealing laugh which drowns the whole house in madness, and sits at the window and stares at the lake for hours on end.

Her gaze fixes on the screen. She seizes the glass, drinks from it ever more greedily, but it's no good, not this time. She throws it against the wall when she realises it contains only water.

No juice, nothing sweet, not this time.

Her gaze. The recognition. The understanding. So much expression in that gaze. At that moment he feels a love for her such as he has never felt before.

It is the best film he has ever made.

38

No sooner had the car door clicked shut than the dog was making a fuss. Kirie reared on her hind legs, pressed her front paws against the passenger door and barked at the window, which steamed up immediately. Nor did the barking stop when Rath opened the door, only now the dog was also wagging its tail, and jumping up and down agitatedly on the leather upholstery. He could barely grab hold of her collar to put her back on the lead.

'Looks like you're coming with me,' he said. 'So behave yourself! We don't want you peeing on a stranger's carpet.'

As it turned out they didn't get that far. Before passing through to the rear building, Rath rang the caretaker's door. It wouldn't hurt to get a little information about the tenant before their visit. A woman in a stained apron opened the door and looked at them suspiciously, first at the dog and then at Rath. Her face was clearly divided into horizontal and vertical lines: the nose a narrow strip, beneath it thin lips pressed together.

'If you're here about the flat—you can forget it!'

Rath sighed and showed his badge. 'Rath, CID,' he said. 'I have a few questions about one of your tenants.'

'What's all this about?'

'I'm afraid I can't tell you that. A little incident at Ford, we're looking for witnesses, and . . .'

'Ford, you say? Then you'll be wanting Schmieder.'

'Correct.'

'Afraid you're out of luck there, Superintendent . . .'

'Inspector . . .'

'. . . Schmieder spends his weekends with his fiancée.'

'That's a pity. It's quite urgent.'

'Should I ask him to get in touch?'

'When's he back?'

'Oh, Sunday usually, and generally pretty late. It depends what shift he's on.' She leaned a little closer to him, as if the dog wasn't supposed to hear what she was saying: 'He's head over heels, I'm telling you. The whole week, he can barely wait to see his Gertie! Even went on Thursday this time.'

'Love's a funny thing. How do you know so much anyway?'

'Please! You have to keep an eye on your tenants.'

'Then no doubt you can give me her address too, Schmieder's girl-friend . . .'

'Fiancée . . .'

'. . . fiancée then. Does she live in Moabit as well?'

'No idea.' She shrugged her shoulders. 'All I know is Frau Hagedorn must live somewhere near Stettiner Bahnhof. That's where he always heads.'

'Thank you,' Rath said, and tipped his hat. He wrote down the name as soon as he returned to the car: *Hagedorn (Gertrud?)* and underneath: *Stettiner Bahnhof.* He thought about heading back to the Castle to check the address with the passport office, but then his gaze alighted on Kirie. Until now the dog had coped with his driving, but Rath was in no mood to tempt fate.

'Shall we?' he said and started the engine.

He made a quick stop in Spenerstrasse but neither Charly nor Greta were home on a Saturday afternoon. 'Well, Kirie,' he said, as they descended the steps, 'you'll just have to meet her tomorrow.'

The journey from Moabit to Kreuzberg passed without incident. Before allowing the dog inside the flat Rath took her for a walk through the gardens of the filled canal basin towards the Engelbecken, the expanse of water that had been retained so that the dome of Sankt Michael could be reflected in it. Kirie enjoyed the exercise, pulling on the lead as if she were a fully grown husky.

Back at the flat, Rath gave the hungry dog something to eat, along with a bowl of water. He had asked Erika Voss to get him some dog food from Wertheim in Königstrasse, which she seemed to like. While the dog ate its way through the contents of the bowl, Rath looked for something that might be suitable as a bed. He found an old woollen blanket and used it to line the dirty laundry basket which Frau Lennartz came by to collect once a week. Kirie looked at him quizzically when he entered the kitchen with the basket, whose contents he had tipped on the bedroom floor.

Rath placed it in the corner. 'Come on, off to bed with you!' Kirie preferred to curl into a ball beneath the kitchen table. 'As you wish,' he said, 'but don't go complaining I didn't offer you a bed.'

He closed the kitchen door and went into the living room. Straightaway the dog started scratching at the door.

He sighed and opened the door to find Kirie wagging her tail and barking at him. 'I know you've had a bad experience of being left alone. Don't worry, that won't happen here, but you do have to stay in the kitchen. The rest of the flat is off-limits.'

He left the door ajar and went back to the living room, leaving the dog to gaze after him through the crack. He had just put on a record and sat in his chair when he heard a pitter-pattering in the hall. Kirie came in and made herself comfortable under the living room table.

'Stay here then,' he said. 'There's no point in training you anyway, that's your mistress's responsibility. If we find her, that is.'

The dog curled up and fell asleep.

When the record came to an end, Rath took the telephone back to his chair. His mother answered. 'Son! Fancy that! How are you?'

'Fine. Is Father there?'

'It's so nice to hear your voice again! Father says that you . . . that there's a woman . . . Aren't you going to introduce us? Does she cook for you too?'

'There's no woman anymore.'

A brief silence at the other end of the line. 'Oh,' she said, 'I'm sorry to hear that.'

'There's no need for you to be.'

'I had been hoping you'd get engaged again. You're not getting any younger, Gereon, and a family is . . .'

'I know, Mama.'

'I'm only saying. Are you eating well?'

'Mama, the station in Berlin has a canteen. Besides, there are more than enough restaurants.'

'Still, there's nothing like a good, home-cooked meal!'

'I'm doing just fine. Can I please speak to Father now? This is a long-distance call!'

He heard her place the receiver to one side. It took a moment or two before Engelbert Rath came on the line.

'Son! Nice of you to telephone your mother. You wouldn't believe how happy it makes her.'

'My pleasure. I have a request. It's about Adenauer's list. It only contains men.'

'So what?'

'Can you please ask Adenauer, along with his friends at the bank, if they know a Fräulein or Frau Hagedorn? First name probably Gertrud.'

'Do you have a lead?'

'If the name means anything to Adenauer and his friends, then yes.'

'I'll take care of it right away, my boy. How are things otherwise?'

'Busy.'

'Your fian . . . girlfriend . . . Mother said she had . . .'

'*I* left *her*. It can happen that way too.'

'How many women is that now? Take care that you don't become an old bachelor. You should think about getting married soon if you want to make a career for yourself.'

'Gennat is a confirmed bachelor as well as Prussia's best criminal investigator.'

'Well, they say he wasn't so successful in Düsseldorf, the infallible one. And he's never made it past superintendent.'

'Yes, Police Director, Sir!'

'Listen, my boy, I know how highly you regard Gennat. Nothing against the man, but I'm not sure he's the best role model for you. Someone of your capabilities should be aiming for Scholz's position.'

Police Director Hans Scholz was head of the Berlin CID.

'You don't get posts like that unless you belong to the right party.'

'That's what I've been telling you, my boy.'

'Papa, leave it. You won't catch me in your beloved Centre Party. And there's no way I'm joining the Sozis either. I'm not a politician. In fact, I despise politics.'

'Politics is the order of the day, my boy.'

'Politics is making our neighbours kill one another. Turning our streets into a battleground.'

'You're talking about its excesses. Nazis and Communists might call each other politicians but that's not what they are.'

'It's what they want to be.'

'It won't come to that.'

'Let's leave it there, Papa. You know conversations like this don't lead anywhere. Call me if you find something about Gertrud Hagedorn.'

He hung up, turned the record over and poured himself a cognac. He tried to think: about Jeanette Fastré, whose disappearance was ominously reminiscent of Vivian Franck's, even if Böhm wouldn't admit it; about Felix Krempin and his unhappy death; but his thoughts kept coming back to Charly. Should he call her? Control yourself, he thought. Bad enough that you almost ambushed her at her house earlier. You're seeing her tomorrow, and that will have to do.

Just don't show any weakness, don't lay yourself open—was that something he had from his father, Police Director Engelbert Rath, the man who always knew how to save face? He was pouring another cognac when the doorbell rang.

Rath looked at the time—almost nine. A little late for a visit. He stood up and opened to find a telegram boy in leather gear, motorcycle goggles pushed onto his forehead.

'Telegram for Gereon Rath.'

'Thank you.' He fished two ten-pfennig pieces out of his trouser pocket and gave the boy a tip. As soon as he had closed the door he tore open the envelope and read. Sent from Cologne Hauptbahnhof barely four hours ago:

arrive tonight 22.35 potsdamer bahnhof STOP staying at hotel excelsior STOP time for a beer STOP look forward to facing your (w)rath STOP paul

He hadn't seen Paul since his birthday last year and now here he was coming pell-mell to Berlin. He still had an hour and a half in which he searched out a fresh suit, quickly showered and changed. He had hoped to leave Kirie in the flat, but the dog kicked up such a fuss that he had to take her with him.

'They should call you Clingy, not Kirie,' he said, once the dog had taken its place on the passenger seat, panting away happily. 'It's much too late for little things like you.'

This time he was in luck, finding a parking space directly in front of the station, despite the chaos at Potsdamer Platz. By twenty past ten, Rath was already at the barrier showing the conductor his platform ticket. He had no idea which car Paul was in, so stayed at the start of the platform.

'Sit,' he said to the dog and, contrary to expectations, she obeyed. One cigarette and the train would be here. Rath picked an Overstolz out of his case and immersed himself in his thoughts.

It was on this very platform that he had stepped from a train a year ago himself. No one met him at the station. Scarcely anyone knew he was in Berlin. He felt lonely, but freed of a burden as he made his way down the platform, everything around him as unreal as a dream. The station spat him into the cold night and, gazing at the lights, the cars and the people on Potsdamer Platz, he understood that this was the start of his new life. Now, for the first time, someone from his old life was coming to visit him in the new.

The train rolled in a few minutes early and came hissing to a stop. What a welcoming committee, Rath thought, as he caught sight of his reflection: an exhausted inspector and an abandoned dog.

He trod the cigarette out. The doors opened and between one moment and the next the platform contained twice as many people. He scanned the milling mass pushing towards the exit and eventually found Paul, who looked the same as he always had: blond hair that resisted any effort at grooming and was kept in check by a hat, a nose that was slightly too big, and an impudent grin.

Paul had long since spotted his welcoming committee, and his grin grew wider as he approached. They stood looking at each other as the crowd pushed and shoved around them, surveying one another, as if neither wanted to be the first to grow sentimental.

'No flowers?' Paul said.

'The dog ate them,' Rath replied.

They embraced a little awkwardly and clapped each other on the shoulder a little too hard.

39

Sunday 9th March 1930

It is pitch-black in the yard, but he has no intention of striking a light. If it remains dark, no one will see him. He switched his headlights off on the road outside. No one saw him open the gate and drive the car into the courtyard. Now the gate is closed again, and he has switched off the engine. He is safe here, no one can wander in or see inside. There might still be a few night owls passing the main entrance, but they won't see what is happening behind the billboards.

He finds the keys even in the dark. The company has so many he simply took the ones that looked right and sorted them out before coming. He hasn't used them in a long time, there have been no films shown here since Christmas.

The moon, his friend, finally appears from behind the clouds, sketching pale contours in the night. The lock is a little stiff, but the key turns. Slowly and carefully, so that the hinges don't creak, he moves one leaf of the heavy steel door, which once served as an emergency exit, into the auditorium. Only now does he open the van. There she is, lying between empty film cans, peaceful in the moonlight that falls upon her face. It's a shame he can't film this moment.

He feels very close to her as he carries her up the six steps to the auditorium. Only once he has closed the door again does he switch on the flashlight. He has already assigned her a space, and it is there that he now carries her.

He doesn't just lay her down. No, he makes a bed for her so that she looks more beautiful than ever. He pulls a little at her dress to arrange the folds, takes a step back and looks upon his work with satisfaction. That is what she is now: his work.

They needed too long to find the first. How long will they need this time?

He must tear himself away. He wants to be at home when the early risers emerge from their houses. He locks the door carefully as he leaves, and goes straight to the gate, checking the road before steering the car out. All is quiet. Not a soul nearby. He is satisfied with his work. In the car he removes his leather gloves.

Before he goes to bed he will open a bottle of wine and watch her films over again.

40

Something warm and damp slobbered on Rath's cheek, rousing him from a deep, dreamless sleep. Kirie was crouched next to the pillow, smiling at him with her tongue out. He started when he saw the black, shaggy hair and held his head in his hands. A throbbing pain protested the speed with which he had sat up.

He didn't have the energy to chase the dog out of bed, but Kirie jumped out of her own accord, wagging her tail and barking at him gamely. 'Not so loud,' he said. The dog gave a short bark before pitter-pattering out of the room.

He tried to recall but there was nothing. He must have left the door open when he came to bed, but where had the dog slept? Hopefully not in bed with him! His alarm clock showed half past eight.

In the bathroom, he splashed cold water on his face and washed an aspirin down with half a litre of water. He hadn't been this bad for a long time, but it was no use; he had to take Kirie out. There was no time for coffee. He threw on yesterday's clothes without taking a shower and put her on the lead.

He wasn't the only Sunday stroller on Luisenufer, but he was the only unshaven one. The morning sun had already enticed a few people out, above all dog owners. He had arranged to meet Charly at eleven, and needed to be on top form by then. His head was still pounding, but it was set to be a fine day.

What on earth had happened last night? He must have been drinking the wrong stuff, and far too much of it. Yet they had started with beer in the Europa-Pavillon, right next to Paul's hotel. They had stayed there, precisely because he didn't want to run the risk of coming a cropper somewhere after touring the local pubs. That much he could still remember.

As they strolled northwards through the gardens the memories rose to the surface. Yes, they had started with beer, which ought to have told Rath where the night was heading. It probably had, too, only he had deliberately ignored the signs. Perhaps because he was in the mood to get drunk as they listened to the sounds of the Manhattan-Band playing pretty decent American jazz. At some point, Paul ordered the first cognac.

They hadn't seen each other for over a year and had a lot to talk about. Only that's not what they did. They chatted, of course, but only about trivial matters, about the band onstage, about the new records Rath had received from New York, all the new talkies he hadn't seen—even if he did know a few actresses who wouldn't be signing any more autographs. Paul had talked about his work too, the wine dealership he was proposing to expand into the imperial capital. He had a meeting on Monday with buyers from Kempinski.

'You should look in on the Kaiserhof as well, they could use a few good wines.'

'I've reserved two days to go door-to-door canvassing,' Paul had said. 'Who knows, perhaps Wittkamp will open a branch in Berlin.'

Apart from chatting about work they hadn't talked about themselves. Everything was exactly as it always was whenever he saw Paul. Perhaps *because* of that, Rath felt as bound to this blond, unassuming and frivolous man as he did to anyone on earth. Excepting Charly perhaps, but that was different. They were the only two who allowed him to forget his loneliness. They made the knowledge that life was a journey you travelled alone seem, however briefly, like a lie.

By the end of the night he was, more or less, incapable of standing. Paul—perhaps not entirely jokingly—had offered him a share of his double bed back at the hotel, but Rath had asked the barman to call for a taxi. He remembered that he had almost left Kirie behind, but the dog had come barking after him and jumped in alongside. How had he managed the stairs at home? Now, *that* he couldn't say; the dog had probably led him up.

Blast, his car was still at Anhalter Bahnhof!

They stopped, and Kirie took the opportunity to use of one of the many shrubs to perform her business. Time was getting on; if he had to pick up the car then he ought to get home now, feed the dog and make himself presentable.

An hour later, emerging from the elevated railway on Möckern Bridge, he was already feeling better. His headache had evaporated along with his fatigue, and the sun was shining. Kirie seemed to be enjoying her second walk just as much as the first. Somehow it was a nice feeling strolling through the morning with a smiling dog on its lead. Yes, it was going to be a beautiful day.

41

Charly was enthusiastic. 'Isn't he sweet?' she said.

Kirie crouched on the rear shelf behind the seats where Rath had tied her, panting curiously at the new passenger. 'He's a she,' he said.

Charly got in facing backwards and, instead of sitting, knelt on the passenger seat and stroked the dog. 'What's your name then, little man?'

'Kirie,' Rath replied. '*Her* name is Kirie. A lady dog. I'm looking after her temporarily. Until her mistress is back.'

'Her mistress?'

'A missing actress, but let's not talk about work. It's Sunday.'

At last Charly turned and sat down. She meant to give Rath just a quick hello kiss, but he held her to prolong it, only to be interrupted by Kirie's barking. 'Cut it out,' he scolded.

Charly couldn't help but laugh. 'I see you've brought a chaperone.'

'She probably thinks we've got something to eat.'

'Well, I hope there will be *something* to eat today.'

'Of course, and the lady can choose the location. Where to?'

'Which one? Kirie's a lady too.'

'The two-legged one, if it was up to four-legs here, we'd spend the day digging up bones and chasing cats.'

'How does a long walk by the Wannsee sound? Then Kirie gets something out of it too. We could go across to the Pfaueninsel and have a little something to eat in Nikolskoe.'

'Good choice. We'll treat ourselves to a trip on the AVUS in honour of the occasion.'

They weren't the only ones with that idea. Though they made good progress through Moabit, it was chaos on Charlottenburger Chaussee. The thermometer showed twelve degrees, and the first decent Sunday of the year was drawing half of Berlin to the country. The year before, March had tormented citizens with minus temperatures.

'I didn't know that so many people had cars,' Charly said.

As they passed Vivian Franck's apartment on Kaiserdamm, Rath couldn't help but think of the dead actress. What devil had done that to her, and how would he feel if something like that happened to Charly? He shook off the thought.

'Are you cold?' she asked.

They made a left before Reichskanzlerplatz. Behind the exhibition grounds the road joined the AVUS, and Rath was looking forward to driving the car at full speed when, before they reached the toll gate, Charly asked: 'Why don't we go up the Funkturm?'

'Pardon me?'

'Up the Funkturm.'

Rath pulled over. 'Because of the dead man I told you about?'

'Of course not! What do you take me for?'

'A detective through and through, even if you're studying law and employed by the Castle as a stenographer.'

'Perhaps I wouldn't have thought of it if you hadn't told me about Krempin. Do you really think I want to secure evidence and question witnesses up there?' She sounded outraged. 'It's such a nice day, and I've never been before. Come on! Just a cup of coffee, a little look and then onwards. Lady's choice, you said so yourself.'

'Fine,' he sighed and turned the car. 'A cup of coffee. We can't leave the dog any longer than that, she doesn't like it, and I'm pretty sure we won't be allowed to take her up.'

Though, as expected, Kirie made a fuss when she was left in the car, Charly managed to coax her into acquiescence. The crowd by the Funkturm was considerably greater than two days before. They were made to queue at the ticket office and again outside the lift. As they joined the back of the queue, Rath noticed how the man in the booth picked up the telephone as soon as he had sold them their tickets, ignoring the two Americans behind them, even though the pair were making their presence felt—the woman more so than the man. He felt ill at ease, imagining himself watched by the cashier as he telephoned. When he realised that Rath was looking back, he quickly turned away, making the Yanks see red once and for all.

'There must be free beer up there,' Charly said. 'The queue just keeps getting longer.'

'Whatever it is, it's making those American tourists impatient.'

They entered the lift and, luckily, he didn't recognise the lift attendant. It was tight in the car, smelling of too many different people, and he was glad when they disembarked.

A man in a slightly rumpled dark suit took Rath by the sleeve. 'May I see your ticket please?'

Before he could say anything the man grabbed his ticket. 'It is you!' he said.

Rath didn't know what he was after, but it couldn't have been anything bad since the next thing he heard was: 'Congratulations!'

'Pardon me?'

'May I congratulate you on behalf of the Berlin Exhibition, Trade Fair and Tourist Office. You are the millionth visitor to the Funkturm!'

Charly burst out laughing, and Rath gave a sour grin. 'Just a cup of coffee,' he hissed.

'Perhaps there'll be a glass of champagne in it,' she whispered back, and smiled. Meanwhile a photographer had taken up position in front of them. That was all he needed!

'A photo for the papers, please,' the man in the suit said.

'Do we have to?'

Instead of answering, the man in the suit shook his hand and turned with a grin towards the photographer. Then came the flash. Luckily it wasn't a crime correspondent. Rath didn't recognise the young man who now produced pen and paper. He couldn't have been more than eighteen or nineteen.

'Might I ask for your name?' he said. 'Do you come from Berlin or are you a tourist? Have you been to the Funkturm before? How do you like Berlin?'

'Have you interviewed people before? Or do you always ask all your questions at once?' Rath replied. The boy went red.

'Your name first, please,' he said. 'For *B.Z.* and other important . . .'

'I'm not saying another word to those ink-slingers from *B.Z . . .* Not even good day.'

'Gereon,' Charly said. 'The poor man isn't asking you to divulge police secrets.'

'So you're a police officer?' the boy asked. Rath cast Charly an angry glance.

'Like many thousands of Berliners, I'd like to have a peaceful weekend,' he said. 'If you would be so discreet as to avoid naming any names. The lady accompanying me is a famous film actress and doesn't wish to be identified.'

'An actress!' The young man took his camera and flashed.

Rath pulled Charly away, leaving the young journalist gazing after them in confusion. Soon he would be trawling the editorial archives for the film star he had just photographed.

The man in the suit took their coats and led them to a handsomely decorated table with a prime view of Charlottenburg, only two tables along from where Rath had sat two days before. He couldn't help thinking about Krempin's distorted features, about the unreal sight of his face through the panorama window. At least Charly didn't mention the subject again.

'We have taken the liberty of serving you and your companion a welcoming drink,' said the man in the suit, 'on the house, of course.'

There really was champagne. Own-brand, but not quite as sticky as the bottle threatened, and well chilled. They clinked glasses, although not exactly in a spirit of romantic togetherness. Two waiters stood at their table as well as the man in the suit.

'As a special surprise we'd like to present you with this small gift,' he said, pressing a dark blue wrapped package into his hands.

Rath placed it next to the chair and toasted Charly again. 'Let's get out of here,' he whispered. 'We'll come back when we can enjoy the view in peace.'

Charly nodded and drained her glass in one gulp. She could barely wipe the amused grin off her face, even as she drank.

Rath likewise emptied his glass, took the package and stood up. He shook the man's hand. 'Thank you,' he said, 'for a truly unforgettable experience!'

He pulled Charly over to the lift. No sooner had the door closed than she snorted with laughter. He looked at her briefly, and could no longer keep a straight face either. Unlike Charly, however, he managed to recover halfway down. The rest of the passengers looked on in irritation.

'Ground floor,' the lift attendant said, unperturbed, and opened the door.

'I'd never have thought a visit to the Funkturm could be so worthwhile,' Rath said, weighing the blue package in his hand. Charly still had tears of laughter in her eyes. They linked arms and together made for the exit.

'Gereon?' said a slightly hung-over voice from the queue in front of the ticket office.

Rath turned around. 'Paul? What are you doing here?'

'Small world. I was giving myself a tour of the imperial capital, seeing as you don't have the time. Is this the countryside you were so desperate to get to?'

'Minor detour,' said Rath. 'There's no escaping you, is there?'

'I'd have avoided anything with even the slightest tinge of green today, so as not to see you, but how was I to know you meant the Funkturm? I didn't realise you were so colour-blind.'

'Well, what brings you here then?'

'A tip from reception. First the Brandenburger Tor and Unter den Linden, then up the Funkturm and a little wander on the Ku'damm. That's what they recommend to unsuspecting foreigners.' He peered curiously at Charly. 'Aren't you going to introduce your companion?'

Rath cleared his throat. 'Of course. Charlotte Ritter, Paul Wittkamp, an old friend from Cologne.'

Paul stretched out a hand to Charly. 'Less of the old, thanks. You're showing Berlin to our friend from the Rhine Province?'

'Someone has to,' said Charly.

'What a charming companion. No such luck for me, I'm afraid. I have to explore Berlin on my own.'

'My heart bleeds,' Rath said.

'Why don't you come with us, then you won't have to spend Sunday alone?'

Rath looked at Charly. Apparently, she was serious.

'Paul wants to go up the Funkturm, where we've just been.'

'Perhaps he'd like to change his plans and come with us instead.'

'Before speculation runs wild, perhaps I should say something myself,' Paul interrupted. 'That's a very kind offer, but one I must decline. I've already spoiled Gereon's Saturday evening. He deserves a rest from me today.'

'You won't be spoiling anything,' said Charly. 'If you fancy a little trip to the lake, then come with us. You can see the Funkturm and the Ku'damm another time. Besides . . . you wouldn't believe how much I'd like to meet one of Gereon's friends.'

It didn't take much to break Paul's resistance. 'What can I say? I've no response to an argument like that.' He gave a particularly impudent grin and together they made their way to the parking lot and the car, where Kirie fell over herself with excitement. Rath let her out.

She almost tore the blue wrapping paper to pieces. Rath placed the package in the glove compartment, causing the wig to fall into his hands. He had almost forgotten about it. He stuffed it back in with the package, hoping no one had seen.

'Aren't you going to unwrap it?' Charly asked.

'Later,' Rath said, and went round to the back of the car to open out the foldaway seat. It didn't look especially comfortable, and Paul, who had been allowed use of the passenger seat the evening before, didn't seem too crazy about it. Even if he claimed otherwise. 'No problem,' he said. 'As long as I don't have to take the dog on my lap.'

Charly thought differently. 'We can't go on the AVUS like that, there'll be too much of a slipstream. Let's take the train,' she decided. 'Witzleben is only round the corner. It'll be just as quick.'

Three-quarters of an hour later they emerged at Bahnhof Wannsee. 'We can take the bus to Nikolskoe,' Charly said, 'or go by foot. It's four or five kilometres though.'

'We did want to go for a walk,' Rath said. 'The dog could use the exercise.'

'Can I take Kirie?' Charly asked.

They made their way through the colony of villas, gazing in astonishment. 'Look at these houses,' Paul said, 'each one more palatial than the last.'

'These aren't *houses*. They're *estates*.'

'If only I were rich,' Paul said. 'I'd live on an estate like that, not in some raised ground-floor flat in the Agnes quarter.'

'I think even if I had money, I'd still live in Moabit,' Charly said.

Rath said nothing. On the opposite shore he could make out the towers and battlements of the Marquard villa. Even on a sunny day like this there was something forbidding about it. He'd sooner stay on Luisenufer than move in there. Or he could live with Charly in Moabit.

At some point the line of villas came to an end and they reached the forest. After a time the path led them back to the shore, where they enjoyed fine views of the lake on which the first sailors were testing their rusty boats.

'That's the Pfaueninsel over there,' Charly said. 'Queen Luise's favourite island.'

'You're well informed . . .'

'My father used to bring me walking here,' she said. 'He loves it. You can take the ferry across back there, but I think if we keep going a little longer we'll be in Nikolskoe.'

They continued along the lake with the Pfaueninsel always in view until, suddenly, in the middle of the forest, a church appeared on their left. Soon they were outside a Russian log cabin, which stood in solitary splendour on a little hill above the lake.

'Nikolskoe,' Charly said.

'I'd never have thought we were quite *so* far east,' Paul said.

Inside the log cabin was a restaurant. The terrace viewed the lake, and the landlord had optimistically placed the first tables and parasols outside. They had difficulty finding a seat until a waiter led them purposefully to a wobbly little table.

'Do they speak German here?' Paul asked.

'You can dig out your Russian if you want to,' Rath said.

'The first landlord was actually a Russian,' Charly said. 'Ivan Bockov, the King's coachman. When the cabin was finished, in 1820, he became the custodian. In those first few years it was mostly the King who came for tea but, little by little, the cabin became a popular destination. Bockov provided his guests with hearty food and entertainment, even music for dancing. He was a pretty decent piano player. The King forbade it when he found out, but Bockov continued in secret. Nikolskoe was simply too popular. That's how it all started. It's not exactly your average tourist café.'

The waiter who appeared shortly afterwards at their table didn't give a particularly Russian impression. He seemed more like a sullen Berliner.

'Solyanka's finished,' he said, when Rath tried to order something to match their surroundings. He recommended the Wiener Schnitzel and, given the lack of alternatives, that's what all three chose.

'Is it still illegal to serve food here?' Paul whispered. 'The waiter looks like he just got out of jail.'

'Welcome to Berlin,' Rath said.

'Careful,' said Charly. 'You're here with a Berliner!'

'The exception proves the rule.'

The waiter came with their drinks and a bowl of water for the dog. He was fond of animals at any rate. Paul chose the wine, and it was very good.

'So, you're a travelling wine salesman?' Charly asked.

'I have a wine store which we're hoping to expand, to bring a more high-quality Rhine wine to the capital.' Paul raised his glass. 'Now that we're armed at last, don't you think it's time we dispensed with the formalities? If not, I'll get confused and start calling Gereon "Herr Rath", which is something I've never done. So, I'm Paul.'

'Charlotte.'

They clinked glasses, and Paul gave Charly a kiss on each cheek.

'Can I join in?' asked Rath. 'Even if we already call each other by our first names.'

'Why? You haven't said I should address you *formally*.'

Rath felt himself growing jealous, as if Paul had stolen Charly's laughter from him. They had once clashed over a woman, and it had nearly destroyed their friendship. Since then they had sworn not to let anything like that happen again. Friendship had to take precedence over any love affair.

But Charly wasn't just any love affair. He heard his name and realised that Paul and Charly were talking about him. 'How did you two meet?' she asked.

'In school. I was new to the class, my parents had moved from Neuwied. I didn't know anyone and the first thing Gereon did was throw a wet sponge at my head when the teacher wasn't looking.'

'Pardon me?'

'The only free seat was next to me, and I didn't want the new boy to sit there,' Rath said. 'But the others also wanted him to get the sponge. They passed it back from the front row until it reached me. The thing was soaking wet. I think we'd actually been planning for the teacher to sit on it, old Bremser, but then the new boy came in.'

'And?'

Rath shrugged his shoulders. 'Paul didn't react at all. His face was dripping with chalk-soaked water, but he took his seat calm as you like. The one next to me.'

'Then we had a little chat in second recess, quite an intense one actually. And we've been friends ever since.'

'Me with my swollen lip and you with your black eye, or was it the other way around?'

'No idea,' Paul said. 'We were both marked for a long time at any rate. Something like that creates a bond.'

'Really!' Charly laughed. 'I just hope you don't have to beat each other up every half-year to renew your friendship.'

'We don't see each other that often.'

'What made you throw a sponge at the new boy?'

'Gereon has always been a little headstrong,' Paul said. 'Has he told you about the time he stirred things up at Sunday mass in St Bruno's? In Holy Cologne at that!'

This wasn't a harmless anecdote anymore. This was a test. Paul wanted to know how serious it was between him and Charly. *Very serious, my friend, very serious. You'll see!*

'What happened?' Charly asked.

'Not much really.' Rath lit a cigarette before telling the story. 'My brother and I filled the incense globes with hashish.'

'Hashish?'

'From the police inventory. They confiscated it from some poor artist, and Father brought it home and showed it to us at table. To warn us or something like that.'

'And you swiped it?'

'Not me, my brother.'

'You've never told me about your brother.'

'Severin is four years older than me and has been living in the States for a long time. It was more his idea than mine, but I helped him. Back then I was a server and I opened the sacristy for him, just before mass.'

'And?'

'We waved the incense during the consecration, and by the end Pastor Lippe was saying increasingly strange things. Which didn't strike anyone as unusual, because he was a little strange anyway.'

'But giggling during mass; he never used to do that,' Paul said.

'No one would've noticed, not until Naujoks collapsed.'

'Who?'

'The other server waving the incense. We bore the brunt of it. I wasn't feeling too good either. I felt sick, but I didn't collapse.'

'Was it because of this Naujoks that you were caught?'

'Father figured it out when he discovered the hashish was missing. Apparently, Severin was seen coming out of the back of the sacristy.'

'And you?'

'To this day my father doesn't know I was involved, and he never will. Severin didn't say anything. They knew somebody must've helped him, but he held firm.' Rath remembered the pressure they put on his brother over that stupid prank. He was packed off to boarding school, where things happened that were so terrible he never spoke of them. No sooner had he finished school than he cleared off, as far away as possible from Cologne, his family, his past, everything.

'They really tore a strip off him,' Rath continued. 'In the spring of 1914, just before war broke out, he hightailed it to America. He had only just turned nineteen.'

'My God. I thought it was a *funny* story. That's what drove your brother to America?'

Rath shrugged his shoulders. 'It wasn't the only thing, but if it wasn't for that stupid prank, things would've probably turned out differently.'

'For you too?'

'It pretty much knocked the stuffing out of me, what they did to Severin, and, if they had caught me, it would have been worse.' He stubbed out the cigarette. 'Paul is the only person who knows the truth,' he said finally. 'Now you do too.'

'Welcome to the club,' Paul said, but Charly couldn't bring herself to laugh.

The waiter came with their schnitzels and they ate in silence. For the time being the easy atmosphere between them had been destroyed. Rath looked across at Paul. Why had he brought up the hash story now, of all times? Of course, he had wanted to know how far Rath would go in Charly's presence, what she meant to him. But why now? He could have just asked him. Not that they ever spoke about their women. Yesterday evening Rath had simply told him he had a date, and that he was heading out to the country with a girl.

Paul was first to finish. He ordered another round of wine and asked for the bill. The wine came when Rath and Charly were also finished. The waiter placed the bill on the table. 'Allow me,' Paul said. 'A little thank-you for the invitation and the lovely afternoon.'

'Absolutely not,' Rath protested. 'You paid for last night as well.'

'If I want to pay then surely you can let me.'

'Would the gentlemen care to duel—or do I get my money today?' the waiter asked.

Rath pressed thirty marks into his hand, and Paul added a five-mark note. The waiter bowed. 'Good day, gentlemen.'

They took the bus back to Bahnhof Wannsee, where Paul was suddenly in a hurry to get away. 'You'll forgive me if I leave now,' he said. 'But I think I would like to take a little wander round Berlin after all. It isn't every day you're in the imperial capital.' They said their goodbyes on the platform. 'It was nice to meet you,' he said to Charly. 'Thanks for this afternoon.'

'It was only half an afternoon,' she said.

The train was already rolling into the station as he said goodbye to Rath. 'You won't find another like her,' he whispered as the two men briefly embraced. 'Make sure you hold onto her!'

Paul jumped on-board the train to Potsdamer Platz. 'Perhaps we'll see each other again!' he shouted before the doors closed.

Kirie barked after the departing train and Rath looked at Charly. It was a rather hasty goodbye. She seemed to think so too. 'That's Paul,' he said. 'Not always easy to understand.'

'Says you! I think he just wanted to be discreet and leave us alone.'

'What now? Should we head back and go to the Pfaueninsel?'

'Another time.' She gestured towards the station clock. 'It's almost four. Let's go back to your car.'

'What should we do with the rest of the afternoon?'

'I could think of something,' she said, nestling up to him.

'Your place or mine?'

'Yours,' she said, her lips drawing closer to his mouth. He closed his eyes and kissed her, but at precisely that moment the dog started barking. Their train was coming in.

42

He had hoped the day might end in Luisenufer, and so had cleaned beforehand. Not wanting it to look too much like a bachelor flat he had taken the empty beer bottles down to the cellar, washed the dirty dishes and, above all, placed the bottle of cognac next to the other bottles in the cupboard. He fetched it now, along with two glasses, placed an empty ashtray on the table and put on a record.

'What a treat to be waited on by a man!'

'All part of the Sunday service.'

'Just the *Sunday* service?'

'Try it.'

They clinked glasses.

Kirie had curled into a ball under the living room table, ignoring the basket Rath had so lovingly prepared. She ought really to have been in the kitchen after demolishing a whole bowl of food in record time, but no sooner had he closed the door than she began barking, scratching and whimpering. He had no choice but to open it again.

'Are you training the dog or is she training you?'

'Kirie belongs to a diva, so she can afford to have bad manners.'

Rath put on something slow, a languid blues: Bessie Smith accompanied by Louis Armstrong on trumpet, and they sat for a while, listening.

'Is dancing permitted here?' Charly asked.

Rath stood up, held out his right hand and pulled her from her chair. Nestled closely together, they moved to the gentle, rhythmical beat. He waited for the final chord to take her chin in his hands and kiss her long and hard, until fierce barking interrupted them. An indignant Kirie stood before them.

'This can't be happening,' he said. 'Whenever we kiss, the dog barks. Come on, Kirie, out!'

Kirie lay back down.

Charly laughed. 'I think she's jealous. She objects to you kissing me.'

'Then she needs to go to her basket.'

'You know how much fuss she makes when you shut her in.'

'As far as I'm concerned the whole flat can be hers, but the bedroom is ours.'

Kirie seemed content with her fate. There was no more barking to be heard, no sound of furniture being overturned or vases being smashed and, at last, they could kiss one another.

The feel of Charly's body, the redolence of her scent, was hugely arousing. They undressed each other while kissing only to lose balance and fall onto the bed. He kissed her slender throat, the nape of her neck, slowly working his way down . . . Then the telephone rang and Kirie started barking again, and neither would stop. Charly couldn't help but laugh.

'What have I done to deserve this?' he said, making for the living room in his underwear.

Kirie was standing in front of the telephone table barking at the machine. Rath picked up, and the dog fell silent as soon as the ringing ceased. It was Lange. 'Boss, finally!'

'What is it?'

'You were right!'

'Pardon me?'

'About the cinemas! We have a corpse! The Kosmos in Weissensee. Probably Fastré.'

'Is someone already out there?'

'You're the only one missing. I thought I'd let you know. It was your idea after all . . .'

'I'm on my way.'

Kirie followed him into the bedroom.

'And?' Charly asked.

Rath reached for his trousers. 'The Castle.'

He didn't have to say anything else. She got dressed too. 'Should I come with you?'

'Best not. If people see us together, there'll be talk.'

'Especially now that I don't work at the Castle.'

'Why don't you stay here? You can take Kirie for a walk. It would be nice if you could look after her.' He paused. 'It's probably her mistress we've found.'

'Oh my, poor dog.'

'I'll be back as soon as soon as I can. You can sleep here too.'

When Kirie tilted her head to one side Charly could hardly refuse.

At Antonplatz the ED car was parked behind the murder wagon. The cream-coloured Horch standing last in line looked like that of Dr Karthaus, the younger colleague of Dr Schwartz's. There was no uniformed officer guarding the main entrance, which was anyway protected by a rolling grille.

The Kosmos was one of several cinemas near Antonplatz, but the only one whose neon lights no longer burned. Andreas Lange was waiting for him under the dark letters, looking like someone who refused to acknowledge that he had been stood up, even after the cinema had closed. 'Evening, Sir,' he said. 'We have to go in via the courtyard.'

They didn't encounter a uniformed officer until they reached the concrete stairs at the rear entrance. A metal gate shielded the courtyard from the world outside.

Only inside the auditorium did the extent of the police operation become clear. There were ED men everywhere looking for clues. Meanwhile, the officers from the 271st precinct, who had found the body, were standing idly by.

This time the body was actually on the stage, right in front of the screen: a blonde angel in a sparkling, silvery-white evening dress. There was a flash, and Rath recognised Reinhold Gräf behind the camera. He gave his former partner a brief wave. Bulldog Böhm was speaking to one of the officers as well as a civilian, momentarily interrupting himself when he caught sight of Rath. He didn't seem too pleased that a search he had turned down had led to this success. Next to the corpse stood the pathologist, bobbing impatiently up and down on the balls of his feet.

'If you don't want any trouble with Böhm,' Rath said to Lange, 'tell him you couldn't get hold of me yesterday evening. You don't know anything about my telephone call to the search unit.'

'I told Böhm the truth,' Lange said. 'In my opinion you did the right thing yesterday. It's how we found Fastré's corpse, isn't it?'

'Good of you to back me up. Are we certain it's her?'

'We haven't found any papers and she hasn't been officially identified, but really there's no doubt. She looks just like her billboards.'

Rath drew closer and saw what Lange meant. Jeanette Fastré didn't look like a corpse at all. Her face had been carefully made up and though her eyes were staring up at the ceiling, they seemed more hypnotised than dead.

'Do your work, Doctor,' Böhm said to Karthaus, who immediately ceased bobbing up and down. 'We have everything we need in the can.'

'Evening, gentlemen,' Rath said politely. Böhm ignored him.

'Evening, Rath,' Karthaus said. 'Are A Division having their company outing? I haven't seen so many *earnest* faces in a long time.'

It became clear what he meant when an imposing figure emerged from the darkness and climbed the steps to the stage. Ernst Gennat! So, Gräf was right: Buddha was back, and had even driven out to the crime scene, which only happened once in a blue moon.

'Inspector,' Gennat said, when he caught sight of Rath. 'I hear we have you to thank for this discovery.'

'I'd say the search unit did a good job, Sir.'

'It seems we really do have a serial killer on our hands,' Gennat said. 'The strict information ban imposed by DCI Böhm holds for the time being. There's no need to send the public crazy while we still don't know what's going on. So, not a word to the press.'

'It seems like someone who specialises in film actresses. Shouldn't we at least warn them?'

'We'll clarify that at briefing tomorrow. There's no rush. Vivian Franck was last seen on the eighth of February and most likely killed shortly afterwards. Frau Fastré here has been dead for a few days at most. Our man likes to take his time. There's roughly a month between the two crimes.'

'Assuming there are no other victims we haven't found . . .'

'You checked all missing person cases, didn't you?'

'We've compared everything. Fastré was the first missing actress in years.'

'Then he'll bide his time before the next one.' Gennat gazed thoughtfully at the corpse. 'What do you think?' he asked. 'Why does he kill? A sex offender?'

Rath shrugged his shoulders. 'There was nothing to suggest that with Vivian Franck's corpse.'

'Still, difficult to say, given her stage of decomposition. We've been lucky this time insofar as we have such a well-preserved corpse. I'll be very interested to hear the results of Dr Karthaus's examination.'

Rath looked across at Böhm. He had dismissed the uniformed officer and was now speaking to the civilian, probably the man who had let the police in. Karthaus turned the corpse over. 'How's it looking?' Buddha asked.

Karthaus shrugged. 'No external agencies, as far as I can see.'

'No injection sites?'

'A number of them, but hardly visible, probably subcutaneous. How did you know?'

'Vivian Franck,' Rath said, more to Gennat than Karthaus. 'Schwartz found injection sites on her too. Maybe lethal.'

By now Böhm had joined them, but didn't deign to look at Rath. Gennat seemed to notice, but didn't say anything. 'Can you say how she died, Doctor?' he asked.

Karthaus shrugged. 'On first glance, I'd say natural causes. Let's see if we find any trace of poisoning during the autopsy.' He gestured towards the body that lay before them so angelically. 'I can tell you one thing for sure, however. This corpse has been washed.'

'Seriously?' Gennat was surprised.

Karthaus nodded. 'Normally,' he said, 'corpses aren't particularly sweet-smelling. Not just because of the decomposition—the sphincter fails at the moment of death, but in this case . . . there is no excrement whatsoever, everything is clean. I think she might even have been perfumed before she was left here.'

'Was that the case with Vivian Franck?'

Gennat had addressed the question to both Rath and Böhm. Rath deferred to the senior man, who raised his broad shoulders into a shrug. 'She was made up, but washed? No idea. Schwartz didn't say anything about that, nor did the men from ED. I'll tell you one thing though: Vivian Franck didn't smell good when we found her. She had already been dead for weeks.'

Gennat nodded. 'How long has this one been dead?'

Karthaus considered for a moment. 'Ten hours at the most, I'd say.'

'Are you familiar with the Franck file?' Rath asked the doctor.

'Why?'

'Because we need to know if the two cases have anything in common.'

'I'll have a look at it tomorrow, before I open the corpse.'

'Can you tell us anything about her vocal cords?'

'No,' Karthaus said. 'I'd need to cut her open for that. But I'm not doing it here. You'll have to be patient.'

Kirie was already asleep when Rath got home, much later than anticipated. Charly, on the other hand, was still awake. She was sitting in the living room with a glass of red wine, and placed her book on criminal law to one side when he entered.

He gave her a kiss. 'Thanks for looking after the little one. It would have been a real shock for her to see her mistress dead.'

'So it really was her.'

Rath nodded as he fetched a glass from the cupboard and sat beside her. He poured himself a little red wine and lit a cigarette. Charly was eager to hear everything that had happened. The only thing he didn't mention was that he was at loggerheads with Böhm again.

'Do you think her vocal cords are missing too?'

'I'm almost certain.'

'What does it mean?'

'No idea. With Vivian Franck, I thought it was someone trying to give Oppenberg a shock. That theory doesn't fit anymore, not now that we have a second dead actress who has absolutely nothing to do with him.'

'An actress's voice is her most important tool. If you take it away, then you take away everything.'

'Unless she makes silent films,' Rath said, and Charly gave him an angry glance. She didn't like cynical remarks like that. 'Sorry,' he said. 'The real question is why he kills them at all. Or rather: why does he remove their vocal cords if he means to kill them anyway? Where's the sense in that?'

'It must have a symbolic meaning,' Charly said. 'He's trying to tell us something. The fact that the corpses are in old cinemas has to mean something too.'

'Do you think he's leaving clues about his identity? That he wants to be caught?'

'Don't know, but these are real *productions*. He's trying to tell us something.'

'It doesn't look like he's a sex offender at any rate.'

There was a pitter-patter in the corridor and Kirie poked her sleepy, black head through the door. She came in and curled up at Rath's feet.

'What's going to happen to the dog?' Charly asked.

Rath shrugged. 'Someone will inherit her.'

'But you're not going to let her go to a home, are you?'

'She'll stay with me for now.'

'I'm tired.' Charly yawned and stood up.

'My bed is your bed.'

'You'll take the sofa, will you?'

'As you know, I have a very large bed.'

'But no ulterior motives.'

Rath made a deadly serious face and raised his hand as if giving an oath.

'Seriously,' she said. 'I need to leave early tomorrow, and I'm exhausted.'

'Me too.'

He stood up and took her in his arms, bit her softly in the nape of the neck, and worked his way along her slender throat.

'Don't,' she said, sighing softly. He took her chin in his hands and looked at her. Her eyes were closed, her lips slightly open. Rath closed his eyes too and, just as his lips brushed hers, Kirie started barking. They had to lock her out again, but Kirie gave only a brief protest bark before falling silent.

Rath let Charly use the bathroom first, and drank another glass of wine to the gentle sounds of Louis Armstrong's *Black and Blue*. In the middle of the piece, he nodded off, waking with a start when he heard Charly shout, 'Bathroom's free!'

He took a final drink, turned the record player off and went into the bathroom. She was already asleep when he returned to the bedroom. The way she lay . . . her profile on the pillow, the outline of her body as it gently rose and fell under the sheets. His intentions were thoroughly dishonourable when he crawled into bed beside her, but he was much too tired. Inhaling the scent of her warm body, he understood just how much it aroused him before falling instantly asleep.

43

Monday 10th March 1930

The face of a dead woman gazed out at him, larger than life. Rath instinctively applied the brakes and Kirie slid from the passenger seat. A taxi beeped and overtook. LIEBESGEWITTER, it said under the face, behind which a huge flash of lightning split the sky in two. THE GREAT BETTY WINTER'S FINAL FILM. IN CINEMAS SOON.

The billboard was impossible to miss. It spanned the whole width of a scaffold on Moritzplatz. Rath pulled over to look at the gigantic advertisement in all its glory. Had Bellmann gone completely mad, or simply been very shrewd and unscrupulous? The Winter team had been far too fixated on Krempin and completely ignored the producer. Why hadn't Gräf listened to him? It had been clear from the start that Bellmann was making capital from his star's death.

On the way to Alex he passed two more giant billboards, from which Betty Winter gazed longingly into the morning.

He was raring to go, a feeling that the spring-like weather only served to intensify. He hadn't slept so well in a long time. Unfortunately, Charly was no longer in bed when he awoke. It was the sound of her closing the front door that roused him. Her scent lingered on the pillows. He saw that she had fed the dog, brewed coffee and left a note, which he stuck in his jacket.

I did warn you, sleepyhead: I have to leave early.
Hope we see each other soon. C.

Even the note smelled of her, which was why he had taken it with him. Climbing the stairs in the Castle he greeted everyone with a smile, but no doubt it was due to Kirie, who was pulling on her lead, that he met such friendly faces in return.

Erika Voss already knew who they had found yesterday. 'You poor thing,' she said, bending over towards Kirie. 'Now you don't have a mistress!'

'Is it only dogs we're saying hello to these days?' Rath asked.

'Forgive me, Inspector, but . . . the poor animal! Who's going to look after her now?'

'We are,' Rath said. 'That is, for the moment *you* are. Can you fetch a bowl of water, and perhaps you could take her for a little walk? She needs exercise.'

'Of course, Inspector. Poor Kirie. You don't even realise you're an orphan.'

Kirie was in high spirits and glad of the water, and Rath knew she was in good hands with his secretary. He closed the door to look through the call logs from Saturday afternoon. There wasn't much. The last person to have seen Jeanette Fastré alive was her caretaker. She seemed to have lived quite a secluded life, unusual for an actress. At least the call logs clarified the mystery of her name: she was called Vanhaelen, but had taken her mother's maiden name for the stage.

Before he went to briefing, Rath made a detour to the passport office, and quickly found what he was looking for. Gertie's name *was* Gertrud. Gertrud Hagedorn. There were no other Gertie Hagedorns, at least no other women by that name. The address was close to Stettiner Bahnhof as well: Bernauer Strasse 110. It had to be Anton Schmieder's girlfriend. Rath made a note of the address.

When he entered the small conference room, Gennat was already sitting on the podium studying various files. 'Morning, Superintendent,' he said.

Gennat responded with a grunt, and continued reading. Rath looked for a free seat as more and more homicide detectives poured into the room. Finally Böhm arrived and, right behind him, arm still in a sling, Frank Brenner.

Just you wait, Rath thought, I haven't finished with you.

Brenner cast him a hostile glance as he sat down. Lange was the last to appear, taking his seat next to Rath. The voices in the room died only as Böhm approached the lectern.

'Dear colleagues,' he began, 'before we make a start, allow me to welcome back Superintendent Gennat. He will be taking charge of Homicide again as of today.'

That was the best news Böhm had announced for a long time. Gennat stood up, and the officers drummed respectfully on the table tops and chairs.

'Good morning, gentlemen,' Buddha said. 'It's good to be back.' He cleared his throat. 'I've already seen some of you in Weissensee, yesterday evening. It's quite something to be greeted by a corpse, but we'll come to that later. I'll familiarise myself with all ongoing homicide investigations as quickly as possible. In the meantime, DCI Böhm, please continue as if I weren't here.'

'It's not so easy, Sir.'

Buddha, who really was hard to ignore, took as little offence at the friendly laughter Böhm's words provoked as at the words themselves. He listened as the DCI provided a summary of the preceding weeks, from the Winter and Franck cases to Krempin's spectacular death. In the process it became clear that Böhm was treating Krempin's fall as suicide as much for its public effect as anything else. The press were more restrained when it came to suicide, as long as they didn't know who had died. So, Böhm also considered foul play to be a possibility. Interesting. Next he showed them the work of the sketch artist: a grim-looking face.

'This man was seen at the Funkturm,' he explained. 'He was one of the first to appear by the corpse, along with a journalist . . .' Böhm looked inside his notebook. '. . . Berthold Weinert. The curious thing is that a number of people saw him go *up* the Funkturm afterwards. Curious, but perhaps there's a simple explanation. Unfortunately, we haven't been able to identify the man. This Weinert didn't know him either.'

'He looks like Inspector Rath,' someone said, and everyone laughed. A few people turned to face Rath, who joined in with the laughter.

'I don't think it's so funny!' Lange said, in a loud, firm voice. 'I need to say something here. I find it more sad than funny that every portrait drawn by this sketch artist resembles one of our colleagues. We engaged the man to draw the wanted poster for the stranger in Wilmersdorf, in the Franck case, and the result was a picture that my mother could have hung in her parlour, so closely did it resemble me. These sketches are of limited use. We should leave the man to work as a court sketch artist, rather than consulting him again. The alternative would be to arrest myself and Herr Rath as prime suspects in the two homicide cases.'

'Hmm,' Gennat said, 'perhaps you are right, but that's down to the artist and not the method. In principle, I believe that a wanted sketch will meet with more response than a personal description, but in this case the debate is futile. If we want to keep the matter discreet we cannot issue a description, whether sketched or written. Carry on, Böhm.'

'Since Herr Lange already has the floor,' Böhm said, 'perhaps he can report on what he and Herr Rath learned about Jeanette Fastré when she was still a missing person case.'

Lange knew what was expected of him and let Rath take the initiative. Briefly listing what they had found in the flat, including the dog, he reported on the meagre results of Saturday afternoon's telephone calls. 'She had few friends in the city, if any,' he concluded. 'The last person to have seen her alive appears to have been her caretaker, who isn't too concerned about what's going on around him. That was on Tuesday evening. Yesterday we found her dead in Kosmos, a disused cinema in Weissensee, as part of a search action that I . . .'

Böhm interrupted. 'That's not relevant, Herr Rath. Thank you for your contribution.' Rath sat down.

'Now we come to the corpse,' Böhm continued. 'Everything seems to point to the same perpetrator as with Vivian Franck. That, or the first murder has inspired a copycat, thanks to the press. Again we find ourselves with an actress, evidence of an injection, and a corpse in a disused cinema. It also seems likely that Fastré has had her vocal cords removed.'

Since Böhm wasn't saying anything new, at least not for those who had been in Weissensee yesterday, Lange fetched an apple from his briefcase, polished it on his sleeve and bit into it so loudly that Böhm interrupted his report. '*Bon appétit*,' he said, and everyone laughed. Lange went red.

Rath looked at the apple, and some memory was aroused, some image that refused to let him alone, until suddenly he knew what had been on his mind this whole time. The fruit bowl in Jeanette Fastré's flat that had been plundered by a hungry dog. Apples, oranges and a nondescript fruit with furry brown skin, which only revealed its bright green flesh and little black seeds when cut open. The one thing Kirie hadn't bitten into. 'Yangtao!' he cried out.

'Pardon me?' Böhm said. 'Was that a sneeze, Herr Rath? Or was there something you wanted to say?'

A few colleagues laughed. Böhm was in a humorous mood.

'I just realised something,' said Rath. 'A possible link that I still don't quite understand.'

'Are you going to share it with us?'

'It could be a coincidence . . .' Rath cleared his throat. 'So,' he said. 'It concerns yangtao, the Chinese gooseberry, an exotic fruit. I ate it myself for the first time a few days ago in a Chinese restaurant, when we were asking after Vivian Franck. Just in front of where she got out of the taxi—probably her final taxi ride.'

'And?'

'The staff didn't recognise her photograph, but they did recognise Betty Winter.'

'It's not unusual for actresses to visit exotic restaurants.'

'I think there were a few yangtao in the fruit bowl at Jeanette Fastré's flat. Perhaps Kronberg's people should check it out.'

'I don't have to tell you, I hope, that the Winter case doesn't have the slightest bit in common with the other two cases.'

'Betty Winter was an actress.'

'That was enough for the press to establish a correlation, but not us.'

'But now there is a second correlation,' Rath said. 'The fact that Fastré's fruit bowl contained the same exotic fruit found in Betty Winter's stomach. On top of that, Winter frequented a Chinese restaurant located at the same intersection where Vivian Franck was picked up by her probable killer.'

'So, we should start looking for a triple murderer amongst Berlin's Chinese population? Or what are you trying to say?'

Böhm got a laugh or two, but Gennat cut him short. 'Leave it, Böhm. Herr Rath is not wrong: that is indeed highly unusual. We may not know, yet, what we can conclude from it, but we should keep the information at the back of our minds and, at the very least, verify where these yangatang-things . . .'

'Yangtao,' Rath said.

'. . . where they can be obtained in Berlin. If you could take care of that, Inspector Rath?'

Rath could think of more exciting assignments, but nodded all the same. Gennat having taken his side and put an end to Böhm's mockery was compensation enough.

They were spared Kronberg's report today. The head of ED had already visited the Fastré flat with his people and had only given Böhm a preliminary summary, which the DCI himself had read out. The ED team still hadn't analysed a number of clues. It was certain, however, that there was no evidence of a break-in, just as with the Luxor. If they could narrow down the list of key owners and see whether there was any overlap between the two cinemas, it would be a step in the right direction. Otherwise, the man who had planted the corpses must be a champion burglar capable of cracking complex security locks, which seemed unlikely.

They had found numerous fingerprints, but hadn't even begun analysing them. They were still right at the start, and faced with a giant riddle.

'We might have another lead in the Franck case,' Böhm said. 'The stranger who picked her up on Hohenzollerndamm—Oppenberg, her producer, knew about it because he hired a private detective when Franck was still a missing person case. Inspector Rath, have you spoken to the detective in the meantime?'

Shit!

'Not yet, I'm afraid. I just haven't got around to it, especially since we are now investigating another fatality and . . .'

'. . . you have failed to do your job again . . .'

'It's all right, Böhm.' Gennat had interrupted Böhm for a second time. 'Herr Rath can still look into it. For the time being, there are more important things. Let's use our imaginations instead.' He looked round the room. No one was laughing anymore. 'We're not dealing with an ordinary killer here. So, think about what kind of person it could be.' It was so still you could hear the clock on the wall ticking. 'Why,' Gennat continued, 'does someone plant the bodies of actresses in old cinemas after making them up as if for a film shoot—and removing their vocal cords?' Again, Gennat looked round the room. 'Does anyone have any suggestions? If so, please feel free to share them, no matter how strange. They might just help us track the perpetrator down.'

'A pervert!' Brenner cried without raising his hand. 'He fucked the women . . . I mean engaged in sexual intercourse with them, then killed

them. And, to prevent them screaming: wham! Away with their vocal cords.'
He gestured towards his throat. A few colleagues nodded their agreement.

'We still don't have any indication that a sexual crime has been committed,' Böhm objected. 'We don't even know if he actually kills them, or, at
least, how he does it. Nor is it clear if the second corpse's vocal cords are
missing yet.'

'Then he used a French letter,' Brenner grumbled.

'We shouldn't rule anything out so long as we lack the relevant exclu-
sion criteria,' Gennat said, and Böhm, who was about to make another ob-
jection, closed his mouth before saying anything.

Lange raised his hand. 'Perhaps it's an act of revenge, or sabotage. Film
types waging war on one another, with the help of the underworld.'

Gennat made a few notes.

'The whole thing is staged,' Rath said, inwardly thanking Charly for the
tip. 'Someone's trying to tell us something—us, or more likely, the public.'

'Tell us what?' Gennat asked.

Rath shrugged his shoulders. 'That's precisely what we have to find
out. If we know that, it could lead us to the perpetrator.'

'If that is so, then perhaps we should wilfully misunderstand him,'
Lange suggested. 'How about we inform the press that a dangerous sex
offender is on the loose, someone who has it in for attractive film actresses?'

Gennat shook his head. 'No,' he said. 'You're probably right, Herr Lange.
We might provoke him that way, but we wouldn't have any control over
the consequences. We would most likely trigger another killing, and no one
here can answer for that.'

'We need to get him to make mistakes.'

'Not mistakes other people pay for with their lives.'

Lange nodded and sat down. There were no further requests to speak.

'Gentlemen, I thank you for your contributions,' Gennat said. 'With
that, we have reached the end of our meeting. Your tasks for today will be
allocated subsequently in Homicide, and we will meet again tomorrow. We
will continue to adhere to Herr Böhm's practice of regular morning brief-
ings, at least for the time being. It has proved to be worthwhile. Good work,
Böhm.'

'Thank you, Superintendent,' Böhm said, and turned again to face the
room. 'That's it for now. Any questions?'

That was how the DCI always ended the meetings, yet until now no one had taken his invitation seriously and he didn't realise at first that Rath had stood up.

'If I might say something else . . .'

'Inspector Rath?'

'Even if the Franck and Fastré cases have priority, I would nevertheless like to draw your attention back to the Winter case. In my opinion, it has not been solved with the death of Felix Krempin.' Rath cleared his throat before continuing. 'I noticed something this morning. Heinrich Bellmann has launched a huge advertising campaign for his new film, in which he is exploiting the death of his lead actress.'

'That might be tasteless, but it isn't against the law,' said Böhm, who was already packing his things.

'It's a motive,' Rath said. 'The whole time he's been giving us this sob story, while simultaneously harnessing the media to make headlines out of Betty Winter and her final film. He's been doing it since the day she died. Now, to cap it, there's this publicity campaign fronted by a dead woman.'

He had aroused Gennat's interest again. 'You mean to say that Betty Winter is of more use to this Bellmann dead than alive?'

Rath shrugged his shoulders. 'What I want to know is where all that money comes from. This morning alone I saw three giant billboards. Who can say how many more there are in the city? It must cost a fortune. Usually Bellmann promotes his little films with notices in the daily press, so how do you explain that for this one he's making more of a ballyhoo than Ufa?'

'Some greedy vulture senses the chance of a lifetime and stakes everything on it,' Böhm said. 'That isn't a crime either.'

'True, but it is unusual,' Gennat said. 'Clearly we should be sounding him out a lot more thoroughly than we have done already. Than *you* have done already, Inspector Rath, Chief Inspector Böhm!'

Rath wasn't too worried about Gennat's parting shot. After all, Wilhelm Böhm was the man in charge of the Winter case. Since taking over, the DCI had been far too focused on Krempin, dismissing Rath's doubts about the man's guilt—and finally made sure the case was passed to Gräf, a mere *detective* who was already overworked. All because he had refused to give it to Rath. That would teach him.

Could Bellmann really have something to do with the death of Betty Winter? Rath had long suspected there were skeletons in his closet, ever since he had threatened him with his lawyers. Sounding the man out, as Gennat had put it, couldn't do any harm.

After the briefing Buddha took Rath to one side and asked for his thoughts. Rath told him everything Böhm hadn't wanted to hear: how Krempin's wire construction worked, and that someone who knew the script had most likely made use of it—only on Betty Winter, rather than an expensive film camera. Which assumed, of course, that same someone had uncovered Krempin's plan. All of which could certainly have applied to Heinrich Bellmann.

Buddha had listened attentively. 'I'll take care of the search warrant for Bellmann,' he had said. 'See if you can make any headway with that Chinese lead. See you at two in the morgue.'

Rath sat at his desk leafing through the telephone book for Chinese restaurants. His outburst was irritating him. Even if Gennat had defended him against Böhm, his colleagues hadn't taken him seriously. Not that he blamed them. Still, in the absence of any tangible leads, this was the sort of thing they were obliged to follow up.

For the time being he couldn't get hold of anyone at Yangtao. He asked Erika Voss to call the number every five minutes. Shortly before eleven, she got through.

'Inspector,' she said. 'Your Chinese restaurant.'

'Wen Tian, Yangtao,' said a soft voice that barely sounded the consonants.

'Rath, CID. I was at your restaurant recently, with a colleague. Do you remember? I'd like to know where you purchase yangtao for your kitchen.'

'Want reserve?'

'No, I'm from the police. I just want to know where in Berlin you can get yangtao.'

'Monday rest day.'

'I don't want to eat.'

'Better reserve. Yangtao many guests.'

'I just have a question. I'm not eating.'

'For two persons?'

Rath gave up. 'Police here,' he said. 'I'll be with you in a moment.'

'Monday rest day.'

He hung up.

'I have to go out,' he said. 'Can you look after Kirie, Erika?'

'It's lunchtime soon. Don't you want to take her?'

'The place I'm going they might put her on the menu.'

She looked at him in horror. 'My goodness, where are you going?'

'To the Chinese.'

Before setting off, Rath made his way on foot to the Zentralmarkthalle, which was only a stone's throw away from the Castle. Things were at their busiest here at the crack of dawn, long before the rest of the city was awake, but right now it was quiet. The Zentralmarkthalle actually comprised two market halls, separated from one another by Kaiser-Wilhelm-Strasse. Horses and carts were parked on both sides of the road, and were a constant source of traffic jams in the early hours. Rath found his way by asking; the fruit and vegetable traders were housed in the northern hall. The best goods had long since been sold, only a few lettuce heads wilted away sadly. Rath accosted a red-faced man with a walrus moustache who was stacking cherries under a large company sign.

'What you after?' the walrus huffed.

'I'm looking for a Chinese fruit and vegetable trader here in the market hall.'

'Does that look like me?'

'No, but perhaps you know of one.'

'Who's asking?' Rath showed his badge. 'Leave the poor slit eyes alone! They have it bad enough already.'

'I just need a little information about a Chinese variety of fruit.'

The man looked at him as if deciding whether he could trust a police officer, then said: 'Up on the gallery, just by the middle aisle where the wholesale butchers are, there's a flight of steps. Ask for Lingyuan, he could be the one.'

Rath tipped his hat and made his way through. It was incredible how much food was on sale, even if most traders were only offering what had survived the frenzy earlier that morning. Rath found the steps and climbed to the gallery. This was where the smaller traders were housed, those who didn't occupy so much space, and to whom fewer customers strayed. He found Lingyuan's stand without having to ask again. A large Chinese paper lantern jutting into the aisle showed the way. Lingyuan didn't just offer exotic varieties of fruit and vegetable, but herbs and spices that Rath had never seen before. A few of the smells reminded him of the Chinese restaurant on Hohenzollerndamm. He felt himself transported to another world, a little piece of Asia in the heart of Berlin. The king of this world was a small Chinese man with a green apron over his grey, Western suit, who spoke accent-free German. He didn't even have trouble sounding the consonants.

'What would you like?' he asked.

'Just some information,' Rath said. This time he showed his badge straightaway. The Chinese man nodded humbly and smiled. 'You sell Chinese groceries . . .'

'For more than seven years now . . .'

'. . . do you have yangtao?'

Lingyuan gestured towards a stack of crates. 'Here,' he said. 'What's left of them. Arrived from China two weeks ago.'

'As long ago as that?'

'You have to keep yangtao cool, then they stay fresh for a long time. Up to half a year.'

'Isn't that expensive? Importing them from China?'

'Quantity is the key,' Lingyuan said. 'Do you know how many Chinese people live here in the city? A few thousand. The poorer ones by Schlesischer Bahnhof, the more prosperous in Charlottenburg, the rest spread across the city.'

'And they all buy from you?'

'All the Chinese restaurants, I'd say. As well as two or three Chinese shops.'

'Do you have the addresses?'

'Why?'

'I need to know all the places in the city where yangtao is sold. Are there any other importers?'

'Not that I know of. At least no one else who grows Chinese fruit and vegetables.'

'Here in Berlin?'

'I have a little nursery over in Mariendorf. A few weeks ago I'd have been able to offer you yangtao that I'd picked myself before Christmas.'

'Business is good, no doubt.'

'I get by.'

'How much does a yangtao cost?'

'Let's say a little more than an apple.'

'A delicacy then . . .'

'If you like. Something different at least. Very healthy too.'

Rath showed the Chinese man the photos of Betty Winter and Jeanette Fastré. Lingyuan didn't seem to go to the cinema or read the paper. He shook his head. 'Never seen them,' he said.

'Where could these women have got hold of yangtao?'

'I'll give you a few names,' the man said, reaching for the notepad next to the weighing scales.

Rath left the market hall with the addresses of five restaurants and three shops, but it wouldn't be worth visiting the former today. 'Rest day,' Lingyuan had warned. So, the Chinese shops it was. Two were in Friedrichshain, the third in the west. Rath fetched the car from Alex and drove first to Krautstrasse, which formed the heart of Berlin's little Chinese quarter. He didn't have happy memories of the area. His fateful clash with Josef Wilczek had taken place just a few blocks away, at a building site on Koppenstrasse.

He parked outside the first address. Compared with New York's Chinatown around Pell Street, which he had visited years ago with his brother, this was a disappointing affair: the building fronts a little run-down, barely any cars on the roadside, a few children playing noisily on the pavement, not a single Chinese person. It was a normal street in East Berlin. At least the Chinese shop, in front of whose display he had parked the car, was adorned with red Chinese characters. There were no Latin letters whatsoever; from the outside it wasn't clear if it was a grocery shop, a clothing store or a laundry.

As it transpired it was a mixture of all three, and much more besides, with an assortment of goods as varied as in KaDeWe, but using only a fraction of the space. Alongside food, tea and spices, there were colourful silk fabrics, porcelain, little soapstone carvings, shelves, paper lanterns, all tightly packed in a wild jumble. The old Chinese lady inside the dark cave, which smelled even stranger than Lingyuan's market stall, didn't speak a word of German. Rath tried his luck with sign language, showing her a few photos and pointing towards the floor with his index finger.

'These women here?' he asked. 'Yangtao?' The old lady gestured towards a crate containing a few miserable-looking yangtao. Rath showed the photos again, this time omitting the word *yangtao*, but the woman shook her head. During the entire conversation, if you could call it that, her face under the black beehive hair hadn't displayed an ounce of emotion. Rath was equally unsuccessful in the next shop, just a few houses further along in Markusstrasse. Once again there was yangtao. Once again no one spoke German or recognised the actresses.

When he returned to the car, he found it surrounded by snotty-nosed brats.

'That yours, chief?' one asked. 'Nice wheels you've got there.'

'You can look but you can't touch,' Rath said, climbing in. It was a crummy neighbourhood. He couldn't imagine either of the two actresses setting foot in a street like this. He drove west.

The third shop was in Kantstrasse, and a very different establishment from the previous two. The Chinahaus, this time using the Latin alphabet, was located next to a Chinese restaurant and was bright and elegantly furnished, with fine porcelain vases lining the walls and two stone lions guarding the stairs. The room's scent came from a shelf full of different types of tea. A slender Chinese man with hair slicked tightly back approached him.

'How can I help you?'

'Do you sell food as well?'

'Of course. If you could follow me.'

'I'm only looking for information.' Rath showed the photos and asked his question.

The man reacted to Betty Winter. 'I think I saw her here a few weeks ago, it could have been her. Usually it's only Chinese people who shop here. Occasionally a curious German or two.'

'You don't have any regular German customers?'

'You couldn't call them regulars.' The Chinese man shook his head. 'Apart from this one old man, perhaps. Although he hasn't been here for a long time.'

'And he comes here often?'

'To buy yangtao too, yes, but not just yangtao.'

'Do you have a name?'

'Alfred or Albert, something like that.'

'How about an address?'

A shake of the head.

He gave the Chinese man his card. 'Please let me know if he comes back. Promptly and without delay, that's very important! Try, if you can, to get his name and address.'

'I'm not a policeman. I can hardly interrogate my customers.'

'Discreetly, of course. You could tell him you need to order the goods first, and ask for a delivery address. You'll think of something.'

Since he was already in Kantstrasse, Rath decided to pay Oppenberg a visit. He was in luck, the producer was at his desk and had already heard the news about Krempin. 'Poor Felix,' he said. 'A rather unfriendly colleague of yours came by to tell me. Just dreadful, plunging to his death like that.'

Rath looked at him closely, but there was nothing in his demeanour to suggest that he was responsible for Krempin's death. 'I'm here about Vivian,' he said. 'The underworld lead has come to nothing, but we're in the process of uncovering new links that could be significant. Do you know yangtao, the Chinese gooseberry?'

Oppenberg considered for a moment. 'Could be. The name doesn't mean anything, but I sometimes go to the Chinese along the road. Perhaps I ate it there. You never really know what's on your plate.'

'Then you can't say whether Vivian Franck liked yangtao either?'

'Vivian?' Oppenberg laughed out loud. 'On the contrary. I can tell you that she gave any food that looked Chinese, or at all Asian, a wide berth, and not just because of the chopsticks. I could never persuade her to come to *Nanking* with me.'

Rath thought about what Oppenberg had said as he made his way back to the car. Betty Winter and Jeanette Fastré adored yangtao, while Vivian Franck despised it. It didn't look like a correlation now, just a strange coincidence. Or was the fact that Vivian Franck abhorred Chinese food some kind of explanation?

On the way back to Alex, he took a detour by Bernauer Strasse and rang number 110. *Hagedorn.*

'The young lady isn't here,' a voice said from above. A man in grey overalls was looking over the banister on the half landing.

'Working?'

'What else? Think the bank does a night shift?'

'Perhaps it should. When you think of those bank robbers, the Brothers Sass.'

'Even if it was the fuzz pulling the night shifts, they still wouldn't catch 'em!' The man gave a brief, dry laugh. 'What do you want from old Hagedorn?'

'It isn't important. Strictly private.'

'See that her fiancé doesn't catch you. He doesn't have much of a sense of humour!'

'Herr Schmieder, you mean?'

'Ah, so you know him too?'

'Berlin's a small place. Didn't you know? Isn't Herr Schmieder living here at the moment?'

'Ha, it's almost like his second home. And whenever I say to old Hagedorn, that's enough now, if he's here a day longer I'll have to take money for gas and electricity, he disappears again for a day or two, and the whole thing starts over.'

'Let me guess, you mentioned it to Frau Hagedorn again today?'

'You're a bright spark. Spend the night at the Osram plant, did you?'

Osram light bulbs. The visit had indeed shed more light than Rath could have hoped for. Schmieder's girlfriend or fiancée, or whatever she was, worked in a bank. He hadn't even had to ask the caretaker which one; he had simply asked which branch. But she didn't work in a branch, she worked at the central office in Behrensstrasse and had only arrived at the start of the year—from Cologne.

He knew enough to pay Anton Schmieder a little visit. So, why not now?

The man would be back on nights after a week of evenings. Perhaps he'd be at home? Besides, there was someone else in Moabit whom Rath wanted to surprise. True, Charly had made coffee for him that morning, but she hadn't said goodbye. She could hardly turn down lunch. He climbed the steps to her flat in Spenerstrasse and rang the bell, feeling like a little kid, looking forward to seeing her surprised face.

The door opened and a man grinned at him; he hadn't counted on seeing that face here. Charly's cowboy. Her dancing partner at the Resi, this time without the fringe. Was he the reason she had to leave so early?

'Who is it you're after?' he asked. 'Can I pass on a message?'

Rath was speechless, but managed to mumble something like 'It's fine' before turning and allowing gravity to carry him down the steps.

Back in the car he sat teeming with rage, with no recollection of how he had got there. He would have liked nothing better than to let out some steam on the grinning man upstairs, but he could forget about that unless he wanted to spoil things with Charly for good. He revved the engine, screeching away onto the carriageway.

Five minutes later, he was standing outside Anton Schmieder's flat. 'A message from Fräulein Hagedorn,' he cried, as he knocked on the door for a second time.

When he heard steps inside he positioned himself so that Schmieder couldn't make him out through the crack, but the man was more trusting than expected. He opened the door without thinking, only to turn deathly pale when he saw who was there.

Rath got his foot in the crack, pushing the door inwards with all his might, and causing Anton Schmieder to stumble backwards. 'What do you want from me?' Schmieder asked.

'Why so nervous when the police are round? We wouldn't do anything to an upstanding citizen.'

Schmieder retreated along the corridor, with Rath in pursuit. They wound up in an untidy kitchen.

'Haven't been here for a while, eh?' said Rath. 'Been shacked up for a few days with your bride-to-be.'

'What do you want?' Schmieder seemed halfway composed again. 'You can't just come marching in.'

Rath smiled and rammed his right fist into the man's solar plexus. He doubled over, gasping for air.

'If you're going to blackmail someone, then it's a good idea not to get caught,' Rath said. 'You see, now someone's hurting you and you can't even call the police.'

'You are the police!' the man panted, having caught his breath at last. 'What you're doing here isn't allowed.'

'This is for my own pleasure. I know you aren't going to report me.'

'I still don't know what you want.'

'I want you to stop exchanging letters with one of my friends. No more unfriendly missives written in red pencil and delivered to the State Council mailboxes. Blackmail is a serious offence.'

'Why don't you report me if you think I'm a blackmailer? I'll tell you why. Because if you do, your friend can forget about his dirty deals. Adenauer, that Jew lover, that . . .'

Rath dealt him another blow to the solar plexus. The man was showing far too little respect. He leaned over him as he gasped for air, pulled him up by the collar and spoke directly in his ear.

'You should take this a little more seriously. At the end of the day it's your health. No more letters and no more harassment of any kind. If any details of this disagreeable Glanzstoff affair should reach the public I will hold you personally responsible. Time to impress upon your girlfriend how dangerous it can be to divulge official secrets.'

Schmieder gasped for air and nodded.

'I hope I've made myself clear, for your sake. Because next time, it'll be people who are far better at this sort of thing than I am.'

Schmieder said nothing. He just nodded, again and again, his whole body shaking.

Rath hadn't realised he was capable of inspiring so much fear. He let go of the man's collar and stood up.

Schmieder started sobbing. 'I just wanted for everything to stay the same,' he said. 'What am I supposed to do if Ford closes? When they hired me three years ago, I thought this is it, this is my life really starting. I'll be earning a decent wage. Now you're telling me that's over? Do you know how many unemployed people there are in this city? What am I supposed to do if there's no more Ford?'

'I wouldn't try your hand at blackmail, anyway,' Rath said. 'You don't have the talent.'

He exited the flat, got in his car and drove off. All he wanted now was to get out of Moabit. Out, out, out. He was still beside himself with rage.

Driving east via Invalidenstrasse, he came to a halt at Stettiner Bahnhof in front of a telephone booth. Before getting out he smoked a cigarette to calm himself down. Then he looked for twenty pfennigs and called Ostbahnhof. To his surprise he got Marlow on the line.

'Inspector!' Dr M. sounded pleased. 'Good of you to call. How are you getting on with Deutsche Kraft?'

'Things are moving along,' Rath lied. 'Perhaps you can do me a little favour.'

'So long as you don't demand the impossible.'

Rath gave Anton Schmieder's name and address. 'Nothing too heavy,' he said. 'The man just needs a little scare. Have him tailed by the most frightening men you have, and tell them to bump into him now and again and give him a dirty look.'

Marlow laughed. 'You don't have to tell me how to go about it. How far can my men go?'

'A scare, no more. No physical violence. Under no circumstances!'

'Supposing your man becomes violent, my people have to be able to defend themselves. I can't forbid them that.'

'Don't worry, he won't. He's just a poor soul.'

'If you say so.'

Rath didn't feel good about his pact with the devil, but he was already too involved with Marlow for another favour to make much difference. He found himself feeling a little sorry for Anton Schmieder, the blackmailer of the rueful countenance, but a blackmailer deserved no better. He could count himself lucky not to face criminal charges. Indeed, all parties involved had come out of the matter rather well: Adenauer had his peace, Schmieder wasn't going to the clink and Inspector Rath would soon be Chief Inspector Rath.

If there *was* something in the Deutsche Kraft affair, then he would be doing not only Marlow a favour, but his colleagues too. He thought about why a Ringverein should be involved in a film company, and realised he only knew one type of illegal film. Perhaps he should alert Superintendent Lanke from Vice.

There was an Aschinger at Stettiner Bahnhof too. Rath ate a Bulette on the hoof and drove towards Hannoversche Strasse. He was late. He would have to throw himself into his work to avoid thinking about Charly, and what that cowboy was still doing rattling around her flat.

44

Dr Karthaus had already begun when Rath swept into the autopsy room. Böhm glanced reproachfully at his watch, but Gennat continued listening to the pathologist.

'. . . your suspicion has been confirmed,' he said, giving Rath a nod of greeting. 'The vocal cords have indeed been removed.'

'Just like Vivian Franck,' said Rath.

Gennat sounded as if he had been expecting the news. 'Whether we like it or not, we should get used to the idea that we're dealing with a serial killer.'

Böhm grunted at the phrase.

'To avoid a second Düsseldorf and a fresh wave of hysteria,' Gennat continued, 'we should keep this to ourselves and continue to handle things as you have done so far, Böhm. The press has done enough damage already. If we were to confirm the serial killer theory now . . .'

'What do you mean, confirm?' Böhm said. 'The press is on completely the wrong track. They've thrown together two cases that have absolutely nothing to do with one another.'

'Apart from the strange coincidence of the Chinese gooseberry,' Gennat said.

'You know what I think of that nonsense.'

'On that note. Did you find anything, Herr Rath?'

'Yes, as a matter of fact.' Rath cleared his throat, only to be cut off by Dr Karthaus.

'Far be it from me to interrupt CID business, but aren't you gentlemen here to listen to *me*?'

'Of course, Doctor. Rath, come to my office immediately afterwards to make your report.'

'I . . . uh, at three . . . my appointment with Zörgiebel.'

'In that case come straight after your appointment.'

'Might I continue?' Karthaus asked, sounding slightly agitated.

'On you go, Doctor, on you go,' Gennat said.

Karthaus cleared his throat. 'Seeing as you've mentioned these yangtao that Dr Schwartz found in Betty Winter's stomach . . .' He made a dramatic pause so that the three CID officers realised he had read the Winter case notes as well as the Franck file. '. . . I have examined the contents of the deceased's stomach and can only say that she didn't eat very much before her death, fruit mostly. There is nothing to suggest the presence of Chinese gooseberries . . .'

'I've brought a few along with me,' Rath said, reaching in his pocket for the yangtao the Chinese man had given him.

'Looks like a furry potato,' Gennat said.

'You have to cut it open,' Rath said to Dr Karthaus. 'That's your area of expertise.'

Karthaus took the scalpel, and parted the unremarkable-looking fruit to reveal a bright green centre with small black seeds arranged in a radial pattern.

'Looks very pretty from the inside,' Gennat said.

'Tastes good too,' Rath said. 'And it's healthy.'

'As I said,' Karthaus continued. 'I didn't find evidence of any such fruit in her stomach, but she had eaten other kinds of fruit, albeit many hours before she died.'

'The cause of death? Drugs? Poison?'

'Wrong on both counts,' Karthaus said. 'Ultimately, I can't tell you what she died of.'

'Just like Franck,' Böhm growled. 'Can you at least venture a guess?'

'The examination revealed an excessive acidity of the blood. That's normal with dead people, but the results were uncommonly high . . .'

'Get to the point, Doctor. You must have a hunch.'

'That's really all it is, and I have no other explanation. She could have died of hypoglycaemia, but I can't prove it.'

'Never heard of it,' Gennat said. 'What is that?'

'Extremely low blood sugar.'

'And it can be fatal?'

'Absolutely. However, it usually only occurs in diabetics who treat their illness with insulin. If the insulin dose is too high or the body isn't supplied with enough sugar, then it can lead to low blood sugar.'

'Was Fastré diabetic?' Gennat asked.

Karthaus shook his head. 'I requested her files from her doctor. She was fit as a fiddle, but there are these injection sites. On closer inspection, I found a number of subcutaneous injections, not so easy to uncover.'

Gennat nodded. 'But this stuff . . .'

'Insulin . . .'

'. . . is something only diabetics take?'

'That's right.' Karthaus nodded. 'It's saved the lives of many people. If I may, I should like to propose a little theory.'

Gennat grinned. 'So, you're finally letting the cat out of the bag.'

'Someone administered a number of insulin jabs, either against her will or without her knowledge.' The pathologist paused and watched the reaction of the police officers. 'Subcutaneous injections, as I said. That is, in the subcutaneous fatty tissue, where the active agent slowly enters the bloodstream. She received these injections over several days.'

'Without her knowledge,' Gennat muttered thoughtfully.

Karthaus nodded. 'Nevertheless, her doctor was unable to tell me of any medication she had to take by injection, so it would have been difficult to trick her. Which leaves against her will, although I've found no trace of violence. The final dose, at any rate, was so high it was fatal; and the woman must have slowly but surely gone into insulin shock. After that she clearly didn't get any more sugar.'

'Sugar?'

'The only thing that could have saved her life once the insulin was in her body.'

About half an hour later Rath set off again, with Böhm and Gennat remaining to receive Grunwald, Fastré's producer, who would identify the body. He made good progress and was parked in the atrium by ten to three. Kirie greeted him enthusiastically when he entered the office. He crouched and patted the dog who, in her exuberance, knocked the grey felt hat from his head and started chasing it round the room. Only with the help of Erika Voss and a few cunning tricks did he manage to get it back.

'Any calls?' he asked, as he hung it, now moist and slightly misshapen, on the hook.

Erika Voss reached for the list on her desk. 'Your father said he'd call back. Then a woman who didn't want to leave her name, probably something private . . .' She looked at him expectantly, but Rath's features were as if chiselled in marble. 'And Frau Kling . . . to remind us about your three o'clock. What's it about, do you know? Why does the commissioner want to speak to you?'

'Goodness knows . . .'

'Is it about Brenner?'

'What makes you say that?'

'I'll cross my fingers for you.'

Rath suspected that the whole station knew about his clash with Brenner. The rumour mill in the Castle was working full-steam, and the canteen was its pressure cooker. Erika Voss spent every lunchtime in there, and it couldn't just be for the food.

Before seeing Zörgiebel, Rath splashed a few litres of water on his face to freshen up. He needed a clear head; just maintain his composure and everything would be fine. He positioned himself in front of the mirror and combed his wet hair into shape. The man staring back at him didn't look too shabby. He couldn't be such a bad guy; surely the commissioner would see that.

Brenner was sitting in Zörgiebel's outer office when Rath entered, holding a magazine awkwardly in his left hand. Reading wasn't so easy with your right arm in a sling. The plasters on his face were a little much, Rath thought, sitting as far away as possible. Zörgiebel was clearly still busy; the leather-upholstered door to his inner sanctum was closed. Rath examined the old Berlin cityscapes on the wall with interest, and tried to avoid making direct eye contact with Frank Brenner. Dagmar Kling typed unperturbed, as the two men gave each other the silent treatment. It was safe to say that The Guillotine, as Zörgiebel's secretary was known, had seen worse than two quarrelling inspectors.

The telephone rang and Dagmar Kling answered. She listened and hung up. 'The commissioner will see you now, gentlemen.'

Brenner jumped to his feet and Rath let him go first. In his eagerness Brenner hadn't realised it would be difficult to open the massive double door with only his left hand. Rath didn't come to his aid, even when he fancied Dagmar Kling was staring at him reproachfully. He waited and followed Brenner in at a respectful distance.

Zörgiebel wasn't alone. Across his brightly polished desk, in one of the three leather chairs, sat Superintendent Brückner, Chief of the Fraud Squad. Brenner had been caught out, Rath registered with satisfaction, although he didn't realise it yet. He couldn't have seen his doctor in the past few days. Smiling obsequiously, Brenner gave first Zörgiebel, and then Brückner, his left hand before sitting down. Rath was glad it wasn't Bernhard Weiss leading the discussion, as that would have been a tougher nut to crack. With Zörgiebel he had no such reservations.

Preliminary greetings over, Zörgiebel didn't hang about. 'Gentlemen, you know why you are here, so let's get to the point. An incident occurred on the evening of the first of March in the Residenz-Casino. Inspector Rath, you are alleged to have struck Inspector Brenner on two occasions. What do you have to say to that?'

Rath made a guilty face. 'I did strike Inspector Brenner, and I am sorry,' he said, 'but it is a mystery to me how he could have sustained such serious injuries. I took a couple of hefty swipes at him, but my blows couldn't have been that forceful. I'm not Max Schmeling.'

'We'll come to that presently,' Zörgiebel said. 'So, you are sorry that you struck Inspector Brenner.' The commissioner cleared his throat. 'Then I would ask you to stand up, give the inspector your hand and apologise formally for behaviour that is entirely unworthy of a Prussian police officer.'

Rath did exactly as asked. He stood up and stretched out his right hand towards Brenner, who almost met it with the hand in the sling, before switching to his left. Rath likewise switched hands.

'I apologise unreservedly, Herr Brenner,' he said. 'It won't happen again.'

'Good,' Zörgiebel said after Rath had resumed his seat, 'then let that be an end to this. Inspector Rath, I would like to remind you that one of a Prussian police officer's most important duties is to conduct himself in a fitting manner at all times. Especially now, with the press ready to pounce on our every error.'

'Yes, Sir.'

'Good. Then I won't keep you from your work any longer. Please take this matter to heart and . . .'

'What?' Brenner could no longer keep his rage and disappointment in check. 'That's it? A half-baked apology and the matter is closed for good old Herr Rath? If that's how it is, I'm going to have to seriously consider instituting criminal proceedings against my colleague here for assault. You and your distinguished Vipoprä tried to talk me out of it, and, idiot that I am, I agreed. This isn't the last of it!'

Brenner no longer had himself under control, almost slamming his right hand against the table.

Zörgiebel remained calm. 'Inspector Brenner, I think you should consider very carefully what you are saying. If you institute criminal proceedings I will have to insist upon an official medical examination. Do you really want that?'

Brenner gave a start. 'What are you trying to say?'

'That is something I'd like to discuss with you and Superintendent Brückner in private. That's why I was just asking Inspector Rath to leave, before you interrupted me.'

'My apologies, Commissioner.' Brenner was kowtowing now. Did he sense what was in store? Rath would have dearly loved to stay in the room and hear what accusations Brenner had to defend himself against.

'Can I go now, Sir?' he asked.

'Of course, my dear Rath!' Zörgiebel waved him out. 'Get back to work.'

Rath took his leave with a bow and the friendliest of smiles. This will be hard on Brenner, he thought, strolling past Dagmar Kling's clattering typewriter and out of the office. Falsification of documents, theft. A number of charges had accumulated. Zörgiebel would probably sweep most of it under the carpet, but Brenner would pay a price. Normally they threatened miscreants with a stint in Köpenick, far outside the gates of the city. Rath's costume in the Resi would thus take on a prophetic meaning.

He had just begun to feel pleased at this favourable turn of events when he remembered what had caused them in the first place. Charly and her cowboy. The grinning man who'd opened the door that morning was the one he should have beaten up, not Brenner.

It was twenty past three when he opened the glass doors to Homicide and knocked on Gennat's door. Trudchen Steiner told him that Böhm was still with Buddha. 'I'll ask if you can go in.'

He could. Böhm and Gennat were sitting eating cake.

'Take a seat,' Gennat said. 'Would you like a slice? Trudchen, please bring the inspector a cup of coffee and a cake plate.'

Rath sat down. The fact that Buddha could get stuck into cakes straight after a visit to the morgue testified to a steady constitution. Böhm didn't look quite so happy, but was forcing himself to eat a slice of nut cake.

'So,' Gennat said, 'take a seat and tell me what you found out about these yangatang . . .'

'Yangtao, Sir.' Rath fished one out of his pocket and divided it with the cake knife. 'You can use your fork to scoop it out.'

Gennat tried it and nodded appreciatively. 'It comes from China, you say?'

'I met someone today who grows yangtao here in Berlin, but that's the exception. Otherwise I think you can only get it in China. It's a very exclusive fruit, and not exactly cheap.'

'Just the thing for film actresses.'

'Perhaps it's fashionable in those circles. I still don't know where Fastré bought hers, but the owner of the Chinahaus in Kantstrasse remembered Betty Winter. Curious as it seems, the matter doesn't appear to go anywhere after that. You see, Vivian Franck has nothing to do with yangtao. She never even went near Chinese food, I learned today. On the other hand, she was picked up by this stranger outside a Chinese restaurant.'

Trudchen Steiner entered with coffee and a cake plate. 'Help yourself,' Gennat said.

Rath looked at the cake plate which, despite having already been plundered, still contained a lavish selection. He left the last slice of gooseberry tart for Gennat, Buddha's favourite, and shovelled a slice of cheesecake onto his own plate.

'Well,' Böhm said, having polished off his nut cake, 'we can consign this Chinese gooseberry nonsense to the shelves. I thought it was hogwash from the start.'

Gennat helped himself to some German gooseberry tart. 'Rath has already voiced his doubts,' he said, 'but as far as I'm concerned the matter isn't closed. There remains this curious coincidence . . .'

'Exactly, coincidence!' Böhm thundered. 'The Winter and Fastré cases have nothing to do with each other!'

'. . . this curious coincidence,' Gennat continued, 'and such coincidences always make me uneasy.'

'We should be concerned with facts, not feelings,' Böhm said.

'We might collect facts, but we should nevertheless allow ourselves to be guided by our instincts,' Gennat said. 'I wouldn't have solved half the cases I have if I had limited myself to simply collecting the facts.'

'I'm not talking about limiting ourselves. I'm saying we shouldn't be abandoning ourselves to wild theories,' Böhm grumbled.

'If you mean Rath's theory that it was staged,' Gennat responded, 'then I have to tell you that, of all the observations made by colleagues this morning, it's still the most plausible. We are dealing with a perpetrator who loves putting on a show—perhaps he has a background in theatre or film, which would explain his preference for actresses. If the killer is trying to tell us something with these murders, and the way he presents his victims, then there are a number of questions we need to ask ourselves. Why are the corpses in *these* cinemas specifically? Why are they in cinemas at all? Why film actresses, and why does he remove their vocal cords? We know that he kills them first. So why does he dress their corpses so beautifully afterwards, make them up and deck them out in fine clothes, perfume them even?'

'One way or another we'd have to answer all those questions,' Böhm objected, 'whether the whole thing has been staged, as you believe it has, or not.'

'Then we are in agreement, Böhm,' Gennat said.

'At any rate, he treats his victims better once they're dead,' Rath said. He was thinking out loud, but Buddha listened attentively all the same. 'To me it looks like he loves and hates them in equal measure.'

Gennat nodded his agreement. 'Let's leave the cinema killings to one side for a moment,' he said at last, 'and turn our attention to the Winter case. You both have ground to make up there. If you had collaborated more effectively with one another, gentlemen—and I don't want to hear any excuses, from either of you—then perhaps we would have made more progress.' He took a carefully folded piece of paper from his jacket.

'The search order for the offices of La Belle Film and Heinrich Bellmann's private quarters,' he said, waving the paper. 'I'd like you to lead the operation jointly. You'll head out there today, I've placed a squad of duty officers at the ready.'

Rath and Böhm were both taken equally by surprise and looked at each other in horror. They had to resolve their differences. Buddha had spoken. There was no getting around it.

They couldn't even work separately. Heinrich Bellmann's offices and private quarters were housed at the same address, which was typical of Bellmann. It was just another way of saving money—dispensing with the representative office in Kantstrasse and residing in Pistoriusstrasse, where the rents weren't nearly so high.

The cars rolled up at five on the dot, an Opel containing the CID officers, with Böhm in front next to the driver, Assistant Detective Mertens, and Rath in the rear next to Gräf, whom Gennat had also forced to take part despite being on late shift in the Castle. A police van of squad officers followed, and a pick-up truck to stow the confiscated articles.

Bellmann lived in a solidly middle-class tenement flat in the front building, while the La Belle office was located in the first rear building. A discreet brass plate pointed the way to a kind of studio with large windows that looked as if it had been built for a sculptor who needed a lot of space. Now it was home to desks and a conference table, everything more untidy, old-fashioned and thrown together than in Oppenberg's uncluttered modern office in Kantstrasse.

Rath left it to the higher-ranking Böhm to dangle the search order in front of the astounded producer's face. Bellmann was soon on the telephone to the lawyer he so enjoyed threatening people with, probably the same one who had earned him a load of money in his running battle with Manfred Oppenberg. Barely quarter of an hour later the lawyer arrived, but there was nothing he could do except watch as the officers packed files and reels of film into crates and carried them outside. Time and time again Bellmann protested that if the *Liebesgewitter* premiere had to be postponed he would be holding Böhm and Rath directly responsible, but the protests were half-hearted. For some reason Bellmann's mind seemed to be elsewhere.

In his years of service, Rath had developed an instinct for house searches.

He had learned to read the guilty consciences of people who protested about their four walls being turned upside down, and could distinguish genuine anger from feigned outrage. Bellmann had something to hide, that much was clear. Rath and Böhm took care that no one disposed of anything secretly.

There was a great deal to pack up, mainly document files, and he felt like he was part of a tax investigation. In his private residence, Bellmann had a little study from which they seized all papers and files, as well a few old appointments diaries, notebooks and screenplays. Next to the study was a small projection room, and Rath instructed that all film cans be secured, including the reel that was still in the projector.

They were almost finished when a woman in a grey winter coat swept through the front door, looking around frantically until she recognised Rath. 'What's going on here?' Cora Bellmann asked.

'House search,' Rath said. 'DCI Böhm has the warrant.' He gestured towards the adjoining room where Böhm was currently signing a list of confiscated articles for the lawyer.

'If anything important should go missing,' Bellmann cursed as he scanned the inventory, 'or your people should have broken anything, then . . .'

'. . . then the Free State of Prussia will naturally reimburse you for the damage,' Böhm interrupted. 'This is a summons. Please make sure you present yourself at police headquarters tomorrow morning at ten.'

'You've a nerve! I've got an important meeting tomorrow at ten.'

'You'll have to postpone.'

Cora Bellmann cut in. 'What is the meaning of this?' she asked first her father, who shrugged his shoulders, then Böhm. 'Can you explain to me why you are treating my father like a criminal?'

'If we were treating your father like a criminal he'd be in handcuffs and heading for a night in the cells,' Böhm said.

'We don't have to stand for this!'

'Actually you do.' Böhm remained calm. 'You may accompany your father to the station tomorrow morning should you wish, Fräulein Bellmann. Any questions you have will be answered there. Now you must excuse me. Our work here is done.'

Böhm lifted his hat and pushed his way outside. Emerging through the door he gave Rath a wink before cocking his head to one side, a gesture that could only mean one thing: let's get out of here!

Gräf and Mertens stayed behind to shadow the producer, '. . . but conspicuously, so that he notices,' as Gennat had said. Thus the Opel stayed where it was, and Rath and Böhm were obliged to head back to the Castle in the pick-up, squashed beside each other on the front seat next to the driver. The return journey was a little rough in places, and the pair were shaken around so much that there was no way they could avoid bumping into one another.

Böhm maintained an icy silence, as he had on the journey out. The driver sensed the tension and said nothing. The man was far too easy to offend, Rath thought. If they *had* to work together then they should at least try to make the best of it. He decided to give it a whirl.

'I know I acted improperly the day before yesterday when I set the whole disused cinema business in motion,' he said. 'Lange had told me expressly that it was against your wishes.'

Böhm continued to stare at the Greifswalder Strasse evening traffic, saying nothing.

'I'm sorry,' Rath said. 'I thought the idea was right and wanted to put it into action. If I've offended you by doing so, then I'd like to apologise.'

'It's fine,' Böhm growled. 'The fact it was successful proves you made the right choice.' He turned his head and looked Rath sternly in the eye. 'But if you should disregard a single one of my orders today, even if all you do is refuse to make coffee, I'll slap a disciplinary hearing on your arse so hard you won't be able to recover from it. Is that understood?'

'Understood.'

Despite the serious threat, Rath couldn't help but grin. The atmosphere in the car was suddenly more relaxed. The driver sensed it too, and was noticeably calmer behind the wheel.

When they arrived at Alex, only the late shift was still on duty in Homicide. Henning, who had to step in for Gräf, and Lange, as well as a little black dog. Kirie jumped up as Rath came through the door.

'What's the dog doing here?' Böhm asked.

'Fräulein Voss brought her just now,' Henning said. 'For Inspector Rath, she said.'

'I'm looking after her,' Rath explained. 'She belonged to Jeanette Fastré, the poor thing.'

'Doesn't it belong in a home?'

'She was beside herself with fear when we found her, I had no choice but to get her back on her feet.'

'Just make sure the damn thing doesn't eat any files, and that bringing dogs into Homicide doesn't become a habit.'

Kirie refused to be intimidated and started barking when the first uniformed officers entered with the heavy crates. She sniffed nosily at the pile, and Rath seized her by the collar to pull her back.

'Enough,' he said. 'Sit down and be good!'

The piles grew as more and more crates were brought in. At last, an officer placed the final crate, which contained only reels of film, at the top. 'That's it, Sir,' he said to Böhm.

The DCI nodded. The officer shrugged his shoulders and took his leave.

'That's a lot of timber,' Lange said, examining the contents of a crate. 'Did Buddha . . . I mean Superintendent Gennat, say we have to plough through all this tonight?'

'I'm saying it,' Böhm growled. 'We'll search until we find something.'

'And who's going to watch the films?' Henning asked.

'We'll take care of that tomorrow. The files are more important. Anything that's linked to Betty Winter or her new film. Contracts, fee statements, insurance documents, what do I know . . . ? Anything that provides information about Bellmann's finances and the commercial success or otherwise of his film company.'

'Someone should get to work on Bellmann's private notebooks and appointments diaries,' Rath said. 'Perhaps he made a note of the fact that Peter Glaser's real name was Felix Krempin.'

'You can take care of that,' Böhm said.

'I take it that's an order.'

It was meant to be a joke, but Böhm wasn't laughing. 'Shall we, then?' he said, heaving the first crate onto a desk. 'A crate each. That's the quickest way.' The three men did as they were told.

'I still don't understand,' Lange said, opening the first lever arch file. 'What are we actually looking for here?'

'Ammunition for Superintendent Gennat,' Böhm said.

45

Tuesday 11th March 1930

Heinrich Bellmann hadn't brought his daughter but his lawyer. He appeared in Homicide at ten on the dot, closely followed by Gräf and Mertens, both of whom looked as if they had spent the night in the car. The pair appeared through the glass door unshaven and with rumpled suits, while Bellmann looked spick and span as he took his seat on the wooden bench outside Gennat's office. Trudchen Steiner requested that he wait a little longer.

Gennat had coffee brought for Gräf and Mertens in the outer office, but continued to keep Bellmann in suspense. 'How was your night in Weissensee?' he asked.

'The man was home all night,' Gräf said, blowing on the hot coffee. 'His lawyer left around eight. The daughter stayed in the house.'

'She lives there too,' Gennat said. 'The man made no attempt to escape?'

'Difficult to say.' Gräf shrugged his shoulders. 'He sneaked a look through the window a few times, but probably sensed we wouldn't let him get away so easily.'

'You must have been conspicuous.'

'We didn't have to toot the horn. He saw us anyway,' Gräf said. 'Why didn't you have him remanded in custody if you thought he might try to escape?'

'Because I wanted to see what he would do, and because we don't have anything to justify holding him.'

'Still not?' Gräf gestured towards the chaos of document files and boxes that had spread across the main Homicide office.

'Not what we were looking for, but enough to give him a good grilling.' Gennat went through the connecting door into his private office. 'We'll get going in half an hour. Send Böhm and Rath in,' he said, and closed the door.

They were still working away feverishly in Homicide. Although they had found a few things that would create difficulties for Bellmann, they still hadn't found anything halfway sufficient for a murder charge. That morning they had started again at eight, even though Rath had got home at just before twelve the previous evening.

They had even postponed the daily briefing to the afternoon. One half of Homicide was following up on the few leads they had on the cinema killings, while the other continued to sift through contracts, fee statements and insurance documents, looking for the decisive find. At half past eight Buddha made himself comfortable behind his desk to feed on fresh insights from his colleagues, think and eat cake.

He was still doing so at half past ten when Rath and Böhm joined him. Gennat made no move to admit Bellmann, but instead spoke to the inspectors about what they had learned so far. Rath had come across the name *Borussia* several times in the manual records. The shady film company Marlow had told him about, and in which Bellmann clearly had a stake, seemed to be a lucrative business. After that he had rummaged through the crates with the film reels until he found a few labelled *Borussia,* which they had then proceeded to watch after all. No one knew that they were doing Johann Marlow a favour in the process.

Rath and Böhm each had to have a slice of cake, and only then did Gennat signal to Trudchen Steiner that Heinrich Bellmann and his lawyer could enter. After waiting for three-quarters of an hour the producer was rather flushed.

'This is an outrage,' he said, before even sitting down, ignoring his lawyer, who tugged incessantly on his sleeve. 'How dare you? Do you even know who you are dealing with?'

You couldn't take that kind of attitude with Gennat.

'I think I do,' he said, leafing calmly through the file. 'Heinrich Antonius Bellmann, if I'm not mistaken.'

'Why have you kept me waiting so long? I've been sitting outside for an hour. Do you think I can afford to waste my time?'

'I'm not interested in what you can and can't afford.'

'You had my office searched, and my private residence! Can you tell me why?'

'We'll come to that.'

'My client has the right to know what you are accusing him of,' said the lawyer.

Straightaway Gennat took the wind out of the man's sails. 'What makes you think we're accusing him of anything? Now take a seat, so that we can talk things through sensibly.'

The lawyer had to positively drag Bellmann to his chair before sitting down beside him. The producer cast suspicious glances at Rath and Böhm as the pair stirred their coffees.

'What's all this about?' he asked Gennat, gesturing towards Rath. 'Up until now I haven't complained about the way your colleague here hampered my shoot, but that can change.'

'I'm afraid police work can sometimes be inconvenient,' Gennat said. 'If it has been in any way disadvantageous or caused you a financial loss, then I apologise.' He closed the folder and fired off his first question as casually as he might remark on the weather. 'Was that the case with Betty Winter's death?'

'Pardon me?'

'Did you incur a financial loss as a result of her death?'

'What do you think?' Bellmann turned to his lawyer, who gave his client a nod. 'Betty was my most important actress,' he said.

'Is that why you took out such a substantial insurance policy on her?' Gennat reopened the file, leafing through it until he found the appropriate passage. 'Five hundred thousand marks in the event of her death, accident and sabotage expressly included.'

'You have to protect yourself. I still haven't received any money!'

'You pledged it as collateral to fund your advertising campaign for *Liebesgewitter*.'

'That's hardly a crime.'

'Perhaps not, but it does give a pretty clear indication of how much you gained from the death of your star.'

'What good are short-term gains against the loss of an irreplaceable actress?'

'Her successor is already filming.'

'You mean Eva Kröger? A promising talent, for sure, but what is she against an experienced actress on the verge of greatness?'

'Your first talkie with Winter wasn't exactly a hit.'

'What's that supposed to mean? At least you could understand what she was saying! Unlike all those lisping, stuttering, screen beauties from God knows where.'

Gennat shrugged. 'I'm in no position to judge her abilities. I'm just looking at the figures.'

'You need to be patient with sound film, it takes a while before you make your money back.'

'These foreign versions you're filming seem rather expensive to me.'

'In future we'll only film one additional language version alongside the original. In English.'

'It's lucky that Frau Kröger speaks English so well then. Being able to employ a single actress for two language versions must save you an enormous amount of money?'

'You can't blame me for limiting costs. Do you have any idea how expensive a sound film can be?'

'How you save on costs is your business. It only concerns the police when people are killed because of it.'

Bellmann turned to his lawyer.

'I refuse to tolerate any suggestion that my client is in any way linked to the murder of Betty Winter.'

'No one's suggesting anything of the kind,' Gennat said. 'All I've done is mention two things that are indisputable: that Betty Winter was killed intentionally and that her death has brought more advantages than disadvantages to your client.'

'According to the *cui bono* principle that makes him a prime suspect!'

'You're the lawyer, not me,' Gennat said.

The man blushed and fell silent. As good as he might have been for contractual disputes, Rath thought, he was unsuited to criminal defence.

'What about Manfred Oppenberg and how *he* benefited from all this?' Bellmann asked. 'He's the one who smuggled Herr Krempin into my studio.'

Bellmann's hypocrisy was getting on Rath's nerves. He tried a shot in the dark.

'On the morning of the twenty-eighth of February you discovered that

Felix Krempin intended to sabotage your shoot. Why didn't you tell the police?'

Bellmann looked as if he'd been dealt a blow to the solar plexus. He gasped for air. Bullseye. Rath had him on the ropes and refused to stop there.

'Because then you wouldn't have been able to accuse your rival Manfred Oppenberg of ordering a murder? Because you knew from the start that Krempin never planned to kill Betty Winter, you just wanted to make it look as though he had.'

'How do you know . . . ? Have you arrested Krempin? Is he serving you up these lies, or is it your old friend Oppenberg?'

'Felix Krempin is dead,' Gennat said.

Bellmann's surprise seemed genuine.

'If he took his own life, and there is evidence to suggest he did, then it'll be on your conscience,' Rath said, even though, of all the officers in the room, he was the least convinced by Krempin's suicide. 'You threw him out, and he went underground because he was forced to read about your suspicions in the press.'

'But that's . . .' Bellmann began to stutter. 'I can't help what the press write.'

'That's something you'll have to square with your conscience,' Gennat said. 'Alongside Betty Winter's death.'

'That's nothing to do with me! I barely understand it myself. He disconnected the wire.'

'You're talking about Krempin?'

'Who else?'

'Then you knew about his plans?'

'Yes, but . . .' Bellmann seemed outraged, before checking himself and lowering his voice. 'It's true, I knew what he was planning, but surely you don't believe what your colleague here is accusing me of!'

'How was it then?'

'I told him what I knew about him, and that he should take his things and scram. Before he left the studio he went onto the bridge and deactivated the device.'

'Did you see him do it?' Rath asked. 'How do you know?'

'I don't go onto the lighting bridges. Krempin went up there on his own, but what else could he have been doing? He knew that I'd have called him to account for the damage otherwise. Besides, the thunder machine was working in the morning as usual. It wasn't until midday . . . You know, the spotlight . . .'

'I still don't understand why you let him go,' Rath said. 'Why not report him straightaway? Was it because you already knew that you wanted to lay the blame at his door for something much worse? Namely murder. In the process, you killed two birds with one stone. On the one hand, by directing the worst kind of suspicion imaginable onto your rival. On the other, by getting rid of the increasingly troublesome Betty Winter. Then there's the insurance money.'

'What are you saying? I'm no murderer!'

The lawyer took his client reassuringly by the arm. 'Best not to say anything now, Herr Bellmann, not before . . .'

'Oh, pipe down!' Bellmann shook off the man's hand. 'Do you think I'm going to sit here and be accused of murder?'

'I just mean . . . The other thing we spoke about,' the lawyer whispered.

'That's got nothing to do with it. Really, I don't know why I brought you here in the first place.'

The lawyer fell silent and gazed out of the window, offended.

Gennat's confidence-inspiring voice filled the room once more. 'Tell me in your own time what really happened on the twenty-eighth of February. You wouldn't believe how many people have sat in your place, grateful to unburden themselves at last.'

'There isn't much to unburden myself of,' Bellmann said. 'I'd known there was something fishy about this Peter Glaser for a long time, and had him placed under surveillance.'

'But waited until he had built his wire construction before exposing him?' Rath said.

'I had to have something on him to prove what Oppenberg was capable of.'

'And on the morning of the twenty-eighth you had reached that point,' Gennat said.

'As I said, I had him placed under surveillance, and they told me he was on the lighting bridges far more often than necessary.'

'So, a few of your people were in on it. That means they knew about Krempin?'

'Yes.'

'Who?'

'Just a few lighting technicians.'

'I need all their names.'

'I can give them to you.'

Gennat shook his head. 'And not one of them told us that Glaser's real name was Krempin.'

'I have loyal workers, Inspector.'

'Superintendent.'

'Superintendent.'

Gennat turned to Rath and Böhm. 'What do you say, gentlemen? Shall we believe the man?'

'You have to, Superintendent!' Bellmann sprang to his feet. 'It can't have been me. I wasn't on the lighting bridge for the entire morning in question. In fact, I've never been up there at all. You can ask anyone, I was down below the whole time.'

'You said you didn't realise Betty Winter had died.'

'I was with the sound engineer in the projection room, I've told you that already. When we heard the bang and her screams, we came out right away.'

'Perhaps it was one of your employees, acting on your behalf? They're very loyal, as you say.'

'You overestimate how far their loyalty stretches.' Bellmann sat back down. 'My staff are all good, upstanding people. They wouldn't commit murder, not even for me.'

'We'll see about that once we've questioned them. We'll be checking your alibi at the same time.'

'Feel free, you'll see that I'm telling the truth!'

'The question remains why you didn't report Krempin.'

'You don't have to report everything; things like that can be settled man-to-man.'

'That sounds out of character coming from you. Given that you have brought legal proceedings against your rival Manfred Oppenberg on thirty-seven occasions in the last five years. You let the thirty-eighth opportunity slide?'

'People change, Superintendent.'

'You haven't changed one iota! You just knew that you could do more damage to Oppenberg if you exploited the sabotage attempt for the press. Which you then proceeded to do.'

'I couldn't have known Betty Winter would die!'

'You took advantage of her death all the same, to blacken your rival's name even though you knew it couldn't have been him, and to publicise your new film in a truly macabre fashion.'

'I owe it to Betty that I give her final film the publicity it deserves. That *she* deserves!'

'My heart bleeds,' Böhm grunted.

Bellmann gave the bulldog a vexed look, as if he expected the bulky DCI to launch himself at him at any moment.

'Herr Bellmann,' Gennat said. 'Even if neither you nor your employees are responsible for the murder of Betty Winter, you have obstructed and misled the police in their investigations. You will have to answer for that.'

'My client . . .' the lawyer began, before being interrupted by Gennat.

'For the time being that's it from our side. You're free to go.'

'I can go back to my studio?'

'No,' Gennat said. 'Things don't happen that quickly around here. Superintendent Lanke from E Division would like to speak with you. On examination of your film reels, we uncovered pornographic material.' The lawyer jumped to his feet and began to protest but Gennat continued. 'It's called accidental discovery. Surely I don't have to explain that to a lawyer such as yourself? In such cases evidence is passed on to the relevant authority. E Division is not far from here, on this floor. An officer will show you and your client the way.'

Bellmann looked at his lawyer.

'You see, Herr Bellmann,' the lawyer said. 'There was a reason you brought me after all.'

Trudchen Steiner arrived with fresh supplies of cake as soon as Bellmann and his lawyer disappeared.

'Well, gentlemen,' Gennat said, shovelling slices of cake on Böhm and Rath's plates. 'We've taken one step forward and two steps back.' He made a thoughtful face. 'I think we can safely rule this Krempin out. He's no killer, not even through negligence. The only thing is, it wasn't Heinrich Bellmann either.'

'Can you be sure?' Böhm asked. He was gazing at his cake as if longing for it to be transformed into a Bulette with mustard. 'I don't trust the man.'

'If he was responsible for Betty Winter's death, he wouldn't have told us so much. He might have exploited her death, but he didn't cause it.'

'Somebody must have reattached the wire,' Rath said, 'and it must have been someone familiar with both the studio and the script. If not Bellmann himself, then someone from his company.'

'I don't think any of his employees would commit murder on his behalf,' Böhm said. 'That's one of his few claims that I do believe, the sleazebag.'

'Perhaps not on his behalf,' Rath said, 'but working under their own steam. Perhaps one of Bellmann's employees had a score to settle with Betty Winter.'

Gennat nodded. 'That means we must step up our search for further motives, something that was neglected last week, I'm afraid. The *cui bono* principle, as Bellmann's lawyer so nicely put it: who stands to gain from her death?'

'Bellmann's daughter perhaps,' Rath said. 'I think she has her eye on Victor Meisner, perhaps she wanted to make him a widower so that she could console him.'

'Then it could also have been Meisner,' Böhm said. 'Perhaps together with her. Love has turned many people into accomplices.'

'I don't think he benefits from her death,' Rath said. 'The only reason he still had a career was his wife. He was the one holding her back. It'd be more likely that she killed *him*.'

'Whoever it was,' Gennat said, 'must have known about the construction up on the lighting bridges, and how to reactivate it in next to no time.'

'Good luck trying to prove that!'

'My dear Böhm, I'm afraid you don't always get everything handed to you on a plate. Let Bellmann's employees stew for the time being. Let's see what they say and take it from there. Before we interrogate them, I want each individual reinvestigated. What relationship did they have to the deceased, what do their finances look like, etc, etc, etc? We need to know more about everyone we bring in, more than they know themselves.'

'Perhaps there's another death that can help us,' Rath said.

Gennat looked at him curiously. 'What do you mean?'

'The Krempin case. What do you think of the idea that Felix Krempin knew who had tampered with his construction, or at least had an inkling? Perhaps he was blackmailing the killer and *he* pushed him off the Funkturm.'

'One thing's for certain, Rath,' said Böhm. 'If what happened at the Funkturm was murder, then Krempin knew his killer, or at least trusted him. Everything points to that. There's no way you could throw someone off otherwise.'

Gennat nodded. 'That sounds plausible, but we need to take care these theories don't get out of control. What we desperately need are facts. If only we could find the man who went back up the Funkturm after Krempin's fall. He might be able to solve a few riddles.'

He looked at the two officers. Both had finished their cake, even if Böhm was making a face as if he had just consumed a bottle of cod liver oil. 'I think,' Gennat said, 'we should discuss the next steps with the whole group at two. Then we can allocate tasks.'

Rath and Böhm stood up and moved to the door.

'Inspector, one more thing,' Gennat said.

'Yes, Sir?'

Gennat waited until Böhm had left the room.

'Let me say this to you,' he said. 'Even if it worked today, in future please refrain from interrupting an interrogation that someone else is leading. If you intend to do anything like that again, arrange it with me beforehand.'

46

The chaos in Homicide was beginning to subside. Most of the crates, above all those containing film reels, could now be passed to E Division. Vice came by themselves to pick up the goods. There was no one Rath recognised from his time in E save for Gregor Lanke, the nephew of the division chief. He had been Rath's successor, though the pair had never worked together. It was already clear from Lanke junior's face just how much he was looking forward to the porn films.

There wasn't much material left for the homicide detectives. Rath took his leave. When he arrived in his office, he encountered a frantic Erika Voss.

'There you are at last,' she said. 'I've been sitting here like a cat on a hot tin roof. I've arranged to meet my sister at half past twelve, and I can hardly take the dog to the canteen with me.'

'Half past twelve is still five minutes away.'

'I didn't know when you were coming back. You didn't say anything.'

'Don't forget that you were the one who wrecked things for us with the canine unit in the first place!'

'I didn't mean it like that. I'm just in a rush, that's all. Oh, before I forget, your father called again. And a woman, the same one as yesterday, I think. Then a . . .' She looked at her pad. '. . . a Herr Weinert and a Herr Wittkamp.'

'Thanks. Did Herr Wittkamp say where he can be reached?'

'No, he didn't. He said he'll try again.'

'And Herr Weinert?'

'No, but it sounded like an office. There were typewriters clattering.'

'Many thanks.'

'I'm off to meet my sister,' she said, taking her leave.

Weinert wasn't at the office or in Nürnberger Strasse. It was lunchtime! He tried the Excelsior.

'I'm afraid Herr Wittkamp isn't in his room,' the porter said.

'Did he say where he was going?'

'He's most likely having his lunch. Should I pass on a message?'

'Just *ne schöne Jrooß*,' Rath said.

'Pardon me?'

'Cologne dialect.'

He put Kirie on her lead and took her outside. With its building sites and crowds of people, Alexanderplatz wasn't an ideal place for young dogs, so Rath strolled up Dircksenstrasse past the city railway and towards Monbijou Park. He liked this quiet green oasis in the heart of the city, and this modest little castle that didn't match the pomp the Hohenzollern had otherwise sought to establish in the capital. He came here whenever he needed to think in peace and escape the clatter of typewriters in the Castle and the traffic on Alex. Usually there wasn't much going on: a few mothers strolling with prams, perhaps a few traders from the nearby stock exchange stretching their legs.

He sat down on a park bench near the bank of the river and looked onto the northern tip of the Spreeinsel, where the Kaiser-Friedrich Museum jutted into the river like the bow of a ship, and immersed himself in his thoughts. Kirie sniffed curiously at the wire netting of a wastepaper basket. Rath unpacked the dog biscuits that Erika Voss had bought from Wertheim, and threw the dog one which she caught in mid-air.

'What am I going to do with you?' he said. 'You wouldn't make a good police dog, but perhaps I should keep you anyway. You like me at least.'

Kirie seemed to smile.

After she had taken care of her business, they returned to Alex. It was already late, so Rath ordered three Buletten to go from Aschinger, two for himself and one for Kirie.

He had just bitten into his when he realised she had already devoured hers and was gazing longingly at the paper bag in his hand. Rath looked for some more dog biscuits but couldn't find any.

'Very well,' he said, sacrificing the second Bulette. 'Next time, we'll share more equally. You're much smaller than me, you shouldn't be eating more.'

His stomach rumbled but there wasn't enough time to go back to Aschinger. It was nearly two already.

Since he had to return Kirie to Erika Voss, Rath was the last to appear in the conference room. Gennat interrupted his report while he found a seat. Brenner seemed to be missing again, but this time he wouldn't be off sick.

Buddha summarised the results of the Bellmann interrogation and turned to those investigating the cinema killings. They had a wealth of new information to impart. Assistant Detective Lange reported on those in possession of a key to the abandoned cinemas.

'Upon realising that there was no positive correlation to be found using the initial lists,' he said, in the ponderous officialese that could only be truly mastered at Prussian police academy, 'we made a conscious choice to further our search to include the personal and professional circles in which the relevant keys circulated *prior* to the closure of the picture palaces in question, and, following a comparison of all addresses, uncovered exactly four companies in possession of such keys.'

'You can say cinemas!' one of the older officers yelled. Everyone laughed, and Lange blushed.

'At any rate, it seems we are dealing with a cleaning firm that specialised in picture . . . cinemas, as well as several film labs and distribution companies that must have had access to the pic . . . cinemas. So far, we have been unable to commence our review of these companies, but will endeavour to . . .'

'. . . carry out said undertaking immediately subsequent to the conclusion of this briefing,' the joker suggested, this time earning a reproachful glance from Gennat.

'Excellent work, Lange,' Gennat said. 'We look forward to your results. Are there any duplicates? Keys that were not returned? If you should find anything else today, please let me know immediately.'

'Yes, Sir.'

Lange sat down, having grown at least three inches taller.

Next Czerwinski stood up. The last time that fatso had contributed anything meaningful to an investigation the Prussian police must still have been wearing spiked helmets.

Czerwinski cleared his throat before beginning. He seemed very pleased with himself. 'We researched the history of both cinemas, Sir. The question is why he, the killer, that is, chose to plant the corpses in such dilapidated hovels?'

'And? Did you make any progress?'

'I think so!' Czerwinski puffed out his chest. 'We found a connection.' He made a dramatic pause before continuing, to ensure that everyone was listening. 'It is this: the Luxor was, or is, the cinema in which Vivian Franck's first film had its premiere. That was November twenty-eight. And Kosmos screened Jeanette Fastré's first film in twenty-seven. The two women are . . . or, I should say, *were* in their premiere cinemas.'

'That might be significant.' Gennat gave a nod of appreciation, and Czerwinski sat down, grinning happily. 'Perhaps that's one of the messages the perpetrator is trying to send us with his staging of the corpses.'

'Maybe we should also check where Betty Winter's first film had its premiere,' Rath said. 'I can't shake the feeling that she has something to do with the other two actresses.'

'You believe too much of what's in the papers,' Böhm said. 'Isn't the Chinese gooseberry fiasco enough for you?'

Rath was already regretting having aired his thoughts when Gennat spoke. 'It isn't such a bad idea.' He looked at Czerwinski. 'Could you take care of that? Let me know when you have traced the cinema in question.'

Then Gennat allocated their tasks.

'The Winter case has priority,' he said. 'It's possible we are on the verge of a breakthrough. At any rate, we have a closed circle of suspects, and must apply more pressure.'

This closed circle of suspects was still big enough. All those who knew the production schedule and had access to the lighting bridges—that is, almost all La Belle employees in Marienfelde. As a lone outsider, Manfred Oppenberg might have known about everything through Felix Krempin.

For the time being only a small cast of officers was investigating the cinema killer, as he was now known, since Gennat needed every officer available to seek out possible motives amongst Bellmann's staff. Böhm was to take care of Oppenberg, Gräf would take Cora Bellmann, and Rath was tasked with reinterviewing Victor Meisner. It was Gennat's way of showing the three former lead investigators that he had read the interrogation records and found them wanting. He was providing an opportunity for all three to revisit anything they had previously overlooked.

Rath returned to his office without exchanging a word with anyone.

Meisner, of all people, that snivelling little wretch! This was going to be some day.

Erika Voss was on the telephone again, and Kirie lay asleep under the desk.

'He's just coming now,' she said. 'One minute, Police Director, I'll put you through.'

She pressed a button and hung up. In the next room Rath's telephone started to ring.

'Who is it?' he asked. 'Not Scholz surely?' The head of CID was the only police director he had dealings with at Alex.

Erika Voss laughed. 'No. Way off. Try a little further west.'

'What is this? Some sort of guessing game?'

'My, we're in a good mood today,' she grumbled as Rath stormed into his office.

'Inspector Rath, A Division!'

'You're a difficult man to get hold of, boy!'

Rath cast Erika Voss a grimly apologetic look, which she countered with a smile and a shrug. He closed the door. 'Father!'

'You were right, my boy!'

'Pardon me?'

It was rare that Engelbert Rath admitted his son was right.

'The name, Hagedorn. Bullseye! A Gertrud Hagedorn worked as a secretary for the Deutsche Bank board of directors in Cologne between nineteen-twenty-seven and twenty-nine, and was present at all board meetings where Konrad spoke about these matters with Chairman Brüning. And then this Fräulein Hagedorn . . .'

'. . . moved to Berlin half a year ago.'

'You already know?'

'I've taken action. You can tell the mayor the matter has been resolved.'

'Did you trace the letters' sender?'

'As a matter of fact, I silenced him.'

'Sometimes you really do surprise me, boy. For days nothing happens, and I ask myself whether it was a mistake entrusting the matter to you, and then, somehow, you manage after all.'

'I didn't just manage. I resolved a serious problem and did both you and the mayor a huge favour.'

'Who was it then? Hagedorn herself?'

'Her fiancé. A Ford worker. The name isn't important.'

'Are you sure he'll stop harassing the mayor?'

'Quite sure.'

'We don't want him to go running to the press now.'

'The mayor needn't worry about his good name.'

'Then I hope you're right.'

'Do you have to call everything I do into question? Can't you just believe me for once? Trust me when I say the matter is resolved?'

'Don't be so sensitive. I just wonder how you can be so certain with a matter as delicate as this.'

'Let me worry about *how* I dealt with everything. Just know that everything *has* been dealt with!'

'Good. We'll take care of Fräulein Hagedorn. Or rather: Deutsche Bank.'

'Best leave her alone. If the bank puts her out on the street she'll only seek revenge. It's enough for the woman to no longer take part in confidential meetings.'

'We let her off scot-free?'

'Fear of unemployment is more effective than unemployment itself. As long as Gertrud Hagedorn has her job, the mayor can sleep easy. I just hope he keeps his word regarding my promotion.'

'Of course, my boy!'

47

What filthy weather! Rath had to turn on the windscreen wipers. At lunch-time the sun had been shining, now it was coming down in buckets. To cap it all, soft hail was drumming on the roof of the car. Some pedestrians had been caught out and, without an umbrella, pulled their hats down or held their briefcases above their heads.

He didn't even know if there was any point in this journey, but the secretary at La Belle Film Production had left him no other choice. No sooner did she realise she was talking to the police than her voice had taken on a layer of ice.

'I'm afraid I must disappoint you there,' she said, sounding anything but apologetic, 'but I have no idea where you can reach Herr Meisner today.'

'Isn't he filming?'

'Our production schedule is with you at Alexanderplatz. Why don't you have a look there?'

Rath had chosen to do something else. He had grabbed Kirie and headed for the car.

'Where are you off to?' Erika Voss asked.

'To look for an actor.'

'Then you've got the right search dog.'

Where to start? Meisner's private address or the studio in Marienfelde? Rath decided on the man's private apartment.

Victor Meisner lived in Lietzensee, a nice residential area near Kant-strasse, which was nevertheless right on the lake with a direct view of the park and the swans. The house even had an elevator.

The door still said *Meisner/Zima*. He pressed the button and there was a shrill ring behind the door, but no one answered.

He rang again and waited. Even in the stairwell there was a nice view of the lake and the Funkturm, its steel struts glistening wet in the sun that was just beginning to peer through the grey clouds.

When no one had answered by the third ring, he went back downstairs. There was still the caretaker, or *concierge* as the sign on his lodge described him.

The man even wore a uniform. Remembering Vivian Franck's apartment building, he thought actors probably needed that sort of thing. He knocked on the glass.

The man opened the sliding window. 'What can I do for you, Inspector?'

'I'm looking for Victor Meisner.'

'Herr Meisner isn't at home.'

'I've realised that.'

'If you had asked me just now, instead of waving your badge, I could have spared you the trip.'

'My dog likes to take the elevator,' Rath said. 'Perhaps you can tell me where I might find Herr Meisner?'

'Herr Meisner is working.'

'He's only just completed a film.'

'Herr Meisner is always working. Probably best for him, after the tragedy with his wife.'

'How is he coping?'

'With dignity. In those first few days he was inconsolable. Luckily Fräulein Bellmann was there to look after him. He seems to have a hold of himself again. Still, even with all his acting gifts he can't hide the fact that this quirk of fate has made a broken man of him.'

'A broken man . . .'

That wasn't Rath's impression, but he didn't want to destroy the image the concierge had of his most celebrated resident.

'He no longer needs Frau Bellmann's support then?'

'She hasn't been here for a long time, if that's what you mean.'

'And has he been there?'

'I'm a concierge, not a private detective.'

'What would you say, did he love his wife?'

'You do ask indiscreet questions!'

'It's one of the things I love about my job. So?'

'Of course, he loved her. Even if recently . . .'

'What?'

'Well, Frau Winter . . . I don't think she loved him. At least not latterly.'

'What makes you think that?'

'She was always a little cold, thought she was above people, never greeted yours truly. And it seems she wanted to leave him . . .'

'She wanted a divorce?'

'I'm not talking about that. She wanted to make other films. Without him, with another producer.'

'How do you know that?'

The concierge shrugged. 'I overheard it. They had a fight right outside my lodge. She wouldn't lend her good name to it, she said, he could forget about that.'

'What did she mean?'

'No idea. I'm just telling you what I heard that morning by chance.'

'Which morning?'

'You know, *that* morning. He came back in the evening looking a picture of misery. Must have been reproaching himself for having fought with her on the day she died. Yet the whole thing was her fault.'

'A huge fight on the day Betty Winter died . . . Why didn't you tell us before?'

'Because no one asked. Your colleagues went into the flat last week, and came straight back out. Nobody was interested in what I had to say.'

They were still working in the studio at Marienfelde, and Rath had to wait before the guard let him in. It looked like an adventure film, at any rate a set with windows that had been shot to pieces. Eva Kröger was there again. Had she found a stage name in the meantime? She gave him a brief smile when she recognised him, in contrast to Jo Dressler, whose gaze had followed her smile.

The director rolled his eyes. 'You as well,' he said. 'I hope that's it for today. Your people have been in and out all afternoon. How are we supposed to get any work done?'

'You must have experience of working in difficult conditions by now,' said Rath.

Dressler gave a forced smile. 'Who are you after then?'

'Victor Meisner.'

'In his dressing room; he's finished filming for the day.'

Rath nodded. 'Don't mind me, I know the way.'

'You can't just go bursting in there,' Dressler called, but Rath continued backstage as if he hadn't heard, towards the door with Meisner's name on.

He knocked and entered.

Victor Meisner sat in front of a large mirror, wiping make-up from his brow. He was scarcely recognisable. The pale face that gazed at Rath from the mirror, still partly smeared with greasepaint, had nothing to do with the heroes Victor Meisner embodied on-screen. There was something else that fitted even less with the image of the glorious hero, however, a discovery that instantly put Rath on high alert. The electric bulbs above the dressing table were reflected by a receding hairline.

The actor was clearly embarrassed at being seen like this. He made a grab for his hairpiece and hastily arranged it on his head. Only then did he sport the hairstyle Rath was familiar with. He still didn't look like a hero though, nor did he sound like one.

'Can't you wait until you are invited to enter?' he asked.

'You wear a wig,' Rath said, trying to sound casual. 'I never knew that.'

'Not a wig, just a hairpiece,' Meisner said. 'Nobody knows. I'm warning you, if I should read about it in the press I'll hold you responsible.'

'Don't worry, I can keep quiet.'

'But that's not why you're here.'

'No.' Rath moved a chair so that he could see Meisner's face in the mirror, and tied Kirie's lead round one of the legs. 'You don't have anything against me sitting down,' he said, fetching a notebook and pencil from his coat. 'I have a few more questions for you.'

'Shouldn't you have asked them last week? Then we'd be through with all this.'

'The police are always asking new questions, Herr Meisner, as well as repeating old ones. We know that we annoy people like you in the process, but it's our job.'

'Some job.'

'You're shooting a new film,' Rath said. 'With Eva Kröger, I see. You seem to have coped rather well with the death of your wife.'

'The world keeps turning, Inspector. *The show must go on*, as the English would say. Eventually you have to get back on an even keel. Betty's funeral is on Thursday and, believe you me, that will be hard enough.' He tapped his index finger against his breast. 'Do you have any idea what things look like in *here*?'

'No, but I'd like to.'

Meisner looked at him suspiciously. 'What do you want? Ask your questions and leave me in peace!'

'Did your wife leave you much?'

Meisner let out a brief, jerky laugh. 'Why don't you just say you're after a motive. Well, the inheritance isn't one! Betty left me very little. Feel free to speak to the notary. If you thought that was a motive for murder, then Bellmann would have more reason. He had Betty insured for a lot of money; her death really pays off for him.'

Rath sketched a stick man in his notebook.

'Another question,' he said, still drawing, 'how was your wife familiar with yangtao?'

'I'm sorry?'

'Yangtao.' Rath left the stick man unfinished for the time being and looked up. 'Chinese gooseberry. An exotic fruit.'

'No idea. What makes you think Betty was familiar with it?'

'We found it in her stomach,' he said, and continued with his drawing.

Meisner made a disgusted face. 'Don't you think you're being excessively tactless? You could show a little more consideration. Just because I have myself under control doesn't mean I'm not mourning the loss of my wife. We were married almost five years.'

'You weren't quite so close in recent times, were you?'

'How dare you . . . ?'

'You quarrelled with her. On the morning of the twenty-eighth of February, the day of her death.'

'Who told you that?'

'That's beside the point. Did you or did you not?'

'Who doesn't quarrel in their marriage? It's no reason to kill someone.'

'She wanted to leave La Belle and stop making films with you.'

'And that's why I killed her, so that she might make films with me again? Where's the logic in that?'

'I never said you killed your wife.'

'You know that I killed my wife, and I know it too, but it was a mistake. You ought to find the one who's responsible for the spotlight.'

Rath drew the stick man a little dog, dark and woolly, with a smiling face.

'That's why I'm here,' he said, adding a lead, 'and it's why I need to ask you something else. Where were you . . . ?'

'You know that! I was standing next to her when she died. I had to witness the whole thing with my own eyes.'

'I'm not talking about that. I'm talking about the morning of the twenty-eighth of February. Can you tell me what you did that day?'

'I was filming, you know that.'

'When did you set off from home, arrive at the studio, film your first scene. Which scenes? Can you give me times?'

'Not off the top of my head. I'd need to think about that. Betty's death overshadowed everything else that day.'

Rath took his pencil and waited eagerly.

'We set off from home about half past eight as usual,' he said. 'We must have arrived at the studio just before nine.'

'You went together?'

'Yes. I have a car, and usually gave her a ride.'

'What did you do when you arrived at the studio?'

'The usual. Said hello to everyone first, chatted a little. We had a look at the schedule and went through the scenes we'd be filming that day with Dressler.'

'You started filming straight after?'

'Yes. That is, first we had to go into make-up. The actors, I mean.'

This time Rath really had made notes. 'Thank you, Herr Meisner.' He snapped the book shut. 'That's it for today from my end.' He stood up and took Kirie's lead. 'I must ask you, however, to come to the station tomorrow at ten. Superintendent Gennat would like to speak to you.'

'And the shoot?'

'Most of your colleagues will also be at Alex. Dressler has almost certainly altered the schedule.'

Meisner sighed and continued wiping greasepaint from his face.

'Just one more thing,' Rath said when he was standing in the door. 'Your hairpiece—is it a spare or did you have to get a new one?'

He didn't wait for a response but followed Kirie, who was already pulling on the lead, and closed the door behind him.

On the drive home, he made a detour via Oranienstrasse and picked up supper for himself and Kirie from the local Aschinger. This time he played it safe and bought half a dozen Buletten and a little potato salad. At least Kirie wouldn't be competing for that.

Tonight, their evening walk only took them as far as Oranienplatz. He fetched their supper from the car and took the matted hairpiece along with the little blue package out of the glove compartment. The present from the Funkturm. Charly and her crazy idea!

Charly!

The thought of her cut him to the quick.

The grinning man at her door.

Shit.

'You dogs have it good,' he said, holding the Aschinger bag safely away from Kirie. 'All you think about is eating.'

Kirie looked at him and smiled expectantly.

'Come on then,' he said, and the dog trotted ahead across the yard, turning again and again to look at the bag of food. Once inside the flat he gave her a few Buletten, as well as a little food in her bowl. He fetched her some fresh water and opened a beer for himself.

While the dog ate, he looked at the toupee. It was matted and soiled, but perhaps still of some use. If only to snap that arrogant Meisner out of his complacent self-assurance.

The only problem: in theory he wasn't allowed to be in possession of the hairpiece.

Then again perhaps he wasn't; perhaps someone else had found it, someone who the police already knew had been at the Funkturm that day.

He took his beer and the Aschinger bag into the living room, made himself comfortable at the table with the telephone and, having given the operator the number, took a bite from his Bulette. At that moment Elisabeth Behnke came on the line, his former landlady, who had thrown him out because of Charly.

'Merthold Meinert, bleathe,' Rath said.

'He's eating,' Behnke said, 'as, clearly, are you!' If there was one thing she couldn't abide it was bad manners.

'Jushth a momemt,' Rath munched down the line. There was a click and he heard her shouting: 'Herr Weinert, it's one of your vulgar colleagues.' It took a moment before someone lifted the receiver again.

'My dear Binding,' he heard Weinert curse. 'Surely the matter isn't so urgent that you need to interrupt my dinner.'

'Very urgent,' Rath said. 'The Reich Chancellor has pissed on the government bench in the Reichstag, and we need an exclusive.'

'Gereon, is that you?'

'Careful with my first name! Behnke might smell a rat, and you're the one who'll have to put up with her bad mood.'

'Thanks for the warning. Where were you on *Sonnabend*, damn it? Not in that Dreieck anyway. Or at home either.'

'Something came up, sorry, I tried to ring you,' Rath lied.

'And I've been trying to ring you for three days!'

'Best not to mention your name when you call Alex. The journalist Berthold Weinert is on file as part of the Krempin case. If they find out you know me, we could be in trouble.'

'All right, but back to our abortive meeting. Is the wig no longer of interest to you?'

'Of course it is. That's why I'm calling.' He glanced at the time. 'Can I bring it round tonight?'

'I have a reception with the Reich Chancellor.'

'Tomorrow then.'

'In the evening, I can't manage before. I'm up to my eyes in work, and this time, there's a price.'

'Which would be?'

'I need the car.'

'For Wednesday night?'

'Inclusive of Thursday morning.'

'Come by and pick it up, together with the wig.'

'I'll come straight to yours from Kochstrasse. Around eight?'

'OK.'

'Woe betide you if you should stand me up again.'

'Don't worry, it won't happen again. Cross my heart! Otherwise I'll address you as *Your Worshipfulness* for a whole month.'

'Well then, it must be serious,' Weinert laughed. 'By the way, there was something I wanted to warn you about. There'll be an article on Krempin tomorrow. He'll be mentioned by name for the first time. It couldn't be withheld any longer.'

'So long as *my* name doesn't appear. No matter who asks: I wasn't at the Funkturm.'

'You were on Sunday.' Weinert's voice sounded as if he was grinning. 'A few nice photos landed on my desk yesterday. The Funkturm's millionth visitor. Looks pretty damn similar to you. And that little cutie next to you! A film actress apparently. Seems like it pays to investigate in those circles.'

'Are you going to publish the picture?'

'It's not exactly the silly season, but I think it would be a good filler. Besides, the tourist office has almost certainly sent the press release and photo to the other papers. The millionth visitor is better than the hundredth suicide.'

'Quit joking, Berthold. If the picture appears somewhere, and one of the Funkturm witnesses recognises me it'll be goodnight.'

'I wouldn't be too worried there. The most likely thing is a nice little text report without the picture. Unless, that is, someone finds out who the actress in the photo is.'

'They won't.'

He hung up and ate the Buletten and potato salad. When he had finished he reached again for the telephone. He'd have liked to get drunk with Paul, but the Excelsior informed him that Herr Wittkamp had gone out again.

'We'll have to make do on our own,' he said to Kirie as he attached her lead.

He made his way to the Dreieck with her. The pub was already full to bursting, which wasn't saying much given the building's narrow triangular structure. He positioned himself at the bar and ordered a beer with corn schnapps. He wasn't the only patron with a dog. They clearly served as an alibi for others to get out of the house in the evening. Kirie got along just fine with the alibi-dogs. She sniffed curiously at an ugly Boxer who let the whole thing wash over him with an expressionless face. Schorsch set down a bowl for the dogs, which he filled with water before taking care of his two-legged guests.

With Kirie, Rath thought as he drained the corn schnapps and took his first sip of beer, at least he would find his way home.

48

Wednesday 12th March 1930

Gennat kept the morning briefing short, in view of the round of interviews that was to follow. Rath was doing his best to keep up, but it was difficult. He had tried everything, even a cold shower, but he could still feel the hangover in his bones. Meisner was second in line, immediately behind Cora Bellmann, who was still being treated as a prime suspect since she was the only one police thought might have acted on her father's behalf.

Before that, it had been Lange and Czerwinski. From the cleaning firm Lange had acquired a list of people who had access to both cinemas. Unfortunately, that was a lot of names—but Czerwinski had discovered something which made Rath sit up and take notice. The cinema in which Betty Winter had celebrated her film premiere in 1925, the Tivoli in Weissensee, had closed in December.

'Betty Winter, therefore,' Gennat took up the thread, 'would have been a likely target for our cinema killer. Film actress, under thirty, first talkie just in cinemas—and the Tivoli would have been the ideal location for the final enactment our perpetrator grants his victims. I would ask you all to bear these possible connections in mind when we start interviewing but, above all, the information Detective Czerwinski is about to provide. Please continue, Detective.'

'The Tivoli has already found an interesting new use,' Czerwinski said. 'It won't be turned into a sound film cinema, but rather back into what it was over ten years ago: a theatre. And who will be in charge?' Czerwinski looked round to check everyone was listening. 'Victor Meisner!'

That really was news. Rath was annoyed that Meisner hadn't told him, neither yesterday nor a week ago.

'It will be called The Betty Winter Theatre,' Czerwinski said. 'Not exactly original, but certainly good for business.'

'Thank you, Detective. We'll explore that in more detail presently, during his interview,' Gennat said. 'Now, to work!'

Rath still had time before it was his turn and returned to his office. Better Erika Voss's coffee than the sludge in Homicide. He sat at his desk, taking the occasional sip from the steaming mug, lit a cigarette and reflected on matters.

By now Gennat would have the transcript from his interview with Meisner. It was too late to insert anything about The Betty Winter Theatre. Another black mark against his name, no doubt, but there was nothing to be done. Perhaps he could make up for it during the interrogation. He had to force Meisner into such a corner that his only option was to confess. He stubbed out his cigarette and went on his way.

When he arrived in Homicide, Cora Bellmann and Victor Meisner were already on the bench outside Gennat's office. Rath greeted them with a nod, but they both ignored him.

You won't be so arrogant when I'm finished with you, Rath thought and went inside. Nearly all the officers who were assisting Buddha with the interrogations had assembled in the spacious office. Reinhold Gräf was pacing up and down nervously. Cora Bellmann's was the first name on the list.

Böhm sat behind a desk with customary ill temper, leafing through his files. He didn't seem to have got a lot out of Manfred Oppenberg on this occasion either. When Trudchen Steiner waved Gräf in, Rath realised that he, too, was getting a little nervous. It would be a while before he was called, so he reached for one of the papers on the desk: the *Berliner Tageblatt*. He found a short paragraph on the Funkturm's millionth visitor, without name or photo, and continued leafing through. The report on Krempin's fatal fall was somewhat longer but Weinert hadn't made too much of it.

Though police have refused to confirm it, our sources suggest that the previously unidentified man who fell to his death from the Funkturm on Friday was Felix Krempin, who is currently being sought in connection with the murder of Betty Winter. As yet it remains unclear whether the fatal fall was indeed a suicide, as initially assumed. As has been reported on several occasions in these pages, the fugitive Krempin is suspected of having manipulated the lighting system in Terra Studios, Marienfelde, such that a thirty-kilogram spotlight fell on the famous actress Betty Winter during filming. Winter was seriously injured, and died shortly afterwards of electric shock.

Famous actress. Betty Winter had only become famous after her death. He was interested to see what would happen at her funeral tomorrow. It might put Horst Wessel's in the shade.

He glanced at the time and continued reading. The Association of Prussian Police Officers was campaigning for more trust to be placed in Uniform and for the service to be less military. Meanwhile, the dispute over sound film licences, which Oppenberg had spoken about a few days ago, was entering a new phase. Adopting a rather martial turn of phrase, the *Tageblatt* headline read: SOUND FILM SEPARATE PEACE IN ELECTRICAL INDUSTRY PATENT DISPUTE.

If he understood the complex subject matter correctly, then through this separate peace the American Warner concern had acquired access to the German market. *In future, at any rate, German cinema owners will be able to reckon with an increased selection of high-quality sound films,* the paper summarised.

There must be a lot of money in talkies if a dispute of such magnitude was taking place behind the scenes. Rath couldn't help thinking of Oppenberg's stubborn business associate, Marquard. The diehards were seeing their hopes go up in smoke. Proponents of silent film would soon be fighting a lost cause.

He thought of Anton Schmieder, the blackmailer of the rueful countenance, another one fighting a lost cause.

What was it he had been yammering about?

That he just wanted everything to stay the same.

Things never did stay the way they were. Nothing in life did, not even oneself.

'Inspector?'

Rath looked up. Gertrud Steiner was standing in the door to Gennat's office.

To begin with Buddha said nothing at all and simply leafed through the file. Rath doubted whether that would impress Victor Meisner. The man was in film, and would be used to hanging around. He seemed pretty sure of himself. Rath's parting shot about the toupee yesterday evening didn't appear to have caused him any further alarm, but perhaps it was all an act.

Rath kept to the arrangement and maintained an icy silence. In the absence of a file to flick through he lit a cigarette. Christel Temme was starting to fiddle with her pencil when Gennat finally began. He snapped the file shut and gave Meisner a friendly look.

'Congratulations,' Buddha said.

'Pardon me?'

'I wanted to congratulate you on your theatre,' Gennat said. 'So, congratulations! Did you inherit it?'

'I've already told your inspector all this.'

'You didn't say anything about the theatre. It is your theatre, isn't it?'

'I'm the artistic director,' Meisner said, 'if that's what you mean.'

'Who bought the building then?'

'It's leased.'

'That's a lot of money though, and there's the cost of turning a cinema into a theatre.'

'We only had to tear out the screen, all the stage machinery was already there. The Tivoli was a theatre before it became a cinema.'

'All the same it can't have been cheap. How did you finance it?'

'I'm not anticipating a large inheritance from my wife, if that's what you mean, Superintendent. I told your inspector all this yesterday.'

'Then tell me how it's being funded.'

'I have a silent partner. Cora Bellmann bore the costs, and she also stands to benefit the most financially. I'm only interested in the artistic side.'

'What does Bellmann think about his daughter setting something like this up with one of his actors, and probably with his money too?'

'It was his idea. We'll be able to transfer original material from the screen to the stage, and vice versa. It stands to reason, especially with the advent of talkies.' Meisner came to life discussing his plans. 'The Betty Winter Theatre will be a people's theatre. Not like the one on Bülowplatz for those Communist muddle-heads, but in the truest sense of the word. We'll perform the plays that people want to see when they need a break from the everyday. Plays that speak to the heart, plays in which it's all right to smile every now and again.'

'You'll be making theatre for people who would otherwise go to the cinema.'

'If you like, yes.'

'And the famous Victor Meisner will play the leads . . .'

'Only to start with. I'm the manager, but we need to gain an audience, and that will work best with my name.'

'Then why is it called The Betty Winter Theatre?'

'It's the least I owe her.'

'Did your wife intend to perform too?'

'Smaller roles, perhaps, for my sake, but no more than that.' Meisner shook his head. 'You couldn't talk to Betty about theatre. All she saw was film, film, film. She made far more of an impression on the screen than onstage. It was a wonder how celluloid transformed her.'

'Then why did she want to leave Bellmann's company?'

'Probably because he was too tight.' Meisner refused to get worked up. 'It was about money, of course, but she also saw greater artistic possibilities for herself with this new producer.'

'For herself, but not for you . . .'

'They wanted her, not me. That wasn't at Betty's discretion. When you're married to an actor, that's the kind of thing you have to deal with. I didn't begrudge her it. Unfortunately . . .' He covered his eyes with his hand.

'Who is this mysterious producer who wanted to sign Betty Winter, but not Victor Meisner?'

'She didn't want to say until everything was done. She was superstitious like that. To this day, I still don't know who courted her.'

'But you would have stayed with Bellmann?'

'I *did* stay with Bellmann. I feel very happy there. I'm his most important male performer; I can film anything I want with him, crime adventure, comedy . . .'

'Then why are you opening a theatre? It makes it look as if your film career is stalling.'

'You really don't understand anything about our industry.' Meisner shook his head. 'My own theatre has been my dream for as long as I can remember. It won't stop me from making films. I just might make a few less.'

Gennat nodded thoughtfully.

'We must ask you again to recall what happened on the twenty-eighth of February. Above all, where you were yourself.'

'Your colleague has already asked me that, so I sat down yesterday evening . . .' Meisner took a sheet of paper from his pocket and unfolded it. '. . . I lived through the terrible day for a second time in my mind, and noted everything down: when and where I was, and where Betty was too, so far as I can speak for her.' He passed Gennat the piece of paper. 'I have taken the liberty of writing out a fair copy.'

Gennat looked at the paper as if he had just received an Easter egg for Christmas.

'I must say this is rather unusual,' he began, before Meisner interrupted him.

'It's for you. Take it. I have a copy. You can compare it with the other statements.'

Buddha accepted the paper gingerly and began to read.

Rath was furious. It was time to knock the slippery, pretentious little shit off his perch.

'You wear a toupee, don't you, Herr Meisner?' he asked suddenly.

There was profound silence. Gennat looked on with irritation, while Christel Temme briefly ceased writing.

'You know I do!'

'Why didn't you tell us?'

'Because I didn't think it was relevant. To my knowledge, Bellmann wears dentures. Did he tell you *that*?'

'Where were you on the seventh of March around lunchtime? Do you have that in writing too?'

'What day was that, Friday?'

'You know perfectly well it was Friday!'

Meisner shrugged. 'I'm not so good with dates, hopeless without my diary.'

'Did you follow Felix Krempin up the Funkturm or did you wait for him there?'

Meisner looked at Gennat helplessly. 'Sorry, Superintendent. I don't know what your colleague wants from me, I really don't. Perhaps *you* can explain?'

'We just want to know where you were on Friday lunchtime,' Gennat said. Rath was about to say something else, but Buddha silenced him with a gesture as forceful as it was discreet.

'Friday? I was home between twelve and two. If the schedule allows, then I have a little afternoon nap.'

'Were you alone?'

'I'm a widower. What do you think? No doubt the concierge can confirm I was there. All the same, I don't quite understand why . . .'

'All right, Herr Meisner, that's it,' Gennat said. 'I don't think we have any more questions for the time being. Thank you for coming. Now, you may leave. Please continue to place yourself at our disposal.'

'Of course.'

Victor Meisner departed with a shake of the head and a sidelong glance at Rath.

Gennat waited until he was outside and for a time said nothing, simply played with his file. Then he exploded.

'Am I talking to a brick wall here, Rath?' He shouted so loud that Christel Temme dropped her pad. 'What did I say to you only yesterday?'

'That I should only intervene in interrogations if we have arranged it beforehand, Sir.'

'Correct. Something did stick after all. What in God's name was that nonsense about a toupee?'

'I wanted to confuse the suspect, Sir. Shake him out of his arrogant self-assurance.'

'Well, you did a splendid job, I must say! All you did was confuse *me*! As well as poor Fräulein Temme. You derailed the entire interview.'

'Listen, that stuff about the written alibi is a joke, it can . . .'

'Do you really think I wouldn't have grilled him on that if you hadn't got in the way?'

'He did it, Sir, I know it. Meisner deliberately killed his wife. He knew exactly what he was doing with the water. He meant to finish her off when he saw the spotlight hadn't killed her. He looked so horrified because she was still alive.'

'Why would he want to kill her?'

'Because he hated her. Because she was better than him and the vain little twerp couldn't stand it. He used the opportunity . . . the spotlight . . .'

'If everything you've just told me is true,' Gennat said, 'then you've made an even bigger mess of things than I thought!'

It didn't seem like today was Rath's lucky day. Not wanting to go through Homicide, past Böhm, he took his leave through the door that led directly into the corridor. When he emerged, Manfred Oppenberg was already sitting on the wooden bench. Rath didn't deign to look at him, and the producer likewise refrained from expressing any joy at their reunion.

He was annoyed at Meisner and his performance, but he was even more annoyed at himself and his own stupidity. He had underestimated Victor Meisner. The man wasn't so easy to rattle after all. Those turns as a sobbing bundle of nerves—what a farce. The real Meisner was an ice-cold, calculating, unscrupulous son of a bitch, a series of masks that could be removed in turn, the way you peeled and peeled an onion until nothing of it remained.

He went into his office to fetch his hat and coat. 'Can I leave Kirie with you for a while, Erika?' he asked. 'I have to head back out to question a witness, and can't take the dog with me everywhere.'

Erika Voss sighed, but said yes.

He was in luck; the concierge was sitting in his lodge.

'No dog today, Inspector?'

'Still at obedience school.'

'I'm afraid you're out of luck. Herr Meisner isn't here today either. Didn't you find him yesterday?'

'I have a few questions for you. My colleagues might not have been interested, but I am.' Rath took out his notebook to highlight the importance of the conversation. 'Yesterday you were recalling a fight between Herr Meisner and his wife. I'd like you to tell me what it was about, as far as possible.'

The concierge scratched his head under his bonnet.

'She wanted to make films with another producer. He could forget about coming with her. *I'm not prepared to carry you anymore,* she said. *You're the millstone around my neck.*'

Rath wrote down everything he said. 'You also mentioned something about her good name, and the fact that Betty Winter wouldn't lend it. Can you remember anything more about that?'

'It was about a theatre, if I understood correctly. He wanted her to perform, but she said no. When he asked her what she thought of the name she said: *Forget about it, I certainly won't be lending my good name to that!*'

'Did you catch which theatre they were talking about?'

'I didn't hear a name, but it must be somewhere in Wei . . .'

The concierge interrupted himself mid-sentence and turned bright red. 'Good morning, Herr Meisner,' he said.

Rath turned around. Victor Meisner looked about as friendly as a jar of pickled gherkins. 'No getting rid of you, is there?'

'It's one of my most salient qualities,' he replied. 'For my part, I'm surprised to see you here. I thought you were filming in Marienfelde.'

'The shoot's been cancelled today, thanks to your hard-working institution. There isn't a soul there.' Meisner fumbled the door key out of his pocket and pressed the button for the lift. 'Did your boss give you a good dressing-down just now? Remind you how to comport yourself?'

The lift door opened and Meisner entered.

He made to take his leave with a smile but just before the door closed Rath jumped in beside him. The smile froze.

'What kind of methods are these?' Meisner asked as the lift started. 'Are you going to beat a confession out of me? No point, I've already confessed.' He adopted a familiar whining tone. 'I killed her, I killed her!' Meisner grinned. 'I was good, wasn't I, Inspector? You believed me, didn't you?'

Rath said nothing. He pushed a button and the lift came to a juddering halt.

'What do you want?' asked Meisner.

'The truth.'

'Why don't you just tell me what you think the truth is?'

'You killed your wife.'

'The whole world knows that.'

'Intentionally.'

'Who can see into another person's mind?'

'You made use of Krempin's sabotaging construction.'

Meisner gave an amused smile. 'Go on.'

'Perhaps he told you about it himself. After all, when he left the studio he considered you a friend.'

'Yes, we made friends quickly, anyone will confirm that. I couldn't have been expected to know what kind of person he was.'

'You even helped him escape. That was how you maintained contact with him, and kept him under control.'

'One doesn't speak about favours granted to friends.'

'When he told you he had arranged to meet me, you panicked. You didn't even have to follow him, no doubt he told you when and where we were meeting. Maybe, even, the meeting point was your suggestion, since you live right next to the Funkturm. Maybe you helped Krempin adopt the perfect disguise, that's something you're good at, I hear. Then, while he was still checking the lie of the land before our meeting, you pushed him. Too bad he defended himself and swept the hairpiece from your head in the process.'

'Interesting story. Is that what your superintendent thinks? I find that hard to believe. You can't do anything without evidence, you know that. Otherwise you get into a lot of trouble with the public prosecutor.'

'Maybe I have evidence: a toupee that got stuck somewhere in the course of your exertions. It won't be too hard to find out who it was made for.'

'The toupee you are talking about comes from the La Belle fund. Krempin could just as easily have stolen it. That's not evidence.'

'Do you realise that was a confession? I didn't even have to beat you for it!'

Meisner pressed a button on the control panel and the lift started moving again.

'Who heard it apart from you? You suspect me anyway. It doesn't change a thing.'

'It's always good to hear a confession. In our line of work, it amounts to a round of applause.'

'I confessed to the murder a long time ago, as you know. It was you who said that no judge in the world would convict me for having poured a bucket of water over my poor wife in panic.'

'Why did you do it?'

382 | VOLKER KUTSCHER

'How do you think it feels to be permanently held up as a failure? She couldn't stop herself saying it over and over again, like a goddamn broken record!' He smiled. 'Well. Perhaps I'm not such a failure after all.'

The lift stopped and Meisner opened the door.

'It was nice talking to you, Inspector,' he said and disembarked. 'You must excuse me now, I need to get changed. I have a dinner date.'

'Say hello to Fräulein Bellmann,' Rath said, 'and don't forget I can be stubborn.'

Frau Lennartz looked surprised when he opened the front door. Rath had forgotten it was cleaning day.

'Inspector!' She wrung out the cleaning rag. 'I'll be finished in a moment. I wasn't expecting you.'

'I just wanted to eat lunch at home for a change,' he said.

'Should I bring you something? We're eating in a moment too, Peter and I.'

'Thank you, no.' He lifted the Aschinger bag. 'I'm already catered for.'

'You can't go into the kitchen yet. Could you wait in the living room for a moment?'

He put on a record while he waited, leaving the cognac in the cupboard. It was still too early in the day. Besides, the caretaker's wife mustn't see him drinking.

Five minutes later she poked her head around the door.

'I'm finished now.'

He waited until she was out of the door to turn off the music, went into the kitchen and put on water for coffee. He unpacked the Buletten but didn't have much of an appetite. He could always take the rest in for Kirie, she'd be happy about that. He examined the toupee, but couldn't make out a La Belle logo, inventory number or anything like that, just a barely decipherable company name.

It was difficult to say whether Meisner had been bluffing. It was conceivable, at any rate, that he'd been wearing a theatre wig at the Funkturm, rather than his own. He hadn't just disguised Krempin beyond all recognition, but himself as well. A man as famous as Victor Meisner would have been recognised all too quickly. And his alibi? He lived so close to the Funkturm that it wouldn't have been any problem to sneak out of some cellar or rear door and leave the concierge to believe he had been at home the whole time. The lift, at any rate, also went down to the basement.

Rath took his time brewing the coffee as he thought things through. No matter which way he turned it, there was no getting at Meisner. Maybe if he gave the toupee to the forensic experts in ED . . . but that would mean acknowledging his secret meeting with Krempin.

He examined the tousled hairpiece. Perhaps Weinert would have more luck with it. The man was a good journalist. Why not wait and see what he'd find?

The telephone rang but he didn't answer. He drank two cups of coffee, smoked a few cigarettes and thought some more. He still hadn't reached a decision when he returned to the Castle shortly before two.

Erika Voss wasn't as cross as he'd feared. She had clearly enjoyed spending her lunch hour with Kirie.

'That lady called again,' she said, 'and Superintendent Gennat would like to speak to you. At three.'

'Again? Why?'

'Fräulein Steiner didn't say.'

'If that's the case, I'll take the dog out in the meantime.'

He needed some fresh air, a clear head. No doubt Buddha would read him the riot act after the botched interrogation that morning. He had been hoping to make good on his error. No chance. Today really wasn't his day. As for the lady who had called again, he didn't want to think of her. He debated whether he should try Paul at the hotel, but wasn't in the mood to talk to his friend, or indeed anyone.

Kirie's presence was the only one he could bear. The dog sniffed curiously at every corner as they walked along the railway arches to the Spree. Although it started raining halfway there he continued to the Märkisches Museum, and let Kirie off the lead in the little park. Before they started back, he took out a Bulette and fed it to the dog. Kirie devoured it in one bite and thanked him with a smile.

Gennat sat, motionless as a statue, behind his desk. He wasn't flicking through any files. He wasn't moving his eyelids. Indeed, he barely seemed to be breathing. Rath was reminded of his visit a week before. There was trouble brewing.

'Nice that you could spare a little time for me,' Buddha said at last.

'Of course, Sir.'

'I hope it won't be too expensive. How much do you take an hour?'

'Pardon me?'

'Or do you have day rates?'

'I don't understand . . .'

'How much do you earn as a private detective?'

Shit.

'I don't work as a private detective, Sir.'

'Then you aren't the Gereon Rath who investigated the whereabouts of the missing actress Vivian Franck on behalf of film producer Manfred Oppenberg?'

'Oh, that? I just made a few enquiries. Nothing illegal.'

'You are aware that any ancillary activities are subject to approval?'

'Come off it.' Rath tried to sound relaxed, but was making an increasingly poor fist of it. 'That was a favour, not an ancillary activity.'

'A favour? That's what undocumented workers say.'

'But I didn't take any money for it!'

Rath hoped Oppenberg had said the same thing.

'You think that makes it any better? If you maintain friendly relations to a man connected to two ongoing investigations then you have to tell us, even if it *is* only a favour. Especially when the man's a potential murder suspect. It's called *bias!*'

'I wasn't to know the missing person case would turn into a homicide enquiry.'

'But when it did, you remained silent.'

'Yes.'

Gennat slammed his fist against the desk panel. 'Just where do you think you are?' He had never seen Gennat like this.

'I realise it was a mistake, Sir. It was just . . . After the Winter business, I didn't want to kiss goodbye to the Franck case too.'

'Didn't you consider the consequences, everything you'll be kissing goodbye to now? You should have nailed your colours to the mast at the very latest when Böhm instructed you to find out which private detective Oppenberg had hired . . .'

'That wasn't so easy, Sir. DCI Böhm and I . . .'

'Who says this kind of thing has to be easy? Did you seriously think you'd get away with it? Böhm served me the news this morning before Oppenberg's interview. He wanted to announce it in front of the whole team tomorrow because he thinks it's relevant to the investigation, but I forbade it.'

'Thank you, Sir.'

'Don't imagine I did it for you. A scandal like that would only distract officers from their work.'

'And now, Sir?'

'You can no longer take any part in ongoing investigations. You are relieved of your duties until further notice. What lies in store for you next will be a matter for the disciplinary hearing.'

'Can't we turn a blind eye this time and work it out another way?'

'Where you're concerned, there aren't enough blind eyes to go around. In the matter with DI Brenner you escaped proceedings by a hair's breadth, but this time your luck has run out.'

'Yes, Sir.'

'Do you know what I find most irritating about all this?'

'No, Sir.'

'It's so unnecessary. You are a capable criminal investigator, but you're constantly creating difficulties for yourself with your antics.' Gennat snapped shut the file that was lying on his desk, Rath's personal file. 'Well, you'll have plenty of time to reflect on these matters in the coming days! Goodbye!'

The grey corridor of A Division seemed as alien as another world, although he had passed down it hundreds of times before. Even the name on the door of his office didn't seem to belong to him anymore. He simply walked past, unable to enter.

On the outside things appeared the same, but that was no longer the case; some evil force had drained everything of its familiarity and replaced it with an undisguised alienness. He recognised this feeling and hated it. He had first felt it when Severin simply hadn't returned home one day, and again several years later when a military policeman brought news of Anno's death. Mother hadn't been able to cry, only to mourn in silence like her son and husband. Then about a year ago, his familiar Cologne world had collapsed around him, and even his home city had become alien to him.

Now it was the end of the road after his promising fresh start in Berlin.

Why hadn't he said anything to Böhm? He should have known things would turn out like this. He had stoked so many fires it was impossible to stamp them out. If they should find out that he had been at the Funkturm too, by Krempin's corpse, then it was goodnight. He would no longer get off with a reprimand or a cut in his wages, and really would have to become a private detective.

As Charly had recommended a year ago.

Charly!

He came to a halt and slammed his fist against the wall. An office boy who was just turning the corner gave him a vexed look, but said nothing, simply crept by anxiously.

What am I supposed to do in this bullshit city? he thought. *What am I supposed to do?*

Get your things and scram! Go to Cologne or, better still, New York!

He turned and went back along the corridor to his office. He needed a moment to regain his composure, took a deep breath, put on his best smile and entered.

Erika Voss was typing, he didn't have the slightest idea what.

'You can finish a little earlier today, Erika. I don't need you anymore.'

She looked surprised and ceased typing immediately. 'That's kind of you, Inspector. Then I can do a little shopping.'

'Treat yourself to something nice.'

The telephone on her desk rang. She already had one arm in her coat, but she answered anyway.

'For you, Inspector,' she said, covering the mouthpiece. 'Chinahaus, the man said. Do you want to buy a Ming vase?'

'Probably because of this yangtao thing. Put him through.'

She performed her final duty of the day, before taking her leave and sweeping out of the room.

It was the friendly Chinese man from Kantstrasse.

'You asked me to let you know, Inspector.'

'Yes, of course.' Rath realised he didn't sound especially euphoric. 'What is it?'

'The man was here again.'

'What man?'

'The German man who buys yangtao.'

'Ah yes, very good.'

'Didn't just buy yangtao, but other Chinese specialties as well. Mushrooms, bamboo shoots, glass noodles and more besides.'

'Do you have an address?'

The Chinese man gave a crafty laugh. 'For the delivery. Like you said.'

'Wait a moment, I'll get something to write with . . .'

He reached for paper and a pencil and wedged the receiver to free his hands. When he hung up he realised that he recognised the address.

His thoughts began to race, that feverish sensation that overcame him whenever he was on the verge of making new links, when he could feel, but still not quite grasp them. The fever seized him, and for a moment he forgot that Gennat had sent him packing. Perhaps the yangtao lead wasn't as stupid as Böhm always made out.

'Come on, Kirie,' he said. 'One last trip out to the Wannsee before home. After that we'll take a holiday.'

49

Why is there still nothing in the papers?

He knows they have found Fastré, they were in the cinema on Sunday. Lehmann said the police were there. He didn't know why, of course. Lehmann, the idiot, but that doesn't matter. If they were there, for whatever reason, then they *must* have found Fastré!

So why can't he read about it? It ought to be in all the city's papers. They all wrote about Franck, after all, so why not about Fastré?

When *will* they write about it? The world must learn what has happened and why. Must understand what this is about. So that it can finally end. He can't take care of them all, not every single one.

They have to understand, otherwise it will keep happening. To those who are depriving film of its beauty, its purity. Who are depriving themselves of their own beauty, their own purity.

Only he can ensure both are returned.

But he can't take care of them all; they must see that!

Or perhaps it is his fault? Does he need to be quicker? Not take so much time? Or wait so long?

He has only invited her to dinner, hasn't prepared anything otherwise, hasn't given Albert the night off. But does he really have to speak to her first to know what he must do? He has heard her, has seen how she has destroyed the magic of her own image. What they have sent to him in the lab is ghastly!

When she is on-screen she is the perfect woman, made purely of light—and then she destroys everything because she opens her mouth and the loudspeakers begin to crackle and croak. It was so awful he had to cover his ears. Why is she doing this to him? Why is she doing it to herself?

His decision is made. It will happen today! No time to lose, he must continue, otherwise there will be too many. She is perfect, perhaps the best he has ever invited.

He goes downstairs, the preparations are quickly made, the syringes filled and his tools placed at the ready. He must only prepare the wine for the anaesthetic. And of course load the film.

Upstairs the doorbell rings. He hears Albert making his way through the hall.

It can't be her; he still has a couple of hours.

50

The Chinahaus had delivered as promised. Their van was just turning onto the road as Rath parked the Buick in front of the villa. He climbed out and put the dog on the lead. Better to take Kirie with him than have her make another fuss. The house lay behind a veil of drizzle that spattered the light from the windows into millions and billions of tiny droplets, and seemed even more forbidding than he remembered from his visit the week before.

He felt a tingle as he walked along the path. Still in the grips of the fever, he could sense how close he was to something. Somewhere here was a link between the three women. He couldn't shake the feeling that he ought to know already that this visit was superfluous, that he only need pause and think and he would understand what had been plaguing him since his telephone call with the Chinahaus.

'Be good,' he said to the dog. 'We're in polite company now.'

Kirie sat as he rang the bell.

It took a little while before the white-haired servant opened. Despite his wealth, Marquard didn't keep many staff. The old man ought to have retired long ago, but continued to perform his duties.

'Yes?' he said, gazing arrogantly at Rath.

'I'd like to speak to Herr Marquard.'

'What's it about?'

'It's a police matter.' He showed his badge. Did the old man really not recognise him, or was dim-wittedness to be expected from a servant?

This time at least, the man didn't make him wait outside. They proceeded to the large hallway, which was called the vestibule here, and the old servant disappeared through one of the great double doors into the enormous house. Kirie sniffed at a suit of armour that was done up to look old but couldn't have more than thirty years on the clock. The dog had seemed agitated since she entered the house. No doubt there was a lot for her nose to discover in a place like this.

After two minutes, the servant returned.

'The master will see you now,' he said, 'but he wishes to make it known that he doesn't have much time.'

'If you had let me in straightaway, I'd be on my way by now,' Rath said.

The old man raised an eyebrow. 'I must ask you to leave the dog in the vestibule,' he said, looking at Kirie as if she had rabies.

Rath tied the lead to a halberd that was supporting a suit of armour, and bent down towards Kirie. 'Be good,' he said. 'Remember what I told you outside.'

He followed the old servant through several rooms—almost all with a fireplace, some even with tapestries, into a small drawing room whose great lancet window would have afforded a fantastic view of the lake but for the veil of drizzle. A door led out onto a little terrace.

Wolfgang Marquard awaited him at a small, dark, wooden table on which there stood a bottle of Armagnac and two glasses. He rose to his feet as Rath entered.

'Inspector,' he said, shaking Rath's hand. 'Last time, you didn't come bearing good news. I hope . . . it's nothing to do with Oppenberg, is it?'

'I can reassure you on that front. No bad news. Just a few questions regarding a small, unremarkable fruit.'

Marquard poured himself a little Armagnac. 'I'd like to offer you a glass, but no doubt you're on duty.'

'Strictly speaking I'm on holiday. I'll take a glass.'

Marquard passed him a beaker of bronze liquid. Rath brandished it under his nose and sniffed. Being rich had its advantages.

'To your holiday,' said Marquard. 'I'm curious, Inspector. Why are you here?'

Rath had never tasted such good Armagnac. 'It concerns yangtao, the Chinese gooseberry. Something very exotic . . .'

'Yangtao? A delicacy. Perhaps you have come to the right man after all. You must know that my chef is Chinese, but how does a policeman learn of such an exotic fruit?'

'Purely from duty. Although I did try it recently, and must say it tasted very good.'

'Not many people in Berlin know of yangtao. Unless, that is, you eat

Chinese food regularly, and have the courage to order something unfamiliar for dessert.'

'That's what I was thinking. That yangtao isn't as widespread here as, say, Buletten.'

'A strange comparison, but no doubt you're right.'

'That's why it could be a lead. Things that are rare always make you sit up and take notice, especially if they keep cropping up. I don't know how much Herr Oppenberg has told you about the murders we're investigating. Murders of actresses. Vivian Franck is one of them . . .'

'A tragic case. I always admired Vivian Franck, you know. I still do.'

'She's dead.'

'Her art is immortal.'

'That's hardly a comfort.'

'Do you think? Isn't it the only comfort we have? The immortality of art?'

'Most people take comfort from the immortality of the soul. Don't you believe in that?'

'The soul? That's something you only find in art. In music, in its purest form. But also in paintings, books, films . . .'

'Only not in sound film, if I've understood you correctly.'

'Sound film is not art, it's a spectacle. It shows us how we are, and not how we should be. Where is the art in that?'

From far away there was a clatter, then a bark, and shortly afterwards the servant knocked on the door.

'What is it, Albert?'

'The inspector's dog . . . well, it's rather restless.'

'You have a dog? Why didn't you bring it in?'

'I thought it advisable to recommend that the inspector leave the dog in the vestibule, on account of the cats. However, it has . . .'

'Stop prattling on, Albert! Bring the dog to its master.'

'Very well, Sir.'

The servant disappeared again.

'Strictly speaking, I'm not its master,' Rath said. 'I'm only looking after it. It belongs to an actress. Jeanette Fastré. Do you know her?'

'Of course, that goes with the territory.'

'Personally too?'

'Not as well as I knew Vivian Franck. I've seen her two, maybe three times.'

'But you never invited her for dinner—as you did Herr Oppenberg recently?'

'No. Why?'

'Frau Fastré has a fondness for yangtao. I thought perhaps she had acquired it at your house.'

'I must disappoint you there. Does Frau Fastré have anything to do with the murders you were just talking about?'

Rath nodded. 'Regrettably, yes. As a victim.'

'I haven't read anything about that.'

'We don't want to trigger a hysterical reaction amongst the population. That's why we're withholding the news. I must also ask that you maintain your silence on the matter. The press have already linked the dead actresses Vivian Franck and Betty Winter, and are talking about a serial killer. Never mind that Betty Winter's death is completely different in background.'

'Do you know who is responsible for her death? The lighting technician, as reported in the papers?'

'No, but let's return to the reason for my visit, Herr Marquard. It was I who wanted to ask you some questions, not the other way around.'

'Of course, I apologise.'

'So back to the subject of yangtao . . .'

There was a knock on the door and the old servant returned, dragging a reluctant Kirie on her lead. Only once she had smelled Rath did she give up her resistance, bounding into the room with her tail wagging.

'There you are, sweetie,' he said. 'I thought I told you to behave!'

'I'm afraid nothing could be further from the truth,' the servant said. 'The dog caused the Maximilian armour in the vestibule to fall, and dragged the halberd to the cellar door.'

'Bad dog,' Rath said and turned to Marquard. 'I hope it can be repaired.'

'These suits of armour can withstand a little punishment. That's what they were built for after all. It's just a bit of a slog putting them back together.'

'I should just like to say that it wasn't at all easy to get the dog away from the door. He smelled something there, I only hope we don't have a rat in the cellar. What with Master's film equipment . . .'

'You did a good job, Albert. As for this rat, why don't you see if the gardener can have a look.'

'Very good, Master.' The servant gingerly passed the dog lead to Rath and disappeared again. Kirie sniffed at Marquard's trouser leg, who clearly didn't like it.

Rath pulled the dog away. 'You have film equipment here?' he asked.

'I live for film,' Marquard said. 'It goes without saying that there are times when I have to view a few reels at home. Indeed, my father had a projection room in the cellar . . .'

He was interrupted by Kirie's barking. The dog had been sniffing at one of the chairs and started barking agitatedly, looking over at Rath again and again and running back and forth between him and the chair.

'It's OK, Kirie,' Rath said, but the dog refused to settle. 'I don't know what the matter is,' he said to Marquard. 'I think it's the unfamiliar surroundings. Since we entered the house she's been as agitated as I've ever seen her.'

'We have a few cats here, perhaps it can smell them.' Marquard smiled a sour smile.

'I won't let her off her lead again, I promise.'

Marquard seemed to be weighing up a difficult decision. 'Inspector, I think I need to show you something,' he said. 'It might answer some of your questions on the subject of yangtao.'

Rath raised his eyebrows. 'What is it?'

'Just follow me and take a look, then we'll see if it's any help.'

He had to pay attention that Marquard's warm, charming voice didn't throw him off guard. He shouldn't have had that Armagnac either. It had already gone to his head. As he followed Marquard up a narrow spiral staircase, the exact opposite of the enormous, protruding staircase in the vestibule, he felt for the Mauser in his holster and immediately felt more secure.

There was something about the friendly, refined Wolfgang Marquard that made him uneasy, a feeling only exacerbated by this strange building. He couldn't help thinking about the extent to which the man was clinging to the past. This forbidding fortress-villa in which he had doubtless spent his entire life was part of it too. There could scarcely be anything more out of fashion than imitation medieval architecture.

Kirie was still nervous. He had hardly been able to tear her away from the chair in the drawing room, and now she was sniffing agitatedly at Marquard's feet. The producer bounded up the stone steps so quickly that they could barely keep up.

Having arrived upstairs, they stood in a semicircular room with doors leading off it.

'These are my private quarters. Hardly anyone gets to see them apart from Albert,' Marquard said. 'I hope you appreciate it.'

'Of course,' Rath said. 'I'm curious about what it is you mean to show me.'

In place of an answer, Marquard opened a door and made an inviting gesture. 'What do you think? Did I promise too much?'

Rath looked through the door and was genuinely astonished, startled even. He hadn't been expecting to see that face here. Kirie started barking, and in the same instant he felt something strike the back of his head. There was a flash brighter than a thousand suns, before everything fell into darkness and swept him along with it.

51

He had rung the doorbell. Nothing doing. Then gone to the Nasse Dreieck, whose taciturn landlord had given an emphatic shrug of the shoulders.
Berthold Weinert now made his way back to Luisenufer. He would give
the man one final chance, seeing as he was in the area, but that was it.

This couldn't be happening.

Gereon Rath couldn't, in all seriousness, be standing him up for a second time. He couldn't believe it, but it looked as if it was true. On today of
all days when he needed the car.

As he crossed the courtyard a man and a woman emerged from the rear
building. The woman looked familiar. He must have seen a photo of her in
the office recently, someone semi-famous whose name he couldn't remember. Or . . . the penny dropped.

'Excuse me,' he said, before the couple could escape through the arch-
way. 'Do I know you from somewhere?'

She turned and looked at him inquisitively.

'You're an actress, aren't you?'

The blond man grinned. The woman seemed less amused.

'What makes you say that?' she asked.

'Weren't you at the Funkturm recently with Gereon Rath?'

'Are you from the press?'

'Is it that obvious? How embarrassing.'

She laughed. 'You have to be from the press, otherwise you wouldn't
think I was an actress. So, you're familiar with the photo from the Funkturm. Is that why you want to see Gereon?'

'Not exactly.' Weinert drew closer and shook her hand. 'Perhaps we
should put an end to these guessing games. My name is Weinert. I'm an
old friend of Gereon's.'

'Charlotte Ritter. I used to work with him at Alex. This is another old
friend of Gereon's. Paul Wittkamp from Cologne.'

'A pleasure.' The blond man had a firm handshake. What was intended as a smile somehow turned into a broad grin.

'We hadn't arranged to meet, yet still he dares not to be home,' Wittkamp said, feigning outrage. 'I'm leaving early tomorrow and wanted to say goodbye. I can't even tempt him with the most beautiful woman in Berlin.'

The most beautiful woman in Berlin went a little red in the cheeks. 'I've been trying to reach him for days,' she said. 'But all I've got is his secretary on the line. Paul likewise. Do you have any idea where he might be?'

'Right now? He ought to be here,' Weinert said, 'because I *have* arranged to meet him. But nothing doing. He's not in his local either.' He shook his head. 'Do you know I was sure he wouldn't stand me up again this time. He even made a bet.'

Wittkamp laughed. 'Well, then you can stop worrying. Gereon really doesn't like to lose a bet.'

'I can only think he was called to an operation at short notice.'

'We can find that out easily enough,' Charlotte Ritter said. 'A telephone call to the station will suffice.'

'There's a telephone at Wassertorplatz.'

They made their way there together and, as they did so, Weinert learned that she had once worked in Homicide as a stenographer, but that her legal studies currently took precedence.

'I know Gereon from his old flat in Nürnberger Strasse,' he revealed. 'I still live there.'

'At Behnke's?'

'You know Frau Behnke?'

'Indirectly.'

Weinert drew his own conclusions and fell silent.

They reached the telephone booth where he searched in his pocket for two ten-pfennig pieces. She took the coins and inserted them into the machine.

'Berolina zero-zero-two-three,' she said. 'Homicide please.' She had to wait a moment to be put through. 'Evening, Reinhold. Have you been relegated to the late shift? Charly here . . . Yeah, yeah, lots on my plate 'cause of the exam. Reinhold, the reason I'm calling. Do you have a major operation on? . . . No? . . . OK . . . Just an old friend who wanted to say goodbye to Gereon Rath. You don't happen to know where he is?'

She shrugged when she hung up. 'Work-wise there's nothing unusual going on, and he doesn't appear to be at the station either.'

'What are we going to do with the rest of the evening?'

Charlotte Ritter sounded determined. 'I think we should go to Alex,' she said. 'It feels strange that no one knows where Gereon is.'

'Maybe he's sitting in a pub somewhere getting drunk,' Wittkamp said.

'Not when he's arranged to meet Herr Weinert here. And he hasn't been in touch with us either, even though his secretary must have told him we called. Something's not right and perhaps we can work it out!'

She gave Weinert a look that brooked no argument. 'Do you want to stay here in case Gereon comes home?'

Weinert nodded. 'I've got nothing better to do. Besides, the beer in the Nasse Dreieck tastes pretty good. Perhaps he'll turn up there. Otherwise I'll try my luck every half-hour on Luisenufer.'

'If he should appear, please telephone the station and ask for Charlotte Ritter.'

'If you should hear anything, just get in touch here at the pub. The Nasse Dreieck. Easy to remember. Don't be surprised if the landlord doesn't say anything. It just means you've got the right number.'

52

A throbbing pain fetched him back. He opened his eyes in darkness. Grey contours gradually emerged from the gloom. He couldn't discern much, just the outlines of two large windows, but the night outside was almost as black as the room itself. He couldn't see where he lay, perhaps on a bed or a sofa, at any rate he was comfortable. If, given his situation, one could speak of comfort at all.

He tried to remember. Before being plunged into darkness he had seen the face of a dead woman. Jeanette Fastré, large as life, and so vivid that, briefly, he thought she was standing in front of him. Even Kirie had been deceived and barked at the photo.

Where was the dog? He sat up with a start, worried that something could have happened to her. His head responded with acute pain. He touched it with his hand, almost surprised it was possible. He wasn't bound. The blow had left a large bump.

Wolfgang Marquard had knocked him out, sure enough.

Marquard, the sound film hater.

Marquard, the cinema killer.

What was he up to? Where had he brought him? He couldn't seriously believe that his problems would be solved by striking a police officer?

For the time being though, Rath was the one with the problems. His headache was abating, albeit gradually.

Suddenly, he sensed he wasn't alone. A silhouette in front of the window moved, he heard the rustle of material and then a voice.

No, not a voice, more of a wheeze, a strange hiss, a kind of panting.

It sounded like a laugh without a voice.

'Welcome to my prison,' it said from the darkness.

'Who are you?'

'You still have your voice, that surprises me!'

'Do you . . . are you an actress? Did he remove your vocal cords?'

The voiceless laugh wheezed through the darkness. 'You wait,' she hissed. It was meant to be loud but he had to strain to hear. 'You'll see.'

He heard furniture squeaking and steps in the darkness. There was a click and then the room was light. He blinked and looked around at a dark, wood-panelled room with old-fashioned furnishings, but luxurious nevertheless. A woman was standing in the door. Despite her snow-white hair, she couldn't have been much older than fifty. She returned to her chair and gazed through the window into the night, which, thanks to the light in the room, had become no more than an impenetrable dark mass.

He sat up and his headache launched another attack.

'I'm his mother.'

She continued to gaze through the window as she spoke. In the light, Rath could understand her whispered speech even less. Listening was a strain, and with each attempt his head grew more painful.

'What's wrong with your voice, Frau Marquard? Did your son . . . ?'

'I would like so very much to go out to the lake again. He doesn't let me.'

'Did he . . . did your son remove your vocal cords?'

'He doesn't let me out anymore. Sometimes I stand in the tower and gaze at the lake and dream that I'm down there in the wind.' Her whispering grew quieter with each sentence, as if even this mode of speech would soon no longer be possible. 'I'm condemned to wait here for death, without having sat by the lake again and felt the wind in my hair.'

Rath felt his headache getting worse. He stood up, and for a moment everything went black and he had to lean against the wall. He went to the next door and opened it.

'You won't get out of here, merely enter the next cell of our golden prison.' She turned to face him, looking straight at him. She had a flawless, beautiful face and skin so fair it appeared almost transparent.

'Why do you think you are up here with me? No one gets out if Wolfgang doesn't want them to. You can't even open the windows.' She gave her panting laugh again. 'It's a good prison. My husband built it for Wolfgang. It was him who locked the boy up, not me, but *I'm* the one he takes revenge on. Strange, isn't it?' When she laughed she looked like the evil stepmother in *Snow White*, before she became the rapidly aged but still beautiful woman once more.

He had to support himself on the door frame. His hand shook for a moment, but the moment passed. There was cold sweat on his forehead.

'You need sugar. Otherwise you'll die.'

'Sugar? Am I . . . Did he . . . ?'

'He gave you an injection. That's why he brought you here.' She shook her head as if she couldn't understand such dim-wittedness. 'People are only brought here to die.'

'Then give me some sugar.'

'I'd like to enjoy your company for a little while longer. It's so rare that I have visitors. Just a few old ghosts.' The old lady smiled. 'It would be very nice if you could stay, but that's not in my hands. Soon you'll be gone, and I'll be alone again.'

'You must be able to bring me something! Don't you have any chocolate, or take sugar in your tea?' Rath felt his panic growing. 'Fruit, sweets, juice, there must be something to hand, damn it!'

'I'm afraid I can't help you. There has never been anything sweet up here, no chocolate, no fruit, no sugar, nothing. That's the reason this prison was built in the first place.'

53

When they entered the Homicide office, Reinhold Gräf was at the duty officer's desk reading the evening paper. Behind him a young officer Charly
didn't recognise sat brooding over files.

Gräf put his paper aside and stood up. 'Charly,' he said, and cast her
companion an inquisitive glance.

'Paul Wittkamp,' she said. 'Gereon's old school friend from Cologne—
Reinhold Gräf, Gereon Rath's colleague and partner.'

The men shook hands.

'Delighted to meet you,' Gräf said. 'Partner isn't quite right though.
Böhm broke us up, and for the time being Gennat hasn't done anything to
change it.'

'Then you don't have any idea where he could be?'

Gräf shrugged apologetically. 'He isn't in his office anyway. I just telephoned, but there was no one there.'

'Do you still have a key?'

'Do you think he's fallen asleep over a mountain of files?'

Charly laughed. 'I'd be very surprised, but you never know.'

Gräf went to the hatstand and rummaged in his coat pocket until a key
ring jangled in his hand.

'Here,' he said. 'Should I come with you?'

'Not necessary. I still know my way around.'

The office was locked. 'He even has his name on the door,' Paul said
appreciatively. 'I never knew Gereon was so important.'

Entering, Charly turned on the light. The secretary's desk was tidy in a
makeshift way. She went straight into Gereon's office and Paul followed.
One desk was a gaping void; the other was submerged in chaos.

'Let me guess where Gereon sits,' Paul said.

Charly looked at the desk. On top of the desk pad was a piece of paper with a note written in pencil. It was an address. Sandwerder had to be down by the Wannsee. A name was circled several times.

She tried to remember, hadn't Gereon mentioned the name recently?

'You hold the fort in case he turns up,' she said to Paul and took the note from the desk. 'I'll be back in a minute.'

Gräf was surprised that she was back so soon.

'Are there any ongoing investigations in which the name Marquard features?' she asked.

Gräf shook his head.

'Marquard?' The man at the desk sat up and took notice. 'Why do you ask?'

'I don't know.' She displayed the note. 'From Gereon . . . Inspector Rath. Perhaps it means something.'

'Show it here. Ah,' he stammered and stretched out a hand. 'Lange's the name, Andreas Lange.'

'Ritter, Charlotte Ritter.'

'I know,' Lange said and blushed. He looked at the note and opened a folder. 'I knew it! Wolfgang Marquard is the owner of the film distribution company Lichtburg. The address is identical to his private residence.'

'What does that mean?'

'I don't know if I can say.'

'Come on, Andreas! Charly's a colleague. Just on a temporary sabbatical.'

'So: Lichtburg is one of the four companies that had keys to the cinemas in which we found the bodies of two dead actresses . . .'

'*Had* keys?'

'Supposedly they were recalled when the cinemas were forced to close, but you never know, perhaps they weren't all returned. Besides, you can copy keys like that easily enough.'

Charly nodded thoughtfully. 'That was how you limited the circle of people who could have planted the actresses.'

'Correct. There are hardly any other clues.' Lange looked at the note again. 'I'm surprised Inspector Rath came across this name; as far as I know he's investigating the Winter murder.'

'If we assume that Gereon wasn't working on your list of keys,' Charly said, 'it can mean only one thing. He came across the same name while investigating another lead.'

'Yangtao,' Lange said.

'Pardon me?' Charly asked.

'It's here on the note. Above the address.'

'What does it mean?'

'Some crazy idea of Gereon's,' Gräf explained. 'Yangtao is a kind of Chinese fruit. That's why he spent half of yesterday traipsing around the Chinese quarter.'

'Why?'

'This Chinese fruit was in Winter's stomach and Fastré's fruit bowl.' Gräf shook his head. 'Coincidence if you ask me. The Winter case doesn't have the slightest thing to do with the cinema killings.'

'Who knows?' Charly shrugged. 'Is there really no connection there? What about this Oppenberg who also appears in both cases?'

'Coincidence.'

'Do you know where Manfred Oppenberg received the news of Vivian Franck's death?'

The two CID officers looked at her curiously.

'In Wolfgang Marquard's villa,' she said. 'Isn't that rather a lot of coincidences?'

'You think Oppenberg is the cinema killer?'

'Or Wolfgang Marquard. Or someone they both know. No idea. At any rate, something isn't right and Gereon has smelled a rat.'

'I don't think he's gone out there. He didn't say anything to anyone. Surely you'd take someone with you.'

'Who knows? If he thought it wasn't dangerous because he didn't know the name Marquard had cropped up as part of the cinema killer investigation . . . Was he familiar with the list, Herr Lange?'

Lange shook his head. 'No. He can't have been. The list was here the whole time.'

'Holy shit,' Charly cried inadvertently.

'Are you saying that Gereon Rath has unwittingly stumbled upon the trail of the cinema killer?'

54

A telephone rang. Rath hadn't noticed it until now, even though it seemed out of place in these surroundings. It was an old model. The mouthpiece was still integrated in the body of the machine so that you had to lift the receiver.

'That'll be Wolfgang,' Elisabeth Marquard said. 'No one calls here otherwise. Answer it, it'll be for you.'

He hesitated and she made an inviting gesture. Rath took the receiver from the cradle.

'Yes,' he said into the trumpet.

'Inspector, how are you?'

'You ought to know.'

'I'm sorry, but you left me with no other choice. You shouldn't have visited me tonight.'

'I visited you before. You were perfectly friendly then.'

'You didn't have a dog sniffing around my house.'

'What have you done with Kirie?'

'You should be worrying about yourself rather than the dog.'

'You can still go back. Let me go, spare my life. If I die things will only get worse. You don't seriously believe you can escape arrest? Do you want to have to answer for a policeman's murder, alongside the others?'

'You haven't understood anything, Inspector. This isn't about murder.'

'If I'm not mistaken you have two actresses on your conscience. What would you call that?'

'I didn't murder those women, I made them immortal.'

'Tell that to the judge.'

'The way you're talking, Inspector, shows that you haven't understood anything, not that it matters. I just wanted to let you know that I'm sorry. Now if you'll excuse me, I have another guest to attend to.'

He hung up.

Elisabeth Marquard looked at Rath expectantly. 'Did he send greetings?'

The woman had a nerve. 'No,' he said, and her sense of hope seemed to crumble. He felt his legs suddenly grow weak, but the moment passed. 'Why does he keep you locked up here?'

She shrugged. 'Because he hates me? Really it's his father he ought to hate. He's the one who locked him up!'

'Why?'

'It's how Dr Schlüter wanted it.'

'What reason can there possibly be to lock up your own son, Frau Marquard? Was he dangerous, even back then?'

'Dangerous?' She looked at him as though even speculating that her son could be dangerous was one of the seven deadly sins. With a shake of the head she turned around and gazed out of the window again. 'Wolfgang was fourteen when he fell ill. First it was just mumps, but then . . . the pancreas . . . a serious inflammation. We feared for his life. He survived, but paid a heavy price.'

'Diabetes.'

She nodded. 'Dr Schlüter gave us hope. It wasn't a total loss. The boy could still produce insulin, but too little. A strict diet, the old doctor said, and Wolfgang can live for many years yet. But the boy was foolish.'

'That's why you locked him up? Because he couldn't have kept to his diet otherwise?'

'I didn't lock him up! It was my husband.'

'Where is your husband? Why isn't your son avenging him?'

'Richard has been dead for a long time. Just like Dr Schlüter.'

'Did your son . . . ?'

'No, what are you thinking of?'

Speaking had tired her. She fell silent and gazed out of the window.

Rath was finding it increasingly difficult to form coherent thoughts. He had to look for an escape route, and went through the open door into the next room of their luxury prison. 'Room' was the wrong expression; these were chambers. A bedchamber with a four-poster bed, in which he would never have been able to get to sleep, then a small library and a spacious drawing room. There was dark wood panelling on every wall.

He tried the windows but they were all sealed. Finally, he reached the dining room; here too the windows were sealed. He tried to go through the second door into the adjoining room, to continue his reconnaissance expedition, but it was locked.

He had reached the end of the prison.

Rath threw himself against the heavy door with all his might, but it wouldn't give. All it brought him was a painful shoulder. He tried again, and again in vain. It tired him out more than it should have. Finally, sweating and gasping for air, he let himself sink to the floor.

'What are you doing?'

Elisabeth Marquard had followed him and was standing in the door as pale as a ghost.

'You shouldn't exert yourself so much. It's not good in your condition.'

He couldn't respond, merely gasp for air.

'You won't get out of here, so accept it, and let's use the time you still have to talk.'

She was just as crazy as her son. Rath looked up at her from the floor, feeble and dejected, and in the process caught sight of something in the wall, next to the big side table: a little double door, dark as the wood panelling, roughly square-shaped and at most half the size of a normal door.

'What is that?' he asked.

'That? It's the dumb waiter. That's how they send food up to me. It means the servants don't have to see my face.' She laughed her crazy laugh. 'So that my isolation isn't broken by anything.'

'It's a way out,' he panted.

'Impossible. You need a helper.'

'*You* can help me!'

'Why should I? I'll be alone again. I'm happier with you here.'

'Didn't you just tell me you wanted to see the lake again, and feel the wind in your hair?'

'They're just dreams. I'll die here.'

'How long have you been locked up? How many years? Do you really want to die here? To have both of us die here?'

'What else?'

'Don't just accept what your son is doing to you!'

'He hates me, and I love him. That's my fate.'

'Then take your fate in your hands.'

'I've tried that once already. It doesn't work. Life never turns out the way you'd like it to. You're loved by the wrong people . . . and hated by the wrong people too.'

'Help me escape from this prison and I promise you'll see the lake again. And I'll keep you company as often as you like.'

She seemed to consider, then went to the wall and opened the door. Behind it was a dark crate.

'Perhaps you're right.' She examined him from top to bottom. 'If you curl up tight, you should fit in.'

Her whisper made her sound like a conspirator.

'Then you'll close the door and send me down to the kitchen as if I were your dirty crockery.' She nodded. 'Let's be quick. I don't know how much time I have left.'

He squeezed himself into the narrow crate. 'One more question,' he said, before she closed the door. 'How do I get the door open again?'

'It's a dumb waiter. You can only open it from the outside.'

'Is anybody still in the kitchen?' She shrugged. 'If not, does that mean I'll die a miserable death in this crate?'

'Don't worry. I'll pull you back up.'

'So that I can die a miserable death with you. What a prospect,' he sighed, 'but keep your fingers crossed. We'll give it a try!'

Every bone in his body was aching even before Elisabeth Marquard closed the door.

He began his descent.

55

Charly felt uneasy but Paul's presence alone reassured her. He gave the impression that nothing could go wrong while he was there. Even now a mocking grin was stretching across the corner of his mouth.

To think she had almost left him in Gereon's office. She had been on the telephone to Wilhelm Böhm, had just received the green light for the operation, indeed, had been about to head to the motor pool when she suddenly remembered him and retraced her steps. He hadn't realised.

Böhm had sounded surprised but pleased when she called him at home. 'Good to hear from you, Charly.'

'I'm in Homicide.'

'Oh?'

'We have reason to believe that Gereon Rath is in danger. He paid an official visit to a witness who might have something to do with the cinema killer; who may even be the killer himself. At any rate, he hasn't returned, he's stood up his friend and . . .'

'Rath can't be anywhere on official duty. He's been suspended.'

'No one told me about that.'

'No one knows.'

'Why was he suspended?'

'For any number of infringements. He'll face a disciplinary hearing. I can't give details.'

The news had shocked her. Had Gereon gone and got himself into trouble again? She thought of the thing with Brenner, but what else had he been up to? *Any number of infringements.*

So what, though? Right now, he was in danger.

She had begged and beseeched, but it hadn't been easy to persuade the DCI to place a few people on standby.

'Only because it's you, Charly,' he had said at last. 'Check the lie of the land on your own first, as a private citizen. I don't want the Prussian police making fools of themselves in a Wannsee villa if it should prove to be a false alarm which, this being Rath, wouldn't come as a great surprise.'

'Understood,' Charly said, doing a little jump for joy inside.

Now she was standing outside the same Wannsee villa, which looked more like a forbidding stronghold, unsure whether she was about to make a fool of herself or expose herself to danger. Böhm had given her a whistle, the classic way to summon help.

Nothing stirred inside the house. She rang the bell again.

'Let me do the talking,' Paul said. 'I look less like a police officer than you do.'

She nodded.

At last they heard steps. An old, white-haired man opened the door. 'What can I do for you? We don't buy anything at the door.'

'Please excuse the lateness of our visit,' Paul began in his best wine trader's voice, 'we're not trying to sell anything. We're looking for a friend who left us a message to say he was at this address. Does the name Gereon Rath mean anything to you?'

'You are indeed too late,' the servant said. 'Herr Rath was here, but that was hours ago. It's almost half past ten, in case you hadn't noticed.'

'When did he leave?'

'I can't say exactly; the master saw him out personally. I was preparing dinner.'

'I know it's late, but could we speak to Herr Marquard?'

The servant looked as if he had been asked to dance the Charleston in a banana skirt. 'I don't know if I can disturb Herr Marquard. You can take me at my word, your friend is certainly no longer here.'

'Perhaps Herr Marquard knows where he's gone,' Charly said. 'Please, it's very important.'

She thought the man was going to slam the door in their faces. He did, as well, but first he said: 'One moment please. I'll ask if Herr Marquard has time.'

Paul and Charly looked at one another.

'If it wasn't so sad it'd be funny,' he said. 'I'm beginning to sense our fears were a little premature. It doesn't seem dangerous. They're just unfriendly.'

'At least we know Gereon was here.'

'Yes, but I haven't seen his car. So, he must have left again.'

'But where?'

'No idea.'

'What if they're both lying at the bottom of the Wannsee?'

'Don't exaggerate, there's no reason to panic.'

'I'm not panicking.'

Again they heard steps. The door seemed to open even more slowly this time.

56

Rath didn't know how long he had held this position, but it felt like hours. His hunched back was hellishly sore and, for the moment, even made him forget his headache. He'd have given anything to stretch out but couldn't.

Should he call for Elisabeth Marquard? It definitely made a difference whether he snuffed it in this crate or died a half-dignified death in the golden cage above. What had made him come up with such a crazy idea? Now he was trapped. To die in a dumb waiter! It was some comfort, at least, that he would escape the ignominy of being found there.

Suddenly he thought he heard something. Yes! Someone was whistling a happy tune. There was a hollow, tinny sound as he kicked against the steel door. He had tried it when he first came down, but no one had reacted. Probably because there was no one in the kitchen.

He kicked against the door again, as hard as he could with bent knees and a hunched back. The steps drew closer, and at last he heard someone unlocking the door; light streamed into his dark, narrow cage and he blinked between his knees into the surprised face of a Chinese man. He had no intention of inflicting harm, but he couldn't help it, he had to stretch his legs. In the process he landed his saviour one on the chin.

Rath manoeuvred himself out of the lift and looked around, scarcely able to think clearly. The Chinese man lay motionless on the light grey marble tiles.

On the work surface was a drawer container with white powder. He rushed to try it, ignoring his aching bones.

Salt! This couldn't be happening.

He was in a kitchen, there had to be sugar somewhere! He looked in the cupboards, but found only pots, bowls, plates. Where did they keep the supplies? He looked around increasingly frantically.

Quick, but don't panic! What was he looking for again?

There, beside the dresser. A small, unremarkable door. He stumbled over and opened it. The larder!

At last he had found paradise! Shelves and shelves of food.

Now, quickly, anything sweet, to me!

The first thing he saw was the sorry remains of a marble cake. He gulped down a slice. The cake was so dry he almost choked, but it was sweet.

He wouldn't be able to manage another piece like that, he had to drink something. He found a bottle of apple juice and brought it to his lips, alternating continuously between drinking and eating until the bottle was empty and the cake demolished. I need more fruit, he thought. Fruit was best, fructose, if he had understood Dr Karthaus correctly. He searched for and found a few crates of fruit, grabbed a banana and an apple, and proceeded to eat his way through the rest as if in a frenzy, leaving only the yangtao.

Starting to think more clearly again, he took another bottle of apple juice and went back into the kitchen. The Chinese man on the ground was groaning.

In amongst the groaning, however, was another sound, a wretched, high-pitched whimper.

'Kirie?' There was a short bark in response. 'Where are you, sweetie?'

Another bark, from the corner next to the big fridge.

He couldn't believe his eyes. She was crouched in a tiny cage that must have been intended to transport chickens. He placed the apple juice on the floor and opened the door.

'My poor Kirie,' he said, taking the dog in his arms. 'Were they going to put you on the menu?'

Now he no longer regretted in the slightest having sent the Chinese man to the floor.

'What you want here? I call police!'

He turned around. The Chinese man was standing in front of him, holding his head in one hand and a large kitchen knife in the other.

'I *am* the police!' Rath showed his badge. The Chinese man bowed and laid the knife down. 'Just stay calm now,' he said, 'unless you want me to arrest you for animal cruelty.'

'My dog! Herr Marquard Sir give me!'

'So you can turn her into sausage meat? This is Germany, you know.'

'No sausage, what you talking about? For niece number two. Has birthday soon.'

'Sorry, I didn't mean to offend you, but that birthday present of yours is a non-starter. The dog belongs to me. Herr Marquard . . .'

'Herr Marquard give to *me*, not police!' The man took a step towards Rath and tried to grab the dog. Kirie barked at him, and he started back.

'You see, she wants nothing to do with you!'

'My dog, talk Herr Marquard! My dog!'

The man wasn't about to give up so easily. He made a second grab for Kirie, but she grew even more agitated, and growled at him until Rath could no longer keep hold of her. She leapt from his arms and tore away at great speed.

The man made to go after her. Rath didn't know what else to do, so he dealt the man another quick blow to the chin, knocking him out again. 'Sorry,' he said.

The excitement and effort had caused him a lot of strain. He wasn't out of the woods yet, still didn't have enough sugar in his blood. Or, rather, had far too much insulin. He grabbed the bottle of apple juice and set off in the same direction as Kirie. She would know the best way out.

He could have done with his Mauser and, for a moment, thought about arming himself with a knife from the kitchen. He decided against. He wasn't cut out to be a knife-man.

57

Wolfgang Marquard received them in proper style in front of a flickering fire. He was wearing an oriental dressing gown that looked very expensive.

'Please excuse my appearance. I had already withdrawn for the evening when Albert informed me of your visit. He said it was important. Please tell me what is on your mind, but first let us have a drink.' He took a bottle of Armagnac and poured himself a measure. 'You may retire, Albert,' he said.

'Very good, Master.'

Marquard gave Charly a friendly smile and handed her a glass. She gazed at the man, who cut a dash even in a dressing gown. Slim, a little on the small side perhaps, with a nose that was a trifle large, but that only made his face more interesting. A born seducer, she thought. And then that voice! A voice you could listen to forever, so softly did it fill the air. Why would a man like that kill actresses when he could just as well break their hearts?

They raised their glasses and drank.

'So,' Marquard said, 'what brings you to me?'

'Gereon Rath,' Paul replied. 'A friend of ours—he told us we would find him here.'

'Then he gave you the wrong time. Herr Rath left hours ago.'

'Do you know where he went?'

Marquard shrugged his shoulders. 'I'm afraid not. Home, I suppose.'

'What time was that approximately?' Charly asked.

Marquard considered. 'Six, maybe half past six. Not much later, anyway.'

'What did he want from you? Was he here on official duty or privately?'

'I don't know if I'm allowed to say. He was here as a police officer, and police matters are, I think, subject to discretion.'

'Of course.'

All three gave a start when a dog suddenly and unexpectedly barked.

Then a little black ball of wool came charging into the room and started sniffing the chair Charly was sitting in.

The dog issued another agitated bark. She wagged her tail and looked at Charly with an expression that resembled a smile.

'Kirie?' she said, disbelievingly.

Paul stood up. 'Why is this dog in your house?' he asked, no longer sounding anything like a friendly wine trader.

'Am I to infer that you know this animal?'

The voice sounded just as warm and friendly, only now Wolfgang Marquard was holding a pistol.

58

Where had Kirie got to, the darned mutt? The house was even more labyrinthine than Rath remembered. He had to reckon with meeting Wolfgang
Marquard or his aged servant at any moment. He still didn't know if they
were in cahoots. Whatever the case, he was determined to fell the old man
if he should encounter him again.

Time and time again he was overcome by dizzy spells and outbreaks of
cold sweat, and had to pause to lean against the wall. Sometimes he remembered to take a swig of apple juice, and sometimes he didn't. Sometimes he forgot he was carrying the bottle at all. His thoughts strayed
constantly, wandering through their own private labyrinth. It took a super-
human effort not to lose sight of his goal.

At some point he had climbed a set of stairs, not the large staircase in
the vestibule or the small spiral staircase, but another, and now he had the
chance to go either right or left down a long corridor. He turned to the
right because he thought he could hear Kirie barking in that direction, and
then found himself standing in front of a large, bolted double-leaf door.

This was surely no longer part of the servants' quarters, but something
more formal. He hesitated before opening it. Kirie couldn't get through a
bolted door. He must have taken the wrong turn, so back he went until he
heard her barking again. He could hear her through the door.

He plucked up his courage and carefully opened it only to find himself
in the vestibule once more.

It was dark, but he didn't dare switch on the light. The gleam from the
door through which he had just entered helped him find his way, as well as
Kirie's barking, which now sounded afresh.

If he had heard correctly, it was coming from somewhere he had already
been that afternoon. When he had followed the old servant into Marquard's
reception room. Why had she chosen to go back there, of all places, rather
than dash for freedom through some open door, some open window?

He sighed. To his right he felt the call of the main front door. Just one step and he would be out in the open, where he could call for backup. But he couldn't leave without the stupid dog! Who knew what Marquard might do to her?

If only she would stop barking.

At least Kirie granted him that wish. Since her last bark, when he entered the vestibule, he hadn't heard a thing.

He opened the door which Albert had opened for him a few hours before and stepped into a dark room. If he remembered correctly, he still had to pass through two rooms to reach the drawing room. Gradually he groped his way towards the next door.

Hopefully Marquard had already gone to bed.

Wishful thinking. A flickering gleam of light shone through the crack in the door. Evidently the master was having a little drink by the fire. Kirie had nothing better to do than come running *here*?

You're on your own, Rath thought, you stupid, ungrateful little mutt.

He was about to turn and creep back towards the vestibule, and the main front door, when he heard a voice he recognised.

Charly?

That couldn't be right. What on earth was she doing here?

Perhaps he was mistaken, and it was the latest actress Marquard meant to immortalise, as he put it. Then he heard another familiar voice.

Paul!

What were the two of them doing in Wolfgang Marquard's drawing room?

Or perhaps it wasn't Wolfgang Marquard's drawing room at all? Perhaps he was long since back at home and hadn't realised? There were a few gaps in his memory. They were in there at any rate, his friends, no doubt they'd been waiting for hours already and it was high time he went in. What was he doing still standing out here anyway? He was so tired, he needed to sit down in his chair and listen to music and fall asleep. Yes, that was exactly what he wanted.

He opened the door to his living room, but someone had stolen the record player and put a fireplace there instead. Wolfgang Marquard was standing by the fire. What business did he have here? He ought to let him be, he was the one who was trying to kill him and Kirie. Now he even had a gun. Rath recognised his own Mauser. Did a man like Marquard even know how to handle it? Someone ought to show him.

And there was Paul, who seemed suddenly to take off from the floor and fly, old Wittkamp had never told him he could fly, he was probably showing off in front of Charly, the swine, for Charly really was sitting there.

Charlotte Ritter had returned and was gazing at him with those wide eyes. Those great big, wide eyes. How lovely!

He managed a smile . . . then someone turned the room upside down, just like that, and switched off the lights. The darkness had him once more, dragging him inexorably into its murky depths.

59

Wolfgang Marquard looked at Gereon Rath as if he had seen a ghost. Gereon Rath, who was swaying in the door, with sweat on his forehead and a bottle in his hand, a monument to drinkers everywhere.

He turned towards Rath to cover him, and Paul seized the advantage. He made straight for the hand holding the gun and knocked it with a clatter to the floor, where it slid across the gleaming parquet towards the fireplace.

What did Gereon do? He gave Charly a blissful smile, as if she were everything he wanted from this life, and doubled up like a marionette whose strings had been cut.

What had they done to him? She had no time to think about that now. Paul and Marquard were rolling in front of her on the floor, dangerously close to the fire, each trying to gain the upper hand or get hold of the pistol. At one point it looked as if Paul had managed, but Marquard was strong and resisted stoutly. All the while Kirie danced round the two men barking.

Charly hated physical violence, but she had to intervene or things would come to a sticky end. She approached the tangle of arms and legs, waited until Wolfgang Marquard turned his face towards her and kicked as hard as she could.

Marquard threw his head backwards and stayed down, while Paul looked at her gratefully.

She ran to Gereon, whom Kirie was already sniffing and licking. It looked bad. There was sweat on his forehead, his skin was deathly pale and his pulse was alarmingly weak. She patted his cheeks, spoke to him and finally shouted and slapped him, but Gereon refused to stir.

She ran through the patio door into the dark garden, put the whistle to her lips, tried to orient herself in the direction of the road and blew, kept on running and blowing, running and blowing until, by the time she reached the gate, a group of uniformed officers came marching towards her. Pistols drawn, they stormed in the direction of the house.

'We need a doctor,' she cried and noticed how, for the first time that evening, she was on the verge of losing control. 'Quickly, a doctor!'

Just then a shot rang out from inside.

60

Thursday 13th March 1930

Through a narrow window, just below the ceiling, he can see a patch of sky. It is grey. A heavy grey, heavy with snow. Soon it will snow, he sees it, smells it, for the final time this year it will snow.

He told them everything, those police officers, but they are stupid, they don't understand. They ask the wrong questions, interrupt him, probe at the wrong times, and ignore him at critical points. They don't listen to a word he says. He can't talk to them.

They haven't let him keep anything, not even his syringes. A doctor comes to his cell to give him insulin in the exact dosage. They take his blood regularly, they don't want to get anything wrong.

He stretches out on the plank bed, the snowy sky outside soothes him.

It is over. He must accept that his life is at an end.

For half of his life he perceived his own body as his worst enemy. Since then he is aware just how rarely man realises his potential so long as he is trapped inside his body. To achieve his true essence, man must free himself from that body, must leave it behind. And he can do so only in art. Or in death.

He knows because he has fused the two together.

And he regrets nothing.

Only that they didn't let him finish his final work; it would have been better than ever.

Perfect.

Why have they locked him up, he who can make people immortal—while Betty Winter's killer, who desecrated her and deprived her of her immortality, is allowed to roam free?

He doesn't understand. And they don't understand him. Nothing he has told them, nothing he has done. You can't talk to them.

And if you have nothing to say you should remain silent.

He hears steps and the metallic jangle of a key ring. The lock squeaks, turning in fits and starts, and the door opens. They have come to take him again. They don't realise he is already dead.

61

Rath had no idea where the journey would end, or if it ever would. Darkness everywhere, and yet he could sense movement. In this dark confinement, he recognised a tiny point, barely the size of a pin, growing gradually larger, slowly at first, then quicker and quicker.

He was afraid of the end of the journey, afraid of what he might see, afraid that he might feel sick, and that there would be no bucket at hand. Strangely he wasn't afraid of the pain, and then he lay, suddenly perfectly calm, staring into the whiteness. Free from fear, free from nausea, free from pain. He realised that the whiteness wasn't white, but rather a blotchy, light, eggshell yellow and, in the midst of it all, a forty-watt bulb in a cheap holder that wasn't lit. He could read the Osram logo alongside the wattage.

'He's opened his eyes!'

A shadow obscured his field of vision, and he squinted at it until it took shape. Two faces. One, a stern woman's face, framed by a white cap, the other friendly with dark brown eyes.

The cap face disappeared. 'I'll get a doctor.'

The brown eyes remained. He could have her watch him forever.

She looked so concerned that he had to grin. 'Where are we?' he asked. 'Your place or mine?'

'Oh, Gereon!' Charly squeezed him and hid her face in his breast. He lifted a hand and stroked her hair realising, in the process, that there was a thin rubber tube attached to his arm.

Charly sat up again. Her eyes were moist. 'Do you realise how close you were to death, and you're making stupid jokes already?!'

'It's not a joke. I'd like to know where I am.'

'In Urban Hospital.'

'You're my nurse?'

She shook her head. 'Sister Angelika will be back in a moment to knock that joking streak out of you.'

'Where's Kirie?'

'In Spenerstrasse. She asks after you the whole time! She feels quite at home with me, but don't worry, you'll get her back.'

'I was snatched from the jaws of death, was I?'

'If Böhm hadn't been there, who knows whether . . .'

'Who?'

'Böhm. Wilhelm Böhm saved your life.'

He sat up. 'Couldn't you have let me die?'

'Don't joke about it!' She looked at him sternly. 'It's about time the sister was here.'

'So, Böhm was there too. What happened anyway? I can only remember that Marquard pumped me full of insulin and his mother . . .' Vague memories floated from the depths to the surface. He saw Charly in the fireplace room. And Paul. Next to him Marquard with a pistol. '*You* were there too!' he said, louder than he intended. 'With Paul! What business did you have at Marquard's?'

'That's a long story. I'll tell you when the doctor allows. You look pretty worn out.'

He did feel unbelievably exhausted, as if he needed to catch up on decades of lost sleep. What on earth had that damned Marquard pumped into him?

When Sister Angelika returned with the doctor, he abandoned his resistance and allowed himself to fall back into darkness.

When he awoke, Charly was gone. In her place sat a man with an impudent grin, a plaster on his right temple and a black eye.

'There you are at last, sleepyhead,' Paul said. 'I was just about to get a puzzle book from the kiosk downstairs, out of pure boredom.'

Paul's arm was in a sling. 'What happened to *you*, you big faker?'

'They've given me a clean bill of health,' Paul said. He pointed with his healthy right arm towards its bandaged counterpart. 'A grazing shot, plus a few little bruises from your delightful colleagues who thought I was the cinema killer, when in fact I was keeping him in check.'

'A grazing shot!'

'It didn't come from the Prussian police, although they were a little rough with me.'

'Did Marquard shoot you?'

'No. Just your pistol, God rest its soul!'

'Stop talking in riddles!'

'You're going to have to get yourself a new service weapon. Your old one didn't survive its baptism of fire at Marquard's. Before giving up the ghost it managed a parting shot at me. Thank God it was just a grazing shot.' Paul shrugged his shoulders. 'I ought to be seeking recourse against you. It was your gun, and you allowed it to be taken off you.'

'Who threw it in the fire?'

'I fear that was me. When you made your grand entrance, I knocked it out of Marquard's hand. That's when it must have happened, or during our struggle.'

'What were you doing there in the first place? With Charly?'

'That's a long story.'

'Don't you say you have to get a doctor before you can tell me too.'

'I'll keep it brief. All I wanted was to say goodbye before leaving for Cologne. There was no getting hold of you so I paid your flat a visit along with Charly.'

'Why was Charly there?'

'Because the Reich Chancellor was busy, and I don't know anyone else in this stupid city. Apart from you, but of course you weren't there. We were worried, Charly especially, and once she'd taken up the scent there was no stopping her. I think she'd make a good policewoman. Or a good sleuth.'

'She *is* a good policewoman. Even if she's not allowed to call herself one yet.' He had almost forgotten about the grinning man in Charly's front door. 'Where is she now?'

'She has to revise for her exams at some point, having spent the whole morning and half of last night by *your* bedside, completely ignoring us serious casualties.' Paul shook his head. 'I don't know what you've done to deserve her. You probably haven't realised, which is why I'm telling you now. Charly is the kind of woman you ought to marry. What do I mean *ought*? *Have to*! Don't let anyone pinch her off you.'

Rath gave a weak smile and nodded, but the memory of the cowboy at Charly's door wouldn't leave him alone. 'Thanks for the advice. You sound like my mother.'

'If it wasn't for Charly there's a good chance you wouldn't be alive. We have her to thank for the whole operation.'

'What about Böhm?'

'That fat, grumpy inspector?'

'Chief inspector.'

'He came strolling through the patio door right at the end, long after Uniform had tied Marquard up. We were waiting for the doctor, because you were in a pretty bad way, my friend, and that fatso was the only one who realised what was wrong. He made sure you got fruit juice and sugared water, anything we could lay our hands on, which is what saved your life. So the emergency doctor said at any rate, before putting you on that drip.' Paul gestured towards the tube attached to Rath's arm. 'Before even bandaging me up.'

'And all you wanted was to say goodbye . . .'

'I just hope it won't involve gunshot wounds this time.'

'When does your train leave?'

Paul glanced at the time. 'It should be rolling across Hohenzollern Bridge right about now.' He shrugged. 'What the hell, I've got a compartment booked on the eighteen forty-seven, but I don't want to miss that one too.'

'You're in a rush to get home.'

'And how! I'm positively longing for Cologne. Berlin is far too dangerous for me.'

Paul said goodbye and Rath fell asleep as soon as his friend had exited the room.

The bouquets and bottles of grape juice were mounting on his bedside table. His hospital room had come to seem more like a place of pilgrimage, so many visitors had he received. After Charly and Paul it had been Berthold Weinert's turn. Amidst all the excitement they had completely forgotten about him in the Nasse Dreieck. Rath told the still hung-over journalist a few things about the cinema killer that wouldn't be appearing in rival papers.

'And the Winter case?' Weinert had asked. 'Is it connected or not?'

'I know who killed Betty Winter, but we don't have any evidence. Only the hairpiece from the Funkturm . . . But that will probably be inadmissible.'

'Who lost it?'

'I can't tell you that. It's not even official police opinion.'

'Just as background information. Who?'

'Victor Meisner.'

'The husband?'

'If you write anything along those lines, then it's speculation and nothing more.'

Weinert was gone by the time Rath's colleagues arrived, almost all of them at once. Erika Voss led the way with a large bouquet, followed by Reinhold Gräf and Andreas Lange, then Mertens, Grabowski and finally Henning and Czerwinski, together again at last. Suddenly the little room was chock-a-block.

'I'm afraid I can't offer everyone a chair,' Rath said.

Gräf shook his head. 'What on earth have you been up to, Gereon? It's high time you found yourself a partner. You can't be left on your own for a minute.' The detective passed him a pile of *Kriminalistische Monatshefte*. 'So that you don't get bored without us . . .'

Since Lange and Czerwinski were among the few who were still working on the cinema killings, they had been allowed to assist Gennat during his interrogation of Marquard.

'This morning he talked nineteen to the dozen,' Czerwinski said. 'Now he isn't saying a thing.'

'The inspector doesn't want to hear about work,' Erika Voss said. 'He needs to look after himself. Isn't that right, Herr Rath?'

'Let them speak. It's bad enough I can't be at the station.'

Lange had tried to reconstruct Marquard's background, primarily from his medical records. At fourteen, Wolfgang Marquard, who had spent his entire childhood in that enormous, forbidding Wannsee villa, had fallen ill with mumps. Then came the inflammation of the pancreas and diabetes, all as Elisabeth Marquard had said.

'Those years must have been torturous, if the doctor's medical notes are anything to go by,' Lange said. 'The strictest of diets and the lack of insulin left him little more than skin and bones. When insulin became available as a form of treatment, it must have been like starting a new life after those six years of constant torment. He took up medicine, which would explain his surgical skills, but gave up after a few semesters. At twenty-two he lost his father, that was Christmas twenty-five. Barely half a year later,

in May twenty-six, the family doctor, Dr Schlüter, died as well. Guess how?'
Lange paused. 'Insulin. Hypoglycaemia.'

'And the father?'

'Dr Schlüter recorded it as a heart attack, but no one examined his
blood.'

'Yet they did take a blood sample from Dr Schlüter . . .'

'Schlüter suffered from age-related diabetes and took insulin in small
doses, which is why they collected the sample. A logical suspicion, but no
one could explain why the experienced physician had miscalculated the dose
to such an extent.'

'He probably hadn't.'

'No,' Lange said. 'Probably not. We can't prove anything after all these
years, but we believe these two deaths were Marquard's first murders using
insulin.'

Rath shook his head. 'No,' he said. 'It was his mother, Elisabeth Marquard, who killed them both. Her son found out and locked her up.'

'Why?'

'So that we didn't, or have her committed to an institution. She's mad;
no doubt she'd have given herself away sooner or later. At least that's what
he feared, and so locked her away.'

'Why did he remove her vocal cords?'

'No idea,' Rath shrugged. 'He seems to be rather sensitive where voices
are concerned.'

'It isn't just the mother who's mad in that family,' Czerwinski said. 'Marquard junior is crackers too, that much is clear. Has a full-blown shrine in
his tower room, with photos and posters of all the women he's killed or intended to kill.'

'I know,' Rath said. 'He showed it to me.'

62

Her name! He heard them call her name. Even though they closed the door immediately behind them.

Betty Winter!

He is left speechless and slumps onto the chair next to the door. He supports his head in his hands and closes his eyes, almost dragging the guard to the floor in the process.

'Quickly, Lensing, call the doctor,' the officer says, holding Marquard's arm with such force it's as if handcuffs alone aren't enough. The man crouches beside him while his colleague goes to the telephone; the handcuffs that bind them together leave him no choice.

The police officers inside are speaking loudly, he can understand almost everything. He has closed his eyes and is concentrating on each individual word.

You want things to end up like they did with Betty Winter? the brawny officer cried, and the fat one said something in reply.

Now the brawny one is speaking again. *Victor Meisner has been given advance warning thanks to Rath,* he heard him grumble. *He isn't going to confess to anything now! The way he stood there at his wife's grave this morning, acting the grieving widower . . . disgusting! As if he knew very well we couldn't prove he killed his wife. You really want Rath to mess things up with Marquard too?*

Again the fat man says something he doesn't understand, but it doesn't matter now.

He has heard enough.

He knows what he must do, and opens his eyes.

He is already dead and they still haven't realised. Meanwhile there is another man in this city who doesn't realise that he, too, is already dead.

He sits up again.

'Seems like he's feeling better. Should I still call for a doctor?'

'You're right. Let's not go overboard. In a quarter of an hour we'll be in Moabit, he's being examined there anyway.'

63

Things move so quickly in our age that even the horrors of the Düsseldorf murders have already partially faded from memory. And yet not so long ago we were living almost in a state of war: the struggle of an entire population against beasts in human form, who sought their victims now here, now there . . .

Rath had just begun to leaf through the new edition of the *Monatshefte*. He was reading Gennat's article when he was interrupted by the clattering of crockery.

'Dinner time,' Sister Angelika yodelled, 'but first we need to take some blood.' She placed the tray to one side and felt for his vein.

'I've come to believe you are a vampire,' he said, smiling grimly.

Her response came in the form of a needle, which she thrust into his arm. That would be a *Yes*.

After she had finished, she sat him up and served him chicken with rice. The sister wished him *bon appétit* and let him alone. It didn't taste bad at all.

Superintendent Gennat appeared before dessert.

'I see you've got your appetite back,' he said. 'That's a good sign.'

Rath mumbled something with his mouth full.

'Don't let me disturb you.'

He spooned the tinned pears they had given him for dessert into his mouth, while Gennat set a little present on his lap and looked round.

'I've brought you something,' he said when Rath was finished, and unwrapped his gift. He had evidently stopped off at a bakery and loaded up on supplies. 'They tell me you need a lot of sugar, so I thought . . . You do eat cakes, don't you?'

'Thank you, Sir. Put it on the table for now. Can I offer you a slice?'

'Only if you take some too.'

It was more or less a command, so Rath sat on his sickbed nibbling at a slice of marble cake, while Ernst Gennat savoured his gooseberry tart.

Sister Angelika swept in to clear away the tray and could scarcely believe her eyes.

'That's against your diet,' she said, taking Rath's cake away. She didn't dare make a move on Gennat's plate.

'If it was up to me, I wouldn't allow you so many visitors, Herr Rath,' she said, casting Gennat a disapproving glance. 'The doctor lets himself get talked into things far too easily. Just because it's the police.'

Once she had left again, Gennat placed his cake plate to one side.

'I ought to be giving you another dressing-down,' he began. 'That display of high-handedness yesterday, and after I'd suspended you!'

'Sorry, Sir, but I had a feeling it could be a lead.'

'Well, you were proved right. I'm glad we were able to take the man out of circulation, before he put the whole city in a flurry. Your operation saved the life of a certain Eva Kröger. We found her in the cellar. Marquard had created his own little film world down there: a small cinema, a studio, as well as a kind of operating theatre. He had already drugged Kröger; she could only remember that he had invited her to dinner.'

'Because he wanted to make her a lucrative offer,' said Rath. 'He wanted to make films with her.'

'How do you know?'

'Marquard had already approached Betty Winter, before her death got in the way.'

'Are you sure?'

'Relatively. There are so many similarities with the other cases, it can't just be coincidence. Ask Marquard the next time you interrogate him.'

'If only it were that easy.' Gennat played with his hat. 'He's a tough one. He won't accept that he killed the women. He just talks about film and how it has made them immortal. We found a number of reels. He filmed his victims in the throes of death. Not that you'd know it. That they were in the throes of death, that is. The films are very aesthetic. Perfectly lit, and the poor women all perfectly made up.'

'The man is crazy.'

'You could be right there.' Gennat nodded. 'We've consulted a psychiatrist, but Marquard hasn't said anything.'

'He'll be convicted whether he talks or not. He tried to kill me. I can testify to that.'

'You won't have to testify to anything. I did wonder, however, whether you might like to take part in the interrogation tomorrow. Perhaps Marquard will speak to you. If you ever get out of here, that is.'

'One more night and I'll be ready to escape Sister Angelika's clutches.'

'Good. Then come to Moabit tomorrow at two o'clock. Marquard's in custody there.'

'I thought I was suspended.'

'Your suspension is over from tomorrow morning, though I won't be letting you anywhere near the Winter case. I hope that much is clear; nor will you be spared disciplinary proceedings. Let there be no misunderstandings there! But I think your present conduct as well as your success in solving the cinema killings will work in your favour.'

Rath understood that Gennat wanted him back at the Castle. He didn't want to show how happy he was and so changed the subject. 'Where is Marquard's mother?'

'We had her admitted to hospital. She is probably a case for the psychiatric unit. Why do you ask?'

'I owe her a stroll by the lake.'

Suddenly the door flew open and Assistant Detective Lange came bursting in.

'Couldn't you have knocked? This is a sickroom,' Gennat scolded.

Lange was out of breath. 'I'm glad I found you here, Sir. Wolfgang Marquard escaped during the transfer to Moabit!'

'What!?' Gennat dropped his cake fork. 'How did that happen?'

'He simulated a diabetic attack and then put the guards out of action. They panicked and pulled over somewhere on Invalidenstrasse, because he was no longer moving.'

'And?'

Lange cleared his throat. 'Marquard took Lensing's service weapon off him along with a pair of handcuffs and keys. Then he used the other pair to chain them to the steering column. It took quite a while for a passerby to find them.'

'He has a weapon?' Gennat shouted.

Lange nodded.

Gennat calmed down. 'What the hell? The man won't get too far without insulin.'

'I'm afraid he might.' Lange appeared so dejected it was as if he was responsible for the slip-up himself. 'We've just had a call from his chemist. He's based in Wilmersdorf.'

'Surely he didn't give him insulin, he knows that Marquard was arrested.'

'I'm afraid he did. Marquard threatened him with a gun. Lensing's service weapon, I imagine.'

'How much insulin did he take?'

'The chemist said enough for two or three weeks.'

'Goddamn it!' said Rath.

Gennat patted his arm. 'Don't you worry, my man. If he's out for revenge then he's got no chance. I'll have the hospital placed under guard immediately.'

They had taken blood from Rath again, for the final time today. Then it was lights out at ten on the dot. All at the same time, just like in the clink. He dozed for a while and waited for sleep.

It was a catastrophe that Marquard had escaped. He wouldn't want to be in the shoes of the two guards. He didn't really think the fugitive would turn up here in the hospital, but in Gennat's position he'd have done the same and placed it under guard. The hospital and any other places he might have felt drawn to: his villa, his cinemas, and of course wherever his mother and Eva Kröger currently were. He was in no doubt that Marquard was enough of a megalomaniac to want to bring his work, as he called it, on Kröger to a conclusion.

His thoughts became more and more entangled as the first fragments of dream emerged, and he felt himself slowly rocking to sleep. Sleep, sleep, sleep.

A noise fetched him back to the present. A door handle being pressed down.

The door opened quietly without anyone having knocked. Perhaps Gennat's guards weren't so invincible after all?

He groped for the bell he used to call Sister Angelika. 'Who are you?' he said into the darkness. 'Tell me right now, or I'll call the nurse.'

'Sshh,' a voice hissed from the darkness. 'Do you really want me to fall into Sister Angelika's hands?'

The door closed and the steps drew closer to the bed. Silky hair tickled his face, and he felt a wet mouth on his. Charly!

'Do you know who it is?' she asked.

'Lieselotte? Isolde? Franziska? Hildegard? Angelika?' He fired the names as if they were bullets from a machine gun.

He couldn't help it, he always had to destroy the romance with stupid jokes, but at least she laughed.

'Angelika I'm not buying.'

'You do the rest?'

'You're more closely guarded than the Reichsbank. If I didn't know the two officers outside, I'd never have made it to you.'

'Marquard's escaped,' he said with a scratchy voice, before clearing his throat. 'Gennat thinks he might want to come here.'

'They just reported it on the radio. I don't think he'll get very far.'

'Why's he doing it? Silent in the interrogations, almost as if he's given up, then this?'

'Perhaps he really is finished with everything and just wants to die in peace.'

'If that's true, do you think he'd have stolen so much insulin?'

'I don't know, but I do know one thing. Right now you urgently need protection.'

While she was still speaking she slipped under the covers and kissed him a second time. He closed his eyes as a man flitted past, grinned at him and disappeared.

Screw you, Rath thought. Charly is *here*. With *me*!

64

Friday 14th March 1930

It has snowed in the night; the snow has laid a white sheet over the world, and, at least for a moment, returned its innocence to her. From up here the city looks as if it has sprouted from a white crystal.

A beautiful image. A beautiful, final image.

The wind up here is cold, and prickles his face like needles, but he scarcely feels it. The man beside him is shivering. Ever since he gave him the gun, he no longer speaks, only shivers.

The killer is silent because he has understood. If he shoots they will both be plunged into the depths, no matter who the bullet hits. The handcuffs see to that. He threw away the key as soon as they assumed their position on the parapet. He thinks he might even have heard the soft *pling* as the metal struck the roof of the restaurant one hundred metres below.

The horrified expression of the man at the moment of realisation! They are two dead men sitting on the parapet and there is nothing anyone can do.

He doesn't want to spare him the fear of imminent death, those torturous final minutes knowing that the end has come, and that it is inevitable.

He had to wait the entire night, and when the killer finally emerged from his car half an hour ago on Lietzensee, still intoxicated, and gazed into the barrel of a gun, he had no inkling of what awaited. He pulled out his purse, but soon realised it wasn't about money.

With the gun in his coat pocket he drove the killer onto the Funkturm and into the lift. The attendant didn't notice a thing, and let them out on the viewing platform on the upper floor. 'You haven't exactly picked the best day for it!'

They stood facing each other for a moment in silence, before he forced the killer upstairs, out onto the platform, into the wind and cold. There he took the handcuffs out of his pocket and gestured towards the parapet. The killer still didn't know why, but he climbed to the top of the railing, shivering with fear and cold, and babbling, endlessly babbling, to drown his fear. Then he sat down, knees facing outwards, hands clinging to the rail until his knuckles turned completely white.

A killer frightened to death. Babbling like a child.

For a moment he gazed at the white knuckles before pushing the piston all the way down. A single shot for himself, that's enough, the killer should be fully conscious for his own demise. Then he sat down next to the man, clicked the handcuffs shut and listened to his jabbering.

'What's going on here? This is dangerous! Did Rath send you? Don't go thinking you can intimidate me like this!'

Since he has held the gun in his hands, the killer no longer speaks. He has understood the significance of the gesture. Even a pistol can't help you now.

Victor Meisner will die in the next few minutes, because that's what Wolfgang Marquard wants, and even with a gun in his hands he is powerless to prevent it.

Down below, police cars are circling. They have picked up his trail again. Perhaps the lift attendant did notice something after all.

All the better, let them see it!

It is almost time, the pain is over. He feels the fine film of sweat on his skin. All his muscles relax, completely loose now. He is ready.

Just one question occupies his mind.

Will he be able to hear it?

Can it be heard at all?

Then it comes and answers all his questions, because he *can* hear it. Hear it approaching, as quickly and inexorably as a raging tornado. Hear it ploughing everything else to one side, the roar of the world, the whistling of the wind, even the unbearable racket deep within his own heart until, finally, it arrives.

The silence before death.